Praise for Dreda Say Mitchell

'As good as it gets'
Lee Child

'The most authentic chronicler of crime
and punishment in multiracial London'
The Times

'Awesome tale from a talented writer'
Sun

'A great read written by a great girl'
Martina Cole

'Zippy, twisty plot . . . and a bevvy of
memorable supporting goodies and baddies'
The Sunday Times

'Very enjoyable'
Literary Review

'Mitchell outguns Martina Cole for pure,
shocking East End gangster grit. *****'
Mirror

'Thrilling'
Sunday Express books of the year

'A truly original voice'
Peter James

'Fast, exciting fun'
Sunday Mirror

Dreda Say Mitchell, who grew up on a housing estate in East London, is an award-winning novelist, broadcaster, journalist and freelance education consultant. For more information and news, visit Dreda's website:

www.dredasaymitchell.com
Follow Dreda on Twitter: @DredaMitchell
Friend her on Facebook: /dredasaymitchell

Also by Dreda Say Mitchell:

Running Hot
Killer Tune

The Gangland Girls trilogy
Geezer Girls
Gangster Girl
Hit Girls

DI Rio Wray series
Vendetta
Snatched
Death Trap

Blood
Sister

Flesh and Blood Trilogy Book One

Dreda Say Mitchell

HODDER

First published in Great Britain in 2016 by Hodder & Stoughton
An Hachette UK company

2

Copyright © Mitchell and Joseph Ltd. 2016

The right of Emma Joseph and Anthony Mason to be identified as
the Authors of the Work has been asserted by them in accordance
with the Copyright, Designs and Patents Act 1988.

A CIP catalogue record for this title is available from the British Library

Paperback ISBN 978 1 473 62566 2
eBook ISBN 978 1 473 62565 5

Typeset in Rotis Serif by Hewer Text UK Ltd, Edinburgh

Printed and bound by Clays Ltd, St Ives plc

Hodder & Stoughton policy is to use papers that are natural, renewable
and recyclable products and made from wood grown in sustainable
forests. The logging and manufacturing processes are expected to
conform to the environmental regulations of the country of origin.

Hodder & Stoughton Ltd
Carmelite House
50 Victoria Embankment
London EC4Y 0DZ

www.hodder.co.uk

Blood
Sister

Prologue

2003

Jen picked up a fearsome-looking bread knife and turned to face her sister, who stood behind her. She shook with fury. 'This is your fault,' she spat. 'It's all your fault. It was your bloody idea in the first place and now ... now ...' Her voice broke with emotion, 'And now they've taken my kids. You're a bum and a crim, Tiffany; you always have been, and I must've been off my nut to think of listening to you. Now get out of my fucking way.'

She slipped the bread knife into her belt and put a smaller one in her handbag.

Tiffany moved closer to her. 'No one's been taken. It's a—'

Jen pulled the knife back out of her belt so quickly her younger sister didn't see it until it was waving like a sword in her face. 'So where are they? Where are my girls? Answer me that.'

'Let's give Mum a ring.'

'On what? Two tin cans with a bit of string?' It was true, their mum didn't own a mobile. In fact their mum thought a landline was a bit racy.

Tiffany was terrified. She'd never seen Jen like this before. 'She's probably taken them up Vicky Park or something, or down The Roman, you know. Please Jen, put that knife—'

Slap. Tiffany reeled from the impact of her sister's open palm against her cheek. Pain and shock stung her face.

'Victoria Park or Roman Road Market with all that's going on? You stupid, silly bitch.'

A raging Jen left the kitchen and headed to the toilet. Moments later, Tiffany heard the chain being pulled and Jen emerged with a glint in her eye, heading for the front door.

'Oi, where are you going?' Tiffany followed her sister, her palm rubbing her reddening cheek.

'To get my children. I know where they are.'

Tiffany's stomach churned as she realised what Jen was planning on doing. 'You can't go up there, if that's what you're thinking. Those people are killers; you'll come out in a box. The girls aren't gone. Look, if you're worried, talk to the cops.'

'Talk to the Bill?' Her sister didn't stop her manic pace as she headed downstairs. 'Why? What are they going to do? Those people you've just called killers have probably got the police on their payroll.'

The two women emerged from the damp, dark, piss-stained stairwell into the cool daylight. Jen pulled her car keys from her bag and got into her motor with grim determination. Unable to think of what else to do, Tiffany quickly slipped into the front seat beside her. 'Please, think about what you're doing.'

'Get out.'

'No chance.'

'Please yourself.'

Jen turned on the ignition and the car lurched backwards before shunting forwards again, heading off towards the Mile End Road. When they reached the junction, she didn't hesitate but put her hand on the horn and pulled out in front of the oncoming traffic. Cars braked and swerved to avoid her before sounding their own horns in response to her honking. Jen ignored them, attempting to nose in front of any vehicle in her way, flashing her lights and shouting abuse as required.

Tiffany realised that her sister meant it. She laid her head against the rest. She had an hour, maybe more, maybe less, to come up with a plan. Otherwise . . . She looked at her sister's grim face and the tight icy grip she had on the wheel.

There was no doubt about it. Someone was going to get killed.

PART ONE: 1993

'She's going off the rails and breaking my mum's heart.'

One

Tiffany Miller hadn't picked up much at school, not least because she was never there, but there was one lesson she had learned: never show that you're afraid. No matter how many people you faced, or how they were threatening to take you down, you never, ever showed fear. If you did, you were royally fucked. So when Tiffany headed into the Bad Moon boozer in Shadwell, East London, she moved slowly and kept her face straight, chewing on two sticks of Juicy Fruit and taking deep breaths to keep her heartbeat down. Although she had a reputation on her estate as a hard girl, she was scared.

One of her favourite tracks, 'What's Up?' by the 4 Non Blondes, was blaring away inside, but Tiffany didn't like this pub. It was a rat hole that looked like it hadn't seen a mop and some Flash in years, packed with the type of low life who'd be patting your back as your best mate one day and selling you out on some scuzzy street corner the next. She knew the bloke she was looking for by sight, but didn't know his name. She'd never spoken to him; she wasn't allowed to.

She found him sitting on his own at a table in a dark corner, with two heavies sat nearby who were obviously there to make sure nothing stupid went on. The guy totally looked the part. Middle-aged, he wore the kind of flash clobber geezers in his line of work always wear, and was bling-bling with gold cufflinks, a fat belcher bracelet and a tie chain. A Scotch on the rocks topped off his 'don't screw with me' image. His face was heavy and marked, like a boxer's.

The man and his heavies took their time carefully looking her up and down, then finally he gave her the nod to sit her arse down.

He said nothing for a while but that didn't bother Tiffany. She knew this silence was his way of letting her know who was running things, so she kept schtum.

Finally, he took a slug of his Scotch and said, 'Do you want a drink, Tiffany?'

She popped the chewing gum out of her mouth and stuck it on the top of the table. 'Yeah. I'll have a vodka and coke.'

The man grinned at her but there was no warmth in his eyes. 'Vodka? You old enough to be sampling the hard stuff, girl?'

Tiffany pushed her chest out slightly. 'I'm nineteen.'

The guy's smile vanished as scorn twisted his features. 'You're a lying bitch. You've just turned sixteen.' He looked like he wanted to gob at her feet. 'That's not a very good start is it? You trying to piss straight in my eye? You'd better believe I know all about you little girl – everything there is to know and then some.'

Now you wouldn't be interested in me if I wasn't up for stretching the truth every now and again. But Tiffany didn't say that; she kept it zipped. She almost grinned when he told one of his thugs to get her a V&C anyway.

He left another long silence before raising his glass. 'So, a mate of a mate says you're looking for work. Is that right?'

'Yeah.'

'Did he tell you what's involved?'

'Yeah.'

The man sighed and stalled for a while. 'Well, I dunno whether you're right for it. The way I hear it you're a bit of a nutter.' He paused for a long time before adding, 'I dunno, I just don't know . . .'

He was trying to rattle her cage, trying to get her to beg for a chance, to convince him that she fit his job description to a T. But because she knew that, she merely said, 'Well, that's up to you, isn't it mister . . . ?'

He smirked slightly at this attempt to get him to tell her his name, but he didn't give it. He nodded as if she'd passed the test. 'You got that right, darling. I'll tell you what, I'll give you a try out.' He said it as if he was doing her the bloody favour of the century. 'Go up to that Pied Piper boozer on Saturday evening and pick up a little something for me. You keep it tucked away nice and safe and, if it works out, I'll put some more business your way. You know where this pub is and where to put the gear?' She quickly nodded. 'You understand how messages get passed back and forth between us? You've got your cover story straight if you're picked up the law?'

'Sure.'

'Alright.' He looked at her again and with contempt snarled, 'Drink up and piss off. I'm a busy man.'

Tiffany didn't need telling twice. She knocked back her drink, pulled up the chewing gum on the table and popped it back into her mouth, then almost let out a scream as his big, hairy paw gripped her wrist like a vice and yanked her across the table. He had her so far forward he could whisper in her ear. 'Listen up and listen good, this isn't Disney World and we're not playing Mickey Mouse games here. Don't ever, *ever* try and get in touch with me. Don't ever, *ever* muck me around and don't ever, *ever* start blabbing to anyone – because if you do, you'll pay the usual price and I don't care that you're sweet sixteen. I've had younger than you put in the ground for taking liberties. Do I make myself clear?'

Tiffany stared back, bug-eyed and trembling. 'You don't need to worry about me. I'm no grass. I'm from The Devil's Estate.'

He let go of her wrist and Tiffany drew herself to her feet. 'Good. The Plod pick you up, you don't know me.'

She laughed at him. 'I don't give a toss about the cops, I know how to deal with them.'

It was the first time she saw anything remotely like respect as he looked at her: 'Yeah, I know, I've heard that about you.'

Tiffany Miller was so chuffed with herself on the way home that she forgot to bunk the fare on the bus. As she stared out of the window at the once grand houses on Mile End Road, long since gone to seed, she started to softly sing 'What's Up?' Her voice grew louder as she sang the line about getting real high and some of the other passengers turned to look at her. *Fuck 'em; let 'em stare.* The East End was full of kids like her who wanted to get on the lowest rung of the gangster ladder in the hope that one day they might hit the big time. And now she – little ole Tiffany Miller – had managed it. But this wasn't about her trying to be some East End hood; nah, this was all about the kicks – anything to break the mind-numbing boredom of life on The Devil's Estate with her deadbeat mum and her wannabe snob sister.

TWO

'Please, take your sister with you, Jen; I don't want her ending up down the cemetery.'

Eighteen-year-old Jennifer Miller slammed the hairbrush down on her dressing table by way of reply and then turned to face her mum in her bedroom doorway. Jen had the type of looks that had been attracting the lads on the estate for a long time; not that she had the time of day for them. She folded her arms, defiantly tilted back her head and looked down her nose at her mother. Babs Miller looked tired and weary; it was a look she reserved for when she wanted something, and it usually worked. As her daughter knew, her life was hard enough and Jen was too soft-hearted to make it any harder.

'Please, Jen,' Babs pleaded. 'Take her with you – I'll make it up to you, I promise. She won't be any trouble.'

Won't be any trouble? Who was her mum kidding? Tiffany Miller was built from lumps of trouble left lying around their estate. All Jen wanted was a peaceful Saturday night on the razzle, to spend a couple of hours letting her hair down. A bit of fun, was that really too much to ask for, for crying out bloody loud?

'No way am I taking her anywhere,' Jen continued stubbornly.

Her mum groaned. 'Why not?'

'Why not? For a start she's only sixteen and that means the bouncers will keep me and Bex out of any decent bars and clubs. I'm eighteen and me and Bex have enough trouble getting in places as it is.'

'Your sister could pass for eighteen, easy.'

'Twenty-one, mum, she has to pass for twenty one – and the way she carries on, she couldn't pass for ten.'

'When she's dressed up, she looks old enough. You know that.'

And it was true; Tiffany Miller did look all grown up, when she wanted to. The shame was that her mind didn't usually follow, which is why her older sister didn't want to drag her along. 'Plus she's got no cash which means she'll be poncing drinks off me and Bex.'

'I'll give her a few sobs. I'll take care of that.'

'She swears, she fights and she's a right show-up.'

Babs sounded hopeful. 'I'll have a word with her – tell her to behave.'

Jen shook her head in disbelief. 'Have a word with her? She won't listen to anyone. You know that. She don't listen to you, she don't listen to me, she don't listen to teachers, cops, neighbours, shopkeepers. She wouldn't even listen to the Queen or her flippin' corgis.'

Babs Miller looked properly washed out. She had nothing to say back; she knew her eldest girl was right.

Jen sighed. She hated it when her mum looked like this – like the weight of the whole, nasty world was on her shoulders. It wasn't her fault that she'd given birth to a Class A teenage nutcase. Jen got up, walked up to her mum and put a comforting hand on her shoulder. She whispered, 'And you want to know the main reason why I'm not taking her up West with me and Bex? Because she doesn't really want to go: she's only saying she does because she knows it will wind me up and fuck my evening out.'

Babs sighed, squeezed her daughter's hand as she sat on the bed. 'I know,' she said weakly, like all the life had drained out of her.

Satisfied, Jen went back to her dressing table, picked up her brush and began combing her long blonde hair, which was styled exactly like supermodel Cindy Crawford's, all blow-dried volume with a large wave on one side kissing her cheekbone. She wore a knock-off Dior little black dress, from The Roman. The stallholder had promised her the dress was the real deal. Perhaps he was right and it really was; it certainly looked authentic. Together with a pair of designer heels that someone on the estate had sold her – 'don't ask me where they came from; it's against my principles to tell lies' – she looked the part, ready to strut her stuff in town.

'The thing is,' her mother wasn't giving up, 'the Old Bill dragged your sister home again the other evening when you were out. They rounded up Tiff and her mates down the cemetery and found some leaf in the girl's pocket, a car radio in her bag, and she was tanked out of her head. They're going to let it go this time but if they catch her again, it's going to mean the courts and social workers, probation officers and the rest of it. We don't need that lot poking their snouts in our business, do we? She's only a kid after all. If you take her into town, at least you can keep an eye on her and keep her out of trouble.'

Jen turned on her mother in fury. 'Where is she?'

'Downstairs.' Babs followed her daughter out and shouted after her, 'Don't have a go. She's only a kid.'

While her mum and sister were going at it upstairs, Tiffany was in the front room. A boy who lived on their landing had rung the bell five minutes before and passed her a piece of folded paper. He'd told her that the note had come from a friend and she knew at once which 'friend' it was. She took it off him, stuck it down her top and returned to the sofa to watch *Blind Date*. She had one hand in a bag of salt and vinegar crisps and was using the other hand to play with her Mod style short hair and flat fringe. She had a huge, smartass smile on her face. She'd heard the shouting upstairs and knew what was coming next.

Until her job interview with the guy in the Bad Moon, Tiffany didn't have many pleasures in life. But then, as she often thought, not many sixteen-year-old girls on The Devil did. She liked a slug of something hard and a smoke, pinching stuff and the odd fight, but none of these compared with royally winding her sister up.

Jennifer had ideas above her station. She was constantly giving the bum's rush to the local lads looking for a date, because they had no drive or ambition. Drive and ambition? Where the bloody hell did Jen think she was, talking bollocks to the judges at Miss World? She was always moaning, 'I'm better than this' when something bad happened on the estate. She had all these big, fairy-tale bollocks dreams. Just because she was studying part-time on a fashion course in that college in Whitechapel, it didn't make her better than anyone else. Tiffany loved dragging her straight back down to earth, reminding her she was just another no-mark from the East End of London, like all the other tuppenny birds.

When her sister came stomping through the door, Tiffany looked at her, pulled a face and then shook her head. 'Oh no, sis, I'm not going out with you if you're going to be wearing that. Supposing someone sees us?'

Jen stopped suddenly, as if someone had whacked her over the head. 'I beg your pardon?'

'That dress – it's a bit slaggy, ain't it? Haven't you got something else? I suppose not; you're too much of a tramp.'

Her big sister's eyes gave Tiff a scornful once-over like she was something in the Sally Army shop window. But Tiffany didn't care. She was proud she didn't go around like Jen in pretty-me-girlie gear. None of that shit make-up for her; a tracksuit was way better than a dress that hardly covered your fanny.

Jen took a handful of her sister's hair, pulled her head towards her and hissed, 'You're not coming into town with us so there's no danger of anyone seeing you – and you're not going down the cemetery with your crapster mates either. You're going to stay in and watch telly with Mum. Do you understand?'

Tiffany had the same look on her face that a cat has when it brings a bird into your house – it knows you're disgusted but there's nothing you can do about it.

She faked a pout and wailed, 'But Mum said you'd take me. Otherwise, I might sneak out of the flat and hang out with all the boys and who knows what will happen to me then?'

Jennifer Miller tightened her grip on her sister's hair. 'You ain't coming.'

Unlike most minicab drivers, the one taking Rebecca 'Bex' Blake to meet her friend Jennifer actually drove her onto the Essex Lane Estate – known to all those in the know as The Devil's Estate – rather than stopping on one of the roads that ran by it and refusing to go any further. Perhaps he was braver than the others or perhaps he was new to the job, wasn't from the area and didn't know its reputation. But the fact that he'd asked for the fare upfront suggested that he knew the full S.P. about The Devil's Estate. He skated down one of the estate's drives, beneath the looming dark blocks, and dropped Bex off near the lift that led up to the Millers' flat. Then he drove away at high speed, like a getaway driver in a gangster movie. The local kids weren't above building barricades out of wheelie bins and then demanding a 'parking fee' from any driver that they'd forced to stop.

Bex pulled her Gap coat tighter around herself, making her high-end bra pop up even further (not that her 40C boobs needed more assistance). It was summer and warm but her coat was full length to cover her fake tan legs. No girl walked around The Devil in a short number if she wanted to avoid trouble: filthy catcalls being the least of it. She put her head down to avoid eye contact with anyone who might be hanging around and hurried over to the block's entrance. The door had had its window put through. She opened the door and nearly jumped out of her skin when a man emerged from the shadows.

He held a can of brew in his hand and swayed towards her. 'You looking for some action?' In his boozed-up slurred voice the words came out as, 'You 'ookin' for slum ashion?'

Bex ran past him and belted for the stairs, which she knew wasn't a smart move – all sorts went on in the stairwell of the block Jen lived in, and right enough she ran into a group of three boys smoking joints halfway between the first and second floor. Luckily they were too stoned to make the usual threatening and rude comments so she side-stepped them and kept going until she reached the third floor. She hurried along the landing and pressed the bell on Jen's door.

As she waited, she looked out, over the balcony wall, across the long line of darkened, deck-access flats and blocks that looked like prison wings rather than homes. In the shadows that the buildings threw, dirty deeds were done most nights. Not for nothing was it known as The Devil's Estate for miles around. Bex lived on the other side of Mile End and The Devil made her estate look like a palace. Sometimes she considered asking her friend if they could meet up at Mile End Tube or up

West, to spare her this journey. But that would remind poor Jen what a proper dump she lived in and Bex didn't want to do that. Her friend had enough problems. And she knew what kind of a place she lived in, anyway. Bex totally got why she wanted out, a good job and an honest fella. Getting off this estate might not have been much of an ambition, but it was the only one that counted, until you did.

When Bex knocked on the door, it was Jen's mum who answered it. Mrs Miller smiled and greeted her but avoided making eye contact, which wasn't like her. Babs was always so open and friendly that sometimes Bex wouldn't have minded nabbing her and taking her home to replace her own mother, who never had much time for her, but plenty for the Bingo.

She shouted her daughter's name and Jen came to the door. Bex couldn't help but be gobsmacked at what a knock-out her mate was. She was slim and trim, unlike Bex who carried a muffin top around her middle, currently squeezed into a panty girdle that was hurting so much it made her eyes almost water. It didn't matter how many diets she tried, she just couldn't shift the fat. Big-boned, that's what her mum claimed she was, but Bex knew she was a gut-bucket with a sweet tooth that went berserk come midnight. Still, she could always count on Jen to make her feel like a million quid, telling her that men liked something to hang onto: a nice bit of plump 'n' grind.

The girls gave each other a quick peck on the cheek and that's when Bex noticed that the devil's offspring, the gum-chewing Tiffany, had appeared at the door too. Bex stared daggers at the little bitch. She despised Jen's sister; a mega headache that even a box-load of Anadin couldn't make go away.

'Alright?' The thing next to Jen had the cheek to speak to her, before resuming that cow chewing, her arms folded.

It was only when Jen called out goodbye to her mum and the front door slammed shut that Bex realised that Tiffany was now standing with them on the block's landing, all sulky mouth and slightly hunched shoulders in an Adidas fur-lined hooded parka that was a couple of sizes too big. She also sported a pair of mauve-tinted Lennon style shades. Who wore sunglasses in the dark for fuck's sake? And her Doc Martens were a crime against fashion that Bex wouldn't allow herself to look at. Jen's sister looked like a wannabe Liam Gallagher ready for a ruck. The girl took out a piece of paper and started reading it. *I'm surprised she can even read,* Bex thought bitchily. She looked at her mate who avoided her eyes as her mum had done a few moments earlier. She looked back at Tiffany who had a smirk on her face and then she turned back to Jennifer in disbelief.

'No way Jen – please tell me we're not taking this little slapper with us . . . ?'

Tiffany didn't respond to Tubby Guts' insult. Instead, she screwed up the note the boy had given her earlier and lobbed it over the balcony wall. She didn't need the handwritten note to remind her what it said: *Don't fuck up.*

Three

The huge bouncer studied Bex and Jen hard before announcing, 'Well, you two aren't twenty-one for a start, but no one's going to pull me up for thinking you are, so you can come in. But her ...' He looked at Tiffany who was staring at him with her arms folded and hatred in her eyes, 'I mean, come on; she don't even look like an eighteen-year-old pretending to be twenty-one. Be fair girls – I'm not being unreasonable here, am I?'

This was too much for Tiffany who shouted, 'Sod off you prick, I'm twenty-five. What are you, blind?'

Jennifer swiftly moved in-between her sister and the bouncer to stop Tiff from trying to deck him, then turned on the charm. This was the third club they'd queued for already that evening and things weren't getting any easier.

'Alright, this is it straight up, we're all twenty-one, but my friend here' – Jen gestured backwards at Tiffany with her thumb – 'she's never looked her age. Come on mate, help us out; we're just three girls who want to dance. That's not a crime, is it?'

The bouncer was sympathetic but couldn't help. 'Seriously girls, if it was up to me, I'd let you in, but the cops and the council are busting everyone's balls on the underage thing at the moment. One sniff that we're letting kids in and that's our licence gone. Seriously ...'

He was distracted for a moment by a man with Beckham good looks, dressed in an expensive, slim-line powder blue suit, which made his already piercing blue eyes even bluer. The stranger playfully punched his arm and said, 'Alright bruv, what's occurring?'

'Just another boring night in the life of an underpaid door-man. At the moment I'm trying to explain our club's very, very strict policy on age to these young ladies.'

The young guy laughed. 'You're barring three lovely birds like this? Have you gone gay or something?' Then he drew close to the bouncer: 'Have you seen Dandy? I want a word.'

The doorman jerked his head to the inside of the club and the hottie in the suit swaggered in: 'Catch you later, yeah?' Clearly he didn't have to queue or pay.

As he went up the steps, he caught Jennifer's eye, held her gaze and smiled at her until she looked away, her heart beating like the clappers. He was sporting a pricey diamond earring and his gelled hair was dyed bleach blonde. Tanned, slender and tall, he had confidence in spades.

Behind her, Jen heard Bex whisper, 'Cor, I would . . .'

The bouncer was getting impatient. 'Sorry girls, I can't help. Now move it along please.'

While Tiffany worked up a strop, Jen studied the young man from her vantage point at the door. He was deep in conversation with a shifty-looking guy and whatever they were discussing was obviously serious. There was a lot of nodding, shaking of heads and shrugging of shoulders. Then the sleazy-looking one noticed that Jen was eyeballing them and dug the gorgeous one in the ribs. He turned to look at her, turned back, whispered something and the two retreated into the club.

'Ladies, please,' the bouncer sounded narked now. 'Could you stand aside?'

The two older girls admitted defeat, but Tiffany Miller never admitted defeat. Ever.

She shoved her sister out of the way and tried to get into the guy's face, even though he was at least a foot taller than her. Her voice went stereo. 'Do you know who you're dealing with here? Do you?' Jen and Bex took an arm each and tried to drag her away but Tiffany wouldn't let up. 'I'm from Mile End, dick brain. I know people. I could have you shot, no problem! Watch your back, you little fucker! People will be coming for you, you six-foot wanker . . .'

The bouncer shrugged his shoulders and grinned at them. Like most door staff, he could never understand why people behaved like they'd just been released from some nut house. It only confirmed he'd made the right call to bar them.

'You need some help, gorgeous?' a voice said near Jen. She looked around to find a group of three lads, the one who'd spoken giving her a thorough once-over. He obviously liked what he saw because his tongue licked his bottom lip. 'I can get you into the club and then . . .' he stepped closer to her, 'me and you can get better acquainted.'

Jen wasn't in the mood. She kneed him in the groin. He groaned as he bent forwards, much to the amusement of his friends. Jen knew that she needed to hone the skills of a proper lady if she was going to make it off her estate, but that didn't mean she wasn't able to dip into her bag of Devil Estate tricks when she needed to.

She turned her attention to her wayward sister and gripped her arm. Kicking and struggling, Tiffany was dragged down Charing Cross Road until finally she broke free. She stared at the two other girls with the same look she'd used on the doorman and then hissed, 'Screw this, I'm off.'

Swaggering, Liam Gallagher style, she was soon lost in the Saturday night crowds. But although they could no longer see her, the two friends were not spared hearing her as she shouted over the crowds, 'Oh, and you were right Jen. I never wanted to come in the first place. I only did it to fuck you off. West End? Wanker's End, more like.'

Bex made a half-hearted attempt to go after her but Jen took her by the arm. 'Don't bother; it ain't worth it. She'll find her own way home . . . eventually.'

'Your sister keeps shouting the odds and she's going to be in real bollocks bother one of these days.'

'Yeah, I know,' Jen agreed, grasping full well that her sister was going to mouth off at the wrong person soon enough and live (or die) to regret it. She might bitch about her sister, but in her heart she loved her really. As far back as she could remember, she'd tried to look out for Tiffany. That's what you did when you were the oldest; you made sure that the rough stuff never touched the young ones. Of course you would expect to get into a bit of verbal with each other, every now and again – that's what happened in families – but at the end of the day, loyalty was everything. Everything.

'She's going off the rails and breaking my mum's heart,' Jen continued softly, 'but what can you do? I've tried having heart-to-hearts with her, but it goes in one ear and comes out the other. The worst of it is, Mum blames herself. She thinks the stupid girl would have grown up straight if she'd known our dad, instead of him doing a flit when she was a baby.'

'Your dad?'

But Bex should have known better than to ask that question. She'd asked it many times without ever getting an answer. All anyone knew was that Stanley Miller was long gone and the family never talked about it. And as far as Jen was concerned, that was the best way to keep it. Her dad had left the family home when she was a toddler. She didn't really remember him, but what she did recall was their flat being freezing, very, very cold indeed. How she could remember this when she'd been so young she didn't know, but then it was funny what stayed with you from your childhood.

Arm in arm, the two young women wandered up Charing Cross Road until Jen suddenly jerked Bex to a stop outside a clothes shop. She hadn't expected to see one here; Charing Cross Road was famous for its bookshops. Jen looked longingly at the mannequins dressed in such pretty clothes. That's what she wanted, to be a fashion designer; it was going to be her way of getting off The Devil. After leaving school at sixteen, it had taken her a whole year before she got the confidence to enrol at college part-time on a diploma foundation fashion course. She'd left school with no qualifications, so her dream was to one day hold a certificate in her hand.

'How's it going up at college?' Bex asked.

'My tutor says my work's really good. Next time you come round I'll show you my portfolio.'

'Portfolio?' Bex nudged Jen playfully in the side. 'Is that the name of a new cocktail?'

Both girls looked at each other and burst out laughing. Bex dragged her away from the shop. There was talk of a club in Leicester Square they could try, but they both knew the evening was a dead loss. Too much had gone wrong already for them to have a good time now. Besides, Jen wanted to get home and let Babs know that her youngest had escaped from her cage and was out in the wild, with no zookeepers to look after her. That meant it would be a long night, just like all the others, until Tiffany either came home juiced-up and stoned or was brought back by the cops (with a 'final' warning). Or she wouldn't come home at all until the next day and then claim she'd been kipping at 'friends'. Sometimes, Jen wondered if the tabloids weren't right and kids like her sister didn't need banging up, or a wake up dose of National Service.

They decided to wrap the night up with a drink and then head home. As they stood together outside a pub, smoking and deciding whether it looked like their kind of place, a hand appeared on Jen's shoulder. Then the other hand appeared on Bex's. Startled, both turned around to find the tasty bloke in the blue suit standing, up close and personal, behind them.

'Hello, girls. Your evening looks like it could do with a shot in the arm from a top geezer – and believe me, ladies, I really am a top geezer.'

Tiffany loitered in the forecourt of a jam-packed Leicester Square tube for ten minutes until she was sure that Jen and Bex had given up on coming after her. Then she walked up the steps to get on with her real business that evening. She'd only tagged along with her sis to cop some spending money from her mum and give herself an excuse to go up West. Now the coast was clear it was time to drop any pretence of what she was doing here. Although she'd promised the geezer in the Bad Moon that she knew the place she was picking up from, the truth was that she only had the haziest idea. She weaved through the streets of Soho and saw a lot of boozers, but none of them were the right one. In the end, frustrated, she decided to do what any lost teenager should do – she asked a cop who was standing with another Bill, getting ready for a long night.

'The Pied Piper?' He looked at her with a mixture of amusement, disgust and alarm. 'Now then, what would a respectable young lady like you want in the Pied Piper?'

Tiffany had a sinking feeling that asking a boy in blue had been a big-time mistake. 'I'm meeting someone there.'

The cop gave her a long look. 'You know what kind of an establishment that is, don't you?'

Establishment? She didn't like the word; it made the place she was meant to go to sound like boring school. But she brazened it out and nodded.

The officer looked at his colleague who shrugged his shoulders. He turned back to the respectable young lady. 'Next left, halfway down the street.'

Tiffany scuttled away as quickly as she could. When she reached the pub, she stood outside and checked it out for a few moments. It seemed normal enough and it was difficult to see what the cop had a problem with. She walked up to the door, but her way was barred by a bow-tied bouncer. 'Sorry love, over twenty-ones only.'

'Oh flamin' hell, not you 'n' all . . . I'm twenty-six.'

The bouncer started laughing. 'Seriously love, I don't care, but the council and Old Bill do.'

'Please,' Tiff pleaded, knowing if she didn't get this job done she'd probably end up pushing up daisies.

The bouncer raised his hands and looked Tiffany up and down. 'You do know what kind of pub this is, don't you?'

Tiff was getting totally ticked off with everyone treating her like a six-year-old. What did she have to do to prove she was a big girl now? Flash her bleeding knockers?

'Yeah.' She rolled her eyes. 'I'm not stupid.'

'Whatever, I don't really think you're dressed for it anyway. I'm doing you a favour by barring you.'

Tiffany couldn't believe it. She was in trouble and she knew it. If the guy in the Bad Moon discovered she couldn't even get into this pub, never mind pick anything up for him, her career would be over before it started. But she was curious too. The pub sounded like a bad place and she was a bad girl, a very bad girl.

When the door swung open to allow someone out, she could hear a woman singing karaoke. She didn't know the name of the song, but she'd heard her mum play that tune. The singer was making a right racket, wailing about standing by your man. The place couldn't be all that bad if it was playing crap music that her mum liked.

Tiffany moved into the side street next to the pub and waited. The bouncer couldn't stand there forever and he was on his own. He'd have to take a piss sooner or later and then she was in. But as she waited, she had a better idea. On the side wall the pub had a series of frosted windows and one of them was open at the top. She walked up to it, gripped the frame and hauled herself up. She looked up and down the street to make sure no one was looking and poked her head and shoulders through. She was skinny and knew she would make it. But as she did so, she came face to face with a man standing at a urinal.

He didn't seem in the least bit phased. Instead he smiled. 'If you've been caught short, the window for the ladies is next door.'

When she got over her initial shock, she said, 'Yeah, you can help actually. Can you help me get in this joint? I had a problem with the bouncer – he thinks I'm too young.'

He looked her up and down. 'Well, you can see why he might have thought that.'

'Oh come on mister – you're not a cop or from the council are you? What do you care?'

The man shook the last drops off his little friend. Tiffany couldn't help looking at it. Weren't they meant to be bigger than that? His would've lost in a competition with a chipolata. He hesitated for a moment before lifting his arms and helping her wriggle her way through the window. He took her by the waist and lowered her to the floor. He looked baffled. 'Are you sure you're in the right place? Only you look like you're dressed for a night out in Romford, love, rather than a pub like this.'

She straightened herself up. 'I'm here to see a man about a dog.'

That must have tickled him because he smiled again at her. 'Well, give him a pat on the head for me.'

'The man or the dog?'

'Either suits me . . .'

There were two bars. One was full of fit and trendy men while the other was crowded with women who seemed to have dressed to avoid the 'night out in Romford' look. The karaoke tunes weren't the sort that filled a dance floor in Romford either. It was then that the penny dropped for Tiffany. She rolled her eyes and whispered, 'Oh hell . . .'

A gay bar. Not that she had a problem with gay people. She was in favour of anything that narked other people off – shop-lifting, gayness, whatever else – as long as someone, somewhere, didn't like it, she was happy. It was just that back on the estates, you didn't meet gay people; you only heard about them as figures of fun or hatred. She'd never met any and this pub was rammed with gayness. She's never seen this stuff up close before, especially the women. A few were danc-ing, most were just chatting, but Tiff's breath caught when she saw a couple tonguing each other in a corner. She dragged her gaze away, suddenly feeling pissed off that she hadn't been forewarned by the boss man in the Bad Moon. Perhaps it was his idea of a little joke. But it took more than a pub like this to get a laugh at the expense of Tiffany Miller.

'I want an absinthe cocktail,' she ordered when she hit the bar.

The trendy barmaid with the gelled back sides and quiff, and Love Heart stud earring, was at a loss. 'A what?'

An absinthe cocktail was the code words she'd been given by the man in the Bad Moon – but this female Elvis lookalike serving drinks didn't seem to get it. So Tiffany repeated her request and added, 'You know what I mean . . . ?' to make her point. The barmaid looked even more confused.

That was until a man, who'd been loitering in the background, enjoying the singing, realised what was happening. What a total Man-donna, Tiffany scoffed as she checked him out – buffed, tanned, good-looking, and he bloody well knew it.

He tapped the barmaid on the shoulder. 'I'll look after this one, Julie. Why don't you refill the optics?' He turned to Tiffany. 'So, you want an absinthe cocktail do you? Follow me and I'll get you one.'

The man, who spoke in the same la-di-da voice as her bore-me-M&S-knickers-off maths teacher, rang the till and took out some notes before leading her to a storeroom at the back of the pub. He ferreted his way through a huge pile of invoices, letters and receipts that no cop or taxman would ever be willing to work through until he found a dog-eared beige envelope. He checked inside and then handed it over, together with a twenty quid note.

Tiffany looked at the score in disbelief. *Someone's having a laugh.* 'Is that it?'

She'd busted a flipping gut to get in here and all she had to show for it was a piddling Demi Moore.

''Fraid so honey. Here's a little tip in life, my dear; always negotiate the fee before signing the contract.'

Smug bastard. Like she needed life lessons from some dick who uses moisturiser.

Tiffany flashed the twenty at him. 'This can't even get me back home.'

'Give over, how much were you expecting? You're not one half of Bonnie and Clyde, are you?'

Tiffany scrunched the note up and shoved it with disgust in her pocket. She tried to flatten the envelope but it was full of bulky paper; at least she assumed it was paper. She tucked it down the front of her grunge, flannel dress, although she was upset to see it made her look a bit fat; she'd be giving Tubby Guts Bex a run for her money. Man-donna chuckled, amused by her amateurish attempts to hide her wares.

'Why don't you stop by the bar and have an absinthe cocktail before you go?'

Tiffany recoiled like he'd gobbed in her face. 'No chance. I ain't hanging around to be eyed up by a bunch of lezzas.' That didn't stop her from looking lingeringly at the ladies part of the bar.

The man looked wistful rather than outraged. 'My, my, you really are from the back end of nowhere aren't you?'

'Mile End actually.'

'Whatever.'

As she made her way out, the guy grabbed her by the collar and dragged her back. 'There's just one other thing.' He tapped the envelope under her clothing with his knuckles. 'Don't lose this or try and sell it on. It's worth a lot of money and if our mutual friend finds out you've let him down, he's going to be very upset. And his employer in turn is going to be even more upset. I'd hate to see your new career ending in the foundations for a motorway flyover. This isn't selling a few pills or nicking stuff from Woolworths, you're playing with the big boys now. Do you understand?'

There was no anger or threat in his voice. He really did sound just like her maths teacher telling her that if she couldn't do long division she'd never amount to anything. And perhaps that was why, for the first time since she'd been hired, she felt a chill in her backbone and butterflies in her stomach.

Four

'Nuts is the name ladies. Not,' Mister Blue Suit hastened to add, 'because I am nuts, but because I've got lots of them.' He raised his eyebrows and winked. 'You know what I mean?'

Hell's bells, Jen thought, I've got a real plastic Casanova on my case. Slowly she checked him out, from head to toe, with a cold, hard look before turning away and dramatically whispering, 'Oh dear, look what the cat's dragged in . . .'

Bex gave him a girlie giggle and fluttered her lashes to show she was into it, but Nuts hardly seemed to be giving her the time of day. His hand was casually draped around her shoulder while he was holding on tight to Jen with the other. Then he seemed to realise that there were only two girls, where there had been three down at the club. 'Where's the girl with the gob on her gone?'

Jen explained. 'She went home.' Then she added, 'She thought there were too many nerky guys in blue suits hanging around; it was creeping her out.'

Nuts leaned into her face with a smile and she caught a whiff of his aftershave as he whispered, 'Woah – hard girl. I like it.'

Jen had already decided that this boy-man was a complete prat but he had in-your-face confidence and wasn't easily deterred; she had to give him that. Nuts gently guided the two women forwards. Bex went eagerly, Jen not so much.

He explained. 'You see, the thing is, my beauty queens, it breaks my good heart to see a couple of classy-looking birds like yourselves being turfed away at crap clubs. You know what I mean? Crap clubs, crap people, crap clothes, crap music; it's insulting.'

All his attention was focused on Jen and he obviously liked a challenge. If she'd been doing the whole hyena giggling routine like Bex, he'd have probably lost interest by now. He needed putting in his place. 'You seemed happy enough to go in there. Perhaps you're a bit crap as well?'

Nuts shrugged his shoulders. 'Had to, babe– Sorry, I didn't catch your name?'

'Simone.'

Nuts looked unconvinced by her lie but went with it. 'Had to, Simone; it's part of my job to knock around in some of these places.'

'And what is your job?' Jen's sarcasm was as thick as butter on the bread of someone with too much cholesterol. 'Only it looked to me, down at the club, like you were some kind of minor league drug pusher; offering a special deal to the staff, were you?'

Nuts' face went stone white. His patter dried up as his arms dropped right away from both women, like he was going to catch something nasty and incurable. 'What are you then, some kind of undercover cop?'

Seeing his look Jen wanted to laugh her head right off. He didn't look so piss confident now. She should prolong and twist his agony by introducing herself as Detective Simone of the Yard's 'Get Men To Keep it in Their Pants' special squad. But she didn't. Not that she felt sorry for him or anything, but she did like the way he smelt, and his eyes.

'No, just a lady who likes to keep her eyes open.'

'So – not a cop then?'

'Don't worry blue eyes, your little secret is safe with me.'

Nuts recovered himself and pressed on. 'Drugs? Oh come on, babe, do I look like an ice pusher?' He looked at his suit as if realising that he did. 'Drugs isn't where the money's at, darling. I work in the City, in finance, loads of lovely spon-doolies, and all totally legit. We lend money to the entertainment industry so all these places want to keep me sweet. Obviously, I don't socialise in them coz they're a bit crap. I'm actually a member of a private members' club in Soho. You know, showbiz types – that kind of thing. That's where I like to hang out when I'm off-duty. I'll tell you what, why don't you let me take you down there? Rub shoulders with some stars? There was that bloke from *EastEnders* in there the other night, you know the one who tried to off his missus and set up his brother to take the fall.'

Jen had had enough; she didn't even watch *EastEnders*; she was a *Corrie* girl. 'I don't think so, Nuts. We're a bit choosy about the kind of blokes we hang out with. We only do designer, not off-the-peg shite.'

Now it was Bex's turn to have had enough as she glared at her friend. 'Could you excuse us for a moment, Nuts?'

She took Jen by the arm, led her a few yards away, into a shop doorway, and hissed, 'What's the matter with you? I'm starting to think your sister's right – you really are a bit up-your-own arse. He's seems a really nice fella. OK, he's a bit flash and full of himself, but so what? He's offering to take us somewhere different and you're acting like Lady Muck. What have you got to lose? You can get the tube back to Mile End if you want, but I'm going with him.'

She flounced off. Jen watched while Bex explained to Nuts that he was only going to be taking her to the club. He looked over in her direction like a cocker spaniel who'd been kicked in the stomach. He looked so disappointed that she began to feel a bit sorry for him. There went her soft heart again. She was also a little worried about her mate. While the guy seemed harmless enough, she didn't want Bex going off on her own. And if she was being honest, at the back of her mind was the nagging doubt that, under the surface, perhaps this young man really was worth fancying, and she might be missing out. It was clearly her he liked, not Bex. As the two of them turned their backs on her and began to walk away, she called out after them, 'Hold up, I'm coming.'

After all, what did she have to lose?

Tiffany jumped the ticket barrier at Charing Cross underground and then bolted down the escalator as two members of staff set off in hot pursuit. Coming from the East End, Tiffany knew that genuine criminals are among the straightest people going, when they're not actually committing crimes. You make sure all the lights on your car are working so the Bill can't pull you over at random. You make sure your books are all in order, so that the Revenue don't start snooping around. You don't get into rucks in pubs, so the law doesn't have a chance to arrest you and get nosey with your business. You keep a low profile and you keep it clean – apart from whatever your crime of choice happens to be. Tiffany knew all that in theory but she had forgotten it when she got into the business of dodging her fare back home.

Pausing only to kick a man who'd told her to be careful when she pushed him and his girlfriend out of the way, she shot off down the escalator and onto the platform. She knew there was no chance of being caught in the heaving, Saturday night crowd. After a short search, the two jobsworths did an about-turn. She couldn't understand why people like that bothered; it wasn't like it was their money. At Mile End station she did the same again but there was no chase this time. A woman in an underground vest merely shouted at her as she vaulted the barrier and disappeared onto the street.

A hundred yards down the road, she went inside a cash and carry to stock up on supplies, but as soon as the guy on the counter clocked her face, he shouted, 'Get out! Get out! You're banned! You're banned! You and your no-good friends . . . !' He ferreted about under the counter, emerged shouldering a baseball bat and came around to confront her.

He looked like he meant business, so Tiffany decided to move on, flipping him the finger and yelling, 'Yeah, yeah, yeah, your shop's full of out-of-date shit, anyway.'

The shop bell jangled behind her and she carried on down the road until she reached another store. She was banned from that one too but that had been three months back and she was hoping there would be no staff there who remembered her mug. She peered in through the window. The guy on the counter looked familiar but she decided to chance it. She was all smiles and seriously Miss Prim and Proper as she walked up to the counter.

'Two bottles of vodka and twenty Benson please – my nan does love a tipple and a fag on a Saturday night.'

It was true what her mother said to her. She could be a lovely girl when she wanted to be. But then Babs would plead, Why can't you be a lovely girl all the time? And Tiffany would roll her eyes and think, Because I'm not a lovely girl and I don't want to be one. She needed excitement not lovely girl syndrome.

'Are you sure you're eighteen?'

It took a huge effort on Tiffany's part to stay a lovely girl and not yell, 'Oh bloody hell, mate, not you too.' Instead she answered sweetly, 'Yes, I'm eighteen; I'm doing business studies at East London College.' She always claimed she was doing business studies in these situations; it sounded so respectable.

He looked doubtful but he fetched the voddy, put it on the counter and then turned to pull the B&H off the shelf. An amateur would have grabbed the bottles and run while his back was turned but she wasn't an amateur and she wanted the ciggies. As the guy rang up the register, Tiffany pulled her dress up to her waist to expose her underwear and then put her hand down the front of her drawers. She pulled out a flick knife from its hiding place, released the catch and, as the blade sprang, she pointed it at her supplies. 'What's this lot come to? Twenty squid? Not worth getting shanked for is it?'

The man's expression reminded her of her mum's when she was acting up: the same weariness and resignation. After a few moments, he raised his hands by way of surrender and Tiffany gleefully grabbed her loot and ran for it. As the door closed, he'd recovered enough to yell, 'You're banned!'

Doubling back, she walked through side streets to get to the local cemetery, a place that she often felt was her real home. The youths who gathered there never asked why she hadn't been to school, they never told her what to do and, most importantly of all, they never, ever asked her if she was sure she was eighteen.

The wrought-iron gates were permanently chained shut while the council tried to work out what to do with the disused site. But further down, the high Victorian wall had been caved in where a lorry had hit it. The local authority had half heartedly filled the gap with wire fencing and tape but kids had soon found a way through and made the rambling and overgrown wasteland Mile End's premier nightspot for teenagers who had nowhere else to go and couldn't stomach being lonely.

For despite all the mates she had here, Tiffany was lonely, and bored. Bored, bored, bored. There was nothing to do, so what alternative did she and the kids like her have but to make up their own excitement – create their own, private place. She liked the booze and the occasional puff because it gave her an adrenaline buzz; it made her feel like she was living a life. Now she had this job going from East London to West, her life had moved up the excitement scale.

In the distance, obscured by gravestones, monuments, trees and undergrowth, she could hear shouts and laughing voices, mixed in with the pulsing beat of Livin' Joy's 'Dreamer' from an ancient ghetto blaster. For those who wanted to come out and play, it was just a case of follow the noise and you can't go wrong. But Tiffany had another reason for coming out this evening. She had a job to do with her envelope, and there was someone she needed to see there who could help.

Five

Babs popped a couple of Benzos as she watched *Dale's Supermarket Sweep* on the VCR, but she couldn't settle. The pills were for what her doctor called 'anxiety'. Sometimes Babs felt like her whole life had been one long stress trip. Some would say that she'd brought that on herself, but no one had the brass balls to say it to her face. She sat down, got up, tidied the room, sat down again. Five minutes later she was back on her feet. She made a brew with a splash of Gordon's, tidied the kitchen and sat down again. Babs was house proud. No one was going to come into her drum and say she was bringing up her girls in a doss house. The dross on the estate might be happy to have folk think their living quarters deserved a visit from the environmental health, but not her.

Still, she knew that tonight's spring cleaning blitz had nothing to do with being house proud. When she was feeling antsy, she tidied up; not that there was anything left to do. Her nerves were shot to pieces by one thing – worrying like crazy about her youngest, Tiffany. She had that awful, unsettled feeling in her tummy, the one she always got when she knew her Tiffany was up to no good.

Her girl had a heart of pure gold, but she was trouble. Whether it was in the West End or Mile End, if there was a problem, her Tiff was smack-bang in the middle of it. It had been a crazy hope to ask Jen to keep an eye on her. Jen couldn't control her sister, and she had her own life to lead anyway. Babs suspected she had been a bad mother to even think that her youngest would be safer in the adult world of bars and nightclubs with Jen than with that bunch of teenage no-hopers who hung around in the cemetery. But the awful thing was she might be right. At least she had her sister with her in the West End, to stop her falling prey to any bad 'uns and the places they went to were policed by staff and bouncers. No one policed the cemetery, not even the police.

When teachers, neighbours and the coppers told her to get a grip on her kid, her answer was always the same. 'What can I do? Please, tell me, what can I do?' She couldn't keep the girl under lock and key 24/7. She couldn't force her to act proper. She couldn't warn her where this behaviour might end. Plus, she just got a mouthful for her trouble. Jen's theory was that Tiff would have to learn from her own mistakes, but Babs was afraid that by the time she did, it would be too late; that had been the story over the years for so many of the local kids walking a wonky line. They'd wake up one day in their twenties or thirties and realise they were in a dead end with nowhere to go – if they weren't already banged up in Holloway or The Scrubs. Babs was desperate for that not to happen to her youngest but she didn't know what to do to put the brakes on it.

They had been a close family once. Tiffany had adored her big sister, trailing after her every chance she got. Once upon a time those two had been as thick as thieves. Then Tiffany had gone to that piss-poor secondary school and nothing had been the same again.

She drifted to her kitchen and peered out of the window onto the communal balcony, willing her girl to magic out of thin air. Fat chance of that happening. But she did see one of her neighbour's kids who knew Tiffany well, walking along past the window, his head bobbing up and down as he went. She went to her front door and called out to him. 'Have you seen my Tiff tonight?'

The kid paused too long before saying, 'No.'

Right. Babs went onto the balcony. 'Is she down the cemetery?' That horrible, sick sensation in her gut told her Tiffany was in the one place she didn't want her to be.

The boy didn't make eye contact this time but stuck like a rat on stinking rubbish to his story. 'No.'

Satisfied that at least she now knew where her daughter was, Babs got her coat, popped another happy pill and headed out across The Devil's Estate, taking care not to catch anyone's eye.

On a side street in Soho, Nuts led Jen and Bex down a narrow flight of steps to a basement entrance guarded by a solid oak door. He rang the bell, a slot opened and two eyes peered out.

'Welcome to the Alley Club,' Nuts said to the girls, as the slot closed and the heavy door was unlocked and opened to reveal an entrance hall and, beyond that, a badly lit space that seemed to roll back forever. The girls could see a bar and a small dance floor where a few couples were grooving to M People's 'Moving On Up'. Nuts made a great play of knowing everyone as he weaved his way through the crowd, proudly whispering to Jen, 'That guy's a singer . . . she's in movies . . . he's an actor . . .'

Jen didn't recognise anyone, but she had to admit that this fella was putting in a real effort. Bex meanwhile had looped her arm through Nuts' arm. He may be after her gorgeous mate, but she figured he'd soon get tired of Jen's snob-with-a-gob attitude and settle for her instead. She'd got used to playing second fiddle to Jen over the years. Bex was good-looking and her curves looked shit-hot in her outfits, but Jen always went one better. That was how it was and they both knew it.

When they got to the bar, Nuts decided he wasn't waiting his turn and waved his hands in the air and called out to one of the girls serving. 'Hey, darlin', how's it hanging? Can you sort us some snorts here? Being glamorous is thirsty work – you know what I mean?'

Flash git. But Jen smiled. She did like a confident man. He insisted on buying some over-the-top cocktails that looked more like something raided from the Amazon Jungle with fruit and leaves hanging off them. He produced a large wad, which he was careful to make sure that Jen saw.

'Is John in tonight?' he asked the barmaid.

The barmaid didn't look comfortable, but she quietly answered him. 'Yeah, he's around.'

'Cool, I'll catch him later.'

As they left the bar area to look for a seat, a waitress bumped into them and spilled a lime-coloured drink down Nuts' jacket. He shouted at her with such blistering venom it shook Jen up: 'Oi, darlin', do you know how much this suit . . .'

But when he caught the fierce expression on her face, he quickly snapped his mouth shut. The woman was a stunner. Black – well, mahogany brown really – with a Naomi Campbell style full-length weave on. The owner of the club thought uniforms were naff so the waiting staff could wear what they wanted, and this one was decked out in a scarlet leather cat suit and heels that only someone with a perfect body and perfect kiss-my-behind attitude could pull off; this woman clearly had both. One hand was studded with bulky rings on four fingers. There was a flash of dark green in her mostly brown eyes and a piss taker might have said that that flash of green, along with the scarlet leather, made her look like a set of traffic lights. But it was clear no one would dare take the rise out of this chick.

She looked Nuts up and down, curling her royal plum-coloured lips before snarling, 'You got a problem?'

Nuts didn't have a problem; in fact, he promptly apologised, although the incident hadn't been his fault. He used a silk hanky to wipe his suit. The waitress looked at him like he was dirt under her kitten heels. She looked at Jen, gave her a knowing smile and shook her head to show what she thought of the guy. Then she was gone.

Nuts looked over his shoulder and whispered, 'Bitch' as she went, although he took care to make sure she didn't hear him. But he was also unable to resist the temptation to watch her pert, tight backside for a few seconds as he did so. *My oh my, that booty knows how to work the room.*

Nuts escorted his guests over to a sofa where he sat down between them. He was now anxious to get rid of Bex but wasn't sure how to do so without looking too obvious. 'John's the owner,' he explained, 'a good mate of mine actually.' He looked around to make sure he wasn't being overheard. 'Although, if I'm being straight, he's well dodgy. A major league Face, he runs his crew out of this club. He's got a finger in everything: you know, motors, naughty deals, the works. He's tried to persuade me to set up shop with him, but I'm not interested, I've got other plans.'

Jen nodded, took a sip of her drink and asked pointedly, 'So, are you well dodgy too then?'

'Me? Dodgy?' Nuts crossed his heart. 'Are you pulling my chain or something? I'm as straight a winner as Oxfam's "straight guy of the year" award.'

He was pleased to see her smile. Not ear-to-ear like a moron, but just a smile that tilted the corners of her delicious mouth. He might not have her hook, line and sinker but at least she was looking at the hook.

'No, I'm going to the top alright,' he carried on, 'but I don't need to break any laws to do it. I'm starting my own firm.' He looked around the club with pride. 'And when I've made my pile, I'll probably come back here, buy this place and get John to work for me.'

Nuts waited patiently for Bex to go to the ladies and when she did, he seized his chance. He snuggled in close to Jen and suggested, 'Listen, why don't you and me lose your mate and head off somewhere a little more cosy?'

He felt her body stiffen. 'I don't think so. Actually we'll be heading home soon.' She performed a yawn for him and explained, 'It's past my bedtime.'

His lips were only inches from her cheek. 'I'm glad you mentioned bedtime, it saves me having to do it.'

'Sorry, it's not your night, I'm afraid.'

'OK, how about I call you then?'

'I'm not on the phone.'

'I could meet you somewhere?'

'I'm very busy at the moment.'

He pleaded with a smile, 'Oh come on, babe, gimme a break. I'm working my arse off here. I'm fully house trained, Scout's honour.'

She turned and gazed into his big blue eyes that looked like a puppy desperate for a pat on the head. And she did kind of like him. It didn't seem to matter how often she knocked him back, he kept bouncing up and that's always flattering. He seemed determined to make something of himself and if you took things at face value, it appeared he was already on his way. He was good-looking and a cut above the caveman East End yob she was used to, who she refused to go out with. Her dreams didn't include having a yob as a daddy to her kids. But there was something about this bloke that wasn't quite right; she couldn't put her finger on it. It was like her mum had always warned her: the flasher the mouth and clothes, the lamer the heart and soul. But when he took a lock of her hair between his fingers and rubbed them together and whispered again, 'Gimme a break . . .' she nearly weakened.

Their moment was broken by the sound of shouting over on the dance floor. They both turned to see the Naomi Campbell-wannabe waitress in a violent argument with a man and his friends.

'You grab my arse again and you'll be leaving minus your fingers,' she growled.

The man let out a raucous laugh, winking at his mates. 'Come on, black beauty, you should be grateful for my attention. It's a step up from being a waitress.'

Without another word, and as other revellers scattered, she clenched her fist and threw a right-hander that caught the well-built man square in the face and sent him reeling backwards. He crashed into a table and chairs where he collapsed in a heap, clutching his bleeding nose and face where her multiple rings had gouged out his skin. As a group of the club's heavies emerged from the shadows to restore order, the woman turned on her victim's friends.

'Do you want some too, eh? Do ya?' She kissed her teeth – the Caribbean equivalent of tutting, with knobs on – dripping derision and disdain.

It seemed they didn't want some. They backed off and raised their hands. The woman turned and delivered a violent kick to the arse-grabber's ribs. 'Learn some fucking manners, you damn fool.'

'Come on, we're out of here,' Nuts said alarmed and grabbed Jen's palm in his. 'John doesn't like trouble in his club and that bird looks like proper trouble and no mistake.'

Six

'Oi, Miller?' the woman growled. 'I want a word with you.'

There were only two reasons anyone walked around The Devil's Estate after dark – either they were looking for trouble or they wanted to avoid it. As soon as Babs heard the voice, she knew she'd found trouble. She stopped walking down the slip road off the estate, that led to the cemetery, and stared hard at the middle-aged woman coming towards her in a right huff.

The woman was Melanie Ingram. She lived in a block on the other side of the estate – thank God – and looked like a reject from the 1980s: big shoulder pads, even bigger teased hair and huge, wild, gobstopper-sized eyes. This mad bitch saw herself as the Joan Collins of The Devil's Estate. Christ almighty, Babs didn't need this now. There had been bad blood between both families since Babs' husband, Stanley, had been around. Really bad blood.

Babs stood with her arms folded while the other woman crossed over. They stared each other out for a few moments before Melanie snapped, 'Keep your skank kid away from my girl or there's going to be a blow up.'

This fat slapper didn't scare Babs Miller. Her husband would have done, but he wasn't around anymore. 'Oh really? From what I hear, your daughter's well trouble on her lonesome and don't need no one else. Is it true that she's got her own team of social workers now? That's a shame, isn't it?'

Melanie Ingram drew closer. 'Whoever you're hearing those fuck-off stories from, you want to tell them to shut their lying gob. But it's gonna be true if she hangs around with your thieving, smacked-up kid. So you tell her straight from me, if she doesn't stay away from our Stacey I'm going to come around your gaff and show her what it's like. Do you understand?'

Babs tutted. 'Hmm – the slacker the bird, the harder the patter. I'll tell you what, sweetheart, any time you feel like coming around and showing anyone what it's like, feel free. We've all got our problems and I fancy taking mine out on an old trout like yourself. By the way, how's that old man of yours? Still popping home from time to time, well bladdered, and giving you a kicking, is he? Or is he too busy now with his much younger piece of snatch?'

Melanie Ingram shook with anger. She was so close now that Babs almost passed out from the stale beer fumes coming off her. 'I mean it. Keep her away from my Stacey.'

'Why don't you get back on your broomstick and fly away?'

Bab stood her ground. She wasn't going to bottle it. She wasn't scared of this sorry excuse for a woman who'd been beaten left, right and centre by life. If she put one finger on Babs – one little touch – everyone would find out who put the name Devil in this estate: she would beat the living daylights out of her.

But she was saved from having to roll up her sleeves when Mel stomped off. In all the years they'd been scrapping, Babs and Mel had never actually come to blows; it was almost as if they had an unspoken agreement not to go there. And there were times when Babs realised how stupid their feud was; both women were in the same boat really, with two tearaway teens who kept head-butting life. But then again she and Melanie Ingram had a history. A bad history.

Babs shook off the past as she continued her journey to the cemetery. Her heart sank and her pace quickened when she saw two cop cars parked by the entrance. The police had unlocked the gate and were trying to manage the growing crowd of teenagers inside who wanted a ruck and were goading the boys in blue with insults from all sides:

'Fuck off, we ain't doing no harm.'

'Why don't you go and help some old dear cross the road.'

'Do you want a drag on my spliff officer?'

When she drew close enough, Babs surveyed the crowd of youths. No sign of her daughter. She slipped past the police and grabbed the arm of a girl she recognised. 'Have you seen my Tiffany?'

The kid shook her head. Babs gripped her arm more tightly and pleaded, 'Help me out.'

The girl gestured with her thumb in the direction of the winding, shadowy paths that led deeper into the cemetery. 'I think she went for a walk with someone.'

Babs tensed up. 'What someone?'

The kid shrugged. 'Dunno.'

Babs let the girl's arm go and started trembling. Someone? Who could Tiff have gone off with? How many times had she warned the stupid girl not to come here at night; there might be pervs and kiddie fiddlers lurking in the bushes. Jesus, when was her girl ever going to learn?

She moved quickly down the rambling tracks that led past graves with white angels and harps mounted on top. Above her, the wind blew through the treetops. The voices and shouts behind her faded as she pressed on. She knew Tiffany would go mental when she discovered that her mum had come looking for her. She anticipated the scream – 'I'm not a fucking kid' – but knew too that she had no choice.

She grew scared at the shapes and shadows that the graves made in the darkness, and the rustling of the leaves. 'Tiffany,' she called out, for her own peace of mind as much as to find her child. Women were attacked in this place in the daylight, never mind at night. Her calls became shrill and desperate.

It was then that Babs spotted a dark figure running amongst the bushes and trees, dodging the gravestones and columns.

'Tiffany?'

No answer. Babs set off in pursuit. It was obviously a youngster as she was easily outpacing the older woman, but when she tripped over a fallen piece of masonry with a squeal of pain, Babs got the chance to draw closer. The noise the kid made meant she was a girl. The kid rose up and turned to see who was chasing her. A gleam of moonlight fell on her face before she turned back and ran, disappearing into the gloom like the ghost of one of the resident stiffs.

Out of breath and wheezing, Babs retraced her steps back to the track. But this time, when she once again shouted Tiffany's name, she got a surly response.

'Over here, Mum.'

Her daughter sat on the stone rim of a grave, her face lit up from the lighter she was using to fire up a spliff, two empty bottles of vodka lying at her feet. 'Yeah, yeah, yeah, I know I'm a wicked girl and I'm in with a bad crowd. Don't go on about it.'

'You little bitch! I'm getting sick of you. Why aren't you out clubbing with your sister?'

Although she couldn't really see her features, it was obvious that Tiff was taken short by her mother's response and she whined, 'As soon as we got to Leicester Square, Jen told me to sod off. She was only making a load of noise about taking me anywhere; she only said so to make a fool out of you, Mum. And I was really up for a night out too.'

The moonlight showed the outline of a sulky pout on her daughter's face. Babs snatched the spliff out of her hand. 'You're smoking grass now are you?'

'It's not weed.' Tiffany's voice was slurred and unsteady. 'It's dandelion leaves we find in the cemetery. We can't afford the real gear, can we? So we tried them. I ain't got no money. I ain't got nothing.'

Babs couldn't believe what she was hearing. 'You mean to tell me you pick dandelions in this place and smoke them? Bloody hell! Dogs and God knows what else have probably done their business all over it and you're smoking it.'

Babs grabbed her daughter by the scruff of her neck and dragged her upright. Tiffany didn't resist; her limp body merely swayed in the wind. But it stiffened when her mum wanted to know who 'we' was.

'I don't know what you're talking about.'

'You said "we", didn't you? Who's the other girl?'

'What other girl?'

Babs shook her by the collar, 'The one who scarpered when I came up the path.'

'No one.' Tiffany was defensive and it was only when she was violently shaken by her mum a couple of times that she coughed up, 'I dunno – some girl. I don't know her.'

'Why did she run away? Why would she be scared?'

Tiffany was on the edge of tears. 'Maybe she thought you were the Plod or something, I don't know . . . How the fuck do I know?' Choking, she wailed, 'Stop asking me questions all the time; you're always asking me stupid questions.'

Babs frogmarched her daughter back through the cemetery, past the approving police who had finally managed to disperse the crowd, and then onto the streets.

Tiffany started grizzling. 'Everyone hates me. There's nothing to do around here. It's shit living on The Devil . . .' On and on she went, like a rainy bank holiday Monday. But Babs wasn't listening; her mind was on other things. Why wouldn't Tiffany admit she knew the girl in the cemetery and why had she been so defensive about it? What were they up to and why had the other girl bolted when she'd heard Babs' voice? Even though she'd caught a glimpse of the girl's face, she didn't need to be Mystic Meg to suss who she was. Stacey Ingram.

Seven

'How's your kid?' John Black asked his right-hand man, Christopher Keston. They stood by the window in John's office, upstairs in the Alley Club. John had a receding hairline, a face that told it straight that he'd come up hard in life, and Paul Smith, stacked-heeled shoes, to give his five-five height a little lift.

'The little man is doing great; he's such a clever boy, you know?'

'I like a clever boy. Shame that the slag we've got here isn't one of them.'

They both looked down at the man lying on the floor choking because John had one of his stacked heels pressed hard against his windpipe. The man was making a horrible noise, but he didn't dare move an inch because he knew what John Black was capable of doing. John pulled his foot off and the man sputtered, dragging in air. John moved over to his desk and picked something up. Then he was back crouching down near the man. Chris ripped the man's shirt open. Two buttons burst free and rolled onto the wooden floor.

'I'm sorry, Mr Black, it won't happen again,' he pleaded, knowing that something bad was about to happen.

John raised what he held in his hand – a long stapler – and waved it in front of his victim like a prize. Then he attached the opening of the stapler around the man's right nipple and clicked down hard. The man closed his mouth tight as his body shook, sucking up the pain; he knew better than to scream in John Black's club. John did the same to the other nipple. He threw the stapler on the floor, grabbed the man by the hair and dragged him to his feet.

He yanked his head backwards. 'My money. I want my dosh. Do you understand? I don't want to hear about the end of the month. I don't want to know who hasn't paid you yet or when you'll be out of the red . . .' He drew back his spare hand, clenched it and punched the guy in the face. His victim's body vibrated briefly before, by way of an answer, he slumped slowly back onto the floor. John crouched down beside him and grabbed his hair again but more gently this time and turned the bloodied face in his direction. His voice was softer. 'Am I making myself clear here? I mean, I'm not talking French am I?' The response was a lolling nod.

John smiled. 'Good.'

He picked up the phone and called reception. 'Send a couple of cleaners up to my office, I've got some rubbish on the floor and I need it tidied up and thrown in the bin.'

Forty-year old John Black – real name Charlie Dalton – had used so many aliases in his time that he sometimes forgot what his real name was. For a while he'd used the moniker John Smith, because tracking someone down with that name was a real problem. Turned out it also meant that people he actually wanted to link up with couldn't find him either. So he changed his name again, firstly to Chico Smith then Blanco Smith before finally settling on John Black. But he preferred to be known simply as 'John'. When he was asked what his surname was he would say, 'Haven't got a clue; I've lost my birth certificate.' And by that stage his reputation was such that no further questions were asked.

John's main club was largely a hobby but it also served as a front for his various businesses, which he ran from his office upstairs. Running a private members' club provided him with the perfect excuse for a heavy door that couldn't be kicked in, and for a security detail that was supposed to keep order in his club, but which really kept friends and enemies alike away from his office. Any raid by the filth meant them elbowing their way past his guests in the bar downstairs which gave him plenty of warning, and the club gave him all the opportunities he needed to launder the proceeds of his various rackets. His business associates were always tickled pink to be admitted to his VIP lounge where he made sure there were always one or two people from the showbiz world hanging round. Like many men in his line of work he prized his connections to the famous and made sure they were always well looked after by his staff.

His club was originally called Tara's after his first wife. When that marriage went tits up he renamed it Jessica's after her replacement. When that one too ended in the divorce court, he changed the name yet again to 'The Alley Club'. As he liked to tell his guests, 'alley' stood for 'alimony', the club being the only way he could afford to pay off the two lazy, greedy, gold digging, bitches who'd ruined his life. John didn't have much in the way of principles but a point blank refusal ever to see the inside of a registry office again was one of them. He usually limited his various girlfriends to two nights a week in case they started to get funny ideas about commitment or family. If they got them anyway, he dumped them. As he liked to explain to baffled young men who worked for him, 'If you're with a dolly bird and she starts hanging around outside jewellers – walk fast and walk far – because she's trouble. Especially if those jewellers are in spitting distance of Hatton Garden. Don't look at me like that, mate; you'll thank me for this nugget of advice later.'

His only regret was he had no young 'uns to pass his empire on to, or at least none he knew about or was willing to acknowledge. John wasn't sentimental about men or women, in fact he didn't like either, but he did dote on kids. That's why he always took the time to ask his right-hand man about his son Nicky. Tragically, Chris had lost his wife to illness shortly after Nicky was born, six years back. John broke all his own rules to ensure that if Chris needed time with his boy, he got it.

'Your lad's going to have to be clever if he's going to work for me,' John announced once the rubbish was dragged by his bollocks from the room.

Chris hesitated, trying to find the right words so as not to give offence. He wasn't a hard man, being the admin and paper man end of the operation, but he knew John's business interests inside out, and was the only person John really trusted. He'd met the boss when they were both banged up in Brixton ten years ago. He'd been in for doing naughty things with other people's plastic; he never figured out what John was in for, and he'd never asked. He simply remembered that he'd been as grateful as shit when John had prevented him getting the beating of his life, when he busted the bollocks of a crew of three guys who had cornered Chris inside the workroom.

It hadn't taken John long to twig that Chris was a man who understood business and numbers. But Chris was always slightly nervous around his boss. 'Well . . . I don't know about that, John. I was hoping my boy would be a doctor or a lawyer or something. You know?'

John looked grim. 'We were all hoping to be upstanding members of society once upon a time, mate. Then real life kicks in and you have to get serious. People like us don't get to do things like that.'

'Well, I'm hoping . . .' Chris tailed off. He didn't want a barney with the boss.

John got down to business. He was proper para about being bugged by the cops or rivals and so he often spoke in code: 'Alright, what's happening with that circus equipment we're sending to the Middle East?'

'It's all sorted. We've got a boat booked and we're shipping next week. I met Javid at the Ritz earlier and he's taking care of things at their end. The consignment's stored in garages out at the usual place. Javid's going to arrange for the payment to be made to one of the new banks in Eastern Europe that don't ask too many questions, then I'll ask our accounts people to bring it back here after a few months. We'll rinse it through the club as private parties for celebrities.'

'I don't think private parties cost that much, do they?'

'You'd be surprised. Catering, champagne, class A extras – it all mounts up.'

John nodded. 'What about the paperwork?'

'Our mutual friend – the one from the East End – has organised a girl to look after it for us. He says she's totally reliable.'

'And is she?'

'I don't know; I haven't met her.'

John looked doubtful. 'She'd better be or I'll have his knackers and hers as well. Alright, you'd better run along and see your kid. Tell him Uncle John will be popping by this weekend and he's got a prezzie for him.'

It always squeezed Chris's heart that the boss took such an interest in Nicky, especially since his child had never known the love of a mother.

'He'll really appreciate that John. By the way, our mutual friend from the East End says he wants to meet up as he's got some projects he wants to run past you.'

John laughed. 'Yeah, tell him to fuck off. I don't deal with small timers like him.'

There was a knock at the door. John dropped the lock with a switch and one of his bar staff poked her head around the corner. 'Mister Black, you'd better come downstairs. We've got a problem. One of the waitresses – black bird – is kicking off.'

Jen and Bex stood with their arms folded, freezing their privates off on the corner of Old Compton Street in Soho, waiting for Nuts. Nuts? Jen rolled her eyes. She was the one who was nuts waiting for him and his so-called motor. He'd insisted on giving them a lift home in his car, which he claimed was parked nearby. Well nearby must be a hell of a way because he'd already been gone ten minutes and there was no sign of him or his drive. She should've known that under all that glitzy gear and charm was moonshine and coke. He was probably trying to unchain his bike to offer them a backy. She'd give him a couple more minutes and then they were off.

Where they stood, they were badly exposed to passers-by. They'd already had a crew of lads from the suburbs, out for a night on the lash, drunk out of their boxes giving them the 'You alright babe, fancy a bevy' routine, which had soon turned into, 'Think you're too good for us? Slappers!' when neither woman had given them the time of day. One had even given them a bare bum salute.

Bex looked at her watch and sighed, 'Come on, let's go. He's not coming back, is he?'

Jen shook her head. 'Give him a chance, give him a chance.'

Now it was Bex's turn to roll her eyes. 'You were right; the guy's a B.S. merchant. Come on, let's go before we get mistaken for a couple of toms.'

But it was because she knew she was right that Jen didn't want to go. She enjoyed being proved right. It was true that Nuts dressed well, knew an underground club in Soho and seemed to have plenty of dosh, but that could all be faked.

A car could be faked too, of course; he could always have hired it for the weekend to impress the more impressionable type of girl. If he drove a kosher motor it might be evidence that he was a genuine geezer. But Jen didn't think it was true, which is why she was smiling to herself, even though it meant she'd have to navigate her way home to Mile End past the drunks and the weirdos, and walk at the other end (because no cab was going to drive on The Devil at what the locals called, 'the witching hour').

A seedy-looking old fella stopped in front of them, looked furtively around and then whispered, 'Are you two girls working the perimeter? I've got the cash-in-hand for a threesome. Got somewhere we could go or do I have to book us a room?'

Bex was speechless so Jen took over. 'Sure, we're doing business. Can't we go back to your place?'

His eyes darted around like he was thinking about the possibility. 'Well, we could, but I don't think my wife would be very happy.'

Jen cosied up a touch closer to him. 'No problem, we can sort somewhere out for you. We cost ten grand an hour. Each.'

He sputtered, 'Ten thousand? Are you taking the piss?'

Jen got right into his badly wrinkled face. 'No, you're taking the piss. Now knob off, you creepy, dirty sod.'

The man couldn't get away from them fast enough. This incident was the end for Bex. 'I'm going to get the tube; you stay and wait for lover boy if you want to.' She walked away but then stopped, 'Oh, and Jen, next time, please leave Tiffany at home will you? I know she's your sister, and you have to look out for her and everything, but she's a total muck-up artist.'

Jen watched her best mate getting smaller in the distance and straight away wished she'd gone off with her. She'd proved her point and there was nothing left to stay for. But as she did so, she was forced to step backwards in a hurry as a car's horn blared. A flash, red, sports Mercedes pulled up on the pavement in front of her. Jen scrambled a few paces back and then stopped in gob-smacking awe when she saw who was at the wheel.

'Alright, Cinderella? Your carriage awaits,' Nuts proclaimed dramatically, a large grin spreading across his chops.

The automatic lock on the passenger side door clicked. When Jen climbed in Nuts put his arm around her shoulder and said, 'You must really fancy me to have waited this long.'

Eight

On the dance floor at the Alley Club, there was a stand-off. The security detail couldn't get the waitress to listen to reason. An attempt to nab her had gone wrong when the three heavies had unwisely tried to manhandle her. One had received a kick to the family jewels, which put him out of the fight; a second was nursing a one-inch stab wound to his arm that she'd inflicted with a small knife, drawn in a single action from her kitten heels. Now the woman was backed into a corner of the dance floor, short blade in one hand, a broken beer bottle in the other, and it was clear she was happy to use either or both. The three security guys stood well back debating what to do next.

The music had stopped; some punters had slipped away while others had gathered close – like they were at a movie premiere – to see what happened next. There was a buzz and hum against the backdrop of silence. And one person seemed to be loving up the mayhem: the waitress in the scarlet cat suit.

The security boys were uncertain. The boss had a strict rule – no aggro and anyone who had the front to cause it was to be dumped outside. But he had another strict rule: he didn't want any violence doled out to the idiot. That way there was never a need for an ambulance or the Bill to come calling.

Dust-ups were bad for business. If word got out that you weren't safe, the showbiz luvvies stopped coming; they were a bit delicate when it came to anything that might mess up their good looks. John chose his staff to reflect his policy. All his men were six foot plus and looked like adverts for the upmarket gay gyms in the area.

They all knew that they were in a tricky situation. Even in her heels, the silly cow wasn't much more than five-eight – tall for a woman, but still small compared to the six plus of all the security staff – and apart from her hips, legs and tits, there didn't seem to be much flesh on her. It was pretty obvious what John was going to make of their failure to deal with her; bottle or no bottle, blade or no blade.

'Come on, love,' the head of security said, 'You don't want to be pissing the boss off.' She raised the jagged-edged broken bottle, kissed her teeth long and hard, and pointed it at him. 'I've got a brighter idea. Why don't you tell the DJ to switch the music back on; you and your pussy boys go for a walk and then I'll leave when I'm good and ready. How about that?'

The guy was about to start at her again but shrank back when he realised that the boss had made an appearance. John wore an expensive dark suit, an open-necked shirt and stacked heels which still left him shorter than the woman with the knife. He pushed his way through the bouncers. 'What the hell's going on? Why's the music stopped?' He noticed the man clutching his arm. 'What happened to you?'

'Just a scratch boss. We've had some trouble.'

All eyes turned towards the woman and John followed their gaze until he realised who the argy-bargy was coming from. He'd seen her around; what man wouldn't notice such a stunning piece of womanhood? He looked at his boys and then gestured towards her with his hand, as if to say, 'What her? A waitress? She's the trouble? Give me a bloody break.'

He called out to the DJ, 'Oi – get spinning some tunes.' Then to the guests, 'Come on, start dancing, drinking and copping off. It's Saturday night!' And then to his security, 'Right, you lot, hop it; I'll deal with you later . . .'

The lights dimmed, DJ Jazzy Jeff and The Fresh Prince's 'Boom! Shake The Room' blasted across the dance floor and the fight's audience drifted away. John walked up to the woman who was still clutching her weapons. As he approached she hitched the bottle level with his face. He raised his hands and smiled. 'OK, OK, there's no need to jump out of your pram. I don't usually appreciate my waitresses behaving like they own the place, but I suspect something's gone on here that I need to know about. So why don't you put that down and let me get you a glass of something sparkling and sweet, and then you can tell me what's twisted you all out of shape.'

She didn't put down the bottle, but said, 'I know I shouldn't have done it, Mister Black, but I don't turn up for work to be dissed. You get me?'

'What's your name, love?'

For a few moments the woman kept up her fighter's glare before it melted into a smile that switched her face from murderous to a hundred watt glow. 'Dee.'

As she put the bottle on a table and slipped the knife back into her kitten boot, John wondered out loud, 'Really? Is Dee short for Demon, or Devil?'

'That's for me to know and you . . .' She teasingly raised her sleek, black eyebrows.

He led her across to the bar, which was now returning to normal, while she explained how the rumble had kicked off. They passed her victim, sprawled on a sofa with a hanky clasped across his nose, getting some first aid from his mates. As Dee finished her story about the backside fondling, John nodded and took prompt action. He walked over to where the guy was lying. 'Fuck off out of my club. I won't have people touching up ladies in my place, especially ladies who work for me. If I ever see you here again, you'll have more than a busted hooter to worry about.'

When he rejoined Dee, he told her, 'That must have been some slap you gave that bloke. A very nice job; I'm impressed. How did you cut his face?'

'With these.' Dee waved her four, large, chunky rings. 'I never leave home without them.'

Smart girl, John thought. Rings could do a lethal bit of damage to a face and there was no law against wearing them. His security crew could take a lesson or two from her. She was a bit of alright this black girl and he wasn't talking about her street smarts. He could well understand why the guy she'd decked had wanted to cop a feel of her rear end. He led Dee to the VIP lounge, ordered her his most expensive champagne and they got chatting.

While John gave it the big 'I Am' about his club, twenty-one-year-old Dee sized him up instead of listening. Despite the receding hairline and wrinkles around his eyes, she almost licked her lips; umm, yes, she liked what she saw. She lived in a cramped flat overlooking the murky water of Limehouse Basin in East London, which didn't belong to her; she was minding it for a mate who was enjoying a few years at Her Majesty's Pleasure. In that flat was her prized possession – her magazine collection. She had copies of *Country Life* from which she'd chosen the beautiful house she wanted to live in. She had copies of *Vogue* from which she'd chosen the clobber she wanted to wear. And she had various motoring mags from which she'd chosen the car she wanted to drive.

At school her teachers had told her that if you wanted to succeed in life you had to put the work in. But Dee knew that just didn't float, not in the world she came from. She'd seen plenty of boys and girls from her gates graft away, day in, day out and end up on a road going nowhere, especially when they were her colour. She decided what she needed was a man who could provide for her instead, and she was ready to pay for the service. Dee knew all about John Black – well, as much as anyone was willing to tell her – and the only thing that needed knowing was he ran his own successful outfit and was unattached. So she set out finding a way to get close to him. But if you asked her if she had anything to do with the Alley Club waitress who had fallen over the stool and sprained her wrist, she'd tell you no. If you asked her if that waitress had fallen because Dee had stuck her foot out, her answer would be the same. How was she to know there'd be a vacancy when she turned up asking for a waiting job at the club the very next day?

When John turned his head to order her another drink, she used her pinkie to pull down the zip on the front of her cat suit to give John a better view of her kitty-kats. She might not have learned much in school but she was a keen student of the male of the species. She knew that they thought with their dicks and that created all kinds of opportunities for a woman with her head screwed on. When John turned back she was proved right. He tried to avoid her noticing where his gaze kept resting, but she noticed anyway.

'Tell me, Dee, do you enjoy working here?'

She flicked her hair over one shoulder. 'If you're asking do I want to be serving drinks for the rest of my days, I think you know the answer to that. Why do you want to know?' She was giggling and girly, a stark contrast to the street fighter she'd been earlier. 'You going to offer me a step up in the world?' If there was one thing Dee had learned it was that sometimes you needed to push a person in the right direction. Plant that seed to allow it to grow.

'I might be able to help you out. No promises mind, but I don't like women under my protection coming to grief right under my nose.'

She wrinkled her own nose; not too much though, she didn't want to look ugly. 'I'm not into ending up on my back if that's what you're offering.'

He smiled as he pulled out a pen and then pushed his drink napkin in front of her.

'Write your number down and I'll be in touch.'

She knew what that meant – he was going to spend a couple of days checking her out.

'I might have just the right position for you.'

As Dee wrote her number down she considered with relish the position she really had her eye on. And as John was to discover, what Dee Clark wanted, Dee Clark always got.

Nine

Nuts enjoyed showing off at the wheel of his Merc, honking pedestrians and shooting lights. When he was out of the West End, he asked Jen where they were going.

She answered with a slight hesitation. 'The Essex Lane Estate in Mile End. Do you know it?'

'No.'

'You might have heard of it as The Devil's Estate . . .'

'No, I don't know it as that either. Bad is it?'

Jen fidgeted in the passenger seat. She was always uncomfortable trying to explain life on The Devil. It made her feel like some green alien living on another planet. 'No worse than a lot of other places. You must know Whitechapel Road? Drive there and I'll direct you. Where do you live anyway?'

'I told you, I live in a company duplex down on the river. I'm saving for a deposit on a place of my own. You can be the guest of honour at my house warming. My clients like a bit of glamour.'

He wasn't giving up but he wasn't being very helpful about himself either. When Jen asked him the whereabouts of his gaff all she got was, 'Oh you know, down on the river. It's a warehouse conversion, porterage, the works. Lovely balcony overlooking the Thames, you know.'

'Yeah, I know. But whereabouts? Wapping or The Island is it?'
He became even vaguer. 'Round there, yeah.'

Jen gave up on grilling him and decided to enjoy her ride
instead. It was certainly a change from waiting for a night
bus with London's crazies after an evening out with a young
lad, even if she hadn't actually had a proper evening out with
this one. As he zoomed through East London she began to
warm to him. He was definitely dodgy but he seemed to be
doing it well. As her mum had once told her, there were two
types of men: the dodgy failures and the dodgy successes. It
was only as the castle-like outline of The Devil's Estate came
into view that she noticed, in the rear of the car, a scattering
of crystal specks on the leather seat in the rear and then,
above that, a plastic sheet that had been sellotaped to the
quarter light.

'What happened to your motor?'

He looked over his shoulder. 'Oh that? I went to visit some
mates in Hackney and some kids broke into it looking for the
usual pickings to nick. And stupid me, I'd left a few sheets in
the glove compartment – my bad. That's the trouble with the
East End; it's full of criminals–'

'Why haven't you had it repaired then?' Jen couldn't keep
the suspicion out of her voice.

Nuts wasn't fazed. 'I haven't had time. No one's gonna
break in it now, are they? Anything worth having would be
gone. I'll take it down the shop next week.' He looked at her
and added, 'It'll all be cushty when I come to pick you up for
our first date.'

Jen turned and looked down. There were still shattered
lumps of glass lying on the mats below the seats. She said
nothing for the rest of the journey. She didn't mind a little
patter and a few fibs to grease the wheels but this boy seemed
to think she'd fallen off a Christmas tree, and that was taking

it too far. He didn't seem to notice her silence though, and kept up a constant barrage of saucy chat and barely disguised nudge-nudge-wink-wink along with boasts about how he was going to skyrocket to the top.

When he drove on to her estate, the first thing they saw – to Jen's shame – was a load of cops swarming outside and in a ground-floor flat in one of the low-rise blocks. She didn't need to be told that it was a drugs bust; that was the third one in that building this year. Five years ago, the whispers were that same flat was a knocking shop. No one was out gawping along the balconies or other blocks; this was the usual usual; everyone had seen it all before.

Nuts didn't seem fazed by any of it. As he drove the car away from the drama he performed a wheel spin for her on a patch of gravel and knocked over a few bollards as an encore before stopping in front of her block. He rejected out of hand the idea that she could manage her way to her front door. 'No way, babe; you ain't going up to that flat on your own. This estate is a zoo and you need a lion tamer as an escort. You know what I mean?'

When they reached her front door, she thanked him for a lovely evening out and the lift home but Nuts didn't seem to notice the sarcasm. He put his arm over the doorframe to stop her going in. 'I'm busy tomorrow and Monday – shall we say I pick you up Tuesday about seven-thirty?'

Cheeky bugger.

'We can say that but's it's not going to happen.'

'Wednesday then?'

She grinned at him. 'You're not getting it are you? You deal drugs with nightclub bouncers, you steal cars and you don't even know where your riverside apartment is? You're trouble, mate. I've got enough of that on the home front and don't need any more.'

Nuts sighed but his smile didn't falter. 'OK, it's confession time. Just to show you I'm on the level: I arranged to get some hooky tickets for a gig for the guy in the club. He needed them and I knew where to get them. OK, strictly speaking, it's probably not legit but if you want to call the Bill, I'll say it's a fair cop and take my punishment like a man. As for the motor.' He raised his hand to show a set of keys that he'd put his finger through. 'You don't put a window through on a car when you've got these, do you? Of course I could have nicked them but then the broken window wouldn't have been necessary. As for my flat, play your cards right and you'll be seeing that soon enough. My bedroom ceiling has a very nice shade of primrose for a start. Now, what about Tuesday?'

He had an answer for everything. But boys like him always did. 'And there's another thing. You told me you didn't know this estate. How come you knew how to drive here without any directions once we got past Whitechapel, and know it's a zoo?'

He leaned into her face as he had at the club and whispered, 'Now you're getting desperate. You told me you lived in Mile End and I know my way there. Once you're in Mile End, this estate sticks out like a baguette on a day-trip to Calais. Of course I knew how to find it then. Come on – give me a chance. I'm not going to weave a web of porkies, only to look a total prat a couple of weeks later, am I?'

She hesitated before saying, 'I'm sorry, Nuts. You're a nice fella but I just want a proper life – a quiet one – and a guy like you is too much of a risk for me.'

He drew back slightly. 'I'll be here on Tuesday, seven-thirty on the dot. Of course you don't have to answer the door.'

They were interrupted by shouting and screaming on the stairwell. Nuts was alarmed when two struggling figures emerged onto the landing.

He turned back to Jen. 'You'd better get inside your flat, treacle. Those two looby-loos look like a right pair.'

Jen's heart sank. 'Those two looby-loos, as you put it, are my mum and sister.'

Nuts decided to leave Jen to it. He passed by as Babs strong-armed Tiffany into the flat. Jen followed her family inside, and the front door banged behind them. Tiffany marched off to her bedroom slamming the door. Babs attempted to follow, then cursed under her breath, suspecting that Tiffany had done her old trick of jamming her bed up against the door. No way was she getting inside.

'I'll kick this door in if you don't come out, my girl,' she shouted, hammering on the door.

'Leave it, Mum,' Jen said, sighing as she triple-locked the front door. 'Talk to her in the morning; it's a waste of time now. Was she down the cemetery?'

Her mother sounded exhausted, but still had some fight in her. 'I thought you were supposed to be keeping an eagle eye on her for me?'

Jen shrugged her shoulders. 'She had a row with a bouncer and then flounced off. What do you want me to do?' She didn't finish by saying, 'I told you so . . .' But then she never did. Her mum was already hurting and she didn't want her words to add any new wounds. Babs slumped into an armchair in the sitting room. Jen fetched a bottle of brandy from the side-board, poured a stiff one into a glass and passed it over. 'What was she up to in the cemetery?'

Her mother took a large gulp. 'She was hanging around with a girl.'

Jen was amused. 'A girl? Well, that's something; at least she won't be telling you she's got a bun in the oven in a couple of months' time.'

Babs tutted furiously. 'It's not bloody funny. The girl was Stacey Ingram. I pretended I didn't know who she was and Tiffany clammed up when I asked about her.'

'Stacey Ingram?' Jen didn't see the funny side of it anymore. 'Why would she be hanging around with her; we don't talk to that lot, do we?'

Her mum took another slug. 'Exactly. The thing is, I bumped into Ma Ingram earlier and we had words. Stacey and your sister must have a habit of hanging about together because the Satanic old bitch was moaning off about it.'

Jen shook her head. 'Well, you know what Tiffany's like. Stacey will probably end up as her BFF – anything to wind up the rest of us.' She topped up her drink and became curious. 'Mum, why is it we don't get on with the Ingrams?'

'Because they're a bunch of bastards, that's why.' When Babs saw the look on her daughter's face, she took another sip and went on. 'Oh, I dunno. I think it was something to do with your dad . . .'

'Our dad . . . ?'

So rarely was Stanley Miller's name mentioned in the flat that Jen was quite shocked to hear him mentioned twice in one day. First of all, when Bex had been fishing for info and now it seemed he was to blame for the feud with the Ingrams. Her strongest memory of him wasn't a face – she'd been too young to remember that – but a smell. Old Spice, his aftershave of choice. It was a hazy memory of him leaning over her bed, clouding her in a delicious aroma – Bay Rum jumbled up with fruits and spices. A dad who'd smelt good but who was, from all accounts, a right bastard. As a little girl, when she'd asked her mum where Daddy was, she'd been told that he was 'away' or sometimes that he'd 'gone to heaven'. Eventually, she accepted it. When she'd become a teenager, she'd taken a renewed interest in her father but any questions to her mother about him were met with, 'I dunno . . . Can't remember . . . Who cares?' When she put the same questions to relatives, she was told, 'Don't worry about him . . . Be grateful he's gone . . . Bad business.'

No one talked. After her husband's mysterious departure, Babs had seen various other guys from time to time but she never seemed to have any luck with men. But then, women on The Devil's Estate rarely did.

Jen attempted to sound offhand as she tried to lure her mother into a chat about Stanley Miller. 'Why would our old man have got into a ruck with the Ingrams?'

But her mum made it clear she wasn't taking the bait, and smartly changed the subject. 'Who was that lad who brought you home?'

'Some spiv I met in Soho,' Jen replied, giving Babs a cold stare, which said, You'll tell me one day.

'He seemed like a nice enough boy . . .' Babs suddenly remembered what she'd seen downstairs and cheered up. 'Eh – was that his fancy motor parked outside? Here! Look at you!'

'Possibly. I think he thieved it actually.'

'He must have liked you to drive on to this estate with a car like that. He'll have been lucky if he got downstairs and found it wasn't on bricks. Hope you're seeing him again?'

'No. He's not my type.'

Her mum's brief moment of cheer disappeared. Jen was only eighteen but her mum took an obsessive interest in her love life. She was happy as Larry when her daughter dated and hit the bottle when she split with someone, which wasn't usually long after. There would be pointed reminders that nice blokes don't grow on trees and that she wasn't Princess Di. It took a while for Jen to realise that her mother was trying to compensate for her own disastrous love life through her oldest daughter's. Perhaps that was why Jen was so determined to avoid her mum's mistakes and all those other women lumbered with dead-beat blokes.

Babs' disappointment shone through. 'You never give a boy an even break, do you?'

Ten

'Will your wife be happy about you buying another woman clothes?' Dee Clark asked coyly, reaching for a wad of cash on her boss's desk, first thing Monday morning.

John's office was much classier than Dee had expected – cushioned carpet; plush chairs around a desk topped with smoky-green glass; Chesterfield sofa backed against a wall filled with framed, signed, black-and-white photos of John grinning with celebs.

He'd called her up yesterday and asked her to pop in for a chat, which had made her ecstatic, knowing that all the calls he'd put in about her had come back with a massive thumbs-up. She didn't blame him for calling around; a man in his position had to make sure he wasn't inviting trouble into his house. Loyalty, keeping your mouth shut and knowing when to look the other way were key assets in the world John inhabited. Dee had no doubt that when he got on the blower, people said she ticked all three. But she was still worried about the type of job he was going to offer her.

She soon found out when she parked herself opposite him at his desk and he got straight down to business.

'I need someone to front my security here. Obviously, I've got the wrong guy in charge at the moment and a bloke like me can't afford to let a situation like that rest. I need someone who knows how to handle themselves and I've seen enough to know you do.' His fingers caressed the glass of whiskey on his desk. 'You'd manage my staff and ensure order was kept. All off the books of course, so you don't need to worry about the taxman. Plus, there will be other benefits. I have to go abroad sometimes on business and I may need someone to watch my back while I'm away, so you'd be coming with me and some of my boys to arrange things. You know what I mean. So, what do you say?'

Dee knew not to agree straight away. Eagerness could be a real weakness in certain situations. She crossed her legs. 'I'm not sure. I mean, what would your security boys say if they had a take orders from a lady?'

He huffed, then took a slug of his drink. 'I couldn't give a fuck. The only geezer with a vote in this organisation is yours truly. And after their performance the other night, when you were giving it large, I don't think they're in a position to say dick about anything.'

Dee stretched her arms to squeeze her breasts together and looked into the middle distance, thinking about what John had said but not in the way he imagined. 'I suppose I could consider the position. There's just one thing – this job wouldn't involve anything crooked now would it?'

'Wash your mouth out, darling. I'm a respectable business-man. What do you take me for?' But he was giving her a knowing grin at the same time.

Dee had to stop herself from grinning back; she was getting exactly what she'd hoped for. 'Alright John, you're on.'

He knocked back the remainder of his drink, slapped the glass down and said, 'Stand up.'

'You what?'

'I'm your boss now.' He raised his eyebrow.

Dee slowly stood and watched as he ran his gaze along the length of her body. If he thought she was going to do a striptease for him he had another thing coming. Well it wouldn't happen yet, anyway. Once she got him exactly where she wanted she'd be happy to give him his own private viewing.

'That clobber has got to go.'

'What's wrong with it?' She'd carefully kitted herself out in a Calvin Klein knit tube dress, which had taken her six months to save up for (none of that fake knock-off shite for her), five-inch mauve platforms and a large turquoise spirit stone on a chain around her neck.

'You want to be taken seriously by my people, you've got to be wearing the right gear.' He pulled out a drawer, reached in and took out a roll of banknotes. He counted off a grand's worth and threw it over his desk.

'Get yourself togged out in one of them designer business suits and a sensible pair of shoes.'

That's when she had made the remark about his wife.

Hearing her question, John's expression glazed over. 'My missus? Which one do you mean? I've had two and they both spend their spare time – which is all of their time – filing their nails and working out new ways to take my financial pants down. I mean, wives? Which reminds me, if any legal beagles from the family division turn up here in pinstripes with a writ in their hands, tell 'em I've gone to Spain. And if their clients carry on killing the goose that laid the golden egg the way they have, I may have to.'

Dee's smile was genuine. No little lady indoors to knock out of the game? That was one less problem to worry about. But the next thing he said made her realise there was a sting in the tail. 'Although I'll be honest, my latest squeeze, my Trish, I do sometimes wonder if it might be third time lucky.'

John leaned back with a dreamy look splattered across his face. Dee made a mental note to make taking care of 'my Trish' a priority.

She returned an hour later in a tailored black suit and cream, ruffle blouse. She wore a pair of black flats to make sure she wasn't too much taller than John. She liked her heels but it had to be done. Some men just didn't like a bird looking down at them. She made sure her look was professional and sexy too but without being too obvious about it.

Satisfied, John took her from the office down to the bar area to introduce her to the staff. They were all lined up in a row, about twenty of them. She studied their faces carefully for some indication of what each one really did, as opposed to what they were supposed to do. She'd realised straight away that John didn't make his living out of this club and he must have a bunch of rackets going on. She needed to find out what they were and get involved in them ASAP. Once she'd made herself indispensable in the club, she would do the same with whatever his real business was, and then it would be easy to move from the boardroom to the bedroom.

Then it would be time to get out her old copies of *Country Life* and *Vogue*.

In the meantime, she was practising smiling, flirting and giggling whenever her employer and future husband was around. And smiling, flirting and giggling didn't come easy to Dee Clark, so she had her work cut out. She stood slightly behind him – which also didn't come easy to her – as he addressed his staff.

'Right, as some of you who were on duty on Saturday will know, there was a bit of a fracas in here.' He massaged his temples with his fingertips to show his displeasure. 'And truth be told I'm a bit peed off that my so-called security team had the piss taken out of them by my bird here.' He used his thumb to indicate Dee. 'I mean, alright, she's obviously a bit tasty in a ruck but even so ...'

She didn't look like she was tasty in a ruck at that moment. She looked like a travel agent who was delighted to be selling someone a cheap holiday in Ibiza.

John turned to his current head of security and stabbed a finger at him. 'You're fired!'

The man was so shocked, he didn't move. That was enough for Dee to drop her plastered, frozen smile for a moment and bare her teeth. 'Are you deaf, mate? Fuck off out of here!'

When John turned and gave her a dirty look, she realised she'd gone too far. Shamefaced for sticking her oar in, she popped the smile back in place.

'His replacement will be Miss Clark here.' Dee smiled and waved at them like the Queen. John went on, 'Any queries on the maintenance or order in this club will go through her and I'm sure you will all show the same loyalty to Dee as you do to me.' He added by way of a joke, 'Even if she is black and a short-arse'.

The crowd tittered while Dee kept smiling. He was right, she was black; but more accurately she was mixed-race and John was even shorter than she, although he didn't seem able to admit it to himself. But even through the grin, she thought, *You'll pay for that remark one day, matey . . .*

In the distance a phone rang. One of John's gophers went to answer it and then returned to whisper in his ear. He turned back to his staff, 'I'm afraid I've got to go and see a man about a dog. Perhaps while I'm gone you'd like to say a few words, Dee?'

She waited patiently, a butter wouldn't melt smile on her face. When John had left the bar, her sweetness died away. She folded her arms and in a low growl said, 'First off, I like to be called Mizz Dee.' She took a menacing step forward, 'But what you really need to get through your heads is this; don't mess me about, because there's only one thing you need to remember, I'm the baddest bitch there's ever been.'

Stacey Ingram was shocked to see her friend in the playground at school. Stacey was pretty like a doll, small and with light chestnut hair whose go-to style was a ponytail. While it was only months until they were all leaving anyway, Tiffany had long made a habit of turning up for registration before disappearing again on the way to her first class. Sometimes Stacey joined her, but that was a no-no now. Even talking to Tiffany was out. She'd been warned by her mum and after the night before, when she realised that Babs Miller was on the hunt for her kid among the graves and they were nearly caught together, she'd decided to give her friend a miss from now on. She shuddered when she remembered Tiff's mum giving chase, and replayed the moment she'd fallen again and again in her mind. Had Babs recognised her?

'Oi, Stace!'

Stacey looked round in horror to see Tiffany slouching propped against a wall waiting for her to leave class. She pretended not to have heard and scurried off but she was soon caught up. 'What's up with you?'

'Leave it out, Tiff, I can't hang with you anymore. You know that. My mum will have my guts for garters and no mistake.'

Tiffany scoffed. 'Scared of your old girl? How old are you? It's a sad, sad state of affairs, Stace, it really is . . .' Tiffany always found it hard to comprehend that her pretty, fragile mate could have come from the same gene pool as ug mug Mel Ingram.

Stacey was looking round like a hunted animal. 'You don't know my mum.'

'A mum's a mum, babe. You have to stand up for yourself.'

'Don't call me babe, it's embarrassing.'

There was no discussion about why the families hated each other; they'd already been through the mystery of what it was all about a number of times. Tiffany had no interest in her father Stanley, who she didn't remember, although her mum said that even though she'd been a baby she'd bawled the house down the day he'd done a bunk, as if sensing her Daddy was never coming back. Mentally Tiffany scoffed at that; it sounded like some fairy tale a parent told her kid to make them feel better. But she knew that this feud went back so long that it might have even lasted since her father was around and it had crossed her mind that he might have been part of it. Given her mum and Jen's sensitivity on the subject of Stanley Miller, she wondered if she might find something out and use it to cause trouble at home. She loved a good row and would do anything to relieve the boredom. But the only explanation Stacey was able to get from her mum was that Babs was a slag, Jen was a flamin' slag and Tiffany was a complete and utter flamin' slag.

As Stacey began to move off, Tiffany caught her by the arm. 'Same time tonight then?'

'You're not listening are you?' Stacey answered through gritted teeth. 'I've told you, it's not happening.'

Tiffany moved up close to her mate's ear, so close she was nearly nuzzling it. 'Don't tell me you're having second thoughts?'

Some of the other kids around were starting to pay them attention, so Stacey drew a line. 'It's too risky. I just want to mind my own business and get on with my life. Is that too much to ask?'

Tiffany shook her head and pursed her lips. 'Disappointing. Really disappointing.' Before Stacey could move off, Tiffany took her by the shoulders, spun her around to fully face her and kissed her, smack-bang on the mouth. There were audible gasps from the spectators. Red with horror, Stacey shoved Tiffany away, drew a deep breath and took off at high speed.

When she was gone, Tiffany turned on the gawpers and shouted, 'What you staring at? Wankers.'

No one dared say anything back. Everyone knew the girl was a spitfire and it was well known that she was 'connected' with some well dodgy youth. What they hadn't known was that she was the type of girl who kissed other girls.

Tiffany headed for the school gates. She'd only dropped in to catch up with a few friends and show Stacey up for a laugh. Although, if she were truthful, Stacey was packing some fuck-off fine lips. She'd kinda liked the kiss, not that she'd admit that to anyone. But as she walked down to the high street, she wondered if she'd gone too far. Maybe seeing those two women tonguing each other for England down the Pied Piper had rubbed off on her some way. Come on, she weren't no geezer bird. She'd just stay clear of the women's section of the bar the next time she went down the pub to get an envelope.

Eleven

The first thing Jen saw that evening when she got in from college was her mother oohing and aahing over the biggest and most luxurious bunch of flowers that she'd ever seen. It was too big for her mum's pride and joy sideboard and seemed a little large for the carpet where it was now resting.

'They for me?' Tiffany sneered behind her.

Jen turned at the sound of her sister's voice. She'd been so knocked out by the floral display she hadn't even heard her sister come home. Tiffany had a smirk on her face that soon turned into a curl of her lip, like Elvis hitting the wrong note, and then she was off to her bedroom. Probably tired out from an afternoon's five-finger discount shopping in town, Jen thought scornfully. In contrast Jen was in a good mood because her tutor had asked to see her and a few other students tomorrow early evening to give them some extra lessons. An excited sizzle went through her thinking that she was well along the road to her dreams of getting into the fashion industry.

Jen looked the bouquet over and then asked Babs, 'Where the hell did that come from?'

Her mum ran her fingers over the petal of a bright yellow flower as if she were touching the finest silk. 'That young man who brought you home the other night popped round with them a couple of hours ago.' She looked up at Jen. 'Lucky he caught me in as I'm off to Bingo with Terri.' Terri was her mate who she cleaned houses with in the square across the road. Babs frowned. 'Why the heck did you tell him your name was Simone?'

Realising her mum would have told Nuts her real name, Jen groaned.

Babs turned back to the bouquet and in a dreamy voice continued, 'I made him a cuppa and we had a nice little chin-wag. Seems like a very, very nice boy. He certainly seems to be making something of himself. He even brought me something.' She pointed at a bottle of Moët champagne. 'He said I could save it for your wedding.'

Babs Miller didn't add what her daughter could read in her eyes: 'He brings you home in a Merc; he buys you a beautiful spray. Still think you're too good for him?' She didn't need her mum giving her the third degree about her choices in life. Jen examined the gilt-edged card that was attached to the bouquet. It read simply: *Will you be my orchid? Love Nuts x*

Jen shook her head and smiled. She'd give him ten out of ten for persistence. This lad wasn't giving up. Her mum went off to the kitchen to give her daughter time to inspect the flowers. When she came back, she was in the mood to read the riot act. 'So, are you going out with him or what?'

Jen wrinkled her nose. She paused before saying, 'Doubt it.'

Babs threw her arms in the air, disgusted. 'What's the matter with you? What's he got to do? Turn up in a Rolls with flashing neon lights? I think you owe him one night out for the bouquet at least; they must have cost a bomb.'

'I'm not a tart.'

Her mum was genuinely baffled. 'I don't get it. He's nice looking. He's got get-up-and-go. He's charming and respectful to your old mum. He's got pots of dosh and he's going places.

He's treating you like Elizabeth blinkin' Taylor – despite you giving him the brush-off – not like some tom on Commercial Street, on her knees for twenty nicker a time. There's so many flowers here, we haven't got enough vases and jam jars to put them all in. You know what the world is like for women like us, don't you? You do realise there's not an endless procession of good, young men to choose from? My mum was right: if a woman can find a decent man in a place like this, she should stick with him. And you won't even go on one date?' Her mother broke off as something caught her attention in the doorway. 'Oi – where the hell do you think you're going?'

Tiffany had reappeared and was shoving on her parka. She flipped the hood up. 'Out!'

'No, you ain't.' Babs marched determinedly towards her. 'You're stopping in here you are.'

Babs' youngest gave her the finger and then banged out of the front door.

Jen was too wrapped up in the flowers to take a blind bit of notice of the same old, same old drama exploding in the passageway. Of course her mum was right. Nuts might be a bit of a plum but he deserved a chance and one night out wasn't going to kill her. She swept up the flowers in her arms and took them into the kitchen to find anything that would hold water. The scent began to cover the musty whiff that seemed to be built into the walls of these old flats. While sorting the flowers, she divided up the plus points of her new suitor. He was indeed handsome. Yes, he did seem to be ambitious and looked like he was doing alright for himself already. He was a laugh – in a rather naff kind of a way. He looked kind and it was a nice touch to bring her mum something. Even his loud clothes marked him off from the herd.

When she went back into the living room, Babs was waiting like a father in a maternity ward. 'So?'

'So what?'

Babs rolled her eyes. 'Are you throwing him a lifeline or not?'

Jen began finding places to put the flowers. 'Well, he is very nice, you're right.' Her mum burst into a joyful smile until her daughter said, 'But I'm not going out with him.'

Babs' face fell. 'Why the effing hell not?'

Jen didn't answer. Instead she handed her mother a ripped card she'd found in amongst the flowers. Although only some of it was left after it had been torn off, it had once clearly said: *Grandad: Rest In Peace.*

'You again? What do you want?' said Tiffany's contact at the Pied Piper, not at all happy to see her. As he'd never given her his name and she'd never asked, in her head she'd christened him Man-donna. Although he hadn't known she was coming she'd had no problems getting in this time, Man-donna obviously having given the nod to the door staff to let her in when she came calling.

Tiffany hadn't expected to be called back to the gay hangout so soon, but she had arrived home to find a kid loitering outside, who she recognised as the runner for the guy she was ducking and diving for. He passed on the message that she was needed back up there, and since she was on her last legs, she paid the fare this time; she was too tired to be arsed doing any running.

'I'm here to collect something,' she told Man-donna boldly as they stood at the bar. The Bluebells' 'Young At Heart' was softly playing in the background.

The man looked at her as if she were talking some language only she understood. 'We haven't got anything for you.'

That butterfly feeling Tiffany had got the first time she came here was back in her tummy. 'Eh? That scrawny little prick on the estate told me you had.'

He stared coldly at her. 'I don't think so. Let me make a phone call. Why don't you have a glass of something while you're waiting?'

Tiffany ordered an absinthe cocktail but had to settle for a V&C when her linkman told her not to take the piss. She took her drink and hid in a corner to spy on the women in the other part of the bar, careful to avoid attracting their attention. No one noticed she was there and after a while, she relaxed a little and began to sneer mentally at all the fashion errors these women had put on display – until she remembered that she wasn't really one to talk about fashion. She was a trainers and trackie girl with untrained hair. She could doll herself up when necessary but with her run-around social life, that wasn't very often.

Man-donna seemed to be taking his time about it and Tiffany began to get brain-numbingly bored. She'd only taken on the gig because she thought it might liven up her deadbeat life a little; now she was starting to go off it. Carrying envelopes around for twenty a pop? There didn't even seem to be much danger of going up against Old Bill, so it was all starting to look a bit pointless. Where was the excitement she craved? The adrenaline rush?

She recalled how amped she'd been when a boy up the cemetery had asked her if she was looking for work. The kid was always shooting his mouth off about being connected and so she guessed it would be a bit iffy. When the boy told her some man was offering her a job – no names asked – and fixed up a meeting with him in the Bad Moon in Shadwell, she was even happier. Not only did it look like serious trouble, it had the added bonus that her mum would go mental if she ever found out. But that was then. Now she was bored.

Man-donna was back. 'Nope, nothing for you – so you can run along.' He flicked the fingers of one hand in a shooing motion.

Tiffany cocked her head boldly at him. 'Where's me money?'

He looked down his nose at her as if she were something manky beneath his Doc Martens. 'What money? You haven't done anything.'

Tiffany showed her teeth. 'I came here didn't I? I want my score or I ain't coming back and you can tell that fat bastard I said so.'

She got her twenty quid. When she left the pub, she noticed a saloon on the other side of the road parked on double yellow lines, watching the entrance. Like a lot of troubled kids, Tiffany had already developed a feral nose for trouble and she knew that's what the two guys were. She turned tail and began to pace up the street in the opposite direction. She registered the sound of car doors slamming and footsteps behind her and broke into a run, but a few yards further down they were on her, taking an arm each.

One of them said, 'We want a word with you.'

Tiffany began to make noise, screaming and shouting. 'Get your dirty mitts off me or I'll call the fucking cops.'

Keeping a firm grip on her with one hand, one of the guys reached into his jacket pocket and produced a card, which he shoved in her face. 'There's no need for that, young lady. We are the fucking police.'

Twelve

Dee got on with the next stage of roping John in. She'd spent the day working hard to impress John that she had the skills for the job he'd given her. She made sure she'd put on a bit more slap, especially lippy to give her full mouth that 'it's going to blow your brains around your knob' look before she went to his office upstairs.

She shook her head back, opened John's office door and was surprised to see that he wasn't alone. There was a young man sporting a baseball cap just getting out of a chair. They looked at each other warily.

John announced, 'Dee, this is Knobby, one of my guys. Does a little bit of . . .' – he tapped his nose – 'you know, for me.'

She knew alright, but still wasn't sure about the particulars. She gave Knobby one of her killer smiles. 'Well, I look forward to putting a drink or two on your tab one day soon.'

Knobby grinned back and then moved past her. Good, Dee thought, he wasn't going to be an awkward customer.

She turned her full attention to John, took a seat and slowly folded her long legs, making her skirt slightly hitch up. She hoped he got an eyeful because she'd taken off her G-string in the Ladies. He listened patiently as she gave an account of her first day on the job. He might be listening but his eyes were doing something else – zeroing in on her boobs pushing against her top.

Atta boy, Johnny.

Dee kept her voice nice and smooth, not sexy though; it wouldn't do for him to think she was some desperate slapper. She gave him a list of her new rules and the strict new regime she'd introduced to stop his staff taking the piss. Even though she was only supposed to be in charge of security, she'd taken the liberty of reviewing some of the other work going on in his joint and she wasn't happy. She'd dished out a couple of final warnings and a sacking.

John was alarmed. 'You can't give people the push. That's my job.'

Dee shuffled forwards in her chair, making her skirt ride up even further. 'John, it was that little ginger bouncer bloke – Ian? He couldn't fight his way out of a wet paper bag and he'd be no good in a ruck. Plus, he's a ginger – the punters can't take someone like that seriously, can they? Let's face it, as soon as someone sees a bloke like that manning the door, they're going to start creasing up and I'm not going to put up with anyone sniggering at you.'

From the expression on John's face she could see he didn't like it. 'I suppose . . . Although my mum – God rest her tender-hearted soul – was a red head. But in the future I want all that stuff run past my door first.'

Dee opened her dark eyes slightly in wide-eyed concern. 'I want to take all that burden off you. You're a top-class business-man with a lot of interests and that's where you need to be keeping your eye, not supervising your staff. There's no need to sweat the small stuff; I like to think that's what I'm here for.' Dee took what she called one of her Marilyn Monroe breaths – deep, throaty and extra long on the way out. 'I expect you've got some important deals on the go and clients to arrange meetings with.'

This was her boss's cue to start blabbing to her about what his deals were and who he might be dealing with, but John wasn't going there. 'OK, I appreciate it,' was all he said.

Some other woman would have taken this as a crushing blow, but not Dee Clark. She'd learnt some tough and hard lessons during her motherless childhood and the biggest one was that if you were going to stand on the edge of the gutter saying *pretty please*, you were going nowhere soon. Begging wasn't her style; taking was. And she realised that the taking of John was going to demand she have more than one card up her designer sleeve.

'Now then,' she said, 'what about this girlfriend of yours?'

He looked puzzled. 'Trish? What about her?'

'Have you bought her flowers lately? Why don't you let me sort that out for you?'

John was horrified. 'Flowers? You off your trolley or what? She'll think I'm serious.'

Dee widened her eyes again and shook her head in mock sympathy. 'You don't know much about ladies do you? Any cash you splash out on the ol' blooms will be amply repaid between the sheets later on. You can't go wrong with flowers. What's her favourite?'

John didn't know. Dee sighed. 'Give me her address and I'll order her some tomorrow. A nice display and then she can choose which ones she likes for next time.'

John wasn't convinced about the flowers but still wrote down Trish's address on a notepad. Dee took the paper, disguising her glee, folded it carefully and put it in her top pocket.

'I know it will be my second day on the job tomorrow and all,' Dee let out tentatively, 'but I already had a prior arrangement sorted, so if it's OK with you, boss, I'm going to need to leave early.'

She could instantly tell from the expression on his face that he didn't like it. 'Maybe I didn't make myself clear when I offered you the job; I'm looking for someone reliable.'

'Alright, not a problem.' She stood up. 'I'll just have to cancel babysitting for my mate. She's had problems . . . You know what I mean?' Shit, Dee wasn't happy. She needed this time to get things set up. But she was going to have to find another way.

She made sure her bum did the business as she moved to the door. As she reached for the handle, John said grudgingly, 'Take yourself off when you need to. But make this the last time, my girl.'

Dee left him with a fat grin on her face. When she got back downstairs she went into the bar area and made a phone call to a good friend of hers and asked if she could borrow her toddler tomorrow evening.

The cops had Tiffany up against the wall. 'What's your name then, young lady?' one of them asked impatiently.

Thank fuck she'd hadn't got an envelope, ID or anything illegal on her, Tiffany thought. Getting picked up by the Plod was the last thing she'd expected after leaving the Pied Piper. It could've screwed her over big time, but she knew they would find dick on her so she felt free to let rip at the two men.

'Mind your own bizz.'

She slouched against the brickwork, her lip permanently curled. She hated the Old Bill; all they ever did was spoil her fun. If they were looking for respect they'd soon learn they'd come to the wrong girl.

A look passed between the two men. The one with the black hair and crooked nose got all sarky. 'We're police officers; anything's our business when we suspect law breaking is going on.'

She pulled the pockets of her trackie bottoms inside out and showed them a handful of few coins and her tube ticket. 'No weed, no car radios, no shooters – looks like you've drawn a blank, don't it?'

The other cop snatched her train ticket and examined it. Now that made her upset, really upset. 'Oi, you can't take that off me; how the bloody hell am I supposed to get home?'

The cop gave her a hard, intense look that said he could do whatever the hell he liked. He was a big bastard and used his bulk to loom over her, but she wasn't scared of him. 'Give it a rest for goodness sake.'

He turned the ticket over. 'Come up from Mile End have you? What are you doing up here then?'

Tiffany scoffed loudly. 'It's a free country; I can go where I like. Listen boys, you ain't got nothing, have you? Now let me go.'

Officer Crooked Nose let out a long-suffering sigh. 'What we've got, young lady, is that we've just seen you emerge from a pub down the road – the Pied Piper. You know what kind of pub that is, don't you?'

'Yeah. It's a butch girl and benders pub. So what?''

'We'd like to know what a young girl of your age is doing hanging around in a place like that?' He was about to add that she might be vulnerable to corruption in there, but he'd already decided, in Tiffany's case it might be a bit late to worry about that.

'I'm . . .' She hesitated; sometimes she forgot how old she was pretending to be. 'Twenty-one. Yeah, twenty-one. I can go where I like. What's your problem with gay people anyway? They ain't doing no harm. Wind your watch up boys, it's 1993.'

The cop reluctantly handed her ticket back. 'Name and address.'

'You ain't getting it,' Tiffany said with huge satisfaction. She drummed her fingers against the wall like this was all getting ever-so boring now.

Big Bastard looked smug like he had her handcuffed and bang to rights. 'We'll take you down West End Central, stick you in a cell and wait for you to be reported missing. I'm sure your parents will be very interested to find out where you go when you're up West.'

Tiffany couldn't resist laughing her head off. 'Do me a favour. No one's seen my Dad since I was in nappies and it'll be weeks before my mum notices I'm gone.' She knew the last was a lie; at least she had a mum who gave two hoots about her, unlike many of her mates down the graveyard. These two idiots were living in another time zone, where kids grew up in families of 2.4 children and Dad set off to work with a briefcase and a bowler hat and Mummy Dearest stopped at home wearing an apron and marigolds cooking chicken casserole for the rest of her life. A woman in an apron on The Devil? She would probably be gunned down for looking like a freak.

The two cops withdrew slightly to confer. Tiffany suddenly noticed that Man-donna was standing outside another bar down the road intently watching proceedings as he sucked on a fag. But when he realised that she'd clocked him, he flicked the ciggie and headed back to the Pied Piper. The strange thing was, Tiffany decided, he hadn't looked at all put out that the cops had grabbed her.

She turned her gaze back on to the Bill. One of them was going through the motions of calling into base and asking if a girl of Tiffany's age had been reported missing. But she knew they were doing it for form's sake. She was in the clear. If they banged up every stray teen they found in the West End they'd need to build a block the size of Trafalgar Square.

'Alright, sweetheart,' Big Bastard said. He slapped his hands onto the wall, either side of her head, crowding her in. Up close he was a terrifying-looking man; the type, she suspected, who would slit your throat in a dark alley, no questions asked. 'We're letting you off with a warning this time. If we see you round here again, especially anywhere near that pub, we're going to run you in. Do you understand? And we'll be looking out for you.'

Tiffany sneered, 'Yeah, yeah, yeah.' The devil suddenly got into her, making her eyes twinkle with merriment. 'Like I said, I'm twenty-one and if I want to go into that pub and tongue the life out of some girl there, ain't dick you can do about it. Dick? No I don't suppose me and my girl will need one of those.'

She smirked as she watched Big Bastard and Crooked Nose return to their cop-mobile. Tiffany laughed hard at them when she realised their plain clothes saloon had been given a ticket while they'd been giving her the third degree.

When they were gone, she returned to the pub and peered in through one of the windows. Behind the bar, her guy was having a serious convo on the phone. She guessed straightaway what had happened. There never had been a package for her to pick up and the local cops had been tipped off that a 'vulnerable' teen would be emerging from the pub, because someone wanted to see how she behaved under pressure. She assumed the person who'd ordered this charade was the gangster from Shadwell. Tiffany had been on the streets long enough to know how these things worked.

Thirteen

When Dee left the Alley Club early on her second day in the new job, she headed straight home to change out of her suit and into dull, casual clothes that made her look like a bit of a Doris. It wasn't easy because she didn't keep clothes like that in her stable, but eventually she found an old pair of slacks that she'd done some decorating in and a naff T-shirt she bought years back down Petticoat Lane Market (or The Lane as most people called it). In the bathroom, she scrubbed off all her Bobbi Brown and Fashion Fair face paint and roughed her hair up, so she looked like one of those washed-out housewife characters on *Jerry Springer* who really should have been barred from inflicting their cry-baby crap on anyone's telly.

Before she left she stared dreamily at a ripped page from one of her mags, taped to the wall. It was a snap of a classic 1950s, two-seater Italian sports car: the Pirano FS. She closed her eyes, breathed deep and hard, and imagined herself in the driver's seat, her long, smooth legs stretched out. She felt the sleek, soft leather seat heating up her hot, brown skin. Her hands gripped and glided around the steering wheel. The motherfucking speed blew her jet black hair into the breeze . . . Dee opened her eyes. This wasn't just a car she was looking at; it was her two-finger salute to anyone who'd ever had the nerve to say that Dee Clark was only going to end up in one place: the gutter.

'Pirano.' The name of the car rolled soft, smooth and slow off her tongue; it came out of her mouth as 'Peeee-rrran-oh.' It sounded like a cocktail straight from heaven.

She almost bounced as she headed out, her confidence in her plans for John at an all-time high. But opening the door, she stopped dead in front of the person standing on the landing.

'Hello, Dee,' said her mum.

Jen was dead excited as she walked through the doors at Eastfield College on Whitechapel High Street, struggling with the large, black, zip folder that held her best fashion sketches. The building didn't have the style or flare of the Whitechapel Library and Art Gallery, just down the road, but it didn't need it; this was the place her dreams were going to be made. Well, that's what her tutor William 'call me Liam' Gilbert told her anyway. He said that her work was exceptional and she was coming here in the evening so he could give her some additional tutoring, along with a select few other students. Plus, he said he could organise the month-long work placement she needed in a proper fashion outfit. She was going to take any extra help she could get, if it meant she'd make it in the fashion world and wave 'bye-bye' to The Devil.

When she entered the second floor art room she was surprised to see only Liam at his usual place behind the long desk at the front. He was one of those middle-aged men who tried to make himself look younger with gelled-back hair and a stud earring. The 'Magnum' 'tash totally spoiled the look but, hey, if the guy wanted to make a prize plonker out of himself that wasn't her business; more important was what he could do to fast-track her fashion ambitions.

'Where's everyone else?' she asked as she looked around the room.

Liam stood up, displaying low-riding, youthful, baggy jeans that were all wrong for his frame. 'They couldn't make it. But I'm not surprised. No commitment. Not like you, Jenny.'

She didn't like him calling her Jenny but she was afraid to tell him because he might take it the wrong way. But his remark about her commitment perked Jen up even more. If there was one thing she had in spades it was commitment. From the age of ten she'd been committed to getting off that dump of an estate.

Liam smiled slowly, showing his slightly coffee-stained teeth. 'I'm glad to see that you bought your portfolio. Bring it over here and you can take me through some of your sketches.'

Jen eagerly walked over to him and laid her portfolio on his desk. He stood very close to her, but she took no notice; she was too caught up in showing him her work. She unzipped the folder and set aside the small bag of pins. 'I've got other portfolios at home, but this one I call my celeb collection,' she gabbled away excitedly. She could feel his moist breath on her neck as she showed him the first sketch. 'This one takes its inspiration from Courtney Love's super-short baby doll dress.' She shifted her finger and pointed. 'I've changed it, so it's not just plain buttons on the front, but military style buttons. Gives it a hard edge as well, if you wear the dress with Doc Martens.'

His hand, sporting his wedding ring, came to rest on the desk near her hip as he shifted himself behind her. 'And this one,' Jen continued as she flipped to another sketch, 'is that Sharon Stone, showing-off-all-your-curves dress – the one she wore in *Basic Instinct*, you know where she . . .' Jen's face went pink. *The last thing I should be talking to my male tutor about is some woman flashing her fanny.*

'Oh, I know,' he whispered by her ear. Jen inched slightly forward. She hadn't realised he was that close to her. It made her feel kinda uncomfortable; probably just wanted to get a better view of her work. 'Anyway,' she continued, but her voice slightly shook. 'I added a zip down the middle.'

'Very inventive, Jenny. Very intense.' Bloody hell his voice was practically down her ear hole. Why was he talking so soft and breathless like he'd been running for the number 25 bus and missed it? 'Makes it so much easier for a man to zip the dress down from the front and take it off.'

Hang on a minute . . . That's when she felt him lean into her and rub . . . No way. Her mind wouldn't let her take it in. He couldn't be rubbing his rock-hard dick against her bum? Yuk! WTF.

She froze, her heart thundering in her chest. 'Mister Gilbert, what the effing hell are you doing?'

Instead of moving away he pressed deeper into her, his breathing more ragged and hoarse. She tried to wriggle free, but he clamped his arm around her middle and slammed her tight to him. She fought but he wouldn't let her go. She could smell the nasty sweat coming off him, mixed with Old Spice and garlic.

'Come on, Jenny, let's not play silly buggers here.' His tongue licked her neck as his fingers dug into her arm. 'You knew that we would be on our own. You're up for it as much as I am—'

'Piss off am I up for it,' she spat, wriggling but only succeeding in rubbing herself deeper against his hard-on. She started feeling scared, the sweat breaking out on her forehead. What if he raped her and she couldn't stop him? People would probably say she was asking for it; what did she expect, meeting a fella on his own?

Stuff what other people thought. Jen gritted her teeth. 'You better get your filthy knob and mitts off me mister or I'm . . .'

He let her go, which surprised her. But she didn't hang around to find out why as she gathered up her portfolio. 'I could make things happen for you, Jennifer,' he coaxed softly; her hand shook as she zipped her portfolio shut. 'I know people in the fashion world, from the West End to East London. I know a place that will be more than eager to take a girl like you for your work placement. With a click of my fingers' – he did just that – 'I could open up a whole new world for you.'

Instead of fleeing she stopped as his words sank in.

A whole new world.

'It's all waiting for you, my sweet girl.' His tone was low and seductive. 'All you've got to do is come and take it.' He unzipped his jeans and his erect cock sprang free.

Jen stared at *it*, revulsion pulsing through her, then back at him. This man could make or break her. All she had to do . . .

Jen made her decision. 'If I do it this once you'll help me?'

'Of course I will.' He smirked. 'Now come here and get on your knees and get that pretty mouth of yours ready for what it's been begging for weeks to do.'

Jen carefully placed her portfolio down and slowly stepped towards him, her breath catching deep in her throat. One of her hands was tightened into a fist. She smiled shyly. 'A girl likes to feel what she's getting.'

He leaned his head back and sighed as her hands reached towards him. In one quick move Jen violently yanked his zip up. As the metal caught into his skin he jumped in the air and let out a noise that didn't sound human. Jen opened her hand and stabbed one of her pins into his drooping willy. His scream was piercing this time as he dropped to his knees.

'You perv,' she spat at him. 'I might be desperate to get out of Mile End, but I ain't that desperate. I feel sorry for your wife.' And with that she grabbed up her work.

'No one will believe a girl like you, you know,' he yelled at her, 'so don't even think about going to the college authorities. Who are they going to believe? A poverty-stricken girl like you or a respectable lecturer like me?'

Jen didn't wait around to hear anymore. By the time she got to Aldgate East tube she was softly crying. He was right, no one would take her word over his. A girl from The Devil? You must be joking. There was no way she was coming back to this college. But what was going to happen to her dream? Of making it off the Essex Lane Estate? As the district line train pulled away, Jen sat tight and devastated in a seat, a single sentence twisting around her head to the rhythm of the train.

A girl like you.

A girl like you.

Fourteen

'What are you doing here?' Dee asked her mum with attitude. 'We agreed to meet on Friday.'

She'd only recently met her mum for the first time and still wasn't sure whether she liked her. How do you like the woman who dumped you as a kid and then got on with the rest of her life? But she'd been the one to hunt her mum down, not the other way around, so she couldn't exactly slam the door in her face.

Her mum looked worried as she took in Dee's slapdash clothing and messed-up hair. 'You don't look too good. Not ill are you? Not got that nasty bug that's been doing the rounds?'

The only nasty bug at the moment is you. Dee felt bad as soon as the thought stormed through her head. The reason she'd found her mum was to get to know the woman and, if she was honest, discover why her mum had given her up.

'I'm fine. Like I just said, what are you doing here?'

Her mum stepped inside and gazed around her gaff. 'Just wanted to see where my baby is living.'

'I'm not your *baby*,' Dee answered in a voice that could chill the sun. Dee so wished now she hadn't given this woman her address, but she'd come over all 'Surprise Surprise' when she was reunited with her mum; as sentimental as heck. She'd even dreamed of them taking a Caribbean cruise, sipping cocktails in the bar, watching the beautiful sunset together. Well, the sun hadn't set when they'd met for the second time. That's when Dee found out that her newly discovered mother was going to keep the door shut on much of her past, including the first few months of Dee's life.

Dee wasn't in the right frame of mind to deal with this right now. 'I'm on my way out so you can't stop for long.'

Dee didn't offer her a seat, too conscious that she needed to go over to her mate's to pick up her toddler. Whatever her mum wanted she needed to hurry it along.

'You've turned into a really gorgeous girl. Look just like . . .' Her mum shut up.

Dee stuck her fists on her hip. 'Like my dad? The same dad that you won't tell me anything about?' She desperately wanted to know who her father was. Although her mum was white, all the world saw when they looked at Dee was a black woman and so it was natural that she wanted to know more about her black dad. She wasn't stupid enough to have built him up to be a saint, but just to know his name would be something very special for her. But her mum wasn't playing ball.

Her mum's voice was soft. 'Dee, let's not do this, honey. We've already been around the houses about this. All I want to do is get to know you.'

'Well I'd like to get to know the man who shoved a load of sperm up you.' Dee knew she was being crude, but this woman didn't deserve her respect, not if she didn't have the common decency to cop to who her father was. 'All I want is a name.'

But her mother ignored her question as she strolled from the passage into the front room. 'Own this place do you? Or renting from the council?' She turned back to Dee and smiled. 'Because you look like a girl who's on her way up.'

'No thanks to you, since you didn't bring me up. What was the trouble, Mum? Scared shit of bringing home a – what was it some of the kids at school used to call me – oh yeah, a half-caste little bastard?'

The other woman's face sagged. 'I'm sorry, so so very sorry that happened to you.'

Dee didn't want her pity; all she wanted was her gone. 'Well I'm a big girl now and anyone who has the brass balls to fling crap in my face will get a fistful of rings.'

'Any chance of a cuppa or something stronger? Let's sit down and have a nice little chit-chat about—'

'Sorry, Mum, you need to leave.' Dee headed for the door and held it open, 'I've got business to take care of.'

Her mum gave her flat one last look and then walked to the door. As she stepped out she said, 'I really wish I could tell you his name—'

Dee slammed the door.

The muffled sound of her mother's voice came through the door. 'We still on for Friday then?'

Dee leaned against the door. 'Yeah.'

As the other woman's footsteps faded away, Dee just stayed rooted to the door. Just seeing her mum drained all the energy from her. She'd grown up in a good family with a woman who took her job as surrogate mum seriously, but somehow that didn't make up for not being held close to her own flesh and blood. Dee shook off thoughts of the bad times, headed back to her bedroom and stared at the photo of the Italian sports car. She couldn't wait for the day when that woman saw her driving it and Dee would make sure she understood that her baby-dumping self would never get to ride in it.

As much as Dee bad-mouthed her mum in her head, she couldn't let her go. Once found, how do you let go of the woman who gave birth to you? The idea that her mum would think she was some no-hoper was crushing. Dee was going to show her what a success she'd made of her life and that meant reeling in the loaded John Black. Dee got her brain back into gear with the plan she was going to carry out – getting John's current gangster groupie, Trish, out of the way.

Dee got into her small run-around and headed over to her mate Marsha's. She'd always owned a car, whether she was skint or flush; it was not a good look to be seen on public transport. Marsha had initially refused point-blank to loan her toddler Kyle, but when Dee explained that she'd been claiming child benefit for a kid that didn't exist and the social were coming round to check in an hour, Marsha hadn't felt able to refuse. Dee was narked at having to give an explanation but when Marsha brought her son out for the loan and she copped an eye on the angelic child, she melted into joy and smiles. It was something she had in common with John; they both had a weak spot for kids. For a few moments, while she lifted the boy into her arms, Dee forgot why she was there. She desperately wanted a child of her own, to create a person that she could rely on one hundred per cent. But she needed the right bloke, and that meant one with the right type of bank balance.

Down on the street Marsha fixed the child into the front seat, fussed over him and made sure his seat belt was secure.

'I want him straight back here afterwards, Dee, you understand?'

Dee reassured her with one of her heart-stopping smiles. 'A couple of hours, tops – you know what the social are like; they'll soon get fed up and piss off. They only want to see a kid in my drum. They're not going to question Kyle are they? Even they're not that sadistic.'

It was a very different Dee that drove little Kyle across London. She sang songs with him, told jokes and rolled the car on the road to keep him amused. It was only when they got to their destination that she became serious again. She led him up the stairs of a new-build block of flats and when she reached a front door on the top floor, she picked him up and hugged him in her arms.

'Now, Kyle, we're going to play a little game called Let's Pretend. I'm going to pretend to be angry and my friend is going to pretend to be upset. Do you get it?'

Kyle got it. He knew all about Let's Pretend. So did Dee.

She knocked on the front door. A woman in a red, silk dressing gown answered it with a towel wrapped loosely around her shoulders. She was just what Dee was expecting: a bottle blonde chick in her twenties, with peachy skin; slim, but well upholstered and with all the fittings that a simple man like John would appreciate.

Trish looked at Dee and then at Kyle. 'Who the hell are you?'

Dee made her voice shake with overblown emotion. 'You might well ask who I am. I have the dubious honour of being your boyfriend's wife and this is our son Tarquin. I suppose you're going to tell me you didn't know about us – you home-wrecker.'

Some of the colour drained out of Trish's face. 'His missus? You're joking; he hasn't got a wife. He said he'd rather stick his todger in a mincer than do the going-to-the-chapel lark again.'

Dee hugged Kyle tighter. 'That's what he told you, is it? You realise that's what he tells all his slags, while me and little Tarquin are sitting crying a river at home. And you were dumb enough to believe him? What kind of idiotic fuckwit are you anyway?'

Trish was nearly snow white. 'I didn't know.'

Dee took a deep breath. 'But you do now. And I'll hope you have the decency to tell my husband that you won't be seeing him anymore and that you won't mention my visit. I've still got my self respect.'

Trish didn't answer but Dee noticed with alarm that some of the colour had returned to her cheeks. Trish folded her arms and firmness returned to her voice. 'Hold on a minute, that kid's white, you're black. And where's your wedding ring?'

Dee considered explaining that she was mixed race and that, with her and John's gene pool mixed together, Tarquin might well have looked white. But instead she decided that was enough of Let's Pretend. She lowered Tarquin/Kyle to the ground and explained in a whisper and with a smile that they were now playing a new game. This one involved him closing his eyes, putting his fingers in his ears and singing 'The Wheels On the Bus Go Round and Round' to himself. When he did so, Dee was triumphant; she always knew she was great with kids.

She rose back to her full height, grabbed Trish by the lapels of her dressing gown and forced her back into the flat and up against the wall. She whipped the towel from the other woman's body and lashed it against the wall next to her. Trish cringed with a squeal.

'Right, bird brain, you listen to me.' Dee smacked the towel against the wall again. 'It doesn't matter to you whether I'm his wife or not, or whether little Tarquin is his kid or not. You're to give him a bell tonight and tell him it's over. Do you get me?' She lashed the towel with such menace and force next to Trish's face that tears sprang into the other woman's eyes. 'Because if you don't, I'll be popping round here again without the kid and that'll clear the decks for some assault and battery – you know what I mean? – as it will if you mention my little visit to him. I'm pretty nifty with a blade and you don't want to end up looking like the Bride of Frankenstein."

Dee stretched the towel against Trish's throat and pressed down. The colour was certainly returning to her cheeks now, but it was a sickening shade of purple.

Trish just managed to choke out 'Yes' before Dee triumphantly let her go.

Dee left, skipping along the balcony with Kyle and cheerfully humming Ace of Base's 'All That She Wants'.

Fifteen

Jen felt crushed as she exited Mile End Station, her hands limply holding her portfolio. And stupid; she should've seen slimy Liam coming a mile off. But that's what happened when you let your dreams take over. Then she remembered that Nuts said he was coming over to take her out this evening. It was almost eight and if he'd turned up he'd be long gone by now. It wasn't that she believed he would actually turn up at 7.30 as he'd promised, but she couldn't be sure. The bloke had more front than the beach on *Miami Vice*.

When she reached The Devil the first thing she saw were two girls slogging it out while a group of lads looked on, laughing. One of the boys was collecting money from one of the others, probably betting on the outcome of the fight. And no doubt the girls were going at it over ownership of one of the boys. Pathetic! The whole spectacle made Jen's lip curl in disgust. She would never go toe-to-toe over some geezer; if he was putting his John Thomas in some other woman, she'd tell the bastard to keep walking. She didn't ever want to be so desperate for a slice of good life she resorted to fighting for it in public.

'A girl like you.' She couldn't get Liam's nasty remark out of her head. Maybe this was what a girl like her really deserved – to live and finally die on The Devil's Estate.

Dejected, she scanned the car park for Nuts' flashy motor, but when she saw no sign of it she made her way up the stairs, home. As she walked up, she couldn't help wishing that he had come. Because, by now the Merc would be on bricks, all its remaining windows would have been put through and half the paintwork would have been keyed off. Unless, of course, it was a blackened wreck (the victim of the second part of third party, fire and theft). Now that would have cheered her up.

But when she got to her front door, she heard the sound of her mother cackling loudly inside. It was obviously not Tiffany causing her to laugh and her mum seldom had visitors. Babs was cautious about who she let into her home: too many light fingers and nosey parkers living on The Devil. Jen backtracked along the landing and checked the car park again. Still no Mercedes there, but she did notice a fuck-off metallic, silver BMW that she hadn't seen before. Sitting on a wall nearby were two local kids who she suspected had been slipped some 'guard it with your life' cash. She walked back to her front door and opened the letterbox. Amid Babs' laughter was the sound of a highly amused Nuts sharing a story with her.

Jen always tried hard to keep the effing and blinding to a minimum. Swearing to high heaven was so common and didn't project the kind of sophisticated image she was comfortable with. But she was badly stressed all over again. 'I don't fucking believe this.' Although she cursed she did buff her hair quickly with her fingers thinking about old blue eyes waiting inside.

She drew a breath, opened the front door, placed her portfolio against the wall and walked into their front room. Nuts was spread out across a sofa with a grin and a cuppa in his hand. He wore a smart, tanned leather jacket, stone-washed jeans and a white T-shirt that had a huge black and gold dragon on it. Who did he think he was? Bruce Lee? When he realised who'd just walked in, he hastily sat up straight, got rid of the smile and put the tea down like a naughty school kid.

Babs was all sunshine and smiles. 'Hello, hun.' She turned to Nuts and continued with pride, 'Jen was getting some extra lessons from her tutor. She's going to be in the fashion—'

'Can I have a word with you a moment? In private?' Jen's eyes snapped at her mother.

The two women went into the kitchen where Jen closed the door. She jabbed a finger at her mother in disbelief as she demanded, 'Mum – what the fuck? I mean seriously – what the fuck?'

Babs held up a restraining hand. 'Now, I know what you're thinking, but the poor boy's just come round to apologise about the flowers. He knows he's done wrong, that you don't want to see him and he accepts that, but he just wants to say sorry.'

Jen reared back, outraged. 'Sorry? He thieves wreaths, Mum – *wreaths*.'

'I know and that was very wrong, but if you hear him out he'll explain why.' Babs put on that mum tone that she usually only used with her youngest and scolded, 'You know it's considered good manners when someone apologises to accept it with good grace.' Then she acknowledged, 'He's a bit of a rough diamond; he admits that.'

Jen looked at her mother still seething and then threw the kitchen door open and strode over to where Nuts was sitting with a hangdog expression. She sat next to him and collected herself. 'Alright, what do you want?'

He gazed at her sheepishly through those memorable blue eyes of his. 'I just wanted to apologise.'

'OK. Well, I accept your apology – now do one and don't come back.'

He pleaded, moving slightly forward in his seat, 'Let me take you down the boozer for half an hour. I'll tell you what happened and then bring you home. Then you'll never see me again. I promise.'

Jen studied his face. He did indeed seem very sorry. But she wasn't fooled. 'You promise? You promise if I do that you won't bother me again or come round here trying to soft-soap my mum?'

'Absolutely, I know I've blown it.'

Jen bit her lip. 'You've got thirty minutes.'

'Enjoying your burger, little man?'

'Yes. We don't get these at home. I don't know why.'

Dee giggled with joy. Even though she knew her friend Marsha would be frantic with worry about where he was, she was enjoying little Kyle's company so much she took him to an upmarket diner she knew. She also wanted to reward him for performing so well at John's now ex-girlfriend's.

She trilled, 'You're a little star, Kyle! You're going to win an Oscar when you become an actor one day and Auntie Dee's going to help you.'

But Kyle didn't want to be an actor; he wanted to be a bus driver. And that, Dee lamented to herself, was the problem with mums like Marsha; they didn't encourage ambition in their kids. Didn't tell them how they could reach for the stars even from a council block in East London. The poor little sod was doomed before he started.

'When I have my little boy, he's going to be exactly like you,' she whispered, tapping him sweetly on the tip of his nose. Except he wasn't going to be no fucking London Transport bus driver.

Kyle peered up at her. 'Are you having a baby, Auntie Dee?'

Dee smiled at him gently. 'Not yet. I've got to marry my fiancé first. He's a big, strong man with lots and lots of money and we're going to have lots of little Kyles to fill up our big house with.' Dee had always acted on the principle that if you behaved as if something was going to happen, it would.

'Did your mum have a big house?'

Dee became wistful. 'My mum? No, my mum was a loser, Kyle.' She only just managed to avoid saying – like yours. 'I'm afraid it all went pear-shaped for my mum. She couldn't find the right bloke. She hooked up with my dad, who I suspect was a prime piece of rubbish.' Kyle was too busy with his burger to listen to what Auntie Dee was going on about. There weren't many people she could or would tell the story to. Little kids, like Kyle, were about the only people she felt she could share secrets with.

'So my mum got herself a new fancy man who she married. Only the trouble was, he was even worse than my dad.' She'd managed to get her mum to tell her at least that part of her history. Her voice became harsh. 'I was kicked to the kerb and farmed out to relatives and the like.' Now her voice resounded with glee. 'But then he dumped her anyway.'

Kyle looked up from his burger again, ketchup smeared at the side of his cute, little boy lips. 'You didn't live with your mum?'

Dee wiped the red sauce away delicately, with a napkin. 'No and it's just as well. I might have ended up like her. I see her every now and again, just to remind myself how not to do things. That's the important thing in life, Kyle. Get yourself the right parents. Get the wrong ones and you're screwed.'

By the time Dee got Kyle back to his mum, Marsha was in a right state. Dee got a choice selection of verbal for keeping the kid out late and she swallowed it because she didn't want Kyle to hear her effing off at his mum. She had rules about cursing in front of children – most of the time.

But Dee had another reason to try and keep Marsha sweet. She needed the phone number of a man her friend had been smooching with for a while, before dumping him because he was a booze merchant, spent half his life in Ladbrokes and nicked money from her. He was a former telecoms engineer who'd been sacked for misconduct, and Marsha was so shocked that anyone would want this guy's number that she gave it to Dee with a warning not to have anything to do with him.

Of course Dee wasn't expecting to trust Jimmy Kite any further than she could throw him, but she did require his services. She'd already disposed of her fiancé's girlfriend; that had been the easy part. Now she needed to become a trusted partner in John's business affairs, so that he couldn't do without her. (A firm basis for any marriage.) And for that, she urgently needed Jimmy's help.

For the final phase of the 'Put John in a Box Called Dee' process she would have to rely on herself.

Jen was in a hurry to get this over with. As she hurried down the balcony to the stairwell with Nuts in tow, she peered over the edge of the wall. 'Oh great. Now I've got her to deal with as well.'

Nuts looked down too. 'Who's that?'

'My sister Tiffany. The girl who put the bitch in witch.'

'Your sister?' He gazed at her amazed, like he couldn't believe that gorgeous Jen came from the same womb as trackie girl downstairs.

'You've met her. She was the mouthy girl outside the club, and the one you called a looby-loo when you brought me home.'

Nuts didn't seem interested. 'Oh, right.'

They carried on towards the end of the balcony until Jen stopped when she saw her sister emerge from the stairwell.

'Where the hell have you been?'

'Knob off,' Tiffany hurled back, not looking at Nuts or missing a step as she brushed past her sister.

'Sometimes . . .' Jen hissed as she stared daggers into her
sister's back.

'Sometimes,' Nuts finished for her, 'you can't save the whole
world.' He chucked his dog end over the landing wall as Jen
decided that he was right. Tiffany was on a one-way track to
trouble and she'd done her best to steer her in the direction of
the straight and narrow.

Pushing her annoying sibling from her mind she followed
Nuts down the stairs, resuming their journey to his car. When
they got there, Nuts nodded to the boys who were keeping
guard on his flash motor.

'That's alright, Nuts. Pleasure doing business with you,' one
of the lads said with a grin. Obviously money had changed
hands earlier. Jen made a note to remind Nuts to pay after the
job got done on The Devil or he'd be ripped off left, right and
centre. Then she almost slapped her forehead. What was she
saying? There wouldn't be a next time.

As they buckled up, Jen said, 'On first name terms with the
local scrotes I see. And where's the Merc then? In the shop
being repaired?' She couldn't help herself from sounding
proper sarky.

Nuts nodded. He seemed weary. 'You still think I nicked it
don't you?'

Jen was upfront with him. 'Yeah, I do actually.'

At this he turned the ignition on the BMW, looked at her
and gave her a grim smile. 'You're right. I did pinch it.'

Sixteen

Tiffany didn't stop at home for long. She decided to head back out again, despite her mother's half-hearted attempt to stop her.

'You're not going down the cemetery Tiff,' Babs ranted. 'The Bill will be there. How many more times do you think you can have a run in with them before they fit you up for something serious?'

'I ain't going to the cemetery, I'm going to see my mate.' Not that it's any of your beeswax, she thought defiantly.

'Which mate?' Babs' features turned stormy. 'Better not be that Stacey Ingram, my girl, or I'll have your hide.' But the front door had already slammed behind Tiff, leaving her mum raving to thin air.

Tiffany scampered down the stairs, stopping briefly to take a drag on the spliff that was being smoked by the two boys who'd kept an eye on Nuts' car. Then she walked the half-mile to a maisonette in a block in another sprawling part of the estate, where Stacey lived with her mum. As she got closer she heard the thump of music from a house party on the top floor and saw the silhouettes of people dancing to Shaggy's 'Oh Carolina'.

She decided against ringing the bell. She knew what response she'd get if fire-breathing Mel Ingram answered the door. So she walked down the road collecting small pebbles and stones, then, one by one, she threw them up against Stacey's bedroom window. It took several hits before her friend's face appeared. She looked down, saw who it was and snapped the curtains shut with horror. Tiffany resumed throwing stones – larger ones this time that sounded as if they might crack or break the glass. Unable to stand it anymore, Stacey came back, threw the window open and hissed, 'What do you want?'

'To hang out,' Tiffany responded happily, swaying along to the music coming from the party upstairs. She loved dancing.

'No chance.'

But Tiffany was in no mood to be sent away with a flea in her ear. 'I'll just ring the doorbell and ask your mum—'

'No, no. I'll come, I'll come,' Stacey cried.

A few moments later, her friend appeared at the front door, closed it gently behind her so it made no sound then grabbed Tiffany by the sleeve and dragged her down to the dark end of the street. 'Are you out of your mind coming round here?'

'Your mum still not happy then?'

'Never mind my mum. My dad's been round; she called him up.'

Even Tiffany was slightly alarmed. Strange as it seemed, she had never seen Mickey Ingram. Sure she'd heard he had a fist-thumping reputation, but he didn't live on the estate and when he was around Tiffany made sure she kept well out of the picture. 'I thought your dad was long gone. I thought your mum hated his guts.'

Stacey shrugged like she just didn't understand the world anymore. 'She does. That's how bad things are Tiff; my mum got my dad round to read me the riot act about hanging out with you.'

'Me?' Tiffany stabbed a finger in her chest.

'Yeah you – or any other dirt bag Miller, as he put it. Please, Tiffany do me a favour,' she pleaded with her friend. 'Leave me alone, at least for now.' Then she suddenly remembered. 'And what were you playing at with the kissing thing at lunchtime? What was that about? You do realise I had to snog Simon Watts in public this afternoon, that dick, just so people don't think I've gone lesbo shaped. I know you like a wind-up, Tiff, but you always have to take things too far. If that got back to my mum and dad, I'd be down the cemetery alright. But for good this time.'

Tiffany looked at her friend and felt sorry for her. She'd moved on but Stacey hadn't. Perhaps that was because Tiffany was more like her sister than she liked to think. Jen wanted to be better than other people and Tiffany wanted to be worse, but it amounted to the same thing really. The world was up for grabs – if you dared reach for it.

'I'm only having a laugh.' Tiffany tried to bring the happy back to their chat. 'Your problem is, you worry too much about what other people think. Stuff 'em.'

'And your problem is you don't think enough. I have to live round here; I have to live with my mum, and now I'm pulling visits from my dad.' Stacey flicked her gaze fretfully towards her front door. 'Look, I've got to go before Mum notices I've gone. I'll see you around . . .'

Tiffany let her go. She knew Stacey would buckle. She didn't have many friends and her mum was a complete bastard. But if that wasn't enough, Tiffany knew the threat of turning up on her doorstep again would be enough to get her back out. She watched as Stacey hurried back to the house, slipped her key into the lock and turned it slowly. Then she went carefully inside. But she hadn't been careful enough. There was an almighty explosion of shouting inside the house that included a man's voice. He barked, 'Who told you to go out? Eh? You slag, I'll show you how it is.'

Tiffany drew closer and shivered as Stacey screamed and the noise of thumping and banging came from the hallway. Then there was silence interrupted only by a mewling and the occasional muffled howl that sounded more like a wounded animal than a human being.

Tiffany's heart filled up with an emotion she couldn't name; her chest and throat felt tight and her tummy muscles crunched together. Trembling and afraid of what she'd see, she drew closer. The front door was wide open and the man's voice was deadly quiet but unapologetic. 'You asked for it, you got it. I'm warning you, girl, if I have to come around here again, I'll give you something to cry about. Stop sneaking out. Stay away from the Millers. You better believe I know all about that family and I'll find out if you draw breath anywhere near them. Stay away from them. You hear?'

A large man emerged from the front door and closed it behind him. Tiffany ducked behind a car. He rearranged his suit, shirt and bracelets, pulled out of shape whilst beating her friend, then adjusted his tie and began walking down the street. Bollocks, he was coming her way. Quickly she crouched low as he went by; she could hear him muttering to himself, 'Fucking women . . .' Further down the street, he got into a car and drove away.

A dazed Tiffany slowly stood up and looked over to the flat. It was only the prospect that she'd cause even more trouble for Stacey that stopped her running up to the front door and offering her support. The thought of her mate – so small and delicate – hurt and probably bleeding, tore her up. Her mum might threaten to raise her hand to her, but that's all it ever was – a threat. Babs Miller would never lay a hand on her. But what could she do about Stacey? Nothing. Plus, she had another problem now.

She walked home, head down. In the days when she still went to school, the teachers had brought in a policeman and former criminal who'd done eight years for armed robbery. This repentant crook had begged the kids not to consider crime as a career option. Gangland is not, he explained, like you see on the TV or in films. It's not tasty geezers running around in fast cars, robbing banks and then going down the pub afterwards for a pint and a laugh. It's a cruel, evil world where terrible things happen and lives are ruined. The cop had backed up what the ex-jailbird had to say. Crime, he promised the kids, is definitely not cool.

The other girls had soon got bored and begun fidgeting and playing with their hair. They were of an age where they discounted anything adults said to them, and they resented having this crook and cop wagging their fingers at them. If crime was so bad, why had this robber spent so much time doing it? They preferred the telly and movie version. But Tiffany had been fascinated. Yeah, this bloke was pathetic and, yeah, he sounded like someone's mum, but he so desperately wanted them to believe him that she'd felt almost sorry for him.

As she walked home with her hands deep in her pockets, she remembered that man. Because he was right. Tiffany realised she was in over her head. Not only did she know there was nothing random about being stopped by the Bill earlier in the evening, she now knew that she had met Stacey's dad before. The man who had just given her friend a vicious hiding was the same man who'd hired her as a courier in the Bad Moon in Shadwell.

They were both Mickey Ingram.

Seventeen

'Alright, my hands are up. I nicked the motor and I nicked the flowers.'

And Nuts had told another lie. Instead of taking Jen to The Old Swan for half an hour as he'd promised, he'd driven her several miles down to the Thames and escorted her to a newly fashionable pub in a part of town where people with money were starting to move into expensive apartments and conversions. But Jen didn't mind. She hated the local pub with its pathetic drunks and punch-ups. She was also enjoying being proved right. She'd known from the start that Nuts was a wrong 'un.

He looked so sheepish she felt almost sympathetic. 'I don't mind being lied to; I get lied to all the time by boys. But lies that insult my intelligence? That I don't appreciate.'

He begged, 'Oh come on. The Bob Marley's my real motor and it really was broken into; it really was down the shop being repaired. All I did was rearrange the facts slightly to suit the situation.'

She pinned him with her hard stare. 'And steal a car.'

'Yeah, alright, I've admitted that. What was I to do? I could hardly offer to put you on a bus after all my mouthing off down the Alley Club, could I? I'd have looked a right plum.' He seemed to feel that avoiding looking like a plum justified what he'd done. 'The owner will get the Merc back, they'll be insured, and whoever turned my Bob over didn't care about me, did they? Cars get broken into and nicked; it happens all the time. It's an occupational hazard of being a car owner. They'll have forgotten about it by next week, just like I will. This is the East End. You're not telling me you've never taken anything?'

Jen didn't answer. She had once swiped a scarf from a store when she was fourteen, but that was a long time ago. Plus, she'd felt so ashamed of doing it that she'd dumped it in the rubbish chute on the landing. But he was right, this was the East End and things got stolen. She thought of Tiffany. Then she went back on the attack. 'And the flowers?'

He avoided her gaze. 'Yeah, I admit that was out of order. I bought you a lovely bunch of flowers in a florist but on the way over to your mum's I thought they looked a bit cheap. I was driving past the cemetery down my way – the extension part, where they've started burying people again – and I saw council workers had picked up all the used wreaths and dumped them on a compost heap by the wall. Some of them still looked in good nick so I pulled over and rummaged through them and put together a bouquet – but obviously I didn't get all the labels off, which was careless.'

Jen pursed her lips with disapproval but there was no anger now. 'Good nick, so you nicked them.'

Nuts pressed on. 'I mean, come on. It's not like I pushed a grieving family and a vicar out of the way, grabbed a wreath off a coffin and ran for it. No one was using them anymore. I was just trying to make a good impression, that's all. You can understand that, can't you?' He started to sound bitter. 'You don't know what it's like trying to impress women. It's not easy . . .' Then he added meaningfully, 'Especially when they look like you.'

He was still avoiding her gaze. Mention of the cemetery made her think of Tiffany again. She knew in her heart that Tiffany wasn't a bad person and she was starting to think that Nuts wasn't either. Perhaps her mum was right. 'And what about the job in the City and the flash flat in Docklands? Did you make that up as well?'

Nuts stared at her now like she'd lost her frigging mind. 'No, I did not.' He opened his leather jacket so she could see the silky, purple lining inside. 'How do you think I can afford this? Then clock my motor in the car park. That didn't cost buttons, did it? What do you think I do for a living?'

She lifted her eyebrows like it was the question of the century. 'I don't know. Maybe you've got a business selling stolen flowers.'

His eyebrows flattened, pulling his face into a hurt expression. 'I'm disappointed. That's cheap, very cheap. I expect better of someone like you.'

She was smiling now. 'Oh, stop feeling sorry for yourself.'

The half hour she was supposed to give him came and went without either of them moving. The Thames turned silver in the twilight and then went inky black after dusk, only reflecting the spotlights on the riverbank. Nuts had her chuckling with the same stories she suspected he'd told her mum. Tales of skulduggery and derring-do in the City and the various people who worked there which he backed up by mimicking their voices and mannerisms. Before Jen realised, it was gone eleven.

He took her back home, keeping up a constant line of patter, and drove her right up to the stairwell where he dropped her off. She made no attempt to get out of the car so he hopefully asked, 'Am I forgiven then?'

'I suppose.' She shyly clutched her shoulder bag.

Nuts shuffled sideways to look at her. 'I know this is really cheeky but I don't suppose I could take you out some time after all?'

She smiled as she got out of the car. 'Give me a call in a week and we'll take it from there.'

As she reached for the door handle, Nuts touched her on the arm and she couldn't keep back the wince of pain as his fingers pressed against the spot where Liam had grabbed her.

'What's up with your arm?' Nuts quickly asked and before she could say anything he leaned over and rolled up the sleeve of her jacket.

'Who's been touching you?' He sounded furious.

She yanked her arm back, sucking in a sharp breath at the renewed pain. 'No one—'

'Don't lie to me, Jen. I know when I'm seeing the marks of fingers against skin.'

The whole awful situation of what had happened with Liam overwhelmed her and she collapsed back onto the seat and started crying. Nuts instantly pulled her into his arms and started gently rocking her and caressing her hair. 'Don't worry, babe, everything's going to be alright now, Nuts is here.'

And, strangely, she did feel that everything was going to work out, now she was safe in his embrace.

'I'm not going to pressurise you, Jen; it's up to you, but I'd really appreciate it if you told me what happened.'

She liked the way he asked her, not demanded she tell him. Now that was a gentleman. And she so wanted to tell someone. Sometimes she felt that her mum and sister were so wrapped up in their own battle, they didn't see her anymore.

Jen slowly pulled out of his arms. 'OK. It was my tutor . . .'

To say that Nuts looked angry by the end of her explanation was the under-statement of the year. His hands were fists, like he was ready to punch out the windscreen.

'I'm not a believer in going to the cops,' he finally said tightly, 'but you should report the bastard for trying to rape you.'

'It wasn't really rape–'

'That's what it would've been Jen if you let him go at you. You didn't ask him to touch you so he had no right putting his hands on you.'

The rage coming off him was electric, so she laid a palm gently on his knee. 'I don't want the Bill involved and, if I'm honest, the only thing that matters is that I won't be able to go to college anymore and get my diploma.' Her hand tightened on his leg. 'Do you know how long I've dreamed of getting off this bloody estate, of being the girl from the East End who made it in the fashion industry? That bastard promised to find me a good placement for a month; without it there's no way I'll finish the course, not that I'm able to go back with that creep still there.'

Nuts surprised her by leaning across and kissing her on the cheek – such a contrast to Liam who'd been pawing and panting all over her.

'I'm going to give you a bell sometime soon.'

Jen stared at him, wishing with all her heart that Nuts didn't have a dodgy bone in his body; if it wasn't for that, he was the type of man she so wanted to settle down with.

Eighteen

Dee was in work early. There was no sign of John who was out for the day on 'business'. What that business actually was had now become her prime concern. Standing outside the Alley Club, in a baseball cap, with a toolbox in hand, was Jimmy Kite. She'd rung him the previous evening and offered him a couple of hundred quid to come and do some private work for her. When he'd asked what the private work involved, she told him it was the same sort of work that had got him sacked from BT.

The club was nearly empty when she led Jimmy through the bar, but she told him that if anyone asked he was to say he was doing handyman work on the instructions of Dee Clark. The staff were already so scared of her, she was confident that would cover it, especially in John's absence. Jimmy was a seedy-looking fella with a complexion that clearly showcased his love of drink. The two of them went upstairs and stood outside John's heavily locked office. Jimmy looked blank as Dee examined the door. 'So what are we here for then? I don't treat wood for dry rot, if that's what you're thinking.'

She gave him one of the looks for which she was already becoming notorious in the Alley Club. 'Yeah? Do you treat noses when someone's broken one for you?' She turned back to the door and gestured at it. 'In this office, there's a phone on the desk. I want you to tap it for me and make absolutely sure the tap can't be discovered. Then I want you to install a listening device in there. Actually, make it two.'

Jimmy was familiar with the drill. 'I can do that for you, no problem. Open up then and I'll get to work.'

Dee looked incredulous, her fists stamping onto her hips. 'Well, I can't open it up, can I? It's locked, Dumbo. That's your job, isn't it? You're the low rent James Bond here.'

Jimmy huffed, looking well pissed off. 'Look love, I'm an engineer not a house breaker.' But he pressed the door with his fingertips. 'Even if I was, I don't reckon I could get in there. That's a proper door, that is. Have you got a diagram of the phone configuration in this place? I might be able to work around it.'

Dee pretended to pat her pockets. 'Of course, I always carry one of those around with me. Oh, would you believe it? Today's the day that I went and left it at home.'

He was taken aback by her sarky tone. 'Alright, love, there's no need to put sauce on my chips. I'll see what I can do.'

While Dee drank coffee in the bar area, Jimmy wandered round the building, tracing the phone lines.

'Alright, Mizz Dee.' At the greeting she turned to find one of John's people behind her. Knobby was not part of the club staff, but one of John's team: a kind of special run-around boy. They hadn't got off to such a good start, but after bumping into each other in John's office they'd soon got a mutual appreciation society going on, built on one simple rule – you keep your beak out of my business and I'll keep mine well out of yours. She wasn't really sure what Knobby did for John, except he was always in and out of the club like a boomerang, which suggested to her that John had something big going on. With Jimmy's techie know-how she could hopefully find out what that was.

'A bit early for you,' Dee said, rearranging her long legs so he got an eyeful. It hadn't taken her long to realise that Knobby appreciated a hot pair of pins. She didn't fancy him – no way – but she needed to keep him sweet; he might be useful in her quest to find out the nature of John's business dealings.

'Ah,' he made it sound like a groan as he copped her exposed skin, 'it's never too early.'

Dee giggled. 'Doing something nice I hope.'

'Just a quickie upstairs and then I'm off to the Pied Piper.'

Pied Piper. Dee stored that piece of info away. 'There's a workman doing a spot of DIY for us, so just ignore him.'

Knobby grinned, making him appear even more boyish, and was on his way just as Jimmy reappeared. He gestured to her with his head. She followed him back upstairs and he led her into the general stores room, where he explained his plan. He showed her a telephone line that came down from John's office before being fed through the wall to a telegraph pole across the street. He offered to put a fake junction box on the wall with a recorder inside that would work in the normal way, with the usual buttons. Dee could either listen to the tapes at the box, with a pair of earphones, or take the apparatus away with her and hear it in private. He would give her a key for the junction box. As for earwigging the office itself, he suggested she take one of his own patented devices and hide it somewhere upstairs. He gave her a radio device that was a dead ringer for a walkie-talkie that she could use to listen in or tape conversations. But he did have a word of warning. If the office was swept for bugs, it would soon get picked up.

Dee told him to get on with the junction box and put the listening device in her handbag.

She hadn't been there for a week but she was already emptying bins and examining the mail in an effort to find out what her fiancé was up to. She knew how important this was because, if she didn't find out what his rackets were, her wedding would be off before John realised he needed to propose. As she sat in the bar with another cup of coffee, drilling and banging echoed from upstairs. More staff were arriving but none of them took any notice. Dee was already enforcing one of her prime rules with staff – that they weren't to notice things. Then, suddenly, the sound of the work stopped mid-drill. Dee knew instinctively that something was wrong. She put down her coffee and hurried upstairs.

As she approached the storeroom, she could hear raised voices inside. She threw the door open and walked in, as easy as you please. Jimmy was standing with his cap in his hand like a servant in front of the lords and ladies. Tearing a strip off him was John's right-hand man Chris. 'You seem a bit confused, my friend, I don't have to ask Miss Clark anything. Now you tell me . . .'

He stopped mid-sentence to turn and look at her, his eyes riddled with a mixture of suspicion and score settling. Within hours of her promotion the two had developed a mutual hatred based on an understanding that they were going to be rivals for John's esteem and both had already begun plotting how to get rid of the other. And now Chris had found her employee in the process of fixing a phone tap onto the wall. Jimmy was closing his toolbox and getting ready to scuttle. But he stopped short when Dee snapped, 'What do you think you're doing? Get on with the job.'

Jimmy's gaze swung nervously between her and Chris. 'Yeah? You look like you want to have a chat in private with this gentleman.'

'Do what I bloody tell you to do.'

Chris walked across the room and stood in front of her. 'What's going on, Dee?'

He was bigger than John with a lot more muscle and, if she hadn't set her sights on her boss, she might – just might – be up for letting Chris cop a feel. 'Why don't you ask John? He asked the guy to come in. Although I expect he will wonder why someone is questioning decisions. I know I would. I never saw you come in?'

'I came around the back.'

'Just like an alley cat.'

Chris leaned closer and demanded, 'What's. He. Doing?'

Dee wiggled her head on her neck; she wasn't fucking scared of him. 'I could give you the same answer John would – why don't you mind your own business? But the truth is, I don't know. I don't ask questions because I don't think I have the right to question my boss's authority, like you seem to imagine you have.'

Chris flushed. 'I'm not questioning John's say-so. I'm questioning yours. You see, that's the trouble with John. He's too trusting. You've come out of nowhere, exploited his good nature and now you're acting like Lady Dee of the Manor.'

'Lady Dee? I like that, Chris.' She said it softly like she was asking him to do something naughty to her in a porn flick. Then she hardened up: 'You've got a problem with me? Take it up with the boss.'

Chris stepped back and looked over at Jimmy who was hurrying his work on the box.

He turned back to her with a smug smile. 'Oh, I will.'

Dee stood her ground until Chris had gone, then she put a fire under Jimmy, telling him he had ten minutes, tops.

'Who is this John character then?' he said as he tightened a screw.

Dee issued a veiled threat. 'Ask around locally, everyone knows him. Then you'll also understand why it won't be in your interest to shoot your big mouth off about this to a soul.'

* * *

'Oi! You blind or what?' a driver roared as Babs crossed the busy Mile End Road without waiting for the lights to turn red.

He honked his horn furiously at her, but she ignored him, taking her sweet time walking, her workbag swinging gently against her hip. As soon as she reached the other side, she instantly felt like she was in another country. This side of the road was filled with imposing and elegant Victorian and Georgian houses. Admittedly a few looked like they were still recovering from the Blitz, but there was something about those houses that put Babs in mind of a better life. You could breathe, really breathe long and slow in one of those houses – not like The Devil, where everyone and their Pitbull seemed to be fighting for space. She walked on until she got to what she considered the best part of the other side of Mile End Road: Bancroft Square, or, as she liked to call it, Babs' Square. The tall, three-storey Georgian houses were laid in a square around a pretty garden with two iron benches and flowers bursting with life and colour.

Fancy having your own little park to sit in? Mind you, it didn't stop the local scum from using it as a drinking and drugs den, come dark. The council had put a thick chain and padlock on the gate to lock it up at night with only residents of the square given a key. As if a padlock could keep out the junkies and tearaways around here.

'I'd given up on you coming today.' The quick-fire Irish accent came from a woman sitting on one of the benches, smoking a fag as Babs walked into the garden.

Theresa Marshall was a good ten years older than Babs, with a mischievous face with deep lines around her eyes that testified to her loving a good chuckle every now and again. She had six grandkids who made her stick out her chin proudly when she talked about them. Two of her grandbabies lived with her, as Theresa's middle girl and husband – well-known drug addicts – had done a flit one night after selling every stick of furniture in their flat, and had never been seen again.

It was Theresa and Babs' ritual to meet once a week for ten minutes before they started their cleaning jobs. Babs cleaned numbers nine and ten, while Terri took care of number fifteen. They would have a smoke, a chit-chat and, if life was on the up, a giggle or two.

'I got carried away cleaning up my place and forgot about the time,' Babs explained as she plonked herself down beside her friend. She crossed her legs at the ankle and inhaled. Even the air smelt fresher this side of Mile End.

'You'd think you'd have enough of cleaning over here to be spending time on it at yours. You know what that bitch said to me?' That bitch was the woman at number 15 who Terri cleaned for. 'She had the front to tell me – not ask, mind you – that the next time I cleaned that fancy stone floor of hers in the kitchen I was to get down on my hands and knees with a scrubbing brush.'

Babs leaned her head to the side, outraged, as she let out a puff of smoke. 'Flippin' sauce. I hope you told her where to get off?'

Terri's watery, grey eyes twinkled. 'I said to her, sure missus I'll get down on my knees, but if my bad back seizes up I'll have to put in an insurance claim. She shut up in the blink of an eye and I ain't heard another word about it.' She leaned into Babs, merriment stamped over her wrinkled face. 'Not unless that gorgeous hubbie of hers wants to do it to me doggie style.'

Babs laughed so hard a pair of startled robins flew away from their resting place in one of the bushes. 'I wish I could take you home. I need a laugh a minute.'

Her friend's face turned serious. 'Not that daughter of yours again?' She didn't need to say which of Babs' daughters she was talking about.

Babs pulled in her last shot of nicotine, ground the dog-end gently on the bench and then put it in her bag; she would never dream of littering this beautiful garden. 'There's something going on with her—'

'There's always something going on with her,' Terri cut in quietly.

Babs shook her head wearily, feeling defeated. 'She just won't quit that cemetery.' Babs gulped in some air, her lips shaking with emotion. 'She's going off the rails. I'm scared she's on a one-way track to big trouble and one day the Bill will be knocking on my door to give me the news that she's dead . . .' She clamped a hand over her mouth staring horrified at the other woman. Her hand quickly dropped away. 'Terri babe, I never—'

'It's alright, love.' But from the tears brimming in the other woman's eyes, Babs knew it was anything but alright. Terri lived on an estate down the road in Bow, but ten years ago her eldest girl had come to live on the Essex Lane and The Devil had done what The Devil did best – screwed up her life. The rotten place had turned a happy, loving girl into someone who refused to leave her flat when she realised she'd borrowed money on the never-never from the wrong people. A year, four months and three days after moving to Babs' estate, she'd been found hanging when a neighbour noticed a ripe smell coming from her place. What had really broken Terri was finding out that her Maggie had covered her face with one of the green, leaf-patterned pillow cases from the John Lewis duvet set the borrowed money had been used to buy. Babs suspected that's why her mate loved this garden so much; the green leaves reminded her of her lost girl.

'It's good to remember the dead,' Terri punched out solidly, 'because they should remind us how we need to be living.

That's what you've got to do to your Tiff. Get her by the scruff of her neck and drag her, kicking and screaming and spitting and howling, on to the straight path.'

'Bloody hell, Terri, every time I get her she just slips like water out of my hand. Back-chats me, swears . . . I'm tearing my hair out . . .'

'And your heart out, by the look of you,' Terri added softly, seeing the devastated expression on Babs' face. She gathered her mate quietly into her arms. 'Have you ever thought of asking—?'

Babs wrenched herself away from Terri's arms. 'No way. I would never, ever, in a million years stoop so low as to ask Stan bloody Miller.'

'She's his responsibility as well. It's about time that man faced up . . .' Terri stopped with disbelief reading the truth on her friend's face. 'You still haven't told them what happened?'

'I can't. Just can't.' Babs quickly gathered her workbag and started striding out of the garden. But it didn't stop her from hearing her caring friend's words:

'You're going to have to tell those girls about Stanley one day.'

What Babs didn't hear was Terri's whispered, 'And God help you when you do.'

Terri's words still ringing in her head, Babs slammed the door shut on number nine Bancroft Square.

'Anyone in?' she called out as she quickly walked across the old-style, rich red-and-black diamond mosaic hall tiles.

Relieved when she got no answer, she headed into the front room and helped herself to the owners' gin and tonic. She plonked herself down on the soft sofa, kicked off her shoes and tried as hard as possible not to think about one of the biggest mistakes of her life: Stanley Miller.

Nineteen

Heading to his car to go around the corner to Brick Lane for a spot of lunch, Liam Gilbert licked his lips and watched the long legs of one of his female students as she walked away from him. She'd just agreed to meet him tomorrow night for some 'extra' lessons. Natasha or was it Marisa? He could never remember the silly girls' names, which didn't matter; all that mattered was persuading her to blow him off. He never went all the way with them; you never knew where some of these East End tarts had been, and he didn't want to bring something nasty home to the wife. His whole shtick about leading them towards fashion paradise always worked. Well it had until that stupid fool Jennifer Miller. At least the girl had taken his words to heart and hadn't showed her face again.

Smiling to himself he opened the car door and slipped inside. He popped his key into the ignition and then got the shock of his life as a young man shoved open the passenger door and settled, nice as you please, beside him.

'What the—?'

The touch of the younger man's palm on Liam's thigh cut short whatever he was going to say next. The heat from the intruder's hand felt more scary than a knife being waved in his face.

The man dug the pads of his fingers into Liam's leg as he finally spoke. 'Me and you are going for a little ride.'

Scared as hell, all Liam could do was nod.

John returned to the club pissed out of his head. He staggered straight up to Dee and kissed her, like he was trying to suck the lips right off her stunned face. He'd obviously been drinking in a dive somewhere; his coat reeked of beer and baccy, the perfume of a rough pub.

'You're a proper piece, Dee. My kind of woman.' He sniffed her. 'And you smell bloody gorgeous too.'

'John,' she protested, shooing him off her. 'I'm not that kind of girl. Plus, you've got a lady.'

He curled his lips as his face went red. 'Stuff Trish, the bitch.' His right eyebrow hiked up, 'Did that rhyme?'

Dee rolled her eyes. She saw Chris loitering around near the back of the room. The best way of dealing with an attack was to get the first shot in. 'Chris wants a word with you. He thinks I've been snooping.' She said it loud and clear for John's right-hand man to hear.

'Snooping?' came out as souping. John swayed as he drunkenly turned to Chris. 'What you banging on about?' He turned back to Dee and cupped her chin tenderly in his hand. 'My precious Black Pearl? Her wish is my command.' He tried to do a theatrical bow to her, but his feet got muddled up and he would've pitched over if Dee hadn't caught him.

It was the first time that Dee had been in John's arms and she was surprised at how she liked the warm feeling of his body. It made her think of the real comfort you got from a peaceful family life, the kind she had never experienced.

'I like you, Dee,' John whispered.

Dee caught his gaze and surprised herself by whispering back, 'I like you too.' John wobbled again.

'Easy boss.' As she righted him she beckoned Chris over with her hand. 'Get some strong coffee down him upstairs.' She knew she was treading a dangerous line, letting Chris get John alone, but at the same time she was showing Chris she didn't have anything to be worried about. She wanted him to know that he was wasting his breath blabbing to John about her. For heaven's sake, she was the guy's black fucking pearl. Dee tilted her lips in a tiny smile. She kind of liked the name. For all his rough and tumble, John did make her smile. She hadn't expected him to be able to do that.

Half an hour later, Chris reappeared. 'The boss doesn't want to be disturbed because he's got some important calls to make.'

Dee raised her hands in a peace offering. 'I've got nish to hide, Chris.'

He stared daggers at her and then left the room. She was tempted to go to the storeroom, put her earphones on and catch John's calls in real time but she knew she had to be patient. She wanted both Chris and John out of the club before she played any tapes. An hour later John appeared again. The guy looked like he hadn't slept in a month of Sundays. And, for the first time, Dee realised how much older he was than her. There was one thing marrying a man to get access to the good life, but it was a totally different thing ending up with a man and having to mash up his food and feed him before she reached forty. She pushed her doubts away as John called out to Chris, 'You'll have to drive me home mate. My head's all over the shop.'

Chris and Dee exchanged meaningful glances. John's right-hand man propped him up and helped him out of the club. Then she went directly to the storeroom to retrieve the tapes, took them to the room that served as her makeshift office and listened intently to his calls. He was drunk. He might have been careless on the phone.

To her fury the first call was to Trish:

'*Treacle! It's John. I organised some flowers for you. Did you get them? Only I ain't heard nothing . . .*'

Dee hissed under her breath, 'I'll give you fucking treacle, you bastard. What a prick this guy is, honestly.' She shut up to catch the rest of the call.

There was a pause and then John's voice turned slightly menacing. '*You know who I am; don't twist my tail. People who end up doing that end up getting bitten.*'

Dee was glad that John had given her rival the put-down but the problem was he had spoken in such an intimidating tone that maybe Trish would be so scared she'd call him back. And John hadn't exactly given her the goodbye brush-off because he hadn't heard from her. Perhaps she'd underestimated John's attachment to the woman; perhaps Trish was more of a threat than she thought and wouldn't go quietly. Worse, she knew what Dee looked like. If Trish turned up at the club, it would make life very difficult. But Dee was confident she could deal with that, and that a two-bit slapper like Trish would soon find another wealthy man to chisel.

There followed a series of business calls. All were carefully phrased and revealed nothing. Some seemed to be about the club, others about his real trade, but all were conducted using coded language, with references to our 'friend' or 'friends', the 'product' or 'consignment', and the 'destination'. There was a lot of talk about 'ice'; Dee couldn't imagine her intended being involved in the freezer business. There was nothing she could understand in the calls to pinpoint exactly what John's trade actually was. But then, right near the end of the line of calls, when his earlier boozing finally made John lose the run of himself, Dee managed to get something helpful:

'*Rocky? What's up? Listen, mate, I went and saw Ingram this afternoon down Shadwell . . . I know, he was playing the plastic hard man as usual, the little prat . . . I know, Ingram couldn't spot a tit in a row of cocks. Anyway, I'm not best pleased about this girl he hired to do errands for us. She picks stuff up at the pub around the corner and then looks after them. Turns out this girl is only sweet sixteen and a bit of a nutter . . . That's right – can you believe it?'* He let out a loud belch.

'I mean, what the fuck? As a precaution, I did arrange with my guy at the Pied Piper to call the cops and tell them there was a vulnerable teenager knocking around with all them benders in there . . . That's right – it's a gay pub. Good eh? Them people don't want anything to do with the law, so it's a good spot to do business in private. Anyway, Old Bill pulled the girl and it looks like she handled herself alright and said dick about ice . . . Nah, she didn't have anything on her, I made sure of that. Anyway, I went down and had a word with Mickey Ingram to find out what he was playing at . . . Thing is I want to cut Ingram out of the loop and get someone else in. Could you look into it and see if you could find someone to run stuff off for me? I'd appreciate it.'

Dee's mind was in a whirl.

Shadwell.

Mickey Ingram.

The Pied Piper.

Ice.

A sixteen-year-old nutter running errands.

At last, Dee had something to work with and she recalled that Knobby was doing something up at the Pied Piper too. She was still confused about what 'ice' could mean; she'd have to really put her head to trying to figure that out.

'Out,' Nuts ordered Liam Gilbert as they reached Epping Forest. He was still spitting mad about what Jen had told him this disgusting rat had done. No one did that to Nuts' girl. No one.

As soon as they were outside, Nuts noticed with satisfaction that the creep looked like he was ready to wet himself.

'If it's money you want—'

'Shut it,' Nuts growled. 'Just keep walking ahead of me and don't stop until I tell you to. Try to run and I'll hunt you down like the filthy animal you are.'

Jen's former tutor started snivelling as he moved. Nuts knew this side of the forest like the back of his hand. His nan would always bring him here after his dad had put his mum in hospital, yet again. It didn't matter what his dad did to his mum – shattered jaw, broken arm, cracked ribs – she'd always go back to him. 'That's just how it is,' his gran would explain to him as they walked through the forest.

'Stop,' Nuts barked as they reached a beautiful, quiet clearing where as a child he'd romped around while his nan sat on a log drinking Sanatogen's Tonic Wine straight from the bottle. 'Take all your clothes off.'

The other man's face went even paler as he started to beg, 'Please. I don't know what this is about, but I'm sure we can get this all sorted out like gentlemen—'

Nuts stormed up to him in three, big strides. 'You want me to take your fucking eyes out with my bare hands you're going the right way about it.'

Liam furiously threw off his jacket, so Nuts stepped back until the other man stood naked as the day he was born. Nuts wrinkled his nose at the flabby skin on display. 'On your knees.' He smiled grimly. 'Isn't that what you told Jen Miller to do? Get on her knees so she could suck your diseased dick?'

Liam shook his head like crazy. 'She got it wrong. I would never—'

Nuts pulled back his fist . . . Liam got on his knees. He shook so badly that Nuts thought he was going to fall down. 'You're a dirty old man through and through, preying on young girls who are just looking to better themselves. I should really cut your tackle and balls off . . .'

Liam started crying; great, hulking sobs that shook his body from head to toe. Nuts leaned down and whispered in his ear, 'It doesn't feel good, does it, when someone has control over you? They can do what they want and there ain't a bloody thing you can do about it.'

Nuts pulled himself straight, suddenly feeling a wave of disgust that he was breathing the same rotten air as this pathetic man. He got on with what he had to do. A few seconds later he started peeing all over him. Liam collapsed as he bawled like a baby.

Nuts kept up a steady stream as the words poured out of his mouth. 'That's all you're good for, Liam boy – to be pissed on. Makes you feel dirty, don't it? That's how every girl you've ever forced to touch you feels. Dirty. If I was you, I'd hand in my notice tomorrow and never set foot in the East End again, because let me tell you, if I set eyes on your ugly mug again and hear that your willy's been going walkabout, you're going to find out what I can really do with a blade.'

Satisfied he'd put the fear of God into this snivelling excuse of manhood, Nuts finished up and cheerfully whistled as he walked away.

Twenty

'I want to see the guy in charge,' Tiffany demanded boldly to Man-donna in the Pied Piper.

Tiffany might be giving it the big 'I Am' to his face, but inside she wasn't so full of it. When the message had arrived for her to pick up another package she got dead worried about the cops, and Mickey Ingram. If she put a step wrong she knew that Mickey was going to have her. She could still hear Stacey's screams and moans in her head, sending a chill through her. What an animal. If he was willing to give his daughter a kicking, what would he do to her, someone who was no blood relation? He wasn't the type of geezer she could walk up to and say she wanted out. And Tiffany wanted out. Revenge on Stacey's dad would come later. For now, saving her own skin was enough and that meant having a little chat with the man in charge. She'd triple checked once she got near the pub, to see if there was any law around, and when she decided the coast was clear she'd gone in there and made her demand.

The buffed, smooth-skinned man in front of her let out a nasty laugh. 'The guy in charge? You mean the landlord?'

'No, I mean whoever's running the envelope business.' Tiffany was hanging tough but it was coming out wrong and she knew it. 'I ain't taking nothing until I have a bit of face time.'

'Oh I see; you want to talk to *him* do you?'

Tiffany's confidence grew and she nodded, like she was the big girl on the block. 'That's right.'

Abruptly her contact turned and started walking away.

'Hold up, where are you going?'

'I thought you wanted to talk to the boss?' he answered without turning back. 'Better follow me then, hadn't you, sweetheart.'

Tiffany followed him to a corridor in the back and up a narrow staircase until they hit the top floor. He stopped at a door and shoved it open. Hand still on the doorknob he ordered, 'In here then.'

She hesitated for a few seconds, then got her confidence back into gear and waltzed past him into the room. The room was empty except for a wreck of a chair, a battered-looking table and partially opened window.

Tiffany swiftly turned back around, saying, 'What the heck—?'

But she never finished because he grabbed her by the back of the head and frogmarched her towards the large, single window. Tiffany was completely taken by surprise by his actions; he'd looked more like a fella who was interested in a tub of Nivea than getting into a ruck. Tiffany fought him all the way, her fists punching any part of him she could reach, but he might as well have been made out of stone for all the notice he took of her flying fists. When they reached the window he pushed it fully open with one hand and tipped her head out into the cold air.

Tiffany's heart dropped in her chest. Her life flashed before her eyes. She remembered the number one lesson she'd learned about life – never, *ever*, show you're afraid. But fear nearly crippled her when he started lifting the lower half of her body up. If she was going down, she was going down fighting. She tried to thump him a good one in the balls but he held his body back and at an angle that made it hard for her to connect to him. She flicked a foot backwards to kick him in his belly, but all she met was empty air. He pushed her once, twice, then she was hanging out of the window.

'I thought you were alright and didn't ask silly questions.' He growled. 'And now you come strolling in here, as cool as you like, and ask to speak to busy people who are out of your league. I'm afraid that's rank bad manners. Now why don't you catch some air and have a think about what you've said?'

The blood rushed to Tiffany's head making her dizzy as she viewed the world upside down. She'd seen the world from this position once before when she and her mates had played Dare Ya on the roof of her block. But no one was being dared here.

Her arms hung heavy and hurt as they swung by her side. Her hair stuck out, including the wisps on the back of her neck. She clawed against the walls, scraping some of the skin off her palms, as if that was going to save her. She was terrified but she still had enough spit to scream, 'I'm going to rip your bloody head off.'

Above her came a snigger and the loosening of the grip on her ankles. She dropped lower until she was hung out by her feet, like a piece of meat in the butcher's. She cried out as she bounced into the wall and then back out again.

'Having a think about things down there, are you? Is the fresh air clearing your head?'

'Sod you!' she screamed back.

One of his hands released her so that she was dangling by one leg. Tiffany's heart fell lower into her body. Mistakes happened in these kind of games. Victims ended up dead. If her broken body was found in the courtyard below, the staff would sort a story out: *'She was a suicidal druggie, officer. We tried to save her, but what could we do?'* Then she'd be forgotten. Only her mum would know better, stroking her hair down the morgue and whispering, '*Stupid girl. If only you had listened to me, Tiff, you'd have never come to this.*'

'Have you done some thinking?' her tormentor shouted.

Tiffany held back the stream of curses in her mouth. 'Yes, I've done some thinking, I've done some thinking.'

He had the nerve to laugh at her and grabbed her other leg so she was more secure. 'Just do your job, love, and keep your snout where it belongs. And don't come up here again with any silly requests, wasting everyone's time.'

'I only wanted to talk to him—'

He shook her. 'You don't need to talk to anyone. Do you understand?'

'Yeah, I get it.' Her tummy started to roll; if she didn't get inside soon she was going to puke.

'That's more like it. You see? I knew you could be a good girl if you put your mind to it.'

She let out a thankful breath as he started reeling her back in. Inside she collapsed against the wall, her legs too shaky to hold her up. He loomed over her like a figure from a night-mare. 'Do you know how many people would kill to get a job like yours? There's a queue a mile long of them. Fuck off downstairs and wait for me by the bar. And don't make me do that again, or you really will get to meet the big guy – and there won't be any talking going on, let me promise you.'

Tiffany got to her feet and staggered towards the door. On the next floor down she bumped into two women who were holding hands. They looked shocked by the state of her. One of them asked with mother hen softness, 'Are you OK? What happened?'

But Tiffany wasn't in the mood to explain herself to no one. She'd been a prize plonker. Even at her age, she should have known better than to ask to see the top dog. And there was always the danger that word would get to Mickey Ingram and then she really would be in the doo-doo. She slumped up against the bar, her weakened legs barely able to support her weight. The place had filled up since her little adventure upstairs. As she waited for the envelope, she noticed a woman she hadn't seen before sitting on her own in the corner, watching her intently while stirring the drink in front of her. Tiffany avoided her gaze.

Man-donna arrived with her envelope, but nothing else.

'Oi, where's my dosh?' Tiffany cried out.

He pasted a nasty grin on his face. 'It's been decided that little girls who come in here shouting the odds don't deserve no pocket money. Your reward is that you're still able to walk.'

Tiffany didn't argue. Through tight eyes she watched him go off to the other side of the bar and start chatting to someone else. She wasn't interested in who he was jarring with, and the guy's face was obscured in any case. She needed to try another tack and she wasn't sure what that was going to be.

As she left the pub, she couldn't resist turning to check out the woman who'd been eyeing her up. She was still there, watching Tiff with hooded, clinical eyes. A paranoid Tiffany picked up speed, reached the door and opened it, turning once again to look at the woman. But this time, the woman was gone.

On the other side of the bar, John Black's guy Knobby only half-listened to Jeff as he stared hard after Tiffany's retreating figure. He knew the teenager hadn't seen him, but he'd seen her.

Jen was halfway through washing her hair when there was a knock at the front door. She groaned. Why, oh why, did someone have to come now? She'd been feeling really down about her fashion dreams going down the pan and was trying to pep herself up with that conditioner Bex had gone on about – the one that promised to give her Cindy Crawford look a bit of 'bounce and shine'.

'Mum!' she yelled, before remembering that Babs had gone across the road to her cleaning job. There was no point shouting for her sister who would only curse back at her.

The knock came again, so she wrung out her hair and headed for the door.

'Nuts!' she exclaimed. He was suited and booted and had a big grin plastered over his face. She touched her dripping hair self-consciously, knowing she looked a real fright.

He bustled inside without her asking, but made no move to go to the sitting room. Instead he proclaimed, like he was in front of an audience. 'Get your coat, my one and only, we are going on a trip.'

Jen frowned, 'What are you going on about? You said you would call me.'

'Ah ha, all will be revealed if my queen will allow me to escort her to my chariot.'

Jen couldn't help grinning back; he did make her laugh. Not that that meant she was going to start dating him or anything.

'Even if I wanted to – which I'm not saying I do – I couldn't go out with you; I'm flippin' dripping all over the shop.'

'Shop,' he gave her a hundred watt smile and raised a finger dramatically in the air. 'The magic word.'

'Magic . . . ?' Jen shook her head in confusion, with a touch of frustration. 'I haven't got a clue–'

'Please, Jen.' His smile had disappeared replaced with that lost puppy expression that squeezed her heart.

'But I look like I've been dragged out of the canal in Vicky Park.'

Those gorgeous blue eyes of his began to glow. 'You could

have chickenpox all over your face, babe, you'd still look heaven to me.'

Nuts certainly had the patter to turn a girl's head, which she liked. None of that moronic 'How about it then?' that came out of the mouth of the likely lads around here. 'OK, but I've got to blow-dry my hair first.'

Twenty minutes later, with Jen dressed to kill and Meatloaf's 'I Would Do Anything For Love' playing on the car radio, they were motoring away from Mile End towards ... well, Nuts wouldn't reveal where they were going. They kept up a steady stream of chatter until Jen realised they were in the West End.

'You taking me to that swanky club again?' she asked, buffing up her hair.

'Better than that.' He mischievously winked at her.

Jen didn't know what he was up to, but he'd taken her mind off the disaster that had become her never-gonna-happen fashion career and she was grateful for that. Her face lit up when she realised that they were just off her favourite place in the world: Bond Street. If you were starting in fashion this is where you wanted to be – among the high-end, exclusive fashion shops. Oxford Street did clothes; Bond Street did designer. She'd often come down here on her own, wander around with her head stuck in cloud nine, staring dreamily into the shops. Sometimes she would close her eyes and see herself dolled up, all pretty and elegant, working in one. Then her eyes would sadly open. A girl from the East End was more likely to get an invite to the Queen's tea party than end up working on this oh-so-famous London street.

Nuts parked his Merc on a side street near a small Greek restaurant. 'You bought me all the way here for some nosh?'

He just smiled. She was getting a bit tired of him smiling and not letting on. 'Your palace awaits you.' Jen rolled her eyes and got out of the car after him. Nuts grabbed her hand

and hustled her quickly along the street and then turned into
Bond Street. The place was teeming with people and the occasional flash car with a chauffeur in peak cap standing beside
it. This was the life – if you had plenty of poke in your pocket.
Jen couldn't help the excitement that throbbed through her as
her eyes darted around. Gucci, Versace, Lagerfeld – they were
all here.

She couldn't stop the excitement in her voice as she turned
to Nuts. 'Is that what we're doing here? You going to buy me
a classic bit of clobber?'

Nuts just laughed as he pulled her along, then he took her
into another side street and stopped halfway down, outside a
designer shop. It was called Dominique, the name in bold, gold
letters underneath a large pane window that showcased
designer women's wear and some jewellery. Inside a security
guard was stationed near the glass door. Before Jen could
question Nuts, the security guard smartly opened the door and
he pulled her into Dominique's. The soft light from the fancy
light fittings and central chandelier gleamed on the ultra-
clean, marble-tiled floors. Clothing was laid out like it was art
and there were rows of neatly folded clothes on teak wooden
shelves. Two shop assistants were fluttering over a customer
who was a walking advertisement for money.

'So this is the young girl you told me about?' Hearing the
soft, French accent, Jen spun around to find an old woman
with a silver-topped walking stick standing near an open side
door. The woman might be old but she stood straight and
breathed old-style Hollywood glamour. Her grey-haired,
1920's flapper-style bob lay around a strong face, its only
make-up red, red lips. Her dark brown eyes were as fresh as a
person's half her age and her triple-tied pearl necklace showed
off her long neck and simple black dress. Now that's how Jen
wanted to look when she got older.

Nuts gently walked Jen closer to the woman. 'This is Madam Dominique, who knows the fashion industry from top to bottom. She'll show you the ropes, Jen, during your work placement here.'

Jen's mouth opened, but no words came out. She couldn't believe what he was saying. He didn't mean . . . 'You're having me on, Nuts?'

'No he's not, my dear,' Dominique answered as she slowly ran her eyes over Jen, assessing what she saw. She moved slowly towards Jen and then placed a long finger under Jen's chin, lifting her head slightly. The older woman stayed like that, her gaze looking Jen over as if she was administering a test. 'You look familiar . . .' But she shook her head as she lowered her hand. She looked Jen directly in the eye. 'You'll do. For the time you are here, I will teach you much of what I know. You start tomorrow, at eight-thirty on the dot.' Then, with an elegant turn, she moved back towards the door and left the room.

Jen was incapable of speaking. This was a wind-up, right? This couldn't be real. Someone had offered her a placement. On Bond Street. In a designer shop. And Nuts . . . Dizzy with joy, Jen flung her arms around him almost toppling him over.

'Hold up, girl,' he said with a laugh, 'this is a respectable establishment.' He grabbed her hand again and they exited the shop.

Once back on the street Jen finally found her tongue. 'I can't thank you enough. Me, on Bond Street! I can't wait to tell Mum.' The joy slipped away from her face. 'But I can't take it, because I'm not in college anymore—'

'You don't need to worry about that scumbag tutor of yours. I saw him straight.'

'You didn't do him a mischief did you? If the cops come after you—'

'They won't,' he reassured her. 'Let's just say he's learned the error of his ways. You go back to college because he won't be coming back.'

Jen's heart swelled. Nuts had not only got her a placement, he had sorted out that sicko. Jen leaned across and gave him a large smacker on his cheek. 'That don't mean I'm going out with you or nothing,' she warned him playfully. 'But if you call me soonish, I might be inclined to say yes.'

He grinned boyishly back, but then his face turned serious and he gently touched her arm. 'Whatever you do, don't ever ask Madam Dominique about her past. She's been around. She didn't get that lame leg playing marbles. You get me? Don't mention her name to no one, not even your mum or sister; she's a woman who likes to keep a low profile unless you're one of her paying customers. She's doing me a big time favour taking you on.'

Jen felt a wave of shame; she'd got Nuts totally wrong. Sure, he was a bit dodgy, but he was *her* dodgy. He was definitely a man whose arm she wanted to be seen on, so she linked her arm possessively into his as they made their way to his car.

Twenty-One

Tiffany headed straight for her tomb when she got to the cemetery. Most people got the willies being here, but Tiffany felt alive among the dead. They were about the only people who weren't out to get her these days. She wept silently with relief as she walked along the path and through the undergrowth. There was no doubt about it, she was in it up to her neck, with no way out.

None of the regulars were at the gate, and there was no shouting or larking about tonight, which she was glad about. She was in a hurry to hide her envelope and get home. She quickly walked down the pathway towards the back of the cemetery, where the trees were thick and there were two huge tombs. As she walked she heard a noise behind her, like a twig snapping. She stopped and peered behind her but couldn't see anyone. She resumed walking, but stopped again when she heard a rustling noise behind her.

'Who's there?' she called out, the beat of her heart galloping. There was no reply, and she still couldn't see anyone, but she knew from experience that seeing no one didn't mean they weren't there. Fear entered her bones. Every noise was an enemy.

'Johnno and Bazza, is that you?' Sometimes her friends got to playing silly games on each other, especially when they were liquored up. But she got no answer. It's probably the wind, Tiffany thought, turning to check, then nearly jumped out of her skin when she saw the person in front of her.

'Stacey, what the fuck? You frightened the fucking life out of me. How did you know I'd be down here? I thought you weren't talking to me.' (She didn't add, *And I understand why now*.)

She sucked in a hard breath when she saw the cuts and bruises on her friend's face; her dad had really beaten the stuffing out of her. Bastard! Tiffany had stayed away from her mate because she didn't want her dad to go ballistic on her again. But she now knew that Mickey Ingram was playing a game. On the one hand he was shouting the odds about his daughter staying well away from the Millers while all the time he was employing the youngest Miller girl as his runner. Tiffany didn't know what he was up to but it broke her heart to see her friend stuck in the middle of it.

Stacey gave her a grim smile. 'You're always down here, sooner or later.'

Tiffany noticed that she spoke slowly, not the type of slow-mo a voice had when it was boozed up, but something else. That something made Tiffany's heart beat faster. 'Stacey, you ain't been doing that shit again?' she asked furiously. And before her friend could answer she grabbed Stacey's left arm.

She shook her head when she saw the needle marks dotting Stacey's skin. Maximum disobedience was Tiffany's calling card, but the one thing she would never do was go on the needle – especially after Tommy Lewis had OD'd during Mister Hampton's biology class. But Stacey was a different story; she couldn't seem to stay away from the stuff. Tiffany had talked to her until she was blue in the face and, for a time, Stacey had stayed away from the filthy gear. But now she was back on it. Tiffany could bet her life it was because of that nutter Mickey Ingram.

Tiffany grabbed tight to the other girl's hand. 'You're going to end up as a smack bitch if you keep this up. You know what all those druggies look like, who go into number five in my block when it's dark? A right mess, that's what, willing to sell their mum for their next fix. That ain't happening to you, Stace; not on my watch.'

'But my life's shit,' Stacey cried with such hurt, Tiffany just wanted to hold her close.

'You've got me.'

Stacey burst into tears, so Tiffany pulled her into her arms. And before she knew it she was kissing her best friend on the cheek, then at the corner near her mouth.

Stacey twisted away from her. 'I've told you I ain't into no lesbo-shaped malarkey.'

'I know, I know,' Tiffany said quickly, 'nor am I. I just wanted you to feel better, that's all.' But the truth was, she had wanted to kiss Stacey. Desperately. She didn't understand these feelings she was having, but she'd better make sure she kept her lips to herself next time, because Stacey wasn't having none of it. Plus, what would everyone on The Devil say if they found out she liked snogging her best mate? She'd probably get duffed over for being worse than a weirdo.

'Let's get a bottle of voddy,' Stacey said.

Tiffany was about to agree, but then she remembered the envelope. 'I can't. I've got to—'

'You don't like me anymore,' Stacey wailed. 'No one likes me anymore.'

Then she was running like a wounded, wild animal out of the cemetery. Tiffany wanted to follow her but knew she couldn't; she needed to hide the envelope. Bollocks. She didn't like leaving Stace in such a state. Right, she made up her mind, Mickey Ingram or no Mickey Ingram she was going to give her friend a bell when she'd finished up here.

Quickly she reached the largest of the crumbling, grey-white tombs. It had a chipped white angel on the top that stared down at anyone approaching. Tiffany bent down and carefully shifted the stone panel on its side. She pulled out her envelope and prepared to creep inside the structure to find the waterproof box where she hid her envelopes. But as she rested a hand on the angel's foot, a hand coming out of the darkness gripped her wrist like a vice.

Twenty-Two

What John was hearing on the phone was making him mad, bad and liable to rip someone's head clean off. He'd been in a sit-down with Chris about the business when the guy from the Pied Piper – Jeff – had called him up.

'As you know our man from Bad Moon has got some slag running errands for you. Well, the little bitch was up here earlier, mouthing off about wanting to see you. So I took her upstairs for some acrobatics, made sure she understood what was what and told her to piss off with a flea in her ear. Just thought you ought to know.'

'That's your department,' John fired back furiously. 'I set you up so no one should even be mentioning my name. Got it?'

'She didn't say a dickie bird about your name to me. If she's running your name all over the place she didn't get it from me.'

Before John could answer, Chris mouthed, 'What's up?'

John placed his hand over the handset. 'One of Mickey's people is getting above her pay grade and making a lot of noise about wanting a nice, little chat with me. My guy down the Pied Piper swears blind he hasn't given her my name—'

'What about Mickey? He's been known to have a loose tongue when he's got a jar load in him.'

Mickey bloody Ingram, John thought. He'd only given him
a squeeze into the operation because they went years back. In
fact, Mickey was about one of the only people left around
who knew his real name was Charlie Dalton. They'd come up
together as ragamuffins on that rough, rat-infested hole of
an estate in Bethnal Green, that the council had called 'a
model of modern housing'. If it was such a model, why didn't
anyone in the council live there? Mind you, it was two steps
up from The Devil's Estate in Mile End, a tube stop away on
the central line.

Mickey had become a liability with his fists, punching out
anyone who looked at him the wrong way, including his
missus, Mel. So John had cut him loose, until Mickey reappeared a few years back, swearing to anyone with an ear that
he'd turned over a new leaf. John had taken him back in. Now
he knew he'd made the right decision about getting shot of the
twat. That's the problem with remembering the good old days;
it could lead to you falling flat on your face.

John returned to his phone conversation. 'You saying that
Mickey's been blabbing?'

'I ain't saying nothing except what happened down here
earlier.'

'What did she want to see me about?'

'I don't know, boss. I mean, you don't want to see the likes
of her do you?'

John needed to find out what was going on. And if Mickey
had started shooting his gob off he'd . . .

'You prick. Get her back up there and find out what the
problem is. If it's serious, call me.' John paused. 'Second
thoughts, leave it to me. It's about time me and Mickey had a
catch-up.'

John slammed the phone down and resumed talking business with Chris, but something other than Mickey Ingram's

death-wish runner was clearly on his mind. A few moments later, he realised what it was.

'Where's Dee? I've only just taken her on and she seems to think her toosh is working a part-time shift.'

Tiffany was too shocked to scream as she looked with a dazed expression at the brown hand gripping her wrist. She clocked that her assailant was a woman – the hand sported a full set of purple, jelly-polished acrylic nails and was blinged to the max with chunky rings. Usually she'd have cursed the woman back-to-front by this stage and dropped her with a solid one-two, but she couldn't move. Everything was catching up with her – being hung out the window at the Pied Piper, seeing her best mate's battered face, having someone grab her in the darkness. She just couldn't move. She felt so shocked, she didn't even have enough gas left in her engine to scream.

And she should be screaming blue murder because the woman who held her tight looked terrifying, togged out like some badass highwayman, a black hat pulled low over her head and a scarf loosely wrapped across her lower face. When the woman grabbed the envelope from her, that kick started Tiffany back into gear.

'Oi,' she growled, but the woman just pushed her down on the stone that surrounded the grave and sat herself down beside her.

Tiffany reached across to snatch the envelope. 'Give that back to me.'

The woman stared back at her with lethal, dark eyes sending a chill through Tiffany. She'd seen those eyes somewhere before, but couldn't, for the life of her, place where.

'Shut. It.'

Tiffany shut up. This woman was what she and her mates called 'fierce' and that made Tiffany scared to hell. She'd met the type before. Fearless, they would take you down any way they could. Tiffany didn't have it in her to get into a ruck. And why should she fight? Screw Mickey 'fuck face' Ingram.

They sat very close, but the woman hardly seemed to notice that Tiffany was still there. Instead she pulled out the contents of the envelope – a stack of paper. Tiffany was disappointed; she expected something a bit more lively to be honest, like a blade, or at least some leaf.

The woman flicked on a zippo lighter to help her read. She flipped through the papers and then started mumbling to herself, 'I might have guessed . . . Bloody small time, small time . . . You can do better than this, John. Doesn't he realise where the money is at these days?' She paused, looking puzzled and murmured, 'I still don't get what this has got to do with ice.'

Tiffany didn't have a clue what the woman was reading, or about anything to do with ice; it had been worth more than her life to look inside those envelopes.

Finally, her assailant turned to Tiffany and waved the papers at her. 'How many of these have you got?'

Tiffany was burnt out and said nothing. The woman pulled off her hat and scarf and put them on the grave. There wasn't much light from the moon or the streetlights that poked through the trees, but the glow from the zippo's flame confirmed what Tiffany suspected when she'd glimpsed her hand earlier – the woman was black. But what was much worse was when she realised that this was the same woman who'd been eyeing her up at the Pied Piper. The woman must have followed her here. *Stupid. Stupid. Stupid.*

'Who are you?' Remembering where she'd first clocked eyes on this woman she added, 'I ain't into no geezer bird stuff.'

The woman grinned. 'Oh yeah? That isn't what I saw when you were trying to suck your friend's face off a minute ago.'

Tiffany's face got hot with colour. Bloody hell, if this woman had seen her, maybe someone else had as well?

'Don't worry about who I am. You just tell me how many of these you've got. Actually, scratch that, start at the beginning. I want the full S.P. Names. What your instructions were. Who told you to do them. Don't leave nuthin' out.'

Was this woman having a laugh? Become a snitch? No, Tiffany might hate Mickey Ingram's guts for the dog he was, but she couldn't be telling anyone else about his business. Horrible things happened to a grass. Look what happened to Bill 'metal head' Williams, who'd once lived on the estate, after he opened his trap to the cops. His flat was burned to the ground, with him and his family inside. They'd only managed to escape by jumping from the second-floor window.

'I don't have to tell you dick,' Tiffany said back, her words full of false swagger.

Tiffany yelped when the woman grabbed a fistful of her hair and pulled her close. 'Look, I haven't come all the way down here to this zombie hang-out to play games. You'd better . . .' She drew the lighter close to Tiffany's face; the flame swam and cast shadows over her face. 'Fuck me.' The woman loosened her grip. 'How old are you?'

Tiffany was about to lie, but all the earlier exhaustion she'd felt came tumbling back in waves and suddenly she was done telling tales. 'Sixteen.'

'Kiss my arse,' the woman let out in disgust. 'What's my man doing hiring kids of that age? I'll have to put a stop to that for a start.'

Her man? What man? Tiffany thought. She couldn't see this stunning bird being Mickey Ingram's arm candy; that was like pairing Quasimodo with Janet Jackson. Tiffany suddenly clicked; she must be chatting about Mickey's guv'nor. Now Tiffany got interested.

The woman let go of her hair and smiled. 'What's your name, babes?'

'Tiffany.'

'OK, listen up Tiff – can I call you Tiff? Let's be mates, eh? I don't want to cause you any trouble, OK?' She sounded almost motherly. 'But I need you to help me out here. Is that alright? If you do that, I'll help you out . . .' Then she stopped, raised her lighter and examined Tiffany's face. 'They roughed you up in the Pied Piper, didn't they?'

Tiffany blushed with shame. 'Yeah. My contact hung me out of the window because I asked to see the main man.'

The woman was horrified. 'He hung you out of the window? A sixteen-year-old kid? What a bunch of bullies. Blokes who go around terrorising young girls are nobodies. You hear me, nobodies. What's the name of the bloke who did that to you?'

Tiffany shrugged. 'Dunno. He works there. He's a real looker and knows it.'

'First rule of business Tiffany is find out the names of the people you're working with and working for – especially scum who put the frighteners on young girls.'

'I know.' Tiffany was thinking of what had happened to Stacey more than what had happened to herself. She'd come out of the womb being able to take punishment, but Stacey was sensitive, fragile, not able to defend herself against the muck life threw at her.

'Who's Mickey Ingram?'

Tiffany's voice was flat and monotone and it seemed to her that someone else was doing the talking for her and that person seemed to be a small child. 'He's my friend Stacey's dad.' Her voice went thin and high. 'He beat her up for talking to me. Our families don't get on.'

The woman looked like she was about to burst a blood vessel. 'Men who go around beating on their kids deserve to have their hands chopped off.' Then she looked puzzled. 'But I thought it was Mickey who hired you to act as a runner? How's that playing out if he's in a slam-down with your family?'

For Dee it all fell into place. Hiring Tiffany had been a front. With a feud going on, Tiffany was the perfect cut-out for Mickey Ingram. If the Bill ever caught up with him, Tiffany became his deniability; all he had to say was there was no way he would be working with someone from a family he hated. And where did that leave this gullible kid? Smack bang in the middle, probably copping the lot for a crime she didn't even understand.

Dee had nearly been caught in the wringer when she was fifteen, bang in lust with some lad who was getting her to deliver H around town. Her mates told her to watch her step, but she wouldn't hear a bad word said about him. That was, until she walked in on him one day sexing the life out of that pole dancer from the Silk Club. She'd never pulled him up on it, and the tosser didn't figure out she'd starting overloading his stash to a rival for a good few months, until she finished with him.

What was the world coming to when you could only do a bit of ducking and diving by using kids? Dee convinced herself that there was no way her John could have known about this. But then even if she found out he did she'd soon ship him into shape when he popped a ring on her finger.

Dee put her arm around Tiffany and squeezed her gently. 'Listen, how would you like to get your own back on that wanker at the Pied Piper and on Mickey Ingram for trashing up your mate?'

'You can do that?' The girl looked so hopeful it tore at Dee's heart.

Dee smiled. 'Where there's a will, sweetheart, there's always a way. All you need to do is exactly what I say. My name's

Laverne and I'm going to be your friend. We'll fix those people together.'

Dee knew she was taking one massive risk after another; this girl had a rep as an out-of-control nutter. But Dee had come this far already and she wasn't going to stop now.

Twenty-Three

'Tiffany! Get in here!'

Jen was fed up with this ritual every time her sister came home and her mum roared out in anger. But tonight, instead of being the starting gun for a bundle, Tiffany did exactly as she was told. Jen noticed straight away that her sister's usual swagger seemed to have drained away in the hours since she'd last seen her. Tiffany walked with hunched shoulders and her face was pale. The lack of colour in her cheeks showed the marks and bruises.

Babs did a double take when she saw them and her tone instantly softened. 'Where have you been?'

'Nowhere.'

There was silence for a few moments as Jen's sister hung like a puppet in the doorway. Her mum's next question was touched with concern. 'Are you alright?'

'Of course I'm alright.' There was a bit of the old bite in Tiffany's answer.

'Are you sure? You don't look well. You been in a bit of Barney Rubble?' Her daughter brawling was the only explanation her mum could think of. The real problem was who she'd been in a fight with.

But Babs got no answer. After hesitating for a while, Tiffany drifted away to her room like a ghost – a ghost with a limp. There was a whispered conversation between mother and oldest daughter as to what could be wrong. Whatever trouble she'd had in the past had only fuelled Tiffany's fire, but now that fire had gone out. She seemed like a boxer who'd gone too many rounds. In the front room the two women traded ideas. Was she doing those E tabs that the government were always going on about? Had she fallen out with the bad crowd at the cemetery? Been in a ding-dong with a mate? Or even been knocked around by the cops? Jen decided to cut the conversation short and go and find out for herself.

She knocked on her sister's door, got no reply so went in anyway. Tiffany sat on the carpet with her back resting against the built-in wardrobe. She'd rolled her trousers up and was massaging her reddened and swollen ankles. When she looked up and saw Jen looking down at her, she stopped, got up and flopped down on her bed. Jen sat down next to her. 'Been in a ruck?'

Tiffany seemed grateful for the steer. 'Yeah, that's right. Some kids came down from Bow and tried to nick our pitch, so we had it out with them. We saw them off, of course.'

Jen knew this was a pack of pure manure, but there was something going on with her sister that made her forget the questions and instead sit on the bed. She took Tiffany's hand and gave it a comforting squeeze. All the times she'd protected her sister when they were growing up came back to her, especially that time their mum had been drunk, cursing to high hell as she'd finally taken the plunge and started throwing their Dad's clothes over the balcony years after he'd left.

Seven-year-old Jen hugged her little sister tight as they huddled together inside the built-in wardrobe in Tiffany's bedroom. It was Saturday night and Mum was sobbing and swearing as she chucked items of clothes out of their home. Jen had been as snug as a bug in bed when the argy-bargy started. She'd got up and gone to Tiff's bedroom knowing exactly where to find her. She could hear her sister's quiet sobs and couldn't see her anywhere, but she knew the wardrobe was Tiffany's special hideout, her refuge from the world when it got too hard a place for a young girl to understand. Jen pulled the door back and found her sister huddled with her knees drawn up and her small face streaming with tears. It always broke Jen's heart to see her little sister like this. She popped herself down by Tiffany, closed the door and pulled Tiff tight into her arms.

'Where shall we go to today?' Jen asked. This was their secret game, dreaming of being anywhere else but The Devil's Estate.

'Top of the Pops,' Tiffany answered quietly. 'Dancing with Boy George and Culture Club.'

They both loved Culture Club. They loved Boy George's wacky clothes and hair. They'd never seen a geezer wear face paint before. Secretly Jen loved the group even harder after Uncle Fred, their Mum's latest boyfriend, had said he didn't want that poof music in the house. Jen didn't get what a poof was, but it made Uncle Fred really peed off, which was good enough for her to keep liking it.

'What if instead of Top of the Pops, we were making a video with them?'

Tiffany's eyes grew round with amazement. 'We can really do that?'

Jen smiled. ''Course we can. This is our little world; we can do whatever we want.'

The girls leaned the sides of their heads together and softly drowned out the noise of their parents as they sang 'Do You Really Want To Hurt Me'.

* * *

'What's up, sis?' Jen drew away from the past where they had once been so close. 'This isn't like you. You enjoy a rumble; you enjoy being in trouble with the law. You haven't been fighting with kids from Bow. So what is it? I might be able to help. Have you fallen out with someone?'

Tiffany sat up and began massaging her ankles again but it looked to Jen as if this was just a way of distracting her attention. 'Is it this business with Stacey?'

'What business with Stacey?' Tiffany replied, so quickly that Jen almost jumped.

Ah, this is about her mate Stacey. 'You worried that Mum will find out you're still knocking about with her?'

Tiffany snapped, 'No, it's nothing to do with Stacey.' Her tone turned fierce. 'I tell you what it's about – living on this dump of an estate and never thinking I'm going to get out here. I'm bored, Jen, bored.' She twisted her face away from her sister. 'Just leave me alone.'

Sighing, Jen eased up but, just before she left the room, she said, 'I'm going places, Tiff, and you know why? Because I work hard. I don't have time to get bored. I'm already moving in the right direction thanks to college. If you want to stop going the wrong way, I'll help you sort something out when you leave school.'

Her sister remained stubbornly silent, so Jen left, closing the door quietly behind her.

'What did she say?' an anxious Babs asked. She was literally wringing her hands.

'Nothing.' No need to worry her mum; she'd just get frantic and start popping more Benzos like they were Smarties. 'Must be time of the month.' Jen headed for the front door.

'Where you off to, love?' her mum asked.

'To see Bex.' Then she closed the door.

But she wasn't off to see her best mate. She decided to go and pay Stacey Ingram a visit.

'John? Someone said you were looking for me?'

When Dee got back from the cemetery in Mile End, it didn't take long for the bar staff to tell her that the boss was on the warpath, looking for her. She decided to go up to his office and front it out.

'Where the hell have you been?' He sat behind his desk with a full glass of whiskey, looking miffed. His lieutenant Chris sat in a chair to the side.

She came over all breathless and flirty. 'I've been down in the cellar counting bottles. I think some of the bar staff have been half-inching your drink.'

Unseen by John, Chris shook his head and smiled hard at her, as if to say, Is that the best you can come up with? From the get-go, Dee realised pretty quickly that John's right-hand man didn't like her. Whether he'd figured out her game, or he was plain jealous because he wanted his boss all to himself, she couldn't say. What she did know was that, if he stood in her way, he was going to be dealt with. He was probably used to John having girlfriends who were PAP (pass around pussy), who were here one day and gone the next, like that brain-dead bimbo Trish – no threat at all to his status. Well, Dee was going to show him that she had an intelligence rating that was way above her kitty-kat size.

'I'll be the first to admit,' she carried on, looking Chris square in the eye, 'that that's Chris's job really, but he never seems to have the time to do simple things, like check your stock, these days.'

Chris's smile turned to stone on his face. That little jibe was one more mark against her. Good. *You want a street fight, big man? Bring. It. On.*

'That true, Chris?' John asked, falling straight into her ring-covered hands.

Chris kept his gaze on Dee. 'Don't you remember, Dee, you said you'd do it for me as a favour? I had to pick up Nicky from school since his sitter couldn't make it.'

Dee smiled. So that's how he was going to play it in front of the boss; use his kid as leverage (it hadn't taken Dee long to realise how much John doted on Chris's boy), and make her out to be someone who forgot stuff – who didn't know their arse from their elbow.

'Oh, I thought that was last week,' Dee responded sweetly. 'I assumed this was a regular thing because you don't want to get that nice suit of yours all dirty in the cellar.' She turned to John. 'But, boss, you want to be working with people who don't mind getting their fingernails a little grimy every now and again.' Dee flashed her acrylics near her cleavage. Oh yeah, she had John's attention. 'Well, if it's all hunky dory boss I'd better get my hands even more dirty downstairs. On your behalf, of course – unlike some other people.'

And with that parting shot in Chris's direction, she was gone. But not before she heard them chatting about her:

'That's one cocky bint,' Chris said.

'That's how I like my staff – able to handle themselves.'

'You want to keep an eye on her.'

John chuckled. 'No need to worry about that, Chris, my son. I've got my eye on her alright.'

Dee almost laughed out loud when she heard John say the last with sauce in it. She'd better rack up the booty moves in his presence. Funny, at first it had slightly creeped her out knowing he was giving her bum the once-over, but now she quite liked his crinkly eyes burning into her. A flash of sexual heat ran through her. She returned to her security duties in the club. But her fearsome reputation already meant there was little for her to do as everyone was on their toes. No one wanted to cross Mizz Dee.

She waited patiently for a sign that John and Chris were leaving, as she was anxious to get back upstairs and listen to that day's tapes. She got her break when an Arsenal player and his tanned-to-death girlfriend arrived at the club. As a fan, she knew John liked to make a fuss of footie stars, so she had one of the security boys ring upstairs and give him a steer. Within minutes, the boss, with Chris in tow, were down in the VIP lounge high-footballing the player, sharing their thoughts on the state of the league and plying him with champagne. While diabolical referees were bad-mouthed, Dee slipped out of the bar and went up to the storeroom to collect her tapes. But just as she got there she heard a disturbance downstairs. She couldn't ignore it because she was head of bloody security. Whatever it was, she needed to deal with it quickly before John finished with the Arsenal player.

Once downstairs, Dee made her way to the main entrance where the noise was coming from. Then she heard a female voice coming in stereo from outside:

'How are you going to feel if you don't wake up tomorrow and haven't made peace with God?' The question was filled with fire and fury.

A large crowd was gathered at the main entrance to the club leading up to street level. Dee noticed that some of the crowd were laughing, as if this were the best entertainment they'd had on a Saturday night in ages.

'Leave this place of wickedness and join us on our joyful journey to find true happiness,' the voice continued.

'A vodka and tonic, plus an E; that's where you'll find real happiness,' someone in the crowd jeered, raising a snicker from some of the others.

'What's going on?' Dee asked one of the door staff.

'A bunch of Bible bashers on the hunt for sinners. That lot used to come around the Mermaid when I worked there. We'd chase them off; bad for business.' He had a smirk on his face. 'They're some of your lot.'

Dee was not amused and pinned him with a filthy stare. 'What do you mean, *my lot*?'

The bouncer became nervous, realising that he'd put his foot in it with the one person who held his job in her hand. The stern expression on her face dared him to look her in the eye. 'I didn't mean nothing by it, Mizz Dee . . .'

But Dee had already turned her back and was shouldering her way through the people, who were queuing up the outdoor stairs, to the pavement. She knew full well what he meant by 'your lot'; whoever was causing the street drama was black. Childhood memories of all-day Saturdays spent at rousing services at the Pentecostal Church and Bible Studies came back to Dee, and she didn't like it. She was done with waiting for God to give her the life she deserved – she'd left that way back in the past. If you wanted something, you better get ready to take it. She didn't do religion, full stop. If people wanted to get down on their bended knees and find their future in the Good Book that was their business, but if they thought they were going to do it on her patch and make a mockery of John's hard work, that was her business.

Once she was free of the crowd, she saw a trio of older black women standing on the other side of the road. They wore clothing that looked more suited to a 1970s revival session, and had hats perched on their heads. The ringleader seemed to be the statuesque woman in the middle, waving a Bible in the air, preaching loud and clear. 'If you leave this house of sin today, The Lord will be merciful.'

'Right ladies,' Dee called out as she started across the street, 'time to close this fire and brimstone showdown.'

'Desiree?' the tall woman with the Bible said in surprise. 'Desiree Clark?'

'Desiree Clark...'

Twenty-Four

Dee stumbled. Shit. No. Couldn't be. But it was, because the woman continued, her voice loud enough for the Lord Himself to hear in heaven. 'Desiree Clark. The handmaiden of Satan . . .'

Dee knew she had to do something. There was no way her meal ticket to paradise – John – could hear any of this. She quickly spun around, leaned over the stairs and yelled out to the bouncers, 'Get these people in the club. I'm dealing with this situation.'

The crowd were hustled back in line as Dee stormed across the road. 'What are you doing here, Auntie Cleo?' Her voice was breathless, choked with disbelief.

The tall woman looked down at her. Her face was sad. 'So this is what has happened to you. This is why you haven't been back home in the last five years. You've fallen by the wayside, just like your mother.'

Cleo Clark was still a very handsome woman and the only true mother Dee had ever known. She had loved Dee, clothed her and taken her into the house of the Lord, from the day Dee's mother had given baby Dee into her care. Although Dee had recently found her mother, she would always feel that this tough, tell-it-as-it-is woman was her real mother. She'd grown up calling her Auntie, but it wasn't until she reached her teenage years that she realised that Cleo was no real relation to her at all. It was hard to find out the truth, because no one – not even Cleo – would tell Dee about her dad or mum. She'd stopped asking Cleo years ago who her dad was, because every time she did the other woman would simply say, 'Satan disguises himself as an angel of light.' And as for her real mum, her foster mother wouldn't even go there.

Dee furtively looked around to make sure no one was still watching. She grabbed Auntie Cleo's arm and propelled her around the corner. 'Auntie you can't be coming around here.'

The older woman studied her like she was a child again. 'Why didn't you tell me where you were? I've been worried about you.'

'You always used to tell me to choose the right path and this is the life that I want—'

'Looking like a filthy sinner straight from Sodom and Gomorrah,' Auntie Cleo scoffed as she took in Dee's clothes, cleavage and make-up.

Dee smirked. 'From what I hear, Auntie Cleo, you would know all about that. I hear you were a right goer, back in your day.'

The other woman held her Bible high as if she was going to belt it across Dee's face. But then she lowered it. Dee seethed with anger, but didn't retaliate; this was one person she would never touch.

'That's why I'm telling you to get out of this life,' the other woman begged. 'It's going to eat you up. Lay down with the Devil and you'll burn for eternity. That's what happened to your mother.' Auntie Cleo stopped abruptly when she saw the expression on Dee's face. 'You've found her, haven't you? You've seen her. She's weak, Desiree, and she'll make you weak too. It's not too late to turn your back on her and walk away.'

Dee shook her head. 'I can't. She's my mum.'

'Then why did she abandon you, like a piece of rubbish left to find its own way in the street?'

That hurt. It really hurt. And the only way she could deal with that emotion was to leave the old Desiree behind and once again become the Dee everyone feared. She lifted the corner of her mouth into a snarl and stepped back. 'Like I said, don't be coming around here anymore.'

Auntie Cleo gave her a final look, then started to walk away. Just as she hit the corner for the main road, she turned back and said, in a gentle tone, 'I'll be praying for you.'

Then she was gone, and the snarl dropped from Dee's lips. She slumped heavily against the wall, and felt choked up with tears. Turning her back on her old life was one of the hardest things she'd ever done. She'd hated all that Bible thumping and preaching, but because moving on also meant leaving the amazing Auntie Cleo behind. Her foster mother didn't have a place in her new life. Scriptures and sin just didn't tango together. But Dee and John did.

Dee swallowed back her tears as she turned her focus back on her plan. She needed to hear those phone tapes.

Auntie Cleo was long gone by the time she got back to the club. As soon as she saw the bouncer on the door, she pointed a finger in his chest and said, 'You're fired. Know why? Because my lot of people don't include you.'

Jen never arrived at Stacey's house. She saw the girl in the distance as she walked through the byways of the neighbouring block. It was a relief – she didn't know what she would have done if she'd come face-to-face with that mad bird Mel Ingram. Just the thought of it made her shudder. Stacey walked in the shadows, head bowed, as if she'd committed a crime. Curious, Jen began to follow her as she weaved her way along the road. Every so often, Stacey would slow down, reach into her pockets and pull out items of clothing to put on. First it was a scarf, which she wrapped around her neck and the lower part of her face; then it was a baseball cap, which she drew over her forehead. Finally, she stopped to thread the hood of her jacket through its holes before pulling that over her head too. She gave a furtive look around and set off again. Now she looked more like an outlaw.

Jen lost sight of her, then spotted her again, resting against a bollard in the driveway of what was comically described as a 'car park' under one of the tower blocks. Any cars parked there were either abandoned, old models that no one wanted to steal, or burned-out wrecks that the council occasionally towed away. Everyone locally knew what the place was really used for. It was a drop-in centre for criminals, drop-outs, drugs and people who were too stoned or ill to have anywhere else to go. That was why the car park was known as 'Neverland'; no one in their right mind would ever go there. Babs had warned both her girls from a young age to stay clear of the place.

Jen decided to go home. She was worried that her sister's friend might see her and she didn't know what her reaction might be. She took a few steps, then remembered that she was there on a mission – to find out what was up with her baby sister – and the Ingram girl might have the answers. She also felt compelled to stop the kid getting into trouble, because it was clear she was looking for it. Jen turned and called her name. But Stacey was gone. On the other side of the road, sitting and resting against one of the driveway's supports, was a drunk. He looked like he was guarding Neverland but had fallen down on the job and taken to the bottle.

'Did you see a girl in a hood come by here?'

His bloodshot eyes gleamed like rubies in the dark. 'They've all got hoods, love.'

Jen moved away from him and looked down the driveway into the darkened concrete cavern that had only a few grimy lamps surviving, from years of neglect. Never going into Neverland was one of the house rules of parents in the area, like not accepting sweets from strangers. Even Tiffany followed that one. But Jen walked down anyway.

The car park seemed both empty and crowded. Out of her eye-line, Jen could see a group of kids darting in and out between cars. She heard the voices and sniggers of youths but couldn't place them. Determined to go no further, she scanned the bays, looking for Stacey. She felt herself being dripped on: cold drops that felt like the condensation that forms on the ceilings of rank, sweaty nightclubs. Stacey appeared, passing under a light, then turned to shadow as she stepped in front of a van that had collapsed on its wheels. Jen watched intently as the girl met another shadowy figure, and the two appeared to do a brief dance together before they separated. Stacey stepped back under the light and it was clear she was stuffing a plastic bag into her pocket.

Jen walked back up the driveway to the estate. The relief of the fresh air on her face matched the release she felt inside, at emerging from the cut-price hell below. She positioned herself by some bins and waited for Stacey to emerge. The girl came out, already pulling off her hood and cap. She squealed when Jen grabbed her arm with one hand and reached into her pocket with the other. For a few moments she looked at Jen with shock before snatching her bag back. 'What the fuck?'

'You don't share those with my sister do you?'

'Share what?'

'Those Es.'

Stacey pulled a face and snarled. 'They're aspirins. I've got a headache.'

'If you take the piss, you will have . . .'

'What are you, my fucking mum or something? Following me around? Bugger off.'

She tucked the bag into her pocket and got ready to walk away. Then she turned back around and pulled the bag out of pocket. She looked inside as if it were a bag of sweets and took out an orange tablet. She took Jen's hand, put the tab in her palm and then closed her fingers around it. 'There. You've always got a stick up your arse, haven't you? Why not get happy for a change?'

As Stacey walked away, Jen opened her hand and looked at the flaky orange tab with the badly scored heart on it. She watched Stacey go and then threw it, with contempt, into the gutter.

Twenty-Five

Dee listened to the call John received from Jeff at the Pied Piper, and John's response to the Tiffany situation. She decided that knowledge could come in very useful. Then there was a call to Mickey Ingram, demanding to know what the deal was with the girl. Was there a problem? John told Mickey he was coming down to the Bad Moon pub that Friday evening for a bit of a chat; he didn't sound very happy. There was a call to someone called Rocky asking if he'd found a replacement for Ingram yet, as John wanted to give him the push the next day. But Rocky hadn't come up trumps and John decided he'd have to stick with Mickey for now. There were no calls to or from Trish. That problem, at least, seemed to have vanished off the radar.

As Dee heard the last calls on her tape, she realised that the handle on the door was turning and someone was coming in. She whipped off her earphones and let them drop to the floor but the walkie-talkie-looking device still rested on her desk. John came in, looking miserable.

'Hello, boss. Shouldn't you be keeping your footie fella happy?' *Keep it steady, girl.*

'The bastard's done a flit already. Said he had somewhere more upmarket to go. The wanker. All these people do is kick a ball around on a Saturday afternoon. I mean, it's not brain surgery is it?'

'His loss, John. Him and his tarty piece.'

Her boss took a chair on the other side of her desk. The device Jimmy had given her suddenly seemed to be about ten foot tall. John massaged his temples and shook his head. 'I dunno, Dee. I really don't.'

What didn't he know? Dee trod carefully. 'What's up, John? Tell me.'

He looked at the ceiling and then back at her. 'I've got a big deal coming up but I've got a bad feeling about it. I obviously didn't want to involve you in this but what's happening is . . .'

Dee raised her hand to make him stop. Now she had a good idea what his business was, her plan had changed. She could be a touch cleverer about how she was going to rope John in. If anything went tits up, she didn't want him to put her in the firing line with all the other suspects.

'Listen, John, there's nothing I'd like more than to be of assistance with your commercial activities, and I think I could be a real asset, but you probably shouldn't tell me in here. After all, walls have ears; you know what I mean? This place could be bugged up to the eyeballs, for all we know.' She looked at her black box on the desk and then quickly away again. 'Besides, you never know who you can trust, do you?'

'Eh?' He looked at her baffled.

'You never know who's wearing sheep's clothing.'

'What's that supposed to mean?'

'Nothing. Just watch your back that's all. No one's a hundred per cent straight up, are they?'

He leaned back in his seat. 'Even you, Dee?'

She smiled. 'Sheep's clothing ain't my style. I like to be decked out in designer swag only, don't I.'

John didn't press the matter, but Dee formed the distinct impression that her employer had something else on his mind. Her heart sank when he confirmed he did and what it was.

'And there's another thing. This bird I've been seeing, Trish. I'm getting blanked. Can you believe it? She seemed really into it and now she won't return my calls or nothing. I don't understand women, Dee, I really don't.'

Dee trod even more carefully. 'The thing is, John, a man in your position has to use a lighter step with women than he does with business. Let's face it, you're a very good-looking guy, a big splash with your own business and club; you're strong and reliable.' Dee realised, with surprise, that she meant all of what she was saying. When had John turned from the man in stacked heels to a bloke who was good-looking, who was strong? 'Unfortunately, there are a lot of women who just see that and think they can wrap a guy like you around their pinkie and pull his leash, whenever they like. Maybe Trish was one of them and thought there was some other bloke even better than you out there.' Dee gave a light laugh and added, 'As if. Or maybe she wanted to take you to the cleaners and guessed you were onto her.'

John nodded. 'Yeah, I know. That was certainly true of my first two wives.' Dee felt sympathy for his hangdog expression. But that was before he announced, 'Anyhow, I've asked Chris to pop over to hers and see if he can talk some sense into her.'

'You did what?' Dee almost fell off her chair.

Seeing her reaction, he asked, 'Do you think that's a mistake?'

Dee could barely contain her fury. If Trish spoke to Chris and he found out what had happened, she was knackered. 'Of course it's a mistake. Where's your self-respect? Screw the bitch.'

Swiftly she got out of her chair and walked around to his side of her desk. She put a hand on his shoulder, using her other hand to ruffle his receded hair, as if he were a little kid. She leaned over, her warm breath brushing his skin, and whispered, 'Forget her, John. She's not worth it and she's certainly not worthy of a man like you. You deserve a lady who knows how to appreciate you.'

John took her hand in his. 'Thanks for that, Dee. I appreciate it.'

When he was gone, Dee thought about what she'd heard. This couldn't be happening. John was hers, especially now she'd decided looking at him no longer hurt her eyes.

'Go on, give the boy another ring, my girl,' Jen's mum gently urged her. 'There's got to be a reason he hasn't called. A fella doesn't find a girl work in a swanky shop in town and leave her high and dry for no reason.'

When Jen had given Babs the news that Nuts had found her a placement – she didn't mention the Liam incident, or her employer's name – it had cemented Nuts' place in her mum's good books. She was learning so much from Madam Dominique that her head was often in a whirl by the time she came home. She was on her way to the fashion world, and now she only needed the man to complete her dreams; but it remained out of her reach because Nuts hadn't called like he'd promised.

She'd called him five times already today, making her feel like a stalker. But she'd had no joy; he wasn't taking her calls. She couldn't understand why he just wouldn't talk to her. For pity's sake, he'd been the one doing all the running, saying he'd move heaven and earth to go out with her. Maybe he'd found another girl; that made Jen feel really down. Maybe her mum was right and she'd laid on the 'I'm too good for the local riff raff' a bit too thick. But a girl couldn't just go out with anyone; you had to take your time to make sure they were straight-up Kosher, before officially hooking up.

A couple of years back, she'd nearly fallen for a local rat who turned out to have a string of ladies on the go, including Bex. She'd been all systems go, ready to give him her virginity, when some poor woman turned up at their table at the local Chinese one night, with a bawling baby, claiming he was the father. Jen had gone bright red before standing up, turning her back on him (and her sweet-and-sour chicken) and never looking back. She'd asked around about Nuts; no one seemed to know him, which she took as a good sign; if he'd been up to no good, everyone would know who he was.

Jen had finally found the lad who she might want to spend the rest of her life with and he didn't want to know. And it was all her fault.

Anxiously, she picked up the phone and dialled Nuts' number again. Her belly did flip-flops because she was desperate for him to answer. The phone line connected.

'Where the hell have you been? I've been waiting for your call,' Nuts snapped out quickly.

Jen's face lit up like the Oxford Street Christmas lights when she heard Nuts' voice. He'd been waiting for her to call him. Aww, sweet! She gave her mum a quick, triumphant smile and Babs left the room, humming happily to herself.

'Where have I been?' Jen tried to sound stern, but she couldn't keep the blinding bliss from her voice. 'I've been calling you morning, noon and bloody night.'

'Jen?' He dragged her name out.

Jen frowned. 'Er, yeah?'

'Oh, Oh, I didn't realise it was you.'

'Who the bleeding hell did you think it was – Kate bloody Moss?' Only after she'd spoken did the penny drop; Nuts had only picked up the phone because he'd thought she was someone else. He didn't recognise her voice. That hurt so bad; it was like vinegar and salt mixed into a wound.

'How you doing, babe–?'

'Don't give me none of that *how ya doing babe* bollocks.'
The words were foaming at her mouth, like she was a mad
woman. 'You only picked up the blower because you were
expecting someone else on the end of the line.'

'No way, darling, it's always great to hear your voice—'

Jen was in no mood to let him finish. 'If it's so flippin'
wonderful, why haven't you been taking my calls? You said
you were going to call.'

'I've been busy—'

Jen shook back the wave of hair on her cheekbones. 'I *bet*
you have. Busy sniffing up some tart's little black number
more like.'

'No, you've got it totally wrong there—'

Jen didn't even realise that her voice had grown so loud
people could probably hear her at Mile End tube. 'If you didn't
want to go out with me, all you had to do was give me a bell
and tell me all polite like. I ain't that desperate to be seen
around town with someone who doesn't want to touch me
with a barge pole.'

'You've got it all wrong, Jen girl; I've been up to my neck
in a new deal. It's the biggest one I've had, so it's really important. I've got people waiting on me so I haven't had the time
for anything else. I was going to call you in a couple of days.'

But Jen didn't believe a word of it. One minute he's chasing
her all over the place, sending her flowers – nicked flowers –
and finding her a prized placement up West, and the next he's
giving her the silent treatment because of some deal. He'd be
telling her next he'd had to organise a sit down with the Pope
and Britney Spears. No, she wasn't buying it. As far as she was
concerned, he was giving her a major league fob off.

'You know what, Nuts? I'm grateful for you dealing with
Liam and getting me sorted at Madam D's, but – in the words
of my sister – fuck off.'

'Jen, don't be like–'

Jen slammed down the phone.

What a grade A fake-up artist. He didn't have the balls to tell her to her face that he wasn't into her anymore. She'd been moping over him for days while he'd probably been pussy watching and putting his knob in the type of places that made her shudder. The phone started trilling – she looked at it with contempt. No way was she giving him the satisfaction of a second chance. But that didn't stop the tears gathering in her eyes.

'What happened, love?' her mum asked as she placed a comforting arm around Jen's shaking shoulders.

'He don't want to know and so he's trying to let me down gently with a pack of lies.'

Babs shook her head. 'Come and sit down while I brew a cuppa.'

Once they were on the sofa, both nursing a steaming cup of tea, Babs proclaimed, 'But he seemed like such a nice lad. Got his head on straight. You sure you got this right?'

Jen sniffed. 'Told me some cock and bull about being deep in some business deal. Too busy to take or answer my calls.'

Babs placed her palm on her daughter's knee. 'But maybe that's the truth. He's one of us, which means, if he's going to make anything of himself he needs to keep his eye on the ball and sometimes that means he's got to do it twenty-four-seven. People from our neck of the woods don't get golden tickets offered to them every day of the week.'

'If he fancies me so much why didn't he recognise my voice at the start?' Jen sipped her tea. 'No, he's playing fast and loose with my feelings and I am not putting up with it.'

'So he didn't try to say sorry?'

Jen's face pinked up. 'Of course he did, now he's been caught bang to rights. What else was the Muppet going to do but try to brazen it out? Well, it's going to take more than sweet words to get back into my book.'

'Sorry, love.'

Jen put her cup down and stood up. 'You know what, Mum? I wash my hands of him.'

Twenty-Six

As soon as Dee entered the Bad Moon boozer in Shadwell, hours before John's meet with Mickey Ingram later that night, she knew she had a problem. She was the problem. The place went silent and she understood why. There were no other black faces in sight. The vibe she got off this lot was hostile: they probably wanted to drag her off, as the outsider in town, and burn her at the stake. Her usual response would be, Well, let them bloody look until their eyes fell out of their head, but she couldn't play it that way this time. She needed to be in and out quickly, so they didn't remember her.

She looked around, taking in the classic two-room drinking hole. This was another problem: there was nowhere for a stranger like her to hide and keep a close eye on John tonight. Even a disguise wouldn't have helped. She would have been too obvious and John wasn't blind. She did a single circuit around the pub, acting as if she were looking for someone, and attracting hostile and suspicious glances as she passed through.

'You looking for someone?' the barman called out. Dee almost shouted back, 'Yeah, Nelson Mandela,' but shook her head instead, mumbling about getting the wrong pub.

She took a deep breath once she got back outside again. At least there had been no argy-bargy when she got to work that morning; she had expected trouble over that walking advert for a bad makeover, Trish. But the boss had said nothing about Chris's visit to see her, which Dee took as a hopeful sign.

She checked the street outside the pub. It was going to be difficult even to park up and watch who went in and out. Bloody bollocks, what was she going to do? She just couldn't think of a way out of this. She started pacing up and down, digging away inside her brain for an answer. She looked up to the sky for inspiration, and that's when she caught something, out of the corner of her eye, on the opposite side of the street. She zeroed in on it – a builder's sign, hanging outside one of the houses opposite. Dee scanned the place, clocking the builder's bollards outside. Her brain started ticking. What if she could get into the house later and keep the doors to the Bad Moon in view? She'd given up on the notion that she was going to hear any conversation, but there was always a chance she could see who was arriving with whom and what their expressions were like. She could do the same again when they left and, who knew, she might get lucky with a fight in the street or some shouting, which she would be able to hear.

But when she went to check the place over, the house was a dead loss. The downstairs windows were boarded up and metal shutters were in place over the front door. Dee cursed the local squatters who made such precautions necessary. She'd developed many skills over the years but housebreaking wasn't one of them. The only option left was to walk to the next street and see if there were any options for observing the pub from there. Another blank. The rear of the pub was guarded by a high wall. Unless she was going to be sitting on it, she could see nothing and the front of the pub was invisible from the rear anyway. It looked like her plan had failed before it even started and Dee began to see what the attraction of the Bad Moon was for the Johns and the Mickeys of this world.

As she came back onto the pub's street, she saw a truck trying to make its way down without hitting anything while being tooted by a car that was stuck coming the other way. She saw the truck back up outside the house she had looked at earlier, and watched, with a smile, as it lowered a skip into place. The builders came out and put a plank up against it before pulling wheelbarrows up. At the same time, another guy began pulling canvas over the other end.

Dee walked past the skip and peered inside. It probably wasn't the ideal place for a spot of spying, but sometimes she couldn't help thinking the gods smiled on nosey parkers.

Jen wavered near the door to Dominique's, on her way to the phone box around the corner. For what felt like the millionth time, she stopped herself from going in. The security guard, Pedro, shot her a sour look, as he was about to reach for the door, just like all those other times she'd approached and then turned away. The plain truth was that instead of washing her hands of Nuts, she couldn't stop thinking about him. He couldn't be all bad if he'd sorted her out a spot in a place like this. Maybe she wasn't being fair to him and should give him another chance.

'Jennifer.'

Jen inwardly groaned at the sound of Madam Dominique's voice, but she turned around quickly, not wanting this kind, old woman to think she was taking the mickey and not doing her work.

'Madam Dominique, I'm so sorry—'

'Come with me please.' Without waiting for a response, Jen's shoulders slumped as she followed the other woman. *You've done it now,* the voice in her head screamed. *You've lost your placement because you can't get that boy out of your brain.*

She was surprised to see that they were entering a part of the building that none of the girls were allowed in, which led up to Madam's private office. The older woman took her time climbing the narrow staircase to the first floor. They entered a room that surprised Jen with its plain and simple décor. She'd always imagined Madam's office to be full of bright curtains and colourful rugs but the walls were white, except for one covered in a large, blue cloth, and the only furniture was a desk and two chairs.

Madam Dominique waved a hand at a chair as she too sat down. 'I can see the surprise in your face when you look at my room, but I like to keep things simple. All the show and colour is to entice my clientele to empty their pockets. You started as such a good worker, but I suspect that your life is anything but simple and has become very complicated.'

Jen squeezed her hands into her lap. 'No,' she said, in a rush, 'I'm as into this job as I've ever been.'

'Then tell me what is going on.'

Jen didn't hesitate; she wanted to get her problems with Nuts out into the open. Once she'd finished, Madam Dominique remained silent for a while, then she quietly said, 'Do you yearn for him?'

Yearn? Yeah, that was the word. Jen hesitated, then nodded.

The older woman smiled. 'Then go get him. Simple. Now that is out of the way, you must apply yourself to your work. Remember, you are here to learn.'

Once Jen had gone, Dominique slowly rose from her chair and moved towards the simple, blue cotton cloth covering one wall. She swept the cloth aside revealing a door, which she opened into the room that was her real private haven, containing many of the relics of her old life. She pulled off one of the many photos on the walls. As soon as she'd discovered Jennifer's last name, she knew that her instincts were right when she first met her, that she knew that face. But she couldn't turn the girl away, once she'd made a promise. She looked at the photo of her younger self, standing arm in arm with Stanley Miller.

Twenty-Seven

'I thought you were doing a bit of retail therapy?' John asked Dee when she got back to the Alley Club.

Dee had deliberately waited for John to come downstairs – she wanted it to look like she hadn't been out at all but in the cellar. 'No, too busy. By the way,' she took his arm, squeezed it, dreading the answer to the question she was about to ask. 'How did Chris get on, round your girlfriend's?'

His face darkened. 'She was obviously in there but wouldn't answer the effing door. The bitch.'

Dee had to restrain herself from smiling. Instead, she patted his arm. 'I know – the bitch. You've sent her flowers; she's probably holding out for you to send her your wallet next. Stuff her, John, she's not worth it.'

Triumphant, Dee went upstairs to listen to John's phone calls. There was only one. A menacing call to one of Mickey Ingram's associates telling him to pass on the message that he'd be down the pub at 7.30 sharp and warning Mickey not to be late. John also insisted that Mickey needed to 'bring the team' with him as he wanted to speak to all of them.

Later that afternoon, Dee did go shopping. She bought a no-brand tracksuit, some washing-up gloves and a cut-price pair of trainers, and got ready to drive down to Shadwell.

She wasn't the first to arrive on the street that evening. There was already a solitary heavy, standing outside the entrance to the Bad Moon. She parked her car at a distance and then walked down to the skip, which she ducked below. After waiting several minutes for the guy on the door to lose interest in the empty street and pop inside for a moment, she loosened the rope that tied the canvas on top and climbed inside, crunching and clattering her way over the broken bricks, plaster and rotten beams until she found a half-comfortable spot to lie down, raise the canvas and keep an eye on proceedings.

Several locals appeared at the entrance where they were stopped by the heavy and subjected to questioning.

'Private party,' Dee heard the goon on the door say.

One of the locals had the unfortunate audacity to answer back. 'I don't remember any mention of a private shindig.'

'Do one, boys, if you want to keep your matching ears.' The locals scurried away. So it was going to be one of those meetings: customers kept out, big boys allowed in. Just as well she'd found an alternative to trying to spy inside the pub because she wouldn't have got in anyway.

Next, a flash Harry turned up in a pinstripe suit with a silk hanky poking out of his top pocket, wearing enough gold jewellery to keep the Royal Mint ticking over. The jowly man looked like he was going to a fancy dress do as a cockney gangster, but the respect he was shown by the guy on the door, and the size of the two men who accompanied him, suggested he was the real deal. A few other, more anonymous blokes appeared and went into the Bad Moon before the first of two cars arrived.

A BMW pulled up directly in front of the pub and a youngster in a tracksuit, trainers and a baseball cap got out. The cap was pulled low, which made it impossible for Dee to see his face. He was subjected to an interrogation and pat down by the guard who eventually allowed him in.

Finally, at 7.30 on the dot, a sleek, black Jag appeared. The driver jumped out to open the back doors. Slowly, Chris and a bit of muscle got out. They scanned the street like they were the Prime Minister's protection duty and only when they were satisfied did John emerge. He straightened the tie that was the same colour as his black suit. The bodyguard stood at a respectful distance while John and Chris stood huddled close, no doubt having a quick, pre-meeting chat. Dee was frustrated she couldn't hear what was being said. The heavy on the door virtually bowed to John and held the door wide open for him.

Dee let the flap of canvas fall back. She assumed that the plonker in the pinstripe suit must be Mickey Ingram but that wasn't really helping much. In fact, none of this was helping very much and she was beginning to wonder why she had come. But then her interest was aroused again when she heard someone shouting so loud, inside the pub. She knew that voice: John.

'So anyway, these three geezers come down to this boozer in Hackney, right?' John was not happy that he could hear that fat cunt Mickey Ingram's voice, as he and Chris made their way through the empty public bar to the saloon bar at the back. Who did that twat think he was? A cross between Al Capone and Jack the Ripper?

Mickey's voice got louder as they got closer. 'Mouthing off about some money I owed them, they were. So I says to them, You want your money, boys? I'll give you your money. So I reached inside my jacket, pulled out my shooter, shot the fuckers, two bullets each. And down they go – bosh, bosh, bosh – stone cold dead, right? Straight up. So I has a look around the pub so everyone sees my face, and I say, My name's Mickey Ingram, if anyone's interested. And then I walk out, cool as you like. Old Bill comes down there, mob-handed, and they interview all the pricks who was in the pub. And you know what? No one saw anything, no one heard anything. A hundred people that was – straight up. Thing is, right, people know better than to grass on Big Mickey. You know what I mean?'

The tosser juggled a pint and a whiskey chaser in his hands, and John was fucked off to see him with his two-tonne arse at the head of the table. John considered that his place.

Mickey waved his arms wide when he clocked him. 'Great to see you, pal – what can I get you to drink?'

John looked around the bar to make sure there were no unfamiliar faces. 'Orange juice and lemonade.'

Mickey started grinning. 'No, come on, John, don't muck about mate. Have a proper snifter; it's all on me this evening.'

John wasn't grinning back. 'No thanks. I'm like the police, I don't drink when I'm on duty.' He looked at Mickey's two drinks which were nearly empty already and added, 'It's sloppy and unprofessional.'

Mickey's smile slipped slightly, letting John know his nose was well and truly out of joint. Mickey heaved his bulk up and walked over to the bar to collect John's bevvy from the landlord. While he was gone, John made himself nice and comfy in Mickey's chair at the head of the table. When Mickey spotted what John had done, the tension in the room heated up. *Go on, I fucking dare ya*, John thought, *I'll rip your brainless head off*.

But Mickey played it safe and took another chair on the other side of the table. He was soon holding forth on the shipment he was organising for John and how the tentacles of his operation reached everywhere; he even had people at Tilbury who would keep everything cushty.

John listened to him in silence before saying, 'Don't worry about Tilbury; I'll have my guy Chris down there, keeping an eye on that.'

Mickey looked none too pleased as he eyed up Chris. 'I thought we were here to talk about Tilbury?'

John stared hard at him. 'No. I'll tell you what we're here to talk about. I asked you to take care of a simple job for me. Find a courier to pick up my paperwork for me and then keep it safe until I need it for the shipment.'

Mickey still didn't understand. 'That's right. And . . . ?'

John brushed his fingers lightly against the bottom of his tie. 'Thing is, bruv, obviously I left the choice to your discretion, because you have to trust people – no matter how crap they are. But now I hear you chose a sixteen-year-old kid, with a reputation for being a bit of an off-the-trolley merchant, who's constantly getting pulled up by the law. In other words, just about the worst possible person you could have picked.'

Mickey brightened. 'But that's the beauty of the plan, John. Thing is, my family have been in a major league strife with her family for years and she don't know who I am anyway. If she gets lifted by the Plod, there's no way she could be traced back to me. Good eh?'

John's hand smoothed against his tie. 'Well, as long as you're alright, Mickey, we won't worry about it.'

The sarcasm went flying over Mickey's head. 'Exactly!'

John looked Ingram squarely in the eye. 'You really are a fucking idiot, aren't you?'

Finally, the penny dropped for the Shadwell gangster. He spread one hand on the table and started jabbing a finger from the other in John's direction. 'No, I'm sorry, John, you can't come down here to my manor, shooting your mouth off to me like that, thinking you're the dog's bollocks.'

'Your manor?' John shoved his drink to the side with an impatient sweep of the back of his hand, while his other gripped his tie. 'Your manor's the four walls of this pub and you don't even boss that. Let me put you in the picture here. You finish this job for me, and then I never want to clap eyes on you or your keystone cops' outfit again. And if anything goes wrong with my job, whether it's your fault or not, I'll be holding you personally responsible.'

This was too much for Mickey. 'No, I'm sorry John, in that case bollocks to your job – and I'm going to have to ask you–'

In two quick moves, John pulled out a razor blade hidden inside his tie and had it pinned between Mickey's spread fingers on the table. The sharp edge touched the inside of one of Mickey's fingers ready to slice. The air filled with the sound of chair legs scraping against the hard floor, as both men's people shoved out of their seats.

'You were saying, Mickey?' John said very slowly and calmly.

Sweat pooled on the other man's forehead and started dripping down his face. Mickey looked at John's minders. They were smirking. Then he looked at his own, who were avoiding his gaze. They were realists, well aware of the pecking order of London's underworld; they weren't interested in taking on the much bigger man.

'Alright, mate, alright,' Mickey finally uttered, his tone filled with panic. Out of the corner of his eye, Mickey could see that his security detail had decided they had other business to attend to and were leaving. 'We go back years, to when we were nippers. Let's not destroy a good friendship over some teenage halfwit. I'll do the job, you'll see, you'll see.'

The tension sizzled. Finally, John straightened up and placed his razor in his pocket. As soon as he turned his back, Mickey was up, out of his chair and heading for the door. But

John spun around: 'Oi, Ingram – back here, I haven't finished with you by a long shot.'

Dee was watching the entrance closely. Two guys appeared and bolted down the street quickly followed by Mr Pinstripe who was also in a mighty hurry to get away.

John appeared at the door to the pub and yelled, 'Oi, Ingram – where do you think you're going? I'm talking to you.'

Mickey Ingram picked up his pace and didn't look around. John shouted after him. 'Hiring sixteen-year-old head-cases for a job like that? What's the matter with you? Why don't you go back to shoplifting, you ignorant little fucker.'

But he made no attempt to follow; he obviously didn't think Mickey was worth it.

Dee felt a surge of pride at her man's behaviour. This was the kind of thing she liked to see in her guys – not the horse-whipped pussy, wringing his hands over dopey cow girlfriends. But then, both sides worked to her advantage. She needed a wealthy man who could go head-to-head with men but not with women. And in John, she'd found one.

Chris and the bodyguard came out of the pub and exchanged a few words before Chris walked up the street to hail their Jag and John slipped the heavy a few quid from his pocket. The car reversed down the street and John and his party climbed in. The Jag stood motionless for a few minutes before it slowly crept up the road and disappeared into the night.

Dee got out of the skip, walked around to her car, got changed and went back to the Bad Moon. She knew it would be empty now and was hoping to catch any gossip the bar staff might be swapping, or, if she got lucky, she might strike up a conversation with them. But it proved to be a wasted journey. The pub was empty alright and the bar staff were relieved and relaxed now that the boys were all gone. But they were going about their business quietly. They didn't seem bothered about a black woman being here anymore.

Dee ordered her favourite tipple – rum and coke, iced to the max. She downed it quickly and got ready to get back to the Alley Club. As she turned, she bumped into a young man, the same one who'd come into the pub wearing a baseball cap.

He looked at her with surprise. 'Mizz Dee? What are you doing here?'

Twenty-Eight

Dee was struck dumb as she stared at the man in front of her, thinking that the game was well and truly up. Without his cap on, Dee pegged him immediately – Knobby, one of John's boys. He gazed at her with suspicion. *Shit.* All of John's people knew that Dee wasn't involved in the bizz side of things. She was just supposed to handle security in the club, and was happy to give that impression. But with her plan about to come to a climax, she felt like a trapeze artist. If she lost her grip now, she would plunge towards the ground and there would be no safety net to catch her. This boy was not going to disrupt her smooth landing.

'What's your real name, son?' He wasn't that much older than her, but she needed to maintain the hierarchy of their different positions on John's power ladder.

The kid was clearly embarrassed. 'You know that everyone calls me Knobby.'

'And how did you get that nickname?'

'It's just what John calls me.' He looked even more embarrassed before admitting, 'It's short for knob head.'

'Your real name, honey.' She needed to keep him sweet.

His face got even redder. 'It's Leonard.' When he saw the look on Dee's face, he added, 'I know. I prefer Knobby if I'm being honest.'

Dee hustled him over to a table. Once they were seated she made a real, slow drama of leaning forward so that her crop top with the bondage studs around the neck put some skin on display. It did the trick because the lad couldn't take his baby blues off the top of her breasts. Poor boy looked hungry: obviously not getting a big enough portion indoors. 'I shouldn't be telling you this, but John asked me to wait around the corner and then to come in and double-check no one's called the cops or are saying anything out of turn.'

Knobby got suspicious again. 'Eh? No one in here is going to call the law, are they? If they did that they wouldn't have any punters left.'

Dee had already discovered an effective way to shut this Doubting Thomas down. 'You questioning John's orders?' His face went pale. 'I don't ever utter "why" when the boss tells me to do something. Word of advice, Knobby love, saying nothing about anything is a good policy where your boss is concerned.'

'Leave it out, Mizz Dee, I don't put my bugle where it don't belong. The guv knows that; that's why he chose me. He knows I keep this,' he pointed to his mouth, 'shut.'

'So Mickey Ingram fucked out of the meeting with John?' Dee asked. She was putting herself right in the shitter if this info was wrong.

Knobby looked puzzled again, then cocky. 'You just told me not to say anything about nothing.'

He was smirking at her. The little prick. She needed to make him understand that he was dealing with his worst nightmare if he crossed her. Abruptly Dee stood up. She shook her head sadly at him. 'I thought you were brighter than this. That's what the boss says to me: "That boy is one clever spark." Now I'm going to have to go back and tell him – right now – that he got it totally wrong, that you're trying to mug him off–'

'That ain't true–'

'That's not what I'm hearing, Knobby.' Dee sat back down again. 'I'm in the loop. I wouldn't know about Mickey Ingram and the Pied Piper, otherwise. Plus, you don't seriously think John's hired me just to keep the bouncers in order, do you? You couldn't get a bit of fag paper between John and me.'

Knobby's voice lowered. 'Well, that's certainly the rumour going round John's crew. Word is, he's lining you up to replace Chris as his right-hand man. I mean bird. Oops, woman.'

Dee's glee knew no bounds, until Knobby added, 'But I don't believe it. Chris has been with him for aeons. They're as thick as thieves – so to speak. Anyway, the boss came down here to have it out with Mickey Ingram. I mean, Mickey's a nice enough bloke but he's a bit out of his depth. You know what I mean? To cut a long one short, John let Mickey hire a bird to look after the documents for the shipment–'

'Tiffany?'

His blue eyes nearly jumped out of his skull. 'How did you know that?'

She gave him a lazy smile. 'Told you, John tells me everything.'

'Only now, word has got back that this girl's a nipper and keeps having run-ins with the law and that she's not the full ticket. If Mickey had admitted he'd made a mistake, it would all have been sweet, but instead he starts mouthing off about how John can't come down to his manor, giving it large. So John squares up to him and then Mickey does a runner with his pathetic boys, which has pissed John right off, even more. I mean, if a bloke can't look after himself, he's no good to anyone, is he? Anyway, John gave him the old heave-ho.'

Dee wondered why Knobby was needed at the meeting. The boy was fit but he didn't look handy. 'So what did he ask you to come down here for then? You're not on the muscle side of the ice operation are you?' She still wasn't sure what 'ice' meant, but she used it anyway to make Knobby think she knew what she was talking about.

Knobby's nose was put out of joint by the slight, but he admitted, 'John had a job for me, an address and that. He needs to fulfil the quota before the shipment goes next week. So he told me to come down. The thing is, the soddin' tube workers are on strike and the job's in Richmond so I don't know how I'm supposed to get down there.'

'Why don't you drive? You brought your car didn't you?'

He was baffled and maintained, 'I said I'm on a job . . .'

Dee nodded. If there was one thing in life she had learned it was, when a door opens you jump through it. And this boy had flung one wide open for her. 'What about I drive you down there?' Then she had another thought. 'Why didn't John just give you the address in the club later?'

'He's got a date. Some bird has blown him out and he's going down to her gaff to talk her round with flowers and choccies. I know he wouldn't bother normally but I've heard he's got the hots for her. Trish, I think her name is . . . Err – are you alright? You look a bit funny.'

With one sweep of her fist, Dee sent the drinks and the ashtray flying across the table to the bar-room floor. Knobby stood up in alarm. 'Oi, take it easy bird . . .'

Dee grabbed him by the ear and yanked his head towards her. 'Don't call me bird, you little tosser. Now put your silly cap on and I'll meet you outside.'

Once Knobby was gone Dee made a quick call on the payphone near the toilets.

'Get your skates on; we're ready to rock 'n' roll.'

A nervous Jen stood outside the Alley Club in Soho. She was dressed very simply in a long, black, float away, daisy-print dress, low heels and a yin and yang necklace. She barely wore any make-up – just some eyeliner and sparkling lip gloss. She didn't want to overdo it because she was here for one reason only: to find Nuts and sort out once and for all whether they should make a go of it. Her mum had become a needle stuck on a record called, 'Give The Boy Another Bloody Chance'. As far as Babs was concerned, she should have taken his apology at face value. Plus, Madam Dominique said she should just go and get what she wanted. What if the poor bloke had really had the deal of a lifetime on? Jen had to admit that if she had something that important on in her life, she'd probably have acted the same. Still, she felt a tad silly because she had never in her eighteen years on this earth run around after any boy.

There was another problem – this was a members-only club and Jen wasn't a member. But she already had a plan for that; she came from The Devil's Estate after all, where telling a tale or two was an art form. She spotted a lone Joe approaching the club and went in for the kill, before he reached the entrance.

'You alright, mate?' she said with a big grin on her face.

He looked at her, puzzled. 'Do I know you?' His accent was uptown.

Jen came over, all big brown eyes and soft smile. 'You could if I got inside the club.'

He grinned back at her. 'You look like a nice enough girl. The only problem is, the type I want to know have got stubble and are packing a whack-a-do of a surprise in the trouser department.'

Jen's face fell as her cheeks got red. 'Sorry, mister.'

Dejected she started walking away but his voice made her stop. 'I didn't say that I wasn't going to assist a damsel in distress.'

Jen couldn't believe her luck. She wasn't even going to have to flirt or show a bit of leg to get inside.

'I'll only do it on one condition,' he continued.

Jen should've figured out there was going to be a catch; there always was. 'What do you want?'

'Tell me, why do you need to get inside?'

Jen stuck with the truth. 'My boyfriend – at least I think he's my fella – we've had a bit of a set to–'

'He's a paid-up member of the club and you want to make sure he's keeping his love stick to himself.'

Jen grinned; she liked this guy. 'Something like that.'

'Come on then. But a word to the wise, my dear. If you catch him with his pants down, don't make any trouble. The owner doesn't like trouble.'

Jen remembered that's exactly what Nuts had said when that black woman had kicked off inside the club. After the gentleman (and he was a gent, Jen decided; not many blokes would go out of their way to help a girl they didn't know from Eve) had signed them in, Jen got down to the business of trying to find Nuts. Lulu's heady lung power on Take That's 'Relight My Fire' greeted her as she walked into the bar.

She spent the next five minutes searching, but couldn't see him anywhere. Frustrated, she discreetly asked one of the waitresses if she'd seen him.

The other woman looked a bit put out. 'I don't know no Nuts.' Before Jen could say anything, the waitress had gone about her business. Jen asked the same question of the bar staff but got the same guarded response. Funny that. The staff had seemed to know Nuts the night he'd taken her here. Oh well, there was nothing for it but to head back home. Well girl, Jen thought, as she headed for the exit, that was the end of your big romance. Her mum would probably pat her on the shoulder and tell her there were plenty of fish in the sea, but as far as Jen was concerned there was no fish like Nuts. She'd never seen a fish with gorgeous blue eyes like his.

As she stepped into the foyer, a group of men burst into the club.

'Police! This is a raid. Everyone remain where you are.'

Only Jen remained rooted to the spot. She watched as chaos descended onto the club. People started running like they'd been caught short for the toilet. Only after she heard one too many toilets being flushed did Jen realise that punters must be trying to get rid of drugs. Other people fled out the back. Jen saw the posh guy who'd got her into the place jump the wall at the back, but a minute later he was being dragged back into the club. Five minutes later, the cops had restored order.

'I'm not interested in what you're shooting up your arms tonight,' called out the cop in charge, 'or who you're shagging; all I want to know is, where is John Black?'

'He ain't here,' the barman replied, with attitude and a load of lip.

The cop waltzed over as easy as you please to the barman, grabbed his head and slammed it against the bar. Jen and everyone else gasped. The barman's head came up, blood streaming from his now broken nose.

The lead cop turned to one of his other men. 'Did you see that, detective? That man tried to attack me.'

'I did, sir.'

Jen wasn't surprised by what she saw. You couldn't live on The Devil and not hear the whispers about coppers who smacked you around to make sure you felt the full force of the law.

'Anyone else,' the cop continued, 'who wants to piss on me and tell me that it's raining while this search goes on, please feel free to step forward.'

Everyone, including Jen, shook their heads and then lowered their eyes to the ground. The search went on for a good twenty minutes, but the barman was right, John Black wasn't in residence.

As they left Jen heard the brutal cop say to his second-in-command, 'No matter, we're rounding up all the other players.'

Who those other players were, Jen didn't care. She scarpered out of there as soon as the filth was gone.

Twenty-Nine

Fit to do murder, Dee shook with anger as she drove Knobby down to Richmond-upon-Thames. She only just managed to resist the temptation to drive by Trish's and see if John's motor was there and, if not, to drop by and give her rival a little reminder of where she stood romantically with her very ex-boyfriend. Knobby meanwhile, because of his professional expertise in the field, was becoming increasingly alarmed at her driving. He began to warn her about red lights, overtaking, speeding and going in the wrong direction up one-way streets. That was until Dee warned him that if he didn't shut his gob it wouldn't be a crash he'd need to worry about but having his skull battered with a car jack. From then on, Knobby kept it shut.

In Richmond, she dropped him off a street away from what he described as the 'target' and then he asked her to hang around in case someone from the target was at home. He'd brought the tools of his trade with him from his BMW and, after picking them up from her boot, he pulled his cap low over his forehead and then set off down the rich, high-end avenue where he hoped to fulfil John's quota.

Dee was still seething about her fiancé trying to two-time her with trashy Trish. But then she realised she had something even worse to worry about. In her rear-view mirror, she noticed a cop car creeping down the road. She sank low in her seat as it passed and watched as it went by. Its driver appeared to be looking for something. Dee didn't give a flying F about knob head, but she was determined that her plan wasn't going down the shitter because he got himself put in cuffs. She gently turned the ignition and without turning her lights on crawled around the corner into the road where her guy was meant to be at work.

She found him outside the door of a house peering through a letterbox with a torch. On the drive outside was a sports car. Dee pulled over and hurried up to where Knobby was trying to feed an extender into the hallway. She whispered, 'You need to get a move on. Five-O are around.'

Poor Knobby nearly jumped out of his skin. He left the extender poking out of the house and hurried down the drive. There was no sign of the police. He ran back and hissed, 'If you hadn't been at the wheel like Evel Knievel on acid maybe they wouldn't . . . Here, hold this.'

He passed her the torch and as Dee directed the beam through the letterbox, Knobby began manoeuvring the extender like a crane. Inside, on a mahogany table under a mirror, Dee could see a set of car keys. 'Are you sure these people are out? Why are all the lights on?'

'Yeah, they're out. John's got a network of snouts in the area – window cleaners, milkmen, those kinds of people, all over the place. You'd be surprised what people like that can find out over time, and how cheap they are to get information out of. They'd probably spy on their grannie if the price was right.'

Like a kid at a funfair full of bright lights and excitement, Knobby tried to catch the keys with a hook on the end of his extender, which shook like a fishing rod.

'Easy!' Knobby beamed as he reeled the keys in.

For a moment, Dee forgot about Trish and John and admired the keys that he held out for her inspection. She looked up and down the road in both directions and there still was no sign of the law. It looked like a successful job.

As he got into the sports car he was stealing Dee decided to ask him the question that had been plaguing her, even though it might make her sound like a first grade plonker. 'What's "ice" got to do with this?'

Knobby laughed. 'I thought you knew what was what?' Then, seeing the stormy look on her face that said she was probably going to thump him one if he didn't answer her question, 'It's one we use in the trade, relieving people of their motors. ICE means In Car Entertainment.'

Of course. Dee nodded her head as she smiled. Clever name. But not clever that her fella was involved in such silly, low-rent stuff. She'd been furious down the cemetery in Mile End when she realised that sixteen-year-old Tiffany was hiding false paperwork for cars: nicked cars. John was a big Face and he was involved in silly little boy games. What was wrong with the man?

'Where are you taking this bit of ice then?' she asked looking at the sports car. 'One of the docks? Tilbury? For the shipment?'

'I wouldn't know about that, Mizz Dee. I just collect the merchandise; I don't do admin.' He gave her one of the smiles that no doubt, Dee thought, melted many a female heart. 'But yeah, to Tilbury. They ain't got time to respray it but they'll change the plates at a garage down there and file off the serial numbers and it'll all be cute.'

'John will be pleased. I think it best you don't mention I gave you a lift.'

'I told you, Mizz Dee, I don't do admin.'

Dee decided she liked Knobby. She liked him a lot. He was obviously very nifty as a car thief, cool under fire and very loyal and because of that she didn't want him getting caught up in the firestorm that was going to hit from her plans. Plus, maybe she and John could use him in the future.

'Do you understand the phrase, "One good turn deserves another"?' she asked him.

Knobby looked confused, but nodded. Dee whispered and cautioned, 'In that case, take my advice and make yourself scarce for a while after you drop that motor off. You get me?'

He was even more baffled. 'No.'

'You will soon . . .'

Since they seemed to be getting more friendly, Knobby whispered, 'By the way, feel free to call me by my proper nickname in future, the one all my real mates call me.' He came over a touch shy, as he added, 'That's if you want to, of course.'

Dee smiled. 'Why not? I didn't think you used Knobby on a day-to-day basis.'

'Nah, course not. My mates all call me—' but he never finished as a voice roared from one of the house's upstairs windows, 'Excuse me but what the hell do you think you're doing?' A man with a mane of bushy white hair leaned out of the window. 'Darling, call the police!'

Dee loved the 'excuse me' but the guy didn't appear to want to come downstairs to confront them. Knobby grinned at Dee; he seemed to be in no hurry. 'What a bull-shitter. We've got ages before the Bill turn up.'

'I don't think so,' Dee added quickly, remembering the cops she'd seen earlier and she was proved right when a police car started coming down the avenue. It had no blue lights flashing or siren blaring but it was clearly looking for trouble. Knobby swung into action. 'Go and get in your car, then wait five minutes and let me deal with this.'

The bloke in the window upstairs was frantically signalling to the police by waving his arms and screaming, 'They're over here. Over here. Hold on! He's stealing my car!'

As Dee made her escape across front gardens, head down, she heard the ignition on the sports car start and Nuts revving the engine in a style which made it sound like a light plane on a runway. She turned to see him reverse down the drive, wheels spinning like propellers but instead of fleeing in the opposite direction, he turned to face the police and then, headlights full on, hand on the horn, he careered down the road towards them so they were forced to brake and veer violently to avoid a collision. Almost upon the cops as they mounted the pavement, Knobby brought the stolen car to a halt, wheels squealing. He leaned out of the window and beckoned with his hand at the shocked driver of the police car. 'C'mon, boys! C'mon! What you got!!??'

Cocky sod, Dee thought with maximum respect.

With that he reversed the sports car again, did a three-point turn and mounted a grass verge, before taking off down the road at high speed, as the police set off in full pursuit. Dee crept through the gardens and returned to her own car. She waited until the rear lights of the two other vehicles had disappeared in the distance before starting her own motor and slipping away with her lights switched off. Only as she drove away did she realise she hadn't found out what Knobby's real nickname was. Probably 'Ice Man' she thought smiling.

Dee knew there was something up at the Alley Club as soon as she got back because there was no music to welcome her when she stepped inside. There was smashed glass in the reception hall and staff were running around like headless chickens.

'What's been going on?' Dee asked one of the security team.

He gave her a dirty look. 'The one night we needed you to be here.'

Dee almost landed one on his chops to wipe away the smart-arse look he was giving her. 'Don't get in my face; just tell me what happened.'

'The cops raided the club when John wasn't here. Made a total mess of the place. John's upstairs. He's been looking for you everywhere and – by the looks of him – he's not a happy bunny about you not being here to protect his club.'

Thirty

'John, you can't be here,' Dee insisted, as soon as she joined him inside his office upstairs.

She stayed close to the door, her chest heaving, as her boss paced the office. This was a John she had never seen before. The angry heat coming off him was nuclear. His nostrils were flared, his face was growing so red she thought he was bound to do himself some damage.

'Who gives the fucking filth the right to come into my place and stamp all over it with their jack boots?' His voice shook the room. Dee didn't even know if he could see her, he was spitting so much fire. And then he went crazy – picking up his chair and smashing it against the floor, toppling over the steel cabinet, and knocking the framed, celebrity portraits off the walls. Strangely enough, the only thing that he didn't touch was his desk, and when Dee saw what was on it, fear ran through her blood, as it never had before. There, sitting pretty, were the phone-tapping wires Jimmy had installed in the club.

Dee had to get the upper hand before things got out of control. She moved quickly towards John and placed her hand on his arm. She felt the burning heat of his flesh and realised she had made a mistake. He twisted her arm up against her back, making her cry out in pain, and then pushed her backwards onto the desk.

She was done for. He'd either found out that she was behind the phone tapping or someone had been blabbing to John behind her back. Maybe Knobby had been caught by the cops and he'd grassed her up to the cops, or John, or both. Or had John caught up with Tiffany and heard about the black woman who'd followed her to the graveyard? Or, worst of all, had that slaggy, gold-digger Trish finally thrown open her door in floods of tears and told him about the visit she'd received from the wife impersonator – the menace who had the brass neck to involve a kid in her threats. Or was it a combination of all three?

John lowered his head towards her. His face looked . . . he looked . . . Flippin' hells bells, if this had been any other situation, Dee would have been turned on like hell. His breath was hot against her face. She wanted to jump him and do the dirty on the desk.

'And where were you, Dee, when all this fuck-up was going on? I took you on as Head of Security to look out for my place—'

'John listen—'

'You better have a good—'

'Fucking listen, will you,' she screamed. 'I had to meet my mother. Remember I told you she dumped me when I was a baby. Well, I just found her again.' She looked pleadingly at him. 'What did you want me to do? Tell her to fuck off?' She let the emotion charge through her voice. 'I couldn't do that. No way.'

The anger abruptly left him as he pulled her up and let go of her arm. 'I'm sorry, Dee—'

She shook her head. 'I'm the one that should be on my knees here. What I don't get is why the coppers would have done your place over tonight.'

John shoved his fingers through his receding hair. 'I found this lot.' He pointed to the wires on the desk. The tone of his voice revealed nothing. Was he toying with her, cat and mouse style?

'What is it?' She knew her heart was racing like it was doing a circuit of Brands Hatch.

'It's a bug for a telephone. Someone, somewhere has been taping my calls. Right under my nose. Can you believe this?'

'Have you spoken to Chris about it?'

John shook his head. 'He's doing some bizz for me.' Which meant Chris hadn't grassed her up. Yet.

John leaned forward and picked up a piece of the equipment. He inspected it before putting it down again. 'I've got a mega problem, Dee. I've got a little wrinkle going on – an export wrinkle – and the shipment goes tonight. I'm as careful as you like on the phone but if the law are onto me, I'm fucked. Everything's moving into place at this very moment. I've got Chris down there, sorting out the logistics and one of my boys picked up the final piece of the jigsaw tonight. It's too late to stop now. And now this . . .'

Dee let out a silent sigh of relief, and drew a silent breath of triumph. Now everything was in place for her own little wrinkle. She picked up the tape that was lying on the desk and shook her head. 'It's not the law, John. Look at it – it's an amateur job. Like I said, I don't know anything about this stuff but it doesn't look like the gear they use in the movies. How did you find it?'

'I rang Trish this morning and when I got the dial tone, I heard a recording of a call I made earlier in the background. So I called the phone people and they sent an engineer over this afternoon. He found it when he checked the line.'

Dee winced twice, once for Trish and a second time for that rank amateur Jimmy Kite. She made a mental note to track him down, give him a kicking and get her money back. She looked her boss in the eye. 'This is an inside job, John. Someone in this club has been keeping tabs on you.'

He shook his head stunned. 'Bollocks – no one in here
would dare do that. My people are totally loyal.'

Dee thought carefully before suggesting, 'You know what
the woman who brought me up said to me once? Never trust
your best friend with your fella.'

'What's that got to do with anything?'

She took a step closer to him. 'I hate to say this, but maybe
your backstabber is Chris.'

'Fuck right off,' he stormed, hands going up, like he didn't
know where to put them. 'My Chris? My old mucker? What are
you suggesting? You came in here to work for me yesterday,
babe. Chris and me go way back. You're bang out of order–'

'Calm down, John, I'm not saying he was doing a badness.
He might have been monitoring your calls as a precaution for
security reasons, just to check nothing was being said out of
turn. That's all I'm suggesting.'

John was still angry. 'Well, keep your suggestions to yourself.' But then he had a think before adding quietly, 'He's down
in Essex anyway until the shipment goes and we're keeping
radio silence until then. When he gets back, I'll ask him if he
knows anything about it.'

Dee grabbed his arms. 'Think, John. You've had the Bill
banging about in here and you've had someone tuning in on
you. That's why I told you not to tell me about your
business–'

'The walls have ears,' he uttered softly, remembering her
words.

Dee let her hand caress his arms. 'I've got a bad feeling,
boss. Say something else happens? You can't be here.'

'And where the fuck am I going to go?'

Dee tightened her fingers. 'Somewhere where no one is
going to find you.'

Thirty-One

'Tiff's been arrested. I'm down West Central nick.
I need you here with me.
Mum'

The handwritten note her mum had stuck on their front door
told Jen that her troubles were far from over. Jen seethed.
She was flat-out fed up with her poxy sister, always bringing
heartache to their door. Sometimes she wished that the cops
would just lock Tiff up and chuck away the key. Then Jen
saw, in her mind, that copper viciously breaking the barman's
nose. Say something awful like that happened to her baby sis
if she got banged up? No, she wasn't going to allow that to
happen, so she was going to have to go down to the cop shop
and get this sorted out. But how was she going to get down
there? It was gone midnight and the tube would be packing
up for the night, so she couldn't jump on a train. A cab
wouldn't come out this time of night to the estate; only trouble called out-of-hours from The Devil to make a quick
getaway. She didn't want to knock on the neighbours' doors,
begging for a ride, because this was private business and if
there was one thing Babs hated it was the Millers being the
talk of the town on the estate. But she needed to get a lift
from somewhere.

Jen opened the door and went straight to the phone. There was only one person she could ask. She started to dial.

Knobby knew something bad was kicking off by the time he got home. As soon as he walked through the door a call had come through from the Alley that the Bill had tossed the place over and smashed up Frank's face. But the tale got worse when he was told that the whisper was the cops were getting ready to take everyone down. Bollocks. That was one of the reasons he never used the moniker his mates called him, or his real name. If the cops were looking for a Knobby, they wouldn't track him down. Well, not unless someone blabbed. But then the only three people who knew about his involvement in the shipment were the boss, Chris and Mizz Dee and he would bet his life that they'd never say a word. Turn grass and you might as well have a stamp tattooed on your head that read Snitch. Or someone would get to you first and carve it for you, with a wickedly sharp razor.

No, he was safe. He had sweet FA to worry about. But that didn't stop him pacing his flat like he was in a cage. Then the phone rang. He stopped pacing. What if it was the Bill? *Course it ain't dipstick; they don't call, they just break your door down.*

On the third ring, he answered the phone.

'What do you want . . . ?' Then he stopped as he heard the person on the other end of the line. 'Jen is that you?'

'I know it's late and all, but I need you to do me a big favour, Nuts.'

Nuts and Jen reached West Central Police Station going on two in the morning. When he heard what she wanted him to do, he'd nearly fobbed her off again. Her sister was the reason he'd stopped seeing Jen. Then he'd seen Tiffany down the Pied Piper as he talked to John's linkman Jeff, and he'd realised that

Mickey Ingram's bat-shit errand girl was Jen's baby sister. He was pretty sure that Tiffany hadn't seen him, but he couldn't take the chance that she hadn't clocked him and then gone blabbing about his real job to Jen. He'd taken a real risk sorting out Jen's perv tutor and arranging a job for her with Madame Dominique, but he couldn't just leave Jen stranded like that. All her dreams up in smoke because some dirty old geezer couldn't keep his mitts to himself? No, that just wasn't right. But after that he'd made himself hang back. If Jen found out what his real occupation was she might ditch him and he was not prepared for that to happen. He really liked her; she fit him to a T.

'I really was going to give you a bell after my deal was over,' he told her as they turned into the street near the nick. 'In fact I was going to give you a buzz tomorrow.'

'You don't have to say that, Nuts. I'm a big girl. I can take being chucked.'

'That's where you're wrong, Jen. I like you. Want to see loads more of you.'

The car stopped a street away from the police station. 'What are we doing stopping here?' Jen asked surprised.

'I don't like cop shops, so if it's all the same to you, I'll wait here.'

'What do you mean wait?'

'Don't think I'm just going to leave you and your mum to get home on some night bus with a deck full of pissheads. I ain't that type of guy, Jen.'

She smiled at him. 'Thanks a bunch, but if I'm not back in a couple of hours you head off home.'

And with that she was gone. But Nuts was going to wait here until daylight, if he had to. Although he was almost one hundred per cent sure Jen's crackpot sister didn't know about his involvement, he had to make sure she hadn't chucked his name into the frame.

Thirty-Two

'My poor girl's innocent,' Babs Miller sniffled into her hanky. 'She's been led astray by that bad lot.'

Tiffany slouched in the chair beside her mum. They were inside what the cop on the desk called 'Interview Room 1', but Tiffany had nicknamed it 'The Grass Room'. That's what the cops were expecting her to become – a snitch bitch. She'd been in these situations before. She was already fed up that her mum was sitting next to her as her appropriate adult, sobbing all over the shop. Tiffany wanted the whole thing to be over, like now! But she did tightly clasp a tissue in her hand; she was planning to do some major league boo-hooing of her own.

The two cops who had dragged her down here waltzed in, set up their recording equipment and sat opposite her. They introduced themselves, using their first names. 'Because we want to keep this nice and friendly, Tiffany,' was the explanation she got. So that's how PC Plod were going to play it – talk to her like she was a friggin' five-year-old.

It was James who did the talking. 'We know you're not to blame for the situation you're in, Tiffany. We know you've been exploited and manipulated and we want to help you as much as we can. If you help us, we can help you. Does that sound fair to you?'

It took all that Tiffany had to avoid saying, 'Oh, fuck off . . .' Instead she whispered, 'Yeah.'

James went on. 'As you know, we found a quantity of cannabis on you when you were arrested—'

'Yeah. That had nothing to do with Stacey, who you nicked me with.' No way was she dragging Stacey into this mess. Stacey wasn't supposed to be there, but when they'd bumped into each other and her best mate had offered her a tote, well, what was a girl like her to do? Turn down a great puff of draw? She would never have done it if she'd figured Stacey was going to be nabbed along with her.

'You were with Stacey flamin' Ingram,' her mum growled. 'I should clip you around the—'

'Mrs Miller, please,' James warned. Babs settled back in her chair and resumed sniffling into her tissue. James carried on. 'Drugs possession is a very serious matter. But we might be able to help with that too, as long as you answer all our questions honestly. Does that sound reasonable to you?'

Through gritted teeth she replied, 'Don't worry, James, I want to make a clean breast of things.'

James looked disappointed and Tiffany knew it was because he was hoping she'd hold out on them, so he could entrap her with his razor-sharp questioning. But she wasn't going to give him the pleasure. When he got over his knock-back, James said, 'That's good. Now, are you OK? Can we get you a cup of tea or a glass of water?'

Tiffany couldn't help herself. 'A vodka and coke would help the party go with a swing.'

James' smile vanished. 'This isn't a laughing matter, Tiffany. You're in serious trouble and you need to understand that.'

'Oh, I do, James. I apologise.' She knew the tone of her voice was too close to piss-taking for comfort but the Plod let it go and began to unpack the outline of the case against her. It was clear the two boys in blue had the lot. They knew all about her visits to the Pied Piper and what she had collected there. They knew she was taking the envelopes to the cemetery and hiding them in a tomb. They knew what was in the envelopes and they even knew how much she'd been paid. She could see from their faces that they also knew what that meant – she was a bit part player, a tiny cog in the wheel. Tiffany also guessed they knew everything else, but were pretending they didn't.

'So tell us, Tiffany, who was it who first recruited you for this job?'

Tiffany paused slightly, looking across at her mother, before saying, 'A guy called Mickey Ingram . . .'

Babs exploded in fury, jumping out of her seat. 'You what? Mickey Ingram? I'll fucking kill the bastard!'

James indicated with his hand for Babs to sit down. 'Mickey Ingram? Tell us about him.'

Tiffany told them all about good ole Mickey – how he'd recruited her down at the Bad Moon; how he'd given her instructions to pick up stuff from the Pied Piper and how notification of the collections came from a runner on The Essex Lane Estate.

'He beat the living daylights out of his daughter Stacey.' Tiffany swiped the tissue under her eyes, surprised to feel real tears gathered there. 'She didn't have nuthin' to do with anything. He only got me on the job because he knew that our families are in a ding-dong, so I was his cover story if he ever got caught. I mean, who's going to believe that Mickey Ingram, of all people, would take me on? And . . .' Tiffany let her voice quiver.

'It's OK, Tiffany. I don't want you to be afraid in here.'

'It was horrible,' she said wiping the tissue under her nose. 'When I'd see him down the Bad Moon, he'd look at me like some dirty old man. You know at my . . .'

'Scumbag,' Babs butted in. 'Perv. Should be locked up and the key tossed in the fucking Thames.'

Then Babs started sobbing again as the other cop, Mark, made more notes. When Tiffany told them about being dangled out of the window at the Pied Piper by 'a lanky streak of piss' the two cops looked horrified and asked for a full description. They made furious notes. Babs was wailing by this point.

Wearily, James looked over at her. 'Should we stop at this point for you to have time to compose yourself?'

Tiffany's mum violently shook her head and tried hard to hold tight to her emotions.

'Tell us, Tiffany, what do you know about John Black's involvement in this conspiracy to steal and sell cars?'

'John Black?' She frowned, making sure her face looked very confused. 'I heard the name. Mickey and the others were always having a laugh at his expense. Said he was a right mug because it was all going on under his nose and he didn't know nuthin' about it. He was a bit of a fall guy. I think he has a club and they used it as a base for the operation. Something like that.'

James looked stunned. 'John Black didn't know what was going on?'

'So I heard.' Tiffany shrugged.

A tense look passed between the two detectives. James turned back to Tiffany. 'You're sure about that, are you?'

'You asked me to be upfront, so that's what I'm being. It's just what I heard. I was told the main guy was called Chris. Never heard no last name. Mickey said I'd be answering to him if there was any trouble and that Chris was a right thug who took care of business.'

James and Mark made notes but as they did so they heard a commotion in the corridor outside. Tiffany recognised Jen's voice and then a woman she didn't know and finally a voice she knew too well. The door handle twisted and rattled as the shouting outside rose to a fever pitch. James turned off his recorder and went to investigate. When he opened the door, three women tumbled in – Jen, a WPC and Mel Ingram. James was too shocked to react and the slim WPC was pushed in the face and flung aside by Mel who pointed her finger at Tiffany and screamed, 'That's her! That's the fucking bitch that's landed my Stacey in the nick.'

Tiffany's silence and the sly smirk on her face turned Stacey's mum into Hurricane Mel as she threw herself at her. But she'd reckoned without Babs who rose to her feet and clenched her fists.

'I'll show you and your husband what it's like.' Babs shoved the other woman sideways. James, Mark and the WPC struggled to restore order but they were no match for the two angry mums who turned the interview room into a wrestling ring. They flew at each other. Stacey's mum went for Babs' hair. Big, big mistake, Tiffany thought; Babs Miller didn't go in for any of that boarding school, prissy girl, hair-pulling malarkey; she had a pair of fists and knew how to use them. Babs belted her one, straight in her big gob. Mel staggered back. Tiffany scrambled out of her seat to stand with her sister by the door. Mel rushed forward and viciously kicked Babs in her right leg. Swearing blue murder, Tiffany's mum jumped the other woman and brought her down. They started screaming and scratching as they rolled around on the ground. The tape machine crashed to the floor.

James ran into the corridor and shouted, 'Get me some big boys down here quick, and tell them to bring batons.'

It took four cops to finally subdue the two raging women. Each was held as they glared and snarled at each other. Mel Ingram was the first to calm down. 'OK, OK, I'm done.' She looked at Babs and then at Tiffany before letting fly a nasty

Thirty-Three

'What is a shooter doing on my kitchen table?'

For fuck's sake, Dee railed inside her mind, she'd only popped out to the club to check that everything was cleaned up after the raid, which appeared to have given his lord and master here enough time to get tooled up. He'd readily agreed to being stashed at her gaff because no one would link his name to it. Word had come through that the coppers were all over John's illegal car scam and that some of his people were already banged up.

John was back to pacing around like a caged animal, just like she'd seen him doing in his office at the club. My Lord, at least he hadn't twigged about her being behind the wiretap.

'I need it. I've got to defend myself, if the law catch up with me.'

'Are you stupid or something?' Dee shot at him, her eyes on fire. She really was trying to hang on to the flirty, girly act, but John's total lack of common sense was sending her into rude-girl-with-attitude orbit. 'Get rid of it. Actually, forget that, I'll get rid of it for you.'

But as she moved, his angry voice stopped her. 'Someone's shafted me proper. Someone's bloody had me over.' He kicked the sofa. Dee had to hold herself back; she'd got the sofa on her plastic and hadn't finished paying for it yet.

laugh. 'At least I won't have to worry about my Stacey being led astray by that bitch anymore.' But Tiffany's smirk was undimmed. And when James told the cops to take Babs and Mel to the cells to cool off, Tiffany called after Mel, 'How's Mickey?'

'What do you ...?' Stacey's mum stopped whatever she was going to say and plastered a fake look of surprise on her face. 'I haven't seen my old man in years.'

'You have to say that, don't you?' Babs taunted, 'Because if the social find out he's been kipping at yours, it means bye-bye to your benefits. Go out and find a fucking job like the rest of us instead of lying on your back all day long,' she finished on a scream.

'Lying on my back?' the other woman bellowed back. 'Don't forget I know all of your secrets, Barbara Miller.'

James stepped in. 'Both of you, shut up.'

Tiffany narrowed her eyes at Mel and taunted, 'When you see Mickey again, tell him Tiff says hi.'

Mel was alarmed. 'What's that supposed to mean?'

But she never got an answer because she was dragged out of the room. With order restored, Jen became Tiffany's appropriate adult as James and Mark had a statement drawn up.

Tiffany signed it.

Then he dropped into the sofa, his hands covering his head. 'I can't do a long stretch, Dee, I can't. I'll go fucking nuts.'

Dee caught her bottom lip between her teeth. She didn't like seeing John broken up like this. She liked his hard, lived-in face and the lines around his eyes when he smiled. She liked the fact he loved kids. If they were going to get through this, she was going to have to be strong for both of them. Alright, she'd be the first to admit *she* started this, but it had been for his own good.

'Nothing's going to happen to you on my watch. Let me get this out of the way and then we'll chat.' She picked up the automatic and took it to her bedroom where she hid it among lingerie in a chest of drawers. But she had no plans to get rid of it; it was hers now.

'They've got sweet FA on you, John,' Dee said, once she was back in the main room. She perched on the arm of the sofa. 'They just want to question you. Do exactly as I say and you've got nothing to worry about. It's too bad for that prick Mickey Ingram and poor old Chris. They'll have been nicked with the stolen motors down in Tilbury. They're goners, John; you can't help them now, but you can help yourself.'

John cocked his head to the side to look at her as he frowned. 'How do you know about Tilbury, chop shops and Mickey Ingram?'

You stupid idiot. Dee could've kicked herself. 'You told me, don't you remember? Just after you found that listening thingie in your office.'

John rubbed his forehead, obviously totally done in. 'Did I? Yes, I suppose I did.'

Dee sighed. Her John looked so tired, poor love. When all this mayhem was sorted she was going to make sure he took some R'n'R time. After that, she would make sure he understood who the real boss was.

'Anyway,' she cut in quickly, moving the conversation along, 'the staff at the Alley told me what type of questions the law were asking. Frank should sue the pants off that officer for breaking his nose.'

John's head sank. 'I can't believe it. How did this happen?'

Dee put her hand on his knee. 'I told you, you can't trust anyone. Anybody involved could've fingered you. Did you fall out with Ingram or Chris? It might have been one of them. Or maybe the cops got lucky. Who knows? The important thing is, we keep you well clear of the shit that's falling down. The others can look after themselves.'

John turned things over in his mind. 'Yeah. Well, I can't hang around here. I'd better book a ticket to Spain pronto until all this blows over.'

Dee was getting fed up with him but tried not to show it. 'You're not going to the bleeding Costa Del Whatever. Do that and you might as well fax a confession to the cops. No mate, you and me will go down the cop station tomorrow and see the guy in charge of this sting they've set up and we'll front it out. Tell them I'm your fiancée and I'll cover for you.' She saw the look of doubt cross his face. 'Don't worry about it. Leave the patter to me.'

His voice softened as he gazed into her big, dark eyes. 'The best thing I ever did was to take you on.'

Dee cupped her palm around his chin. 'The pleasure was all mine, John. You're a great man, a top Face. You're way too clever to end up in the slammer like Mickey and Chris.'

John smiled at her. 'You know what they say, Dee, behind every great man is a great woman.'

Dee slowly let her hand drop. 'You need to get some shut-eye if we're facing the cops tomorrow.'

John got up and shook his coat out and laid it on the sofa. As he went to lie down, Dee gasped, 'What do you think you're doing?' She grabbed his hand and led him into the bedroom. She let go of him and sat on the bed. She patted the duvet cover as she flashed her false lashes. 'You're coming to sleep with me – as far as the cops are concerned, from tomorrow, I'm your fiancée remember?'

'I don't know what I would've done without you,' Jen said to Nuts as they sat next to each other in his motor. They were parked back up near her place. An exhausted Babs, relieved to be released from the cell with a warning, had left them to it and gone up already, no doubt for a swift gin and a sleeping tab. The Plod had decided to hang on to Tiffany until tomorrow morning, which was good as far as Jen was concerned; maybe that would knock some sense into the silly kid.

Jen felt all fingers and thumbs and highly embarrassed; she'd got Nuts so wrong. Who else would've dropped everything and the kitchen sink to come help her in the early hours of the morning? Certainly no one on The Devil; at least, not without a price tag attached. She felt ashamed that she'd doubted him. Nuts was a good and decent man.

His blue eyes looked so kind in his handsome face. 'You don't have to thank me, you silly moo.' She didn't take offence at the last. 'No way was I going to leave you – and your mum – on your uppers.'

'Oh heck.' Jen reached into her bag. 'I've got to pay you for the petrol.' But she stopped when she felt Nuts' hand on her arm. Her skin heated up as he turned her, ever so gently, as if she was one of those orchids he'd sent – OK stolen. Then he lay his lips against hers. And then they were a tangle of arms and tongues as they hugged and kissed.

'Jen, you're the most gorgeous girl I know,' Nuts said gently when they drew apart. 'I could gobble you up.'

Jen laughed out loud. Then she came over all shy again as she slowly started unbuttoning her top. 'Can't leave you starving then, can we?'

Jen let him take a few liberties, but not too many; she didn't want him thinking she was a total scrubber or anything.

As he nibbled along her neck, he said, 'I didn't want to say nothing when your mum was here, but I hope your sister isn't in too much bother.'

Jen let out a contented sigh before answering, 'I think they're going to just keep her locked up for a night to put the frighteners on her, so she behaves in the future . . . Ummm, I like that!' He was doing naughty things to her ear.

'Probably following older kids and taking the fall for them,' he said softly, against her skin.

'No. Silly girl's been fixed up with a neighbour who's bad news and we don't have nothing to do with him and his family.'

He gave her breast a gentle squeeze. 'So she didn't mention no one else?'

'Not from what Mum's said . . . Nuts, your hand goes no further.' His hand was on a one-way track past her belly.

They were interrupted by a knock on the window. Two scruffy kids, who should've been tucked up hours ago, stood near the car.

'Oi, you gotta pay a fee if you want to park here,' one said with cocky bluster. 'Plus, if you want to get your leg over, that's extra.'

'You cheeky–' Jen started, but Nuts finished off for her, 'Do one, you little piss artists, before I knock your heads together.'

They must've read the menace in Nuts' voice because their little legs scarpered into the darkness.

'That's what you're going to get if you go out with me,' Jen told him straight. 'The Devil's going to come as well.'

Nuts just smiled back. 'I'll take you any way I can get you.'

No more words were said as they kissed and cuddled on The Devil's Estate.

Thirty-Four

As the police came into the interview room the next morning, Dee whispered, 'Don't forget, John, leave all the chat to me. Whatever they say, just repeat those two beautiful words – no comment.'

Detective Simpson and Detective Jones, who were Mark and James yesterday with the Miller girl, questioned John but they weren't as cocky as they had been with Tiffany. Chris and Mickey had been caught red-handed with the cars in Tilbury, but both had refused to implicate John. Tiffany had told them John had nothing to do with any car ringing business. Meanwhile the police who were trawling through the paper trail of documents found at the Alley Club had found nothing that incriminated their guy either. Although the police were convinced that John was involved, the two cops could feel their big fish slipping away.

Detective Simpson got down to business. 'Are you sure you don't want a solicitor? It would be better for you in the long run if you did.'

Before John could answer, Dee took control. 'He doesn't need a solicitor; only guilty people need a brief.'

The officer snorted. 'In that case, he doesn't need an appropriate adult either – which I understand is what you're here for. Perhaps you can tell us what your interest in this matter is?'

Dee curled her hand through John's arm and gave her man a hot, loving look. 'He's my fiancé. We're hoping to be married soon – which is why I'm so outraged at your attempt to drag my intended into this unfortunate business, which of course is nothing to do with him.'

Simpson shook his head and grinned humourlessly. 'I see. OK, then. Why don't we just cut the crap here, John, eh? The fact is, a car ringing business was organised out of your club. We've caught Mickey Ingram, Christopher Keston and Tiffany Miller and some of the other Herberts involved. They all say you bossed the operation. Now, why don't you save us all the trouble of confronting you with the evidence, 'fess up and then we can all have a nice cup of tea and see what we can do with the charges – maybe knock off a few and recommend that the judge goes easy on you. How's that sound?'

Before John had finished saying 'No comment,' Dee told them. 'It sounds like bollocks to me, bruv. You ain't got no evidence and you know it. And the reason you ain't got none is because there isn't any. Now, why don't you go and catch a burglar and let my fiancé get back to running his very respectable club with its highly distinguished and influential clientele?'

The detective patted his file. 'I've got plenty of evidence, love.'

Dee was confident that he didn't. 'Let's see it then.'

He ignored her. 'So tell us, John, how well do you know Mickey Ingram? He got the fake docs done for you, didn't he?'

'No comment.'

Dee was providing a running commentary. 'Of course he doesn't know anyone called Mickey Ingram. If I thought he knew anyone with a name like that I'd ban him from seeing him – he sounds right common. My fiancé mixes with London's elite – you know, show people, footballers, business people like that. Not someone with a name like Mickey Ingram . . .'

'OK, John, tell us about Tiffany Miller.'

'No comment.'

As Dee held forth on how a woman with a name like Tiffany Miller must be a slag, Detective Jones interrupted her. 'Listen John, are you planning to no comment your way through this whole interview while your friend here covers for you? You do realise only a guilty man would do that, don't you?'

'No comment.'

Dee rose to her feet, placed both her hands on the table and asked firmly, 'Evidence boys? Have you got any actual evidence?'

Simpson pulled a paper out of his file. He read it and then handed it to his colleague who read it and passed it back. Simpson nodded with approval and then passed it back to his partner. Dee wasn't fooled; she suspected there was fuck all on the paper or it was some other nonsense like the police station's leccy bill.

Simpson paused for dramatic effect before saying, 'Yes, as a matter of fact, we do. We've got a witness who puts you in the Bad Moon pub yesterday with Mickey Ingram, Christopher Keston and a number of other known associates and ne'er-do-wells who are of interest in this case, including a young man we suspect actually stole the cars. So tell us, John, what were you, Mickey, Chris and the gang discussing – the weather?'

John said nothing, not even 'No comment.'

Dee meanwhile was like the black cat who'd got the cream. 'Have you got a time and date and what this supposed witness supposedly saw?'

That surprised him, but he gave her the time and date. Dee was triumphant. 'Utter bollocks. I can tell you exactly where my fiancé was at the time. He was in bed with me, having some hot and steamy lovin'. I was on top and underneath, in and out, shaking it all about; we had it over the dressing table, in the bathroom and on the Persian rug my fiancé gave me as a gift – the lot. Ask my neighbours; they were banging on the wall complaining. Isn't that right, John?'

John said nothing, just turned scarlet.

Dee looked pointedly at Detective Simpson. 'Go on, ask around. People will probably slam the door in your face.'

Both detectives looked disappointed knowing that Dee had probably got the right of it. In the East End, who wanted to be known as a grass? Simpson closed his file. 'OK. That's all for now. We'll be in touch.'

Despite his embarrassment, John was pathetically grateful for Dee getting him off the hook and offered to take her for lunch somewhere smart. When she hailed a cab and ordered it to take them to Hatton Garden, he looked blank and told her he didn't know any decent restaurants in the area. As she relaxed in the back of the cab, Dee explained her plan.

'You can take me to lunch later, darling. First, you've got to buy me an engagement ring. The law will be keeping an eagle eye on you now and your idea that we're engaged needs ring-fencing. And don't skimp on the ice either – and I don't mean "in car entertainment". We need everyone to take us seriously.'

Instead of sitting on the bunk in the cell, Tiffany was on the floor with her back against the stone wall and her knees drawn up to her chest. The excitement of being interviewed by Five-O had long ago fizzled away and she had a gut feeling that life was never going to be the same again. For starters, Stacey's mum would definitely make sure she didn't come anywhere near her daughter; and, if Tiffany was truthful, she wouldn't do it anyway, knowing it would bring her friend heartache. And that's what hurt the most, knowing she wouldn't be able to get close to her mate anymore. She would never touch her face again, never take a tote from a spliff where Stace had just put her lips. Tiffany wrapped her fist against her mouth and started sobbing.

Dee was sporting a larger-than-life, emerald engagement ring when they got back to her flat. She was dizzy with triumph; she couldn't believe that she had pulled it off. John might think this was a fake engagement for the cops' sake, but he'd soon learn differently.

'Well, I'd better be off,' John said smartly, moving towards the front door.

But Dee was around him in no time, her open palms placed swiftly on his chest. She'd been diddled out of a night of amore last night when he'd fallen asleep as soon as his head hit the pillow. She wasn't allowing that to happen again. 'What's the hurry, John? Kick your heels back and take one of the six-packs from the fridge while I go and find that shooter you gave me. You can have it back and tuck it up somewhere safe.'

Five minutes later, beer shot out of John's mouth (all over that sofa Dee hadn't finished paying for), as he clapped eyes on Dee artfully posed in the doorway. Most women wanting a portion would have a flirty baby doll on, a bit of lingerie, or maybe just a G-string. Dee had learned that if you were going to do something, you went all the way, and that's why she stood on display for John, in her birthday suit.

'Bloody hell, Dee,' he choked, wiping the beer from his lips.

'Don't you like what you see, John?' She moved towards him in sleek strides, jiggling anything she had that moved. When she reached him, she firmly pushed his chest back into the sofa. 'You know what they say, John – the blacker the berry, the sweeter the juice.' Then she lifted one leg, hooked it over him and lifted the other leg and did the same. John was sweating buckets. She almost laughed out loud when his hand clutched her bottom. She stretched and then lowered her boobs to his face. Within two seconds he had her flat on her back, his knob out; then he went in for the kill.

Dee was expecting the sex to be a bit bish, bash, bosh, with John howling to high heaven and her faking it to the hilt. But that's not what happened. Instead, John spent the next half hour showing her not how to have sex, but for maybe the first time in her life, what it meant to make love. By the time they slid off the sofa and collapsed on the floor, Dee was speechless, dazed and, yeah, confused. Most of the boys and young men she'd been with had left her feeling nice and warm, but John had blown her mind. Fancy that: John Black of all people.

She was startled when he got ready to leave.

'John, you can't go.' She scrambled off the floor. 'We've got to make sure we give a good show for the neighbours so that Bill and Ben down the station believe our story.' *And I want to do it again.*

John shook his head. 'I've got to go, darling.'

Dee was narked. 'Oh I get it. I get you out of trouble with the Rozzers and my thank you is wham bam thank you mam.'

''Course not. You know I'm grateful. The thing is, I've got, let's just call him a friend, who might have some info for me. Plus, the way I'm hearing it, Chris is out and about.'

Dee couldn't stop the shock showing on her face. 'Chris is out? Surely they had enough evidence to keep him banged up?'

'I don't know if it's true, but I'm going to find out. See you later at the club.'

And with that he left. Dee slumped on the sofa. If Chris was out, Dee knew the game might be up.

Thirty-Five

Jeff walked arm-in-arm with his boyfriend as he left the Pied Piper. He'd managed to wiggle out of all that screw-up that went down with Mr Black's car op. He had given the cops some claptrap about hiring a solicitor to sue them for harassment for being gay and, knowing they had dick on him, they had to let him go. Right now, he was thinking it was time for him to leave the pub and find new, fresh green pastures. Maybe . . .

'Are you Jeff from the Pied Piper?' He left his thoughts behind as he was confronted by someone wearing a black crash helmet, speaking through a visor.

'Never heard of him.'

'Well, I say you are.'

And before Jeff or his boyfriend could do a thing, the stranger head-butted him, with the helmet breaking his nose. His boyfriend yelled as he dropped to the pavement, blood gushing down his face and onto his clothes.

'Next time,' his assailant declared, 'leave little girls alone.'

Then the head-butting maniac was gone, marching down the road the other way.

Once she got around the corner, Dee pulled the helmet off and shook out her hair. That would teach him to terrorise sixteen-year-old kids.

* * *

'Well, I hope that you've learned your lesson, my girl,' Babs said sternly to Tiffany, who the police had let out early.

She sat with her two girls in the sitting room of their flat on The Devil's Estate. The telly had been switched off, and there was no music blaring from the stereo system; this was just some quiet time for Babs and her daughters. It seemed like this flat hadn't been quiet for ages. It felt good. It felt like a real home.

Tiffany said nothing, so Babs carried on (it was her right as a mother): 'My girl, banged up? I still can't believe it. The shame of it. I'd never have been able to show my face again on the estate if people had found out. And don't forget you've still got to go up before a judge.' Suddenly, a horrifying thought struck her. 'They didn't touch you in that cell did they? You know, slap you around?'

Tiffany tutted. 'Come off it, Mum.'

'Well, you never know these days. You hear all kind of stories about what happens behind the walls of a nick. In my day you knew where you stood; they'd just give you a kicking in public.'

'Talking about kicking, Mum, you really laid into that Mel Ingram.' Jen sniggered. 'You caught her a good one in the face.'

Tiffany giggled. 'When you took her down, she went crashing like a crate of lard.'

'Mum, you should've seen that cop's face when you went all Genghis Khan on him.' Jen was clutching her belly now she was laughing so hard. 'I thought he was going to keel over.'

Babs' gaze switched between her two daughters. 'I don't see what's so funny. She had it coming for years, that one.'

They all looked at each other and fell about pissing with laughter. It was good to see her daughters happy again. Jen was definitely stepping out with that Nuts, and Tiffany . . .

'Tiff honey,' Babs said, 'promise me you'll never go down that cemetery again.'

Her youngest smiled, just like she had when she was a little nipper. 'After this, Mum, you won't catch me there again.'

John was still trembling when he got to the Alley Club later that evening. He couldn't shake off what had gone on in the last two hours. He just couldn't believe what he'd heard and what he'd done.

'We're unofficially engaged,' he heard Dee saying to one of the girls who worked behind the bar. 'We don't want it spread about, so keep it under your hat.'

'Dee,' he called. She twisted around and her eyes widened when she saw him. 'Let's go upstairs.'

'Did you find—?'

'I said, let's take it upstairs.' His tone was hard, which told Dee straight that he wasn't in the mood for any muck around.

John hit the bottle as soon as the door to his office was shut behind them. He knocked the whiskey back in one swallow. 'I know exactly how the police tumbled the car operation.' The expression on his face chilled her to the bone. 'I've been making some enquiries.' He paused again. 'I had a drink with a pal of mine in the police. He explained the whole shebang. I was grassed up – by someone I thought I could trust. Disappointing.' He fixed Dee with what looked like a flinty and uncompromising stare.

One of Dee's house rules was, never to be on the back foot. 'And you're going to take the word of a cop are you? Disappointing.'

'No, I wouldn't usually. But there's supporting evidence. I got a phone call from Chris this morning . . .' *Here it comes.* Dee waited for the blow to fall as John carried on. 'He talked his way out of it down in Tilbury and he's been released on bail. Mickey Ingram's been booked but Chris hasn't as yet. But Mickey won't grass – he's stupid, but he's no snitch. Anyway, Chris wants to meet tonight to explain his theory about what happened.'

Dee didn't flinch. 'I'd better come too. I'll be interested to hear what his theory is.'

'I don't think so . . .' His gaze had turned from hard to homicidal.

'Why not?'

John looked around as if he was searching for prying ears. 'Because we won't be seeing Chris again – not tonight, not ever. You know what I mean? I mean, look at the facts – there was the phone bug, he was the only person fully in the picture on the operation and then he gets released on *bail*, despite being caught red-handed. I mean, come on. He was probably planning to come wired for sound because the law have got nothing on me. I'm too clever. You won't need to worry about Chris again.'

He didn't mean . . . ? But from the way he was flexing his hands, she knew he did. She hadn't meant it to come to this. Dee felt bad about Chris, but there was nothing she could do now. Bloody hell, what was going to happen to his orphaned son, Nicky? But she couldn't think about that now, she still needed to make sure John was steered in the right direction for the future.

'I'm afraid you've not been clever enough, John. A man like you shouldn't be in the "ICE" bizz. You might as well run a pickpocketing scam. You should be importing real stuff. You get me? That's where the money is.'

He shook his head. 'You need big money to invest in that, and contacts. I don't have them.'

The phone from reception rang. Dee ignored it. 'This club is full of people with money to invest and people who can

arrange introductions. Just leave everything to me.' She picked
up the phone and took the call. Quickly she covered the phone
and with urgency warned him, 'I think it's the law again.' She
chucked him a spare set of keys to her flat. 'Go over the roof
and I'll take care of whoever's downstairs.'

Thirty-Six

It wasn't the law. Dee already knew that it was someone far more dangerous downstairs. She spotted Trish as soon as she got to the clubroom, but made sure she remained hidden in the shadows so the other woman couldn't see her. Her hands tightened around the instant camera she held. She caught the eye of a member of security and beckoned him over.

'John wants Trish to meet him out back.' She leaned over and whispered the rest of the instruction in his ear. He didn't ask any questions; he knew better than to challenge Mizz Dee.

As soon as he was gone, Dee put the camera into her pocket and made her way quickly to the back and went outside. The back of the club was really an alleyway where the deliveries were made and the rubbish put out. Dee walked a few paces forwards, concealing herself once again in the shadows. Her face became grim when she heard the door open and soon Trish came outside, hugging her fur-lined jacket around her against the cold.

'John?' she called out.

She jumped when the metal door clanged shut behind her (thanks to the security guy following Dee's instructions). 'John?'

Dee waltzed into the moonlight. 'No, Trish, not lover boy John I'm afraid, but your worst nightmare.'

Trish went pale and was visibly startled. 'I never said anything about you to John. I swear on my mother's life.'

'I told you loud and clear to use the exit sign on your way out of John's life and to never look back.' Dee rolled her sleeves up. 'You can't say you weren't told.'

The other woman backed away as Dee moved slowly forward. Trish twisted around and started banging against the closed door. 'Help, someone help me.'

'Not even God can help you now, Trish.'

Dee grabbed the other woman's arm and started dragging Trish further into the alley. John's girlfriend yelled and struggled all the way, losing one of her mile-high stiletto heels along the way. Dee shoved her against the wall near a large, grey metallic bin. Dee easily held the squirming woman with one hand as she tossed the lid of the bin onto the floor. Inside was a bulging black bin liner filled with rubbish, but there was plenty of space left inside.

'Noooo,' Trish begged as she cottoned on to what Dee planned to do. But Dee ignored her as she gripped the woman by the lapels of her flash coat and tipped her head first into the bin. Trish let out a muffled cry as her face and upper body toppled sideways and squashed down against the black bag leaving her legs stuck out in the air. Dee ruthlessly jammed them in after her, grabbed the lid and slammed it down on the bin. Then she sat down on top of it and started swinging her legs like she didn't have a care in the world.

Trish beat against the inside of the bin, sobbing. In between her cries she pleaded, 'I can't breathe, can't breathe—'

'Trish girl I want you to imagine,' Dee began calmly, 'a life without spray-on tan. A life without dosh for a new boob job. A life without tottering down The Roman to get your knock-off bottle of Charlie. That's what you're going to leave behind if you keep sniffing around John, because I'm going to make it my business to see you end-up, arse first in the gutter.'

'Pleeeeze, just let me out.'

'The only way you're drawing pure air again is if you promise to leave John alone. He don't even like your skank self, he's only using you as his spunk pump machine.'

'I'll leave him alone, I'll leave him alone, I promise.'

'Cross your heart?' Dee was having fun now.

'Cross my heart.'

Dee knew she should let the interfering bitch out before the stupid cow went and suffocated on her. She hopped off the bin and pulled the lid away.

'Smile,' Dee said. Snap. Flash. With the camera she took a picture of the defeated woman looking crumpled inside the bin, dirty with mascara running rivers of black down her face.

'You tangle with me again and I'm going to make copies of this, enlarge them and post them all over town.'

A frantic and terrified Trish stood on shaky legs and rapidly sucked air into her body. Dee stepped back and Trish got out of the bin and then she ran for her life. Dee noticed her stiletto still on the ground. She picked it up and, with a huge grin, dumped it inside the bin.

Tiffany broke her promise to her mum and jumped the wall at the back of the cemetery so that she didn't have to see her mates on the way in. She didn't want it to get back to her newly appointed social worker that she was prowling around her old haunt, and she didn't need anyone to know about whom she was meeting. Quickly she made her way to the tomb with the angel where her contact was already waiting for her.

'You done good, girl,' the black woman told her. Tiffany suspected her name wasn't Laverne, but she'd already decided that the less she knew about her one-time partner in crime, the better. As soon as Laverne had called her yesterday from the Bad Moon and said, 'Get your skates on, it's time to rock 'n' roll . . .' Tiffany had swung into action on their plan.

'I'm proud of the way you handled yourself, telling the cops all about Mickey Ingram and Chris.'

Tiffany sat down beside her on the cold stone. 'I only said that I heard this Chris bloke's name but didn't know him.'

'Don't worry, babe, that was more than enough.'

Tiffany still worried about who this Chris was. What if he was some big time Face and came gunning for her? Whatever Laverne's reasons for fitting him up, one thing was very clear – she'd wanted to keep John Black well out of it. That's why Tiffany had told the two cops that John Black knew nothing about the job – that, in fact, he had been made to look a fall guy.

As if reading her mind, Laverne said, 'Don't bother yourself about Chris. He ain't going to touch you in a month of Sundays. All you need to think about is that Mickey Ingram won't be around to wallop your mate anymore.'

That's the only reason Tiffany had gone along with Laverne's plan – to make sure Mickey was out of Stacy's life. She hoped that when he was banged up, someone gave him the kicking of a lifetime.

'Did you tip off Five-O about the car shipment?' Tiffany couldn't help asking. The only way her part of their plan would've worked was if Laverne had anonymously tipped the wink to The Bill about the car ring.

Laverne smiled. 'Let's just say that God helps those who help themselves.'

Tiffany realised that Laverne was never going to spell it out for her, but she knew she'd grassed up the car ring. Why she'd want to set this Chris up and keep John Black in the clear, she didn't know. And she didn't want to know.

Tiffany put on her sulky face. 'I didn't get off scot free though; I've got to go up before the judge next month.'

'How come?' Laverne looked puzzled.

Tiffany was embarrassed. 'They caught me with a bit of leaf. It was my mate who I was with; it was hers.'

Laverne's face turned pinched and nasty. 'You stupid idiot. You could've made all our plans go up in smoke. And for what? Some wacky backy? All you had to do was play your part while I called the cops.' She stared even harder at the young girl next to her. 'You never heard that right. You need a lesson on priorities.' She raised one perfectly shaped eyebrow and shook her head. 'I know you don't probably want to hear this, but maybe the judge will give you a break that will set you up on the path of the straight and narrow for life.'

'As if,' the sixteen-year-old scoffed back.

Laverne stood up. 'You look after yourself, kid. And your mum. Good mums are hard to come by.' She started walking away, but stopped after a few steps and turned back around. 'One more thing, babes, you ever see me, I don't know you and you don't know me.'

PART TWO: 2003

Ten Years Later

'Sometimes you only get one chance to change your life.'

Thirty-Seven

'I want you to draw a picture of how you see yourself in the future.'

Bloody hells bells, thought fifteen-year-old Nicky Black, resisting the urge to do a runner as he listened to his fuckwit counsellor. He wore a plain, fully-opened, chocolate brown shirt over a stark white T-shirt and loose khaki pants. His look was topped off with a black Fedora, which he wore at an angle to show off his heart-stopping good looks and hazel eyes. He knew he was a good-looking boy, taking after the birth mother he couldn't remember, and he used it to his advantage any chance he got.

His counsellor was driving him doolally as they sat inside the room his mum called the 'family room' of the huge Essex house he lived in with his parents. But he had no choice in the matter, or his mum was going to do her nut, just like she'd gone ballistic when he'd got suspended from school. Thing is, she was mad with the school not him: 'They just don't know how to handle a boy like Nicholas,' was what she told his dad, despite it being the third school he'd been slung out of. School was a fool's game. He wanted to be rolling on the street with the high flyers, not the low rollers in his class. Except for Chad, of course. Chad might come from one of those high-end families, but he knew how to have fun with a bit of weed.

'Nicholas, are you listening to me?'

He couldn't help but hear her; she'd been chewing his ear off with mind-numbing nonsense since she'd arrived. He slouched back in the leopard-print sofa and nodded. Gail Thornton – 'Just call me Gail; first names are so important to our emotional well-being' – could've been a right looker, Nicky thought, if it weren't for those twit-twoo owl-shaped glasses and her hair tied back, as if she were trying to rip it right off her scalp.

'You want me to draw a picture, do you?' Nicky turned on a mischievous grin, the one the girls liked, at that club he and Chad sneaked off to. His face lighting up, he picked up the pencil and paper on the table and started to draw. It took him all of one minute to finish, and then he shoved it at her with an innocent look.

Gail turned red and her mouth fell open as she gazed at his effort. He'd drawn the outline of a woman with big ones and a massive bush as well.

'That's . . . that's disgusting,' she babbled, not able to take her eyes off the picture.

'But you said to draw how I saw myself in the future. I want to be a Doris, don't I. You know, get one of them sex change things.'

His counsellor stormed to her feet. 'That's it. For the last three weeks I have tried, but this isn't working.' She turned around and pulled the door open as Nicky chuckled to himself. She marched off to the massive kitchen where his mum was.

'Here comes trouble,' Dee whispered to her precious Banshee, a small, fluffy ball of a cat, as she watched a furious Gail Thornton step into the room. She cradled her pet against her cheek, near her massive, gold hoop earring. She'd long since dumped the long weave-on and replaced it with her own hair, straightened and layered close to her head like Halle Berry, with butter blonde streaks on the tips of the fringe. Her body had maintained its trimness, still with that extra bounce on her bum and she worked out to keep those legs sleek and long. She wore a mauve, velour sweat tracksuit, which fitted into the relaxed feeling she always got in one of her favourite rooms in the house. Not that she did any cooking or stuff like that – she left that to the housekeeper, plus she had her gel nails to think about.

With one hand she reached for the fluted glass near her on the counter and took another sip of champagne, savouring the bubbles in her mouth. Oh yeah, this was the life. A million and one miles away from the grotty memories of her childhood. She thought of every one of those twats who predicted she was going to end up gutter-side, and wondered what they would say if they could see her now, in her huge house in Essex. It still sent a thrill through Dee that she had managed to finally get John to tie the knot. It had taken her six months, and some pussy blowing sex after the car ring had been smashed, to get him down the aisle.

After their wedding, she'd wasted no time in getting John to widen his horizons and enter the drugs bizz. She'd even helped him organise his first big deal, which had been signed, sealed and, oh so beautifully delivered during their honey-moon in the Seychelles. John had established himself as a big-time player and she was very proud of him. Now they were well on their way. John was leaving some of the drugs trade behind and investing their money in legitimate businesses.

She watched Gail Thornton with an eagle eye as the other woman reached her.

'I'm sorry,' the counsellor explained, 'but I'm not sure I can do this anymore.'

Christ above, what'd he done now? After Chris disap-peared – that was the word John used to describe what had happened to his former right-hand man and Dee wasn't about to contradict him – his son Nicky had been taken in by his Nan, who was a walking Hammer House horror story. Her rat hole of a flat had smelt like wee, with a kitchen stacked full of unwashed dishes, cans of empty Tennent's everywhere and a toilet in such a state, a young child was bound to pick up an infection. Dee had wanted to do something when she and John had visited the place, but he said they weren't blood, so they couldn't do a thing. Of course what she could never say to her husband was that she was riddled with guilt about what had happened to Chris. If it hadn't been for her, his beautiful little boy wouldn't be in this horrible mess now. But during one grim visit, when Dee had seen maggots crawling near the fridge, she'd whipped that kid into her arms, marched out of the place and vowed to never take him back. Chris's gran had made a loud fuss until John had stumped up enough cash to shut her up. It hadn't taken them too long to adopt him and now Nicky was her boy.

Dee carefully popped Banshee onto the tiled floor. 'Whatever the problem is, I'm sure we can get it sorted.' Each of the other three counsellors she'd paid for Nicky had gone the same way – out the door and never looked back. She was paying this woman a ton an hour and expected results. 'What are you claiming he did this time?'

Gail huffed and puffed. 'Claiming? He drew an obscene picture.'

'He's artistic.' She was dead proud of his arty talent and just didn't get why his school complained about what they called his 'graffiti'; she'd read up about it and told them they should be calling it 'self portraits'. 'Should he be drawing during your sessions? I'm not paying you to run a nursery in my house.'

The other woman had that look on her face that told Dee she was going to use that baby voice she did sometimes, like

Dee was too dim to understand what she was saying. 'It's called art therapy. Sometimes drawing a picture can be an easier vehicle for someone to convey their emotional stress and pain.'

Dee didn't know what she was going on about. The only vehicle she liked was her beautiful motor, sitting pretty outside in the driveway.

'I'm not paying you to turn him into Damien Hirst either, love.' Without waiting for her to respond, Dee marched out of the kitchen, showcasing the glittering logo on her tracksuit bottom – Juicy Bling. She yelled Nicky's name; he knew that when she was shouting for him, he better get his shit together before she got there.

Her heart pinched when she saw him. Aww, he was still her cute little boy. Dee still couldn't get over how that prick Chris – rest his soul – had produced such a gorgeous-looking lad; his wife must've been a stunner. Nicky had gold-blonde hair made for the sun and features that seemed to have been perfectly placed on his face. What stopped him from being tagged as a pretty boy was the small scar next to his right eye that he'd got when he'd fallen when he was younger. That boy was going to be a lady killer when he got older, no doubt about it. He held his Fedora in his hand; now that was respect – to take your hat off in the presence of a lady. Her little saint: and anyone who said different better beware.

Time had proved he was probably the only kid she was ever going to have; she and John hadn't been blessed with any. John had tried to get them to visit one of those private fertility clinics in Harley Street, but no way was someone shoving their hand inside her and telling her she had a dud womb. Anyway, the problem must be John firing blanks; he hadn't had any sprogs with his other wives either.

'Gail here says you're wasting her time, drawing filth.'

Nicky stood up. 'No way, Mum.' He shook his head. 'I wouldn't do that.' He put his hat down and then held out a piece of paper to her. 'That's what I drew.'

She took it from him and her heart nearly broke. It was a picture of a small boy holding hands with a much larger man. At the top of the picture were the words, 'Me and dad.' From the colour of the dad's eyes and hair she knew it wasn't John but Chris. She knew Nicky missed the dad he could barely remember, terribly. John made sure he didn't hold back and told Chris's son all about him: well, the legal bits anyway. Despite her guilt over what happened to his real dad – and she maintained to this day, that's not how she'd wanted it played out – she remembered what her Auntie Cleo used to tell her: 'Sometimes you just have to sweep bad stuff under the carpet.'

Dee held the picture up for Gail to see. 'Does this look like something from a porno mag to you?'

Shock covered Gail's face. 'He must've drawn this while we were conversing in the kitchen.'

Conversing? Didn't this woman know, life was so much better if you just dropped all the la-di-da lingo. Dee walked up to her menacingly, her fists curling at her side. 'You calling my boy a liar?'

The blood drained from Gail's face. 'Of course not.'

Dee nodded satisfied. 'Well then, get on and sort him out. Make him better.' Dee leaned in close and whispered, 'Word to the wise, babes, you might want to stop wearing them black flats on your feet and swap them for some Jimmy Choo's. And make your hemline wiggle up a bit further north. He might start respecting you then.'

Gail reared back. 'Right, that's it.' She flounced across the room to grab her bag and then headed for the door.

'Hold up,' Dee shouted, following her into the hallway.

'I don't know what the problem is. All I said was that you might wanna put more on display in the window.'

The front door slammed.

'I think she needed to have her own counsellor,' Nicky said softly as he came to stand beside Dee. 'I mean, drawing pictures is for five year olds.' He put his arm around her and leaned his head against her shoulder. 'Why do I have to go to back to school? I want to stay here with you.'

It was at times like this that Dee wanted the same thing. But kids needed to be in school to learn and Nicky was no different. She wanted him to have the best. He might've lost his father but he wasn't going to lose anything else on her watch.

She kissed him on the cheek. 'Go upstairs and play with one of your computer games.'

Not long after, John arrived back home. He found his wife in the conservatory out back, having a Bacardi and coke, and a fag. John might've lost all his hair – he'd taken his wife's advice and had it shaved off instead of wearing that comical comb-over in the years they'd been together – but he wasn't losing his business touch. He had fingers in more drug pies than Keith Richards and he was raking in the cash. That's all that mattered to Dee. Blokes with looks were ten a penny, but guys who knew how to keep that ka-ching bell ringing in a girl's life were the real men.

'I thought I saw Nicky's counsellor heading out,' John said as he sat down. 'A bit early for her to be off?'

Dee wearily took him through the Nicky–Gail ding-dong.

'Come on, Dee,' John said. 'He's playing you for a mug. He did what she accused him of.'

Dee glared at him. 'I know that, Dumbo. I'm not a total idiot. But to have thought of a trick like drawing another picture so quickly shows that he's smart.'

'That's why we sent him to one of those posh schools, but they cost money and it's like watching my hard-earned cash go down a black hole.'

'*Our* cash,' Dee cut in. 'He's just a bit sensitive.' She glared harder when her husband snorted. 'Maybe he feels out of place with all those posh boys.'

'What that boy needs is a cuff around the ear. That will knock some sense into his skull.'

'You what?' Dee erupted with fury, almost jumping off her seat. 'You touch that kid and you're a dead man, John Black.'

Her husband quickly held up his hand, trying to calm her down. 'All I'm saying is, spare the rod, spare the child, some would say.' Dee calmed herself down, settling back in the chair. 'A mate of mine was telling me about this boarding school—'

'No way—'

'I hear those places turn boys into men.'

'You must be joking. I wouldn't see my boy until the school holidays. Anyway, he'd probably fire bomb the place.' She shook her head. 'What he needs is someone who understands his situation. Someone who's been there and done it at his age, but managed to sort their shit out and come out smelling like roses.'

Banshee wandered in and started spitting and hissing, baring her sharp teeth when she saw John. Dee took her into her arms and stood up. As she started to leave the room, she mumbled into the cat's fur, 'Who are we going to find for Nicky, my precious Banshee? Who's going to straighten him out?'

The only answer the cat gave was to turn, squint her green eyes at John and growl.

Thirty-Eight

This is the last time I'm doing this, Jen vowed as she clutched tight to her Louis Vuitton knock-off handbag in her seen-better-days Ford Escort outside Brixton Prison. She'd had to park in the council estate across the road because you couldn't park outside Brixton, it being off a main road. She'd be more visible if she stood on the side of the road, but that was asking for trouble, especially in a place like South London; some nutter was bound to think she was touting for business. And that was bound to happen, because, despite her troubles, Jen still drew a man's eye. Her mostly blonde hair was layered into a volumised bob cut with burnished bronze dyed along the bottom half and tips. Her body still looked good in the short denim skirt and jacket, despite giving birth to two kids.

Nuts was coming out after doing bird for six months. The prat had been done for handling stolen goods. Just thinking about Nuts coming out brought back all the terrible memories of him being nicked during their first year of marriage, while she was pregnant with Courtney. It had taken the Plod a while to track him down, but they'd been looking for him for months in connection to a car ringing gang. What had slowed the police in their hunt for him was his use of so many names – including, she learned to her disgust, Knobby. And what a knob head he'd been. She was too embarrassed to tell people the truth, so she told them he was doing a contract job in Wales. This time she'd said Scotland, time before that, Ireland. No one was fooled of course, but as long as they didn't dispute her story to her face, she was fine with that. Mind you, each time he did a stretch, at least her body had time to heal from the punishing bruises he gave her.

After Nuts had been so wonderfully helpful with Tiffany down the police station, they had started seeing each other on a regular basis. He'd wined and dined her at upmarket restaurants, loved to be seen with her on his arm at the local boozer and given her flowers – not nicked this time – on so many occasions, Jen couldn't believe her luck. There had been no how's your father for the first few months; oh no, Jen wasn't giving it up until she knew what she was getting into. But he'd been so sweet, so nice, that when she'd finally gone to bed with him it had seemed right. Typical that she should get up the duff after that first time. They'd gone down the aisle a month later – registry office job – and gone to the council hand-in-hand to get a place together.

That's when Jen's nightmare started. The same month her belly started to show he clouted her one, right across the mouth. She'd fallen against the table, hand protecting her unborn kid, hurt more from the surprise than the blow. How hadn't she seen this about him? Only the coming baby had stopped her from feeling such an almighty failure. Bex was the only person she had told; Jen was too ashamed to tell Babs or Tiffany. Bex said she should boot him out, but Jen couldn't do that; they were having a kid together, for crying out loud. No way was she going to become a single mum like some of the no marks on the estate, even before her kid was born. In the end, she'd given birth to her beautiful, precious baby girl while her baby's dad was banged up.

Jen slipped out of the past as she spotted Nuts coming across the road, a single carrier bag in his hand. She didn't get out of the car, instead she waved her hand from the open window so he knew where she was. He now wore his hair in its natural colour, a solid brown, above a slightly redder complexion, from too many jars down the pub.

Nuts had a big grin on his chops when he got into the passenger seat. 'Let me have a look at my orchid,' he said, using the nickname he'd given her years back. He looked like he'd missed a dinner or two but those blue eyes of his were still the same: bright and shining. His gaze settled on her chest and he started licking his lips like a starving man. 'Jen, do me a favour, love . . .' His hands went to the buttons of his trousers.

Was he having a laugh? As if she'd give him a blow job in public. 'We need to get back. The girls are itching to see their dad.'

'Oh come on, Jen, I ain't had none in a month of Sundays.'

Jen cast him a dirty look before she got her motor into gear. It still astonished her what a selfish prick he was; didn't he get the trouble and strife she and the girls had had to endure, while he was banged up? Her placement at Madam Dominique's had helped her secure a job in a fashion outlet on Oxford Street, but then the place had gone bust and she was now working part-time as a cashier at a large supermarket down the road in Bromley-by-Bow.

'So, how are my little angels?' he asked as they drove home.

'Good. Courtney's teacher said she's a star pupil and Little Bea got a prize at the end of last term for some history project she did.'

Courtney was their eldest at nine years old and had Jen's light hair and her dad's blue eyes. Little Bea was seven and was the spit of her dad. Little Bea's real name was Sasha but everyone called her by her nickname because as a toddler she'd trailed after her Nanna Babs any chance she got. Jen felt such pride just thinking about her girls. They never gave her any backchat or bother – not like many of the other kids on The Devil – and they were the apple of their Nan's eye. Poor Little Bea had cried a bucketful when her dad wasn't able to come and see her receive her prize at the special end of year school assembly. Little Bea might've swallowed her mum's lie but Jen suspected that Courtney didn't buy into it.

When they arrived on the estate, Nuts took in his surroundings, an expression of wonder on his face like he expected the place to have turned into Buckingham Palace while he was inside. Fat chance of that happening. In fact, the place looked worse; the council had stopped doing so many repairs and Jen suspected they had moved some of their more troubled families in. The Devil's Estate did what it said on the tin and always would.

They headed home, which was now on the sixth floor of one of the high rises, a short walk from her mum's.

'Where are my two princesses?' Nuts announced, coming into the flat like Father Christmas with his body slightly bent and his arms out-stretched, like he was about to say, 'Ho-ho-ho!'

Courtney and Little Bea were in the sitting room being looked after by their nan. Babs hadn't changed much over the years and while other women her age were piling on the pounds, she had got slimmer. Her daughters tried to tell her to lay off the booze, but she'd always wave her hands at them, saying they were worrying about nothing. Now she appeared anxious as her grandkids looked at each other and slowly moved towards him.

'Go on, girls,' Babs encouraged, gently nudging Courtney forward. But the girls took their time, looking like they were walking to their doom.

'What, you don't know your old dad anymore?' Nuts said. He turned accusing eyes onto Jen. 'What you been telling them about me?'

But before she could answer, Courtney said, 'Hello, Dad.' Nuts held his arms out and their nine-year-old went into them. He made a big drama of nuzzling her neck as he lifted her off the ground and twirled her around. He did the same to their youngest. Both girls still looked like they'd rather be somewhere else.

'Right,' Babs said, 'Come on, girls, we're going over to mine for a bit.'

Once the kids and Babs were gone, Jen had to deal with the same tension that came into her home every time her old man came back home. Sometimes she just wished he wouldn't.

'You must be starving. I'll pop some tea on.' Jen quickly started moving towards the kitchen, but Nuts grabbed her arm.

'I'm hungry, alright.' Then his lips and hands were mauling her. Jen sighed; she knew the routine inside out. Get her on her back on the sofa. Boobs jiggling in the air, knickers around her ankle, his dick shoved home. He never lasted more than ten seconds. He made it to eight this time.

As he panted heavily, his body squashing hers, Jen warned him, 'This is the last time, Nuts. You get banged up again, you're on your own.'

'Yeah, yeah.' Yuck, he was slobbering all over her ear.

'I mean it.' He could suck on her ear as much as he wanted as long as he got it into his thick head that life was going to have to change.

Thirty-Nine

Dee stared at Marilyn with such amazement and love as she stood in the driveway, she thought she was going to cry with tears of joy. Marilyn was her beloved 1950s classic Italian Pirano FS convertible sports car – the motor she'd dreamed about for years. The car was gorgeous. A sleek black with white trim around the two doors, hexagonal front lights and a hood she kept permanently detached. A hood was no good to her; she wanted people to see her flashing around town. She'd named it Marilyn in memory of Marilyn Monroe. A stunning car deserved to be named after a stunning woman.

John had given her the dream car soon after she'd called him out on it during those early days of their marriage. She could remember the night as if it had happened yesterday. He'd played it cool when she asked where they'd be going to celebrate their anniversary, saying that he was taking her for a slap-up bit of nosh at a restaurant in Mayfair. But after the meal, he'd blindfolded her – to Dee's delight – and guided her out back. Then he'd undone the blindfold and, voila! There Marilyn had been, like a baby waiting for its momma, wrapped up in red ribbon and a massive pink bow on top. Dee's heart had almost stopped. She couldn't believe it. It wasn't just a car, it was a symbol of finally making it to the top. She, Dee Clark, motherless, fatherless, with only a Bible-bashing fanatic to steady her early life, had finally made it. Dee had given John such a seeing to that night, by way of a thank you, he'd complained about only being able to walk bowlegged the next day.

Dee slid her fingertips along Marilyn's satiny side and let out little sighs of electric-shock pleasure. She closed her eyes as her fingers glided to the other side of the car. Abruptly Dee stopped. She moved her fingers again – no, that didn't feel right. Dee shoved her eyes open and looked at her car and almost fell backwards. There was a long scrape along the bodywork of the motor. Someone had hurt her Marilyn.

Dee stormed back inside the house, yelling at full blast. 'Which one of you sorry bastards did it?'

She found John and Nicky in the bar room. 'Which one of you,' she pointed an accusing finger, 'messed with Marilyn?'

She didn't wait for an answer as she picked up the nearest thing to her – a glass vase – and threw it at them. Both men dived for cover, as they always did when volcano Dee blew. Even Banshee cowered behind the sofa. Dee went ballistic, throwing anything that came to hand, including her stiletto heels. Finally, she upended the single sofa that John and the cat hid behind. Banshee meowed furiously as she belted out of the room, a ball of fur running for its life. A heavy breathing Dee looked down at her husband. She saw the guilt written all over his face.

'You bastard.'

John held his hands up. 'Hold on a minute, babe, it was an accident. I was going to get it fixed.'

Dee stamped her foot. 'You tosser! How could you do that to my Marilyn? She'll be disfigured for life.'

'One of my mates' dad is a plastic surgeon,' Nicky said from across the room, sniggering.

'You little shit.' Dee picked up a pint glass and threw it him. Nicky neatly ducked and went the same way as the cat, scarpering out of the room.

John stood up and took a shaking Dee into his arms. 'It's alright, love,' he soothed her. 'We'll sort it – her – out. I know a brilliant garage that will do her up a treat. I'll take her–'

Dee pushed out of his arms. 'No, I will. Give me the address.' She stabbed a finger in his chest. 'From now on, you stay the hell away from my Marilyn.'

She marched into the hallway and yelled up the stairs, 'Nicky, get your coat. We're going for a ride.'

Tiffany wearily threw her screwdriver into her toolbox after fixing a tricky gearbox. She was tired of being a grease monkey. There had to be more to life than doing up people's poxy motors in Watson Garages Ltd, tucked away under the arches near Bethnal Green overland station. Tiffany had dyed her still short hair pitch black. She could usually be seen out 'n' about in three-quarter-length trousers or jeans and a pair of Nikes. Now she wore the deep green overalls that marked her as a mechanic.

She found it hard to recall how much she'd once loved this job to bits. The sentence she'd received for her part in the car ringer crime ten years ago hadn't been getting banged up in one of those secure units for naughty girls, but a twelve-month stint doing community service at an East End garage. Her mum had wept with tears of joy and gratitude; if Babs had been allowed, she'd probably have kissed the hand of the judge and curtsied at the same time. She could still hear the judge's voice as he pronounced sentence on her: 'Since you enjoy working with your hands and obviously like cars, we should put this to good use.' And that's how she'd ended up working for Richard 'Richie' Watson for that first year. Turns out, the judge had his luxury Rolls serviced by Richie.

Tiffany had gone into a right strop about it, at first; getting her hands dirty with oil was not a good look. Plus, in the past, she and her mates from the cemetery had made a real song and dance of pointing and laughing their heads clean off at those community service Muppets as they picked up rubbish in the streets. But, to her surprise, she'd soon found out that she liked working down the garage. Pulling stuff apart and sticking them in the right place again gave her a real sense of pleasure and achievement. And the biggest thing of all – she wasn't bored out of her tree anymore.

Richie had taken her under his wing, showing her the ins and outs of the business on the shop floor. He'd been so impressed he kept her on after her community service stint was finished. Mum was really proud of her. In that first year, she'd still sneaked out to the cemetery, but not as much as before; the gang didn't have the same vibe and Stacey wasn't allowed anywhere near her. The one time she had managed to have a quick word with her friend, she'd been shocked by how terrible Stacey looked and knew instantly that she was still taking that hard shit. She'd tried to explain how she had set Stacey's old man up to get him out of her life, but her mate hadn't wanted to know; she'd turned her back on Tiff and walked away. That had really hurt. She hadn't tried to see Stacey again or gone back to the cemetery.

Tiffany wiped her hands, threw the rag on top of the bonnet and then pulled out a fag. There were signs up everywhere in the place about flammable liquids but – sod that – she needed a nicotine rush, like now. Life in the garage had become one big bore fest since Richie put up his spanner forever and passed the business to his two sons. A bigger pair of Tweedle Dumb and Tweedle Dumb Arse, Tiffany had never met in her life.

They went about business like they shared a single brain cell, so what had once been a profitable business was now on the slide. The younger brother had pulled her aside last week and had the cheek to announce that her wages were being cut. They must think she was stupid or something; she knew all about the off-the-books bizz they did – switching number plates; filing off serial numbers; cars entering one colour and leaving another. Richie would never have stood for that kind of carry on. By rights, she should let her fag drop and watch the bloody place go up in a ball of flames: her two-fingered salute to the slap in the face the brothers were giving her.

Well, she'd had enough and was looking to new horizons – something that could finally get her out of this, and from her mum's thumb at home. Whoever heard of a twenty-six-year-old still at home? It was unnatural. She couldn't even have her girlfriend stay overnight. *'If that's what you are, that's what you are, but that other stuff ain't going under my roof,'* was how Babs put it. OK, she was the first to admit, she'd had a string of girls over the years, preferring the fun of the casual hook-up to long-term commitment. But still, she wanted to make out in her own bed. Tiffany was disgusted with the council who'd told her she didn't qualify for priority housing, not like Jen who'd gone to them with a big belly. After Richie's sons had started playing up, she'd tried changing careers through an evening course, but that had gone nowhere. Was it too much to want her own roof and four walls? To get respect at work? She vowed to get it and that meant she was going to have to say ta-ra to the garage.

Tiffany sucked hard on her ciggie. How was she going to find the route to a load of dosh? Going back to ducking and diving in the cemetery was a no-go because the place now had an education centre that the local schools used for the kids. Who'd have thought the cemetery would turn into (in the words of the council) a nature reserve? That made Tiffany laugh; the way she heard it, you could still find plenty of strange creatures come dark. Including Stacey. Tiffany didn't like to think about her former best mate. It made her too sad.

Just as she was getting ready to lock up, she heard a car roar into the garage.

'We're shutting up,' she shouted as she walked from the office back into the workroom. She stopped and whistled when she caught sight of the car. Fuck me, never seen one of them before. She'd only seen it in motor mags. A convertible Pirano FS. Sleek, slim, in classic black, this one was a limited production, which meant it was worth a mint. Now that's the kind of car she wanted to be seen burning the road up in. The black woman wearing shades behind the wheel looked pretty sleek and slim too. Beside her, in the passenger seat, sat a sulky-looking white teen sporting a black baseball cap with 'Missy Elliott' written in white on the brim.

'You'll have to come back tomorrow.'

'I don't do tomorrows,' the woman snapped back.

That voice ... Tiffany stepped closer. She knew that voice. Where did she know it from? The woman grinned as she slid her long legs out of the car and pulled off her lilac-tinted Oakley vintage sunglasses.

'Well, well, well,' the woman said slowly, 'if it isn't the ghoul from the graveyard.'

Tiffany's mouth fell open as she stared at a woman she hadn't seen in ten years.

Forty

'Get this man another pint,' Kevin O'Connor yelled to the gathering of men, his arm slung around Nuts' shoulder.

When Nuts came out of the Big House, Kev always made sure that he got the welcome home he deserved. His closest friend got the boys together and they took a trip to Sally's, off Commercial Street. Sally's was a clothing outlet in the daytime and the upstairs was a knocking shop come night. 'Touch My Bum' by the Cheeky Girls was playing on a large video screen on one wall, but it was the two naked women – one Asian, the other white – getting dirty with each other on a black, leather sofa, who were making Nuts salivate at the mouth. Now that's the fireworks a bloke needs when he gets out of prison.

'Bet you're as hard as a rock,' Kev shouted. 'Can't wait to get your nuts off.' Then he laughed raucously. 'Nuts. Get it?'

Kevin was spot on. Shagging Jen earlier had been like having his dick mangled; she was that dry. Her cunt had grown a set of teeth. That was no way to welcome your man back home. Jen was no fun anymore. He'd have to remind her who was boss. His pint of whiskey arrived and Nuts sipped as one of the other tarts in the room came over to him, wiggling her assets. She was all double-D plastic boobs and glitter, wearing only a metallic thong and a silver necklace with the name

Monica across it. She was offering him sex on a plate, and he could smell it from here. Maybe he should bring Jen to Sally's, to teach her a lesson or two about how to keep her man happy. He grabbed the tom's arse as soon as she was over him and sucked hard on a raspberry ripple. Bloody hell, he couldn't wait, he had to have her. They were soon bouncing, groaning and moaning while the boys watched and cheered him on. Yeah, this is what it felt like to be a man.

'Come on, Nuts, come on Nuts . . .' the men chanted to the tune of 'Come On Eileen'.

Nuts let rip, blew his load, digging his nails into the woman's super-soft arse. He hadn't taken two breaths before the woman had been dragged off to do someone else.

'Good lad.' Kevin thumped him on the back as Nuts sorted his jeans out. 'I want to thank you again for keeping your gob shut.'

'I ain't no grass, Kev.'

Kevin pulled out a spliff. 'Yeah, but there are those who would have blabbed rather than do another stretch.'

'Partners don't do that kind of shit. When I was inside, one of the guys got a snitch tat across his forehead with a tooth-brush shank for letting his tongue wander. The scumbag got what he deserved.'

Kevin let out a puff of smoke. 'I got another job coming up. Good money—'

Nuts shook his head. 'No can do. I promised Jen I'll keep it clean. She says I'm out on my B-O-T-tom next time. My girls didn't even look like they knew me, when I got home. Mind you, screwing Jen was like jacking off to "The Sound of Music".'

Kevin laughed. 'You down the job centre? That will be like Mother Teresa as one of Sally's girls.' He popped his hand in his pocket. 'I've got one of these for you.'

Nuts looked at the mobile phone. 'That's our hotline,' Kevin continued. 'It's pay-as-you-go.'

'Kev, I can't do it mate.' But Nuts held tight to the phone. 'If Jen finds out—'

'But she doesn't have to know,' his friend whispered persuasively. He touched the side of his nose. 'Strictly between me and you.'

He passed the spliff to Nuts who was soon puffing away. Nuts wasn't looking forward to joining all the other Muppets looking for work at the job centre. All those forms, and the questions that nosey lot down there asked you. But still, he'd promised Jen he was going straight . . . Then all his thoughts disappeared as one of the girls knelt between his legs and started multi-tasking with her mouth and hands.

'Sorry, but I can't touch your motor,' Tiffany said, arms stubbornly folded.

'You what?' Laverne's eyes were brimming with fury. She pointed to her mouth. 'Read my lips; you'll bloody fix it if I have to shove your head in the engine and use your teeth to give it a new serial number.'

The threat was water off a duck's back to someone like Tiffany. 'No can do, lady, because you told me, point blank to my face, if I ever saw you again to keep walking. You remember, that whole "You don't know me, I don't know you" thing. We've got history, you may recall?'

Laverne looked nervously at the kid in the car, obviously to see if he'd heard, but he was hooked up to his earphones, nodding his head away, totally lost in a world of music on his portable CD player.

Now it was Laverne's turn to fold her arms, one of her legs thrust out cockily to the side. 'I could take my motor somewhere else.'

'You can do that if you don't want the job done properly. Decent garages are like decent men, around here.'

Instead of doing her nut, the other woman smiled as she pulled out a roll of notes like a magic wand. 'Forget the history. You get my Marilyn spanking new again and this wonga's straight in your pocket, no questions asked.'

Tiffany didn't even blink at the name this woman had given her car. There were always punters coming in with idiotic names for their motors – Poppy, Alfred and the worst, the absolute worst, had been Mamma Mia.

'What's your real name?' Tiffany asked. 'You're as much a Laverne as I am a Lavinia.'

The other woman squinted at her, her mouth tight. Then her lips relaxed. 'It's Dee.'

'So how much you offering?' Tiffany got back to business.

'Five and two zeros. That's if you get it done pronto.'

Tiffany was impressed with the money. She looked over at the damage on the car. 'Someone key it?'

Dee's eyes blazed. 'Well, it didn't scratch its own itch, did it? Now are you doing it or what?'

Tiffany got down to work, while the kid – who Dee told her was her son Nicky – stayed in the car. Tiffany didn't even blink at the news that a white boy was her son; in the East End she'd got used to seeing all types of families. Dee sat on a high stool with her endless legs crossed at the ankles and a brew that Tiffany had made her in her hand. Tiffany got the job done in fifty minutes straight.

'Strange job for a girl – being a grease monkey I mean.'

'Didn't have much choice,' Tiffany explained, as she wiped her hands. 'The judge dumped me here to do community service. I've tried some other things in the meantime. I did an evening course to get me into youth work with troubled teenagers but they threw me off – I was too rough with the boys on the placements they sent me on, apparently. Imagine that, eh? Too rough for the boys round here.'

Dee unlocked her legs, suddenly very interested in Tiffany's career path. 'Too rough?'

'Yeah, I didn't take no crap from the little bastards – so the course coordinator decided I wasn't "sensitive" enough and he kicked me out. The prick.'

'No crap, eh?' Dee looked over at her car. Nicky had his feet up resting on the dashboard, no longer listening to his music, and was adjusting his cap in the rear-view mirror which he'd bent round for the purpose. Dee screamed, 'Get your dirty trainers off my car!'

Nicky was unimpressed and without looking around sneered, 'Yeah, yeah, yeah.'

Dee turned back to Tiffany and explained in a hush tone, 'My boy's very delicate.'

Tiffany cocked an eyebrow. 'Yeah, I can see that.'

After a think and some hesitation, Dee went on. 'Did you get a certificate for this youth work thing you went on?'

'Nope.'

'Hmmm. But bits of paper don't prove anything, do they?' She paused and studied her son. Then both women looked at Nicky who was now adjusting his seat so it went right back, ready it seemed to take a nap.

Dee turned back to stare at Tiffany. 'Alright, Tiffany, let's be honest here – how do you fancy doing some freelance youth work?' It was obvious what she had in mind. 'The thing is right, we got my boy into one of them private schools, but they don't get him. They can't handle someone like my little Nicky. He's too sensitive and artistic.' Dee's face got all dreamy. 'He's going to be a musician. When my boy plays the piano, he is killing it; it brings tears to your eyes. They're all a bunch of posh bastards up there – stock-brokers, money people, you know the type. They say he's anti-social. Yeah alright, he did whack that kid with a hockey stick, but you can't let people take liberties, can you, babes? Before you know it they'll be in his effing trousers. He only goes around using his fists because he's so sensitive, so he over reacts, doesn't he? I think that Beethoven was the same. OK, so he's skipped a few classes, but he's bored – he's too clever for them.'

Tiffany suspected that when Dee's son played the piano he was killing it a way his mum didn't mean. Artistic? Sensitive? More like a trouble-making toerag, Tiffany thought. And I should know, I was one.

'We're not paying ten grand a term to hear that, are we? You know what I mean?'

Tiffany's mouth did partly fall open at that. Ten Gs, to send some little bastard to school? She looked at Dee and started to take notice. The shades weren't just sunglasses, they were vintage. The dress that showed skin top and bottom was no Top Shop off-the-peg rig. The foxy, huge hoop earrings were platinum, through and through. And the heels weren't knock-off from down The Roman, but up West designer. Dee was living the type of life that Tiffany wanted. Desperately.

'Oh yeah, I know what you mean. The school I went to didn't get me,' Tiffany quickly agreed. 'Fobbed my old mum off with the same kind of bollocks. She kept telling them the only reason I flung chairs around was because they needed to have more lessons where I could use my hands. A bit of woodwork, some cooking. But did they listen to her? You know what they did once?' Dee leaned in. 'They banned her from school for four months, just because she tried to say my art teacher wasn't any good – that's why I was drawing on the walls. Alright, so she was a touch loud and leery, but what's a mum to do when no one's listening to her? I mean, come on, it's parents who know their kids the best, right?'

Dee straightened up, popped off the stool and walked over to Tiffany. 'You work here full or part time?'

'PT,' Tiffany lied.

'Alright, I'll tell you what I'll do. You come up our place one evening and I'll introduce you to my boy and you see if you can act as a good influence on him. I'll be honest with you, babes, I'm at my wits' end. He's going through counsellors like a dose of salts. Now you, you would get him. You speak the same language. I'll make it worth your while, don't worry about that.'

Tiffany did smile then. *Oh yeah, you'll make it worth my while alright.*

A piercing sound like an air-raid siren abruptly cut across their conversation. Nicky was pressing the horn on his mum's car and not letting go. Dee took out some more notes and, over the noise, shouted, 'Here's another onner on top, for the advice. Come around to mine in two weeks' time, on Friday. Wish it could be sooner but we're going for a little family break in Spain. Me and John will be ever so grateful.'

All Tiffany's other thoughts dropped from her mind, replaced by the name 'John'. Her mind skidded back to the past. Wasn't John ... ? She frowned, trying to recall his last name. Oh yeah, John Black. He was the geezer Laverne/Dee had instructed Tiffany to get out of the firing line with the Plod, at the cop shop.

'Is *John* the same John who was involved in that malarkey—?'

Dee cut in, her features stern. 'We don't chat about our

business in public,' her considerable chest proudly puffed out, 'but yeah, that's my John.'

'Does your old man know I was acting as a runner for Mickey Ingram?'

'No, he doesn't and I'd be grateful if you didn't mention it. In fact, don't mention anything to do with the old days; it ain't just my boy who's a bit sensitive.' Almost guessing the next question Tiffany was going to ask, Dee added, 'And don't worry about Mickey Ingram. Once he got out, he found a new perch in Portugal with a new lady and two little ones.'

Tiffany anxiously rubbed her lips together; she needed to think. She'd been well out of the 'other' life for years and had no plans to go back. But Dee wasn't asking her to start toting an AK47, she just wanted someone to put her kid straight. But the old Tiffany couldn't help pressing the fast-forward button in her mind – if you get in with the family . . .

'I'm in,' she said simply, just as Nicky stopped his racket.

Dee's lips spread in a satisfied smile. The women exchanged details and struck a price that left Tiffany grinning from ear to ear.

'You still into girl-on-girl action?' Dee asked.

'What if I am?' Tiffany answered defensively. Over the years she'd met many people, especially on The Devil, who just didn't get her preference for women. But she didn't hide what she was. She'd have one answer for any knockers – stuff you! She looked Dee straight in the eye, hoping she wasn't going to have to say the same to her.

'It will be good if you are, because I don't want my Nicky hanging with some older bird who pushes her strawberry creams in his face. You get me?'

Tiffany smiled with relief. 'No need to worry there; your Nicky's family jewels will be in safe hands.'

Dee popped on her shades and got in her classic sports car as Nicky popped his earphones back on. 'One more thing, I like to be called Mizz Dee.'

Tiffany watched the woman and boy drive away and grinned. Mizz Dee was about to become her meal ticket out of this dump and off The Devil.

Forty-One

Two weeks later, on Friday morning, Nuts slapped some cash down on the kitchen table, startling Jen. She looked at the tens and twenties suspiciously. 'If you've been on the rob again—'

"Course I haven't. I've found myself an honest bit of labour.' He popped on a pleased-as-punch smile.

That's when Jen noticed that he was togged out in a suit. It was the same colour as the one she'd first seen him in: powder blue. Jen was still wary; she'd heard all those tales of men dressing the part for some job that didn't exist. When they got married, Nuts' fancy job in the city had never materialised; his tale was that he'd left it because he wanted to set up his own firm, but Jen knew that was all lies. Nuts couldn't tell a stock market share from a pork pie. What his 'business' was he never told her and, in truth, she never asked as long as he put cash on the table.

'Got another job in the city then?' she said acidly.

She never even saw Nuts move. Before she knew it, he had grabbed her by the front of her dressing gown. 'What's a man got to do to prove his worth to you? What do you want – for me to show you my balls bleeding?' His fist was clenched tight, his face red with fury and violence coming off every part of his body.

Jen quickly shut her eyes, her heart pounding, body trembling. She knew what came next: his fist slamming into her body. It was never her face though; it wouldn't do for the neighbours to know what really went on behind their four walls. She waited, horrified that the girls might walk in any minute. They were still getting ready for school. If Nuts was going to give her a hiding, he always took care that his daughters were not around. 'It ain't right that my princesses should have to see their dad teach their mum some manners,' was the way he put it.

If someone had said that she'd end up with a wife beater, she would've told them where to get off. No way would that happen to Jennifer Miller. Jen Miller had been swanning around like Lady Muck, turning her back on all the local lads because she said they were riff raff. No, Jen Miller was holding out for a prince, a real gent to take care of her, to create a happy home with even happier kids. But Jen Miller had got it wrong. Her prince had turned into a very violent frog.

She just didn't understand where her wonderful Nuts had gone. The charming man who'd driven her around in a plush motor, nicked flowers to impress her. The man who'd defended her honour against her wannabe rapist tutor. God knows she'd tried, tried her hardest to be a good wife, but nothing ever seemed to be right for him. His dinner was too hot; she'd popped on the telly too loud; his white shirt never looked white enough. It had taken her years to admit to herself that she'd hooked up with a monster. And poor, soft-hearted woman that she was, she was too ashamed to tell anyone other than Bex that her marriage was a living hell, full of pain.

He punched her just below her ribs and then twisted his free hand in her hair and snapped her neck back. The pain was awful and tears sprang to her eyes, but she didn't cry out; she couldn't let the kids know what was going on. He marched her across the room and squashed the side of her face into the wall.

'I'm tired of this, Jen,' he growled, 'tired of it. A bloke should feel like a king in his own home.'

Please don't let the girls come in. Please . . .

'I didn't mean nothing by it, Nuts.' She hated the begging, the reasoning, the taking the blame.

Then his hand dropped away and his other hand came up and gently smoothed her hair, like she was the most precious thing to him. 'I've got a job down at a car dealership in Romford. The boss knows I've done time and says that my skills with cars will come in handy. I'll leave the address if you don't think it's kosher.'

He stepped back and gingerly Jen pulled herself off the wall. She could hear the girls laughing in their bedroom. Thank God they hadn't had to see their father treat their mum like a bag of crap.

'You look smart,' Jen finally said. And he did. He looked like the Nuts she'd once known. Of course, Jen told herself, she should never have doubted him. He was the girls' dad and he wanted the best for his daughters.

'That money is a down payment from the boss because I explained that times have been a bit hard and my missus needs money for the kids.'

'That was good of him.'

'I love you, girl.' Jen's heart dropped. When he said that to her, it made all the pain go away.

'I know. I love you too.'

Long after he'd gone Jen sat at the table, rubbing her side, staring at the money. She let out a sigh of pure relief. Her jail-bird of a husband had finally found a job.

Tiffany looked around with wonder when the electronic gates of Dee's house opened to let her in. She'd suspected that her new employer would have a fuck-off house, but nothing like this. She'd seen similar places like this on reality TV and in celeb magazines. Tiffany pressed the bell and tried to look like she'd seen gaffs like this in real life, plenty of times.

Tiffany had expected a housekeeper with grey hair tied back in a bun to answer, but it was the lady of the house herself who came to the door. She held a white cat cuddled against her chest. The cat gazed at Tiffany and purred.

'Banshee likes you. Glad you've come, babes.' Dee ushered her into a large hallway that was pure white on ceilings and floor. 'Since you're going to be working here, let me give you a bit of a tour downstairs.'

And for the next half hour, Dee swanned around her home with Tiffany, like she was the Queen of Sheba. Tiffany was excited by the wealth on display. She'd never seen so many rooms in her life. A swimming pool with water the colour of a tropical sea led into the gym room next door; a kitchen, with one of those old-fashioned stoves; a movie room – which Dee simply called Hollywood – which also had a fruit machine; a family room with a large fish tank across one wall; a snooker room and, Dee's fav room, the bar, done up like an old-style pub. This was the life and Tiffany wanted it.

They came to a room that had a sign that read 'Gangsta'.

'This is Nicky's day room,' Dee explained. 'He's been suspended from school – it weren't his fault, alright. Me and John are working with the school to take him back sooner rather than later. He's keeping up with his studies though.'

Keeping up with his studies? Tiffany wasn't convinced. Behind the door, she could hear the bleeping and blooping of a computer game being played and the hectic rhythm of So Solid Crew's '21 Seconds'. Dee tapped on the door. She didn't get an answer but she went in anyway with Tiffany in tow. The boy was huddled over a desk, punching away at his keyboard taking down the aliens who were invading Planet Earth, his shoulders moving to the music coming from a high-tech mini stereo system.

Dee enquired hopefully, 'Hard at work?'

Nicky didn't turn around. 'I was – but I'm having a break at the moment.'

Tiffany could see from his score on the screen that this break had lasted quite a while already and there was no sign that it would be ending any time soon. There were a couple of unopened text books on the floor that had been kicked to one side.

Dee was positive. 'Well, you need a break, babes; you can't work all the time.'

Nicky said nothing except to whisper, 'Bollocks' when an alien laser beam took out part of his spaceship.

'Anyway, Nicky – remember that woman we met at the garage, a couple of weeks back? Her name is Tiffany and she's going to be your new friend.' Nicky ignored her and carried on playing.

Dee turned to her son's new friend and whispered, 'Pull up a seat, he won't be long. You know what kids are like with their computer games. Apparently they improve eye-hand coordination and help with the development of the right side of the brain. Did you know that? Wish I'd known that as a kid; I might not have gone around thumping so many people with my right hand.' When Tiffany didn't answer, Dee went on, 'Well, if you need me, I'll be in the pool area.'

When Dee was gone, Tiffany pulled up a chair and studied her new charge while he played on. It was a couple of minutes before he paused in his game to say, 'You my new counsellor?'

'No.'

'Good. Coz I don't need one. I know what my problems are; I was diagnosed up London by a top shrink. I've got self-esteem issues dating back to losing my real mum and dad when I was kid.' He picked up a small bottle of tablets from his desk. 'I've got these for it.' Then he resumed playing his game and explained, 'That's why I'm so sensitive. Gotcha, you little green bastard!'

Tiffany had already formed her own diagnosis of Nicky's issues and decided on her own treatment. She stood up, leaned over and pulled the plug out of his computer and threw it on his desk. The PC groaned and desperately tried to save its data before the power drained away. She did the same to the stereo. Stunned, Nicky turned to her. 'What the fuck? What's your fucking problem?'

Tiffany grabbed him by his slim fit Ralph Lauren polo shirt and pulled him out of his chair, pushed him up against the wall and shook him violently. 'I'll tell you what my problem is. Your mum's brought me over here to do a job. You're going to share your troubles with me while I pretend I give a toss. And as in any new job, it's important to start as we mean to go on. You understand?'

Nicky's face went pale with disbelief before he began screaming. 'Mum! Mum! The new counsellor is abusing me.'

But he was brought up short when he was shaken again within an inch of his life. 'I said, do you understand?'

Nicky's shock turned to anger and he snarled, 'Listen, sugar tits, I don't think you know who you're dealing with. My dad's a top gangster. When he finds out you've laid a finger on me, you'll be in with a sack of kittens in the river.'

He was shaken again and Tiffany sneered, 'I don't think so, and you know why? Because your dad is the real thing, and because he's the real thing, he knows full well that you're a soppy little tart. He might play angry with me but deep down he'll be laughing. And you know what? Deep, deep down, that's what your mother really thinks too. You're a two-bit, public school ponce and everyone knows it. I'm here to show you what it's like. Now, I repeat, do you understand?'

Nicky withered a little but warned her, 'I'm hard. I know people. I'll get you taken care of . . .' But his voice was choked off when she grabbed him by the throat and squeezed. His face began to swell and redden. Tiffany loosened her grip slightly to give him the space to splutter, 'OK, OK . . .'

She let go of his throat and Nicky staggered over to his chair and slumped into it. Tiffany walked a few paces and stood over him with her arms folded, her feet braced apart. The boy looked up and whimpered, 'I'll tell my mum; she'll kill you.'

Tiffany shook her head. 'You're going to tell your mum you got roughed up by a girl and then you'd feel no shame? Now – this is my last time of asking – Do. You. Understand?'

Nicky looked at the door and then back at Tiffany. He was a public school ponce but he knew how the pecking orders were arranged.

'Yeah, I understand.'

Forty-Two

'Mum, Mum,' Courtney said excitedly as she and her sister joined their mum in the kitchen. The girls had just got back from school. 'Can I have some pop tarts, I'm starving.'

'Me too,' piped up Little Bea.

Jen was bone weary after finishing a bag full of ironing for one of the more well-to-do families who lived in one of the big houses in the square across the road. This was as near to the fashion industry as she got to now – ironing other people's clothing. While Nuts was inside, she'd had to take in ironing as a second job, to make the pennies stretch. She was ashamed of being someone else's skivvy, but she'd do anything to make sure her girls didn't go around in rags or second-hand clothes from the charity shop. Her eldest didn't wait for an answer as Courtney headed over to the fruit bowl and nabbed a pear. She ate it like a kid who'd never seen food before. Given the speed with which she demolished it, she was in danger of eating her little fingers as well.

'What do you mean you're starving? Didn't you have any school dinners today?' Jen said, watching the two apples of her eye closely.

The fruit froze near Courtney's mouth as she gave her little sister one of those looks they shared when they were hiding something from their mum; well, that's the way it always seemed to Jen.

Courtney swallowed, then said, "Course we had dinner, didn't we, Little Bea?' Her sister quickly nodded her head. 'But I didn't eat much because I didn't like it today. They had that horrible rice pudding stuff for afters.'

'But I thought it was roast dinner Friday. They usually have Jam Roly Poly.'

Her girls couldn't get enough of that pudding. Jen wasn't a bad cook, but she was a bit rubbish at making the dessert her kids loved so much; she just couldn't get the suet right. Jen swung her gaze slowly between her girls. There was something going on here and she would bet her last quid it had something to do with the letter she'd just received from the school.

'Have you been paying the dinner money I give you?'

Courtney nodded furiously but didn't speak.

'Taking it to the office like I told you?' Jen got another nod.

'Please, Mum,' Little Bea said softly, 'can I have a pop tart? I'm hun—' But she never finished the word as she looked at her sister. But Jen already knew that she was going to say 'hungry'. Why did both her kids look like they needed Bob Geldof to raise money for them to get money for food? Jen didn't know what the effing hell was going on here, but she was going to go down that school right now with the letter and find out.

'What do you mean the dinner money hasn't been paid?' Jen asked, amazed at the school office management. It didn't help that she stood opposite a poster announcing it was National School Meals Week. The manager, Mrs Lamont, was one of those women who always rubbed Jen up the wrong way. Fake la-di-da accent, twin sets and pearl clothing, and a way of looking down her nose that suggested that Jen shouldn't be sharing the same planet as her.

That awkward feeling came over Jen. She felt like she was a girl in a navy blue uniform, back in school. She'd got through her school days, but she'd always felt like she didn't fit in there. She'd never done a bunk or given any backchat, like Tiffany had, but she'd just felt like a lump in class, getting by but not understanding half the stuff the teachers went on about. Not that the teachers seemed to care whether she understood or not, just as long as she kept nodding. Of course, that didn't mean she didn't take her responsibilities for her kids' education seriously. Jen attended parents' evenings, bought the girls the right P.E. kit for school, came to workshops held especially for parents; if the school asked her to do something, she did it.

'The school must've made a mistake.' Jen's arms were folded elastic tight against her chest.

Mrs Lamont shook her head. 'All the dinner money is collected during registration on a Monday morning. All of our teachers make sure that each child's money is put in the money box with the appropriate paperwork.'

The metal boxes stood side by side in a neat line on a low filing cabinet behind the office manager. Each had the names of the classes printed on them. Courtney was in Emerald class and Little Bea was in Diamond.

'Yeah, but what if the teachers have made a mistake and got muddled up with the names of the kids?'

The other woman stretched her neck in indignation. 'I can assure you, Mrs Taylor, that our teachers do not make mistakes.' She leaned over and checked her computer. 'The school would never let a child go hungry, so your daughters are fed at lunchtime, but we have to make sure that proper procedures are followed. We've already written to you twice about the arrears.'

Jen hated that word 'arrears'; it made it sound like she owed the council a wagon-load of rent. 'You what? Two letters before I got this one?' She waved the letter in her hand. 'I haven't ever received any letters before this one. Now come on, if you'd been sending them they would've been posted through my letterbox. Mind you, the post can always be a bit hit and miss where I live.'

Last year, the Post Office had put the brakes on mail being delivered to the estate after the postman was attacked by a gang of youths armed to the teeth with knives and pitbulls who snatched his mailbag looking for cash and giros. But that was all sorted now.

'I notice from our records that you live on the Essex Lane Estate.'

Jen swallowed. It was never a good sign when someone mentioned The Devil. Everyone tried to forget that it existed, much less talked about it, including its residents.

'Yeah, what about it?' Jen said defensively.

Mrs Lamont didn't answer her but instead gave her a letter. The first line put Jen's back up, straight away: *'If you are in need of financial assistance, the school recommends . . .'*

Jen almost threw the letter in this condescending woman's face. Instead she raised her chin. 'Oh I get it, everyone who lives on The Devil's . . . The Essex Lane are lazy good-for-nothings. We're either on the dole or on the make, working and fiddling the social at the same time. Well, let me tell you, I have never been a member of the JSA crew.' Seeing the look of confusion on the woman's face, Jen added, 'That's Job Seekers Allowance to people like you. I've got a perfectly good job, thank you very much. The wages might be crap, but I'm working.'

'Then I suggest you pay your children's dinner money.'

Jen left the school steaming. She screwed up the letter and pitched it into the gutter where it belonged. If the girls weren't giving the school the money and were too scared to tell her what was happening, that was not good. Anyway she had pretty much figured out what was happening to her girls. And she was going to put a stop to it.

Forty-Three

Tiffany lit up and then passed the spliff to Nicky. 'Remember what I said. You need to inhale deeply,' she told him.

They sat in Tiff's motor around the corner from Nicky's house in a lane dark enough that no one could see what they were doing. They had come back from one of their 'evenings out'. Tiffany had told Mizz Dee that she was taking her son up West to see *Pirates of the Caribbean*. Dee had liked that and started chuckling when she found out that the movie's other title was *The Curse of the Black Pearl*. Only Tiffany hadn't taken him to Leicester Square but to the garage under the arches in Bethnal Green where she still did a bit of part-time work at the weekend. Dee was now employing her through the week to see to her son's needs, because she was really pleased with the progress Tiffany was making with him.

If there was one thing Tiffany had sussed out quickly, it was that the boy was bored out of his box. She remembered what that had felt like, wasting her teen years down the cemetery. His mum smothered him with anything she saw he wanted, but what the kid really wanted was a slice of real life. So Tiff took him to the garage to get a feel of the ole East End.

Now it was time for him to step up to the next stage of his education, Tiffany Miller style.

'What you waiting for?' she asked as Nicky stared, fascinated by the spliff he held in his hand. 'It ain't going to bite your nose off.'

Nicky slowly placed it at his lips, pulled in and exhaled on a splutter and cough. 'That's flippin' disgusting,' he let out, wiping his mouth.

'It's always like that to start with. You'll soon get used to it.'

So the kid took another tote and this time he didn't cough but started to frantically spit. 'Uh, it tastes like shit. All my mates said it should taste kind of mellow.'

'Well, your friends weren't smoking the real deal. They probably got some of that cheap rubbish dealers palm off to gullible kids.'

Tiffany sat back as Nicky kept puffing away at his smoke. Suddenly his cheeks blew out like a squirrel with nuts and he quickly opened the door and puked on the ground outside. Tiffany smiled. She hadn't given him weed but Rizlas rolled up with parsley. He wanted to experience smoking some herb so she'd given him some – the cooking variety. Now every time he thought about defying his parents by smoking some leaf he'd think about throwing up; well, that was her reasoning. That's what so many parents didn't get: you want your kid to stop doing naughties, no point ranting and raving at them. Instead, introduce him to a slice of life your way.

A heavy breathing Nicky leaned back in the car, his face very pale indeed. He looked at her. 'That weren't weed, was it?'

'What do you–?'

'Come off it, Tiff, I've had a joint before. All those fancy boys at school are into it.'

Tiffany squinted at him. 'You been pulling my plonker?'

He grinned, despite still looking green. 'Thought you might have some hot shit gear I haven't done before. What was that stuff?'

Tiffany grinned. 'Parsley.' Then she became dead serious. 'I just want to make sure you don't go down that bad road. When I was your age, me and my mates would smoke dandelion down the cemetery because we didn't have the readies to buy the proper stuff. And just as well, because I think if I'd had a regular stream of real ganja, I don't know where I'd be now.' She stopped thinking about what had happened to Stacey.

'I wanted to thank you,' Nicky said shyly, the green on his face replaced by blushing red.

'Nicky thanking me?' Tiffany said with mock amazement, 'Quick someone, get me a camera so we can preserve Nicky saying ta to me, for all eternity.'

He grinned. 'For showing me where my dad was probably born – that's what I wanted to thank you for.'

'I didn't know that John hailed from Bethnal–'

'Not *my* dad, my *other* dad – Chris.'

The blood drained away from Tiffany's face. 'I didn't know that your real dad was called Chris.'

Nicky started talking but Tiffany didn't hear a word he said. Oh bloody hell. Her mind was dragged back ten years to the plan that she and Dee had put together where she had to stitch up a geezer called Chris and keep John's name well and truly out of the frame. She didn't need to ask if it was the same Chris; hadn't Dee told her, on the quiet, that Nicky's father had been John's right-hand man? But the other woman had never told her his name.

'I'm so sorry, Nicky.'

He gazed at her confused. 'It ain't your fault about my dad.'

Maybe it is, Tiffany thought, guilt eating her up. But she kept her thoughts to herself.

'Someone's bullying the girls, Mum,' Jen told Babs as she headed for the bottle of light blue Bombay Sapphire gin on the drinks cabinet. She'd left it a couple of weeks before coming to her mum to tackle how to stop the problem with the dinner money. What her daughters didn't know was that she'd paid the dinner money in full until the end of the month, but she'd still given the girls their dinner money on the last two Mondays. Courtney should have been bringing the money Jen gave her back home, because the school would have told her that the money was already paid. But instead her daughter came home every Monday saying she'd paid the dinner money. Whoever was pinching her kids' money was still at it.

Jen and the girls were frequent visitors to her mum's. Even though she had her own flat in another block on the estate, this place still felt like her real home. Every couple of weeks she'd bring the girls and they'd stay for the whole weekend. Babs adored her grandkids and they adored her in turn.

'Bullying my girls?' Babs said indignantly. 'You give me the names and I'll sort the toerags out.'

Babs Miller hadn't changed much in the last ten years, but two things worried Jen about her mum. She knocked it back like a fish and seemed even more obsessive about keeping her home neat and tidy. Even now she held a cloth midway through a polish routine for dust Jen could never see.

Jen took herself and her drink and sat heavily on the sofa. 'But I don't know who they are, Mum.'

Babs joined her on the sofa, placing her duster across her knees. 'So how do you know they're being bullied?'

Jen ran her mum through the dinner money saga. 'It's the only explanation,' Jen concluded. 'Some bastard brat must be waiting for them before they get to school and ripping them off.'

'I know you don't want to hear this, but I've always said Jen that you're too protective of those girls. It's a rough world out there and they've got to learn when to stand their ground.'

Jen bit her lip. 'But once you start teaching them to use their fists that's how they might deal with life every time they find themselves in a tight spot.' Jen couldn't help thinking of Nuts and the way he brutally used his fists on her every time they got into a bit of verbal. No way did she want to encourage her kids to go around decking other people. 'I don't want them to be like the other young 'uns around here, thinking the only way to go through life is to punch their way through it.'

Jen didn't even realise she did it, but she smoothed her hand across her side where Nuts had punched her a couple of weeks back.

Babs took note of her daughter's hand and worry lines creased her forehead and around her mouth. 'You hurt yourself, love?'

Jen instantly dropped her hand, but wouldn't meet her mum's gaze. 'It's nothing. I think I hurt myself when I knocked into a table or something.'

Babs leaned over and stretched her hands towards her eldest child. 'Let me be the judge of whether it's nothing.' She touched Jen's top. 'Let me have a look—'

Jen stormed to her feet, but couldn't stop the tears forming in the bottom of her eyes. 'I said it's nothing, Mum. Now please, leave it out.'

Stone-faced, Babs got to her feet, the duster dropping onto the carpet. And in her mum voice, that Jen hadn't heard for years, ordered, 'Jennifer Miller, you stay right where you are.'

Jen pulled in a strong breath as her mum lifted her top. She looked away as her mum gasped at the fading blue-black-yellow bruise. She was too ashamed to look at her mother. Babs tenderly touched her fingertips to the bruise. The tears began to fall at the care her mum was showing her.

'It ain't . . .' she gulped as the tears came stronger, 'what you think, Mum.'

'And what do I think, baby?' The last time her mum had
called her 'baby' was when she was ten and scraped the side of
her face when she'd fallen off her bike. Babs had gently cleaned
her face and whispered soothing words in her ear.

Babs pulled herself straight and looked her daughter in the
eye. 'I tell you what I think. I think that bastard of a husband
of yours is using you as a punch bag. And don't lie to me
because my mate Terri had enough of these in the early part of
her marriage – until her brothers made her old man see the
error of his ways. How long, Jen?'

'When I started carrying Courtney.' The tears and emotions
overwhelmed Jen and she collapsed in her mother's arms and
started sobbing as if her heart was breaking. Babs soothed and
caressed her, like she was that ten-year-old again. Eventually
she got her tears under control and allowed her mum to steer
her back to the sofa. But Babs didn't sit down, instead she said,
'Let's make you a nice cuppa.'

When Babs left the room Jen slumped back against the sofa.
She was consumed by relief. It was like a large stone had been
lifted from her chest. All the years when she'd had to hold
back the pain, and wear long sleeves to cover the bruises and
swelling on her arms, were now in the past. Just knowing that
her mum was now in the picture made her feel strangely safe.
But the safe feeling disappeared a minute later when she saw
her mum headed for the door.

Jen jumped up and rushed into the passage. 'Mum? Mum,
what you doing?'

Babs turned displaying the rolling pin in her hand. Her eyes
spat fire. 'I tell you what I'm doing,' she growled, 'I'm going to
find that no good son-in-law of mine and beat some sense into
him–'

Jen frantically shook her head. 'No, Mum, you can't do
that.'

'I want him to know what it feels like to be beaten like a dog in the street.'

'Mum, stop.' Jen could see her mother was shaking with rage. She placed her hand gently on Babs' arm. 'Please, Mum. I don't want any argy-bargy.'

'But you don't understand.' Her mum's face was so filled with pain that Jen regretted coming here. 'It's all my fault. I encouraged you to go out with the slimeball even when you pegged him for a bad penny.'

'No, Mum. The only person to blame is Nuts. Those hands he hits me with belong to him.'

'Stanley Miller might've been the Devil's disciple from hell, but he never, *never*, laid a hand on me. Never laid a hand on you or your sister.'

Her mother rarely talked about the past or her dad, so seeing an opening, Jen asked, 'So why did he do a bunk from our lives when Tiff was a baby and me not much older?'

A silent Babs looked at her eldest. Her shoulders slumped, as if the life had been drained out of her, and she moved slowly back into the sitting room where she dropped back on to the sofa. 'I only ever tried to do my best.'

Jen was instantly sorry. It wasn't Babs' fault she'd been dumped and had to bring up two children on her own. 'I know, Mum. You done good.' She hated her mum looking like this – like she'd aged a good twenty years. Her mum had lived a hard life and she didn't want to make it any harder.

She eased down on the sofa again and took the rolling pin away from her mum and placed it on the carpet. 'Don't worry about me and Nuts. Things are going to get better because he's got a job now. Maybe he's been feeling frustrated, but now his mind's going to be occupied, he'll be a hell of a lot happier.' She touched her mum's arm. 'Promise me you won't let on to Tiffany.'

Babs nodded.

'What am I going to do about the girls and their dinner money?'

Babs looked across at her. 'Have you told ...' Her mouth twisted, then spat, 'Nuts?'

Jen made a disgusted noise. 'No point, he'll only say that's the mum's department to get sorted.'

'There's only one thing you can do, Jen. Follow them when they leave the house for school on Monday morning with the dinner money.'

Forty-Four

Jen kissed both her daughters goodbye and then followed them as they set off to school. She wore her hair tucked under a hat and kept a respectable distance so the girls were less likely to notice her. The school was about a fifteen-minute walk from her home, across Mile End Road, in a little turning off the Georgian Square where Babs cleaned a few houses. Jen had initially been worried about the girls crossing to the other side of the street, because Mile End was such a busy road, but the only alternative had been to send them to the school around the corner where she and Tiff had gone. She knew first hand what that place was like and wouldn't even send a dog there. She nodded her head with approval as she saw Courtney take her little sister's hand when they got to the crossing. That's what she'd told her Courtney – always keep your little sister safe. Just like she'd done with Tiffany when they went to primary school.

Jen held back, giving them time to get to the other side. As she got to the middle of the crossing, she saw a group of three other kids approach her girls. Right, I've got you, Jen thought triumphantly, I'm going to bloody wring your necks. She watched closely as the other children reached her daughters. Jen waited for Courtney to get out the dinner money, but it never happened. All the children did was laugh and chat. Jen quickly crossed over, but held back. She recognised two of the group as Courtney's classmates. One of them was Dexter Ingram. He was a really good-looking kid, mixed race with dimples in his cheeks and big brown eyes. Shame he was a bloody Ingram because that kid had manners, respect and was always nicely turned out, unlike the rest of his clan. Mel Ingram claimed he was her cousin's kid who she'd taken into her home out of the goodness of her heart when her cousin died, but the estate jungle vine told a different tale. People speculated that his real mum was the eldest Ingram girl who had had him when she was fourteen. Who the father was, no one knew. Still tea leafing was in his blood and he was going to rue the day he started on her daughters, if he turned out to be a bully.

Jen was astonished to see both her children let out loud giggles. Her girls wouldn't be spinning a joke or two with a bunch of bullies. Then the other children left the girls and walked away. So, they weren't the ones robbing her kids. In fact, what Jen saw was her Courtney gazing all dopey eyed after Dexter Ingram. Courtney was sweet on the boy. There was no way – no way – her girl was getting ideas about an Ingram.

But before Jen could ponder that some more, her daughters were on the move again.

Just as they got to the street their school was on, the girls stopped at the corner as if they were waiting for someone. Jen stopped and tried to hide herself by moving to the side of the pavement. A man in a hooded top seemed to appear out of nowhere and was in front of the girls in seconds. Jen couldn't make out his face, but she could make out Courtney passing him the small envelope with the dinner money inside. Bastard. Probably some junkie terrorising her kids to sort out his next fix. Not on her watch. Jen started barrelling forward just as Courtney leaned up and planted a kiss on the man's cheek. Jen stopped in her tracks. What the hell was going on? The man turned and Jen caught his face.

Nuts.

Stunned, Jen stumbled around and quickly walked back the other way. She couldn't believe it. Nuts had told her he was working in a car dealership in Romford. But he wasn't. He was ripping his own kids off, the dirty low life. No wonder the girls had kept schtum; they didn't want to grass up their dad to her; they loved him to bits. Poxy cunt. Every curse word Jen knew battered around her head. She followed him and saw him get in a flash motor with tinted windows so she couldn't see who was inside. Probably some bird with boobs as big as her bimbo hairdo. She wasn't surprised; the stories of Nuts sticking his wick where it didn't belong had reached her years ago. She could live with that. She could live with him knocking her around. But what she couldn't, and wouldn't, live with was him literally taking the food from her daughters' mouths and making a liar of them into the bargain, just so he could shag his useless life away.

Jen immediately got the overland train to Romford. She used to come out with Bex and some of the other girls back in the day, to shake a leg and paint the town redder than red on a Saturday night. The high street was the same, but also different. The Liberty Shopping Centre she knew well, but she didn't know what the large building called The Brewery was all about, and she didn't have time to find out. From what Nuts had told her, the car dealership he worked in was near the market at the top of the High Street. She looked for almost half an hour and didn't find the address. In the end, she asked an older woman who was passing by.

'Car dealership?' The woman looked baffled. 'I've lived here for thirty years love and if there was a car place up here I'd know about it.'

Jen thanked the woman and started walking away. Car dealership my arse. Nuts had been having one over on her. He never had any job, the kiddie-money-nicking bastard. She didn't feel rage, anger or fury. Instead her mind was calm as she got the train back. One of the other passengers had his CD portable on too loud so she caught the tune he was playing – Destiny's Child's 'Survivor'. Yes, Jen decided, taking a leaf out of Beyoncé and her girls' advice – she was better than this. She made a life changing decision.

Nuts was going to have to go.

'He'll fucking kill you, Jen,' Bex warned her friend.

They sat at the back near the foot spas, in the nail bar Bex managed in Roman Road Market. Bex was still a good-looking girl, but boy had she piled on the pounds over the years. She looked more like a Buddha than a Bex. Plus, she'd had a baby with some Turkish bastard who had conveniently forgotten to mention he already had a missus tucked up indoors. And when his wife had gone gunning for Bex with a baby oil bottle, filled with acid, the poor girl had been left with a scar on her face for the rest of her life.

But Bex spoiled that boy of hers something chronic, believing she had to make up for his absent father. Meanwhile, she tried to keep herself looking hip, with clobber she got from one of the more trendy stalls in the market and high-end perfume (that Jen couldn't afford, although she couldn't say she liked the scent Bex was smothered in today).

'Mum told me that too,' Jen said, as she watched Bex lick her fingers after eating a family bag of Doritos Chilli Heatwave.

'You'd better listen to her. If you go to the authorities about Nuts or go to one of them women refuge places, he'll track you down and squeeze the life out of you.'

'But he's bloody filching from his own kids and pissing all over me, taking me for a mug.' Tears sprang to Jen's eyes. 'He crossed his heart and swore that job was the real deal. I can't live like this anymore, Bex. I've got to get out.'

Bex started on another pack of Doritos. 'Only thing I can think of is for you to leave the country. Got any people in Spain?'

Jen slumped back in despair. Bex wasn't saying anything that her mum hadn't said already, apart from do a bunk out of the country. The message from her best mate was clear – if she tried to leave Nuts he was going to murder her. And she wasn't joking. You didn't have a laugh about that kind of stuff in East London. Who could forget poor Maureen Ryan, who'd lived on The Devil? A gentle woman, bit of a Jack Daniels follower but went out of her way to be respectful to everyone and always took care that her kids were done up nice and tidy. But that bastard of an old man of hers had beat her black and blue like it was his hobby, even in public. She'd finally left him and taken the kids with her to some refuge in Whitechapel. She didn't even last a week; he found her and snapped her neck. The fucker went down for life and poor, dead Maureen's children ended up going to live with their nan and grandad in Ireland. The thought of Courtney and Little Bea being brought up by other people twisted Jen's heart more than her own death.

She looked pleadingly at her friend. 'I've got to do something, Bex. If I don't I'm going to go mad.'

Bex licked her fingers again. 'But what, Jen? What are you going to do?'

Forty-Five

When they arrived back at John and Dee's after a special evening out – a treat to the local chicken 'n' chips eating hole, because Nicky had been readmitted to school – Tiffany took him to one side before they went into the house.

'Don't forget to be humble and promise you'll be a good pupil from now on. Do you hear?'

'Whatever . . .' He was smiling his teeth off.

Tiffany was confused. 'What are you beaming about? You can't be that happy that the school's taking you back, surely?'

Nicky was radiant. 'Nah, two fingers to school – but I'm bound to be on a sweetener from mum and dad now the posh joint's taken me back. Stands to reason, they had the right hump when I was slung out – now I'm back in, they'll be giving me a little reward.' He rubbed his hands eagerly together. 'Can't make me mind up what I want, but I fancy a motorbike to tell you the truth, Tiff.'

Tiffany rolled her eyes. 'If anyone deserves a reward, it's the school, not you. And you're only fifteen – too young to be on the back of a motorbike, you little runt. And stop calling me Tiff; I'm not a fucking charwoman.'

'I can ride a bike – Tiffany. We ride them around the local playing fields. Piece of piss.'

They found Dee, John and Banshee in the cinema room watching the carry-ons on *Big Brother*.

'That bimbo's a right twat,' Dee announced. 'They shouldn't wait for a vote but throw her arse out the door right . . . Oh you're back.'

Then Dee went into overdrive, still on cloud nine that her son was going back to school. She greeted her little soldier as if he'd just won a couple of gold medals at the Olympics. Squealing with joy, like a teenager who'd seen her idol at the stage door after a concert, she threw her arms around him. 'John! John! The school's admitted they've made a mistake and they've taken Nicky back.'

John was skipping the celebrations. He sat in an armchair with a glass of his favourite tipple – whiskey. Tiffany overheard him muttering, 'Yeah and I'm sure that donation I gave to the school's sports fund had nothing to do with it. If I'd tried that trick anywhere else the Bill would have run me in for extortion.'

When she'd finished fussing over her son, Dee got serious and told him to get in his room and start swotting up so he wasn't behind when he went back to class. She also gently reminded Nicky that he was to apply himself from now on and there was to be no more hitting other boys with any types of sticks. Like an eager puppy, Nicky promised he was going to be kosher at school from now on. Then he stood, pointedly, with his arms folded and a big smile on his face like a dustman who'd just wished a resident a Merry Christmas. Dee didn't get it and furrowed her brow. 'What you looking at me like that for?'

Nicky didn't get the fact that she didn't get it. 'Well, you know . . .'

'No, what don't I know?'

Nicky realised he'd drawn a blank on his sweetener and the smile faded to a frown and he began to stomp off.

'Oi,' Dee said, 'get back here.'

Nicky turned around and Tiffany was surprised to see the smile on his face instead of his usual sulky routine when he didn't get his own way.

Dee pointed at her cheek. 'Ain't you forgotten something?'

Nicky dutifully kissed her and left the room to begin swotting, mumbling under his breath.

Dee didn't like champagne – she liked to compare it to fizzy apple juice from a bargain store – but she had a sense of occasion and she opened a bottle from the room that she used as a bar when she had guests. She shared it with Tiffany and John while hunting around in a drawer where she found a grand, in assorted bank notes. She folded them together and gave them to Tiffany. 'Get yourself something nice, babes. You've done wonders with my boy – hasn't she, John?'

John ignored the question, but he did look up like he was listening out for something. He then shook his head and returned back to his newspaper. Dee and Tiffany kicked off their shoes and swapped stories about schools, kids, ambitions and their respective mothers.

'You ever thought about having any little ones?' Dee asked. 'With you being a you-know-what?'

Tiffany guzzled some bolly before saying, 'Being *you know what* don't mean I haven't got the necessary equipment if I wanted a kid or two.'

Out of the corner of her eye, Tiffany noticed that John kept looking up from his newspaper, his eyes and body alert.

'So, you going to have some?' Dee persisted.

Tiffany mulled the question over. 'If I'm truthful, I ain't really thought about it. I kind of like life on my own.'

'I only knew my mum when I got to be an adult.' Seeing the look of surprise on Tiffany's face, she added, 'It's too long a story, but I've always wanted to . . .' Dee stopped as she watched her husband suddenly get up. 'What's up with you?'

'I dunno . . .' He walked up to the heavy drapes that covered the picture window with its commanding view over their drive and front garden to the countryside beyond. Dee knew that look he wore; as a successful criminal he had a sixth sense for danger. He pressed a button to open the curtains and then peered out. It was pitch black outside. The lights, which usually burned by the gates to the property, were switched off. John pursed his lips before going to pick up his jacket from which he took a flick knife. He put it into his back pocket.

Dee stood up, alarmed. 'What's up?'

'There's someone out there.'

'How do you know?'

'I just know.'

But as he went to the door, their garden flooded with light from a set of headlamps and a car engine roared into life as its accelerator was pressed right down, making it sound like a light plane readying for take-off. John rushed for the front door while Dee ran to the window. A shocked Tiffany followed, and for a few horrified moments she thought she was going to have to physically restrain Dee from crashing through the glass into the garden outside. For there, in full view – thanks to the lights John had switched on – her prize possession, the car she valued more than anything else in the world, was being manoeuvred past John's Range Rover and Tiffany's far more modest hatchback. The thief wore a balaclava, keeping his face hidden despite the glare of the lights.

Dee shrieked like a character in a horror film and made for the door. Tiffany watched as John ran across the drive, jumped on the bonnet of Dee's car as it swept by and was thrown off by the driver swerving. He ran to his own vehicle and set off in pursuit, his wife running after him on foot. Then there was silence and the noise of the two engines and their lights faded into the distance.

Tiffany stood alone, stunned and horrified by what had happened. It seemed like an age before she heard the front door slam shut. Dee appeared again in the front room. Tiffany flinched at the burning hatred in her eyes.

'Someone's going to die for this.'

Forty-Six

John drove like he was in pole position at a Grand Prix, confident he was going to catch the tea leaf. He knew he had no chance on an open road; he'd easily be outrun. But on the narrow country lanes that surrounded his property, Dee's car wouldn't be able to pick up speed and the complicated road pattern meant the driver would be unsure where he was going and would be caught out by hidden junctions and other hazards. Only if the car thief found his way down the A13 would John be royally fucked.

There was no doubt the guy was a proper pro. He held to the road and covered any gaps that would allow John to get by and overtake where the road widened. When John tailgated him, putting his lights on full beam and sounding his horn for minutes at a time to spook the other driver, the guy kept his nerve. He avoided the obvious mistake of slamming the brakes on so John would crash into him and damage his engine, allowing the fugitive to escape; the car he'd stolen was too valuable to be sacrificed like that. It had clearly been stolen to order, in the same way John had once arranged for high-end motors to be TWOC-ed. No normal thief would take it; it would be too difficult to sell on the UK market and you needed contacts to sell it abroad, the sort of contacts he'd once had. While John sighed at the grim irony, the thief slammed on his brakes and took a violent turn to the left and then vanished into the night.

John's Range Rover squealed as he put his foot to the pedal and hurriedly reversed back up the lane to where he'd last seen his quarry. He noticed an open gate in a fence and went through it. The field behind was black with no sign of his quarry. Lights full on, he drove in a circle. So well disguised was Dee's car, huddled up against a tree and bushes, that he nearly missed it. John carried on turning to mislead the thief and then returned to the gap in the fence. He drove back through it and headed off up the lane at high speed, lights aglow, horn blaring in deceptive frustration. A half-mile down the road, he stopped and did a three point. Then he turned off the lights and engine and rolled gently forwards on the incline back towards the gate in the fence.

He brought the Range Rover to a halt covering the gate and then got out. In the black shade, he crept along the hedgerows until he was close enough to see the outline of Dee's car where it was still parked.

John smiled and whispered, 'Gotcha, you bastard.'

With the entrance covered, he pulled the flick knife out of his pocket and opened it and began his approach. It was possible that the guy had fled across the fields but John thought that was unlikely. Dee's car was too valuable an item for a pro to give up lightly. But as he closed in, he turned when he realised that another car was coming up the lane at high speed. He watched in horror as it accelerated and then swerved wildly, its brakes screeching before it hit his Range Rover and shunted it down the road with a roar, the bodywork of both vehicles buckling and caving in.

Silence followed, except for the hissing of an engine. John knew he should run and help the other driver but he was now doubly determined to give the thief who'd cost him two vehicles a hiding. But the decision was made for him. The lights on Dee's car came full on, blinding John. The ignition was turned and with insulting slowness, the car drove around him and nosed its way towards the gate. It stopped briefly for the driver to inspect the accident a few dozen yards away, before turning and heading away at a leisurely speed in the direction from which he had come.

Dee paced the family room like a lioness who hadn't had her lunch, her Motorola flip-lid mobile jammed to her face as she waited for her call to connect. Tiffany stood just inside the door, really shaken by tonight's turn of events. Banshee rubbed herself against Tiffany's leg and purred softly as if she understood her distress. Tiffany had a good idea who Dee was calling and didn't think she should do it.

'Mizz Dee, I don't think you should call the cops. I don't think John would want the Filth sticking their beaks into your business.'

Dee blinked, flashing her bold eyelash extensions at Tiffany like they were two yobs in a pub squaring up, and she was about to launch straight at her. 'We ain't done nothing wrong and it's their job to sort this out.' The call connected and she shouted with fury and rage down the phone. 'You're bloody right I want to report a crime. Some scrote has nicked my motor. I want every cop car in Essex looking for the scumbag and get your helicopters on the case as well. You need to set up road blocks and get in reinforcements . . . Yeah, you heard me, I want you to track the bastard down and when you get him, beat the fucker up; string him up. That's what I'm paying my taxes for . . . You what?' Dee stopped pacing. 'Are you having a laugh? You'll write a report and tell your cars to keep an eye out for it?' Her voice rose to full level that should've had the walls of the house shaking. 'You're all a bunch of fucking wankers. Don't know why I bothered to call you in the first place.' She terminated the call and hurled the phone across the room. Dee clenched and unclenched her hands as her breathing got harsher and louder.

'Bastard! Bastard! Bastard!'

The cat rushed behind Tiffany's legs as if knowing what was coming. And when it did, Tiffany understood why people called Dee 'Demon' and 'Devil' behind her back. She started tearing the room apart. Tiffany had thrown some mega wobbles in her time but she'd never kicked off like this. Dee's assault on the room left it looking like Buckingham Palace had moved to the North Peckham Estate. No way was Tiffany going to get in her face to try to stop her. She'd probably try to hack my head off with her bare hands, she thought. No, the best thing to do was let super storm Dee blow itself out.

Dee tore the stuffing from the sofa cushion; yanked pictures off walls; smashed the telly screen with the curtain rod. Not the fish tank . . . Tiffany could hardly bring herself to watch as Dee aimed the curtain pole at it . . . Thank God, Tiffany thought, relieved as Dee threw her makeshift weapon to the ground. Dee's attention had been caught by something. Tiffany followed her gaze and saw that it rested on a heart-shaped photo of a beaming Nicky back in his primary school days, wearing his uniform. Dee picked it up and wrapped her arms around it as she held it to her chest.

'John doesn't get it, you know,' Dee said quietly, the raging puff gone from her, keeping her back to Tiffany. 'Thinks that Marilyn's just a car, a hunk of shiny metal that I roll around in.' Something about her voice compelled Tiffany to move across the room and stand behind her. 'So many people told me I was going to be a nothing – do sweet FA with my life. I was going to prove every last one of them wrong. And do you know how I did it, babes? I started to stick my dreams on the wall. Got 'em out of magazines. The gaff I was going to live in; the clobber I was going to wear and . . .' Her voice caught with emotion. 'And the first time I ever saw a picture of a Pirano FS, my heart started racing like I'd just snorted some charlie. I just knew that if people saw me riding around in it I was going to get maximum respect.' Finally, she turned to Tiffany. The younger woman thought Dee would be all blood-shot eyes from crying, but her eyes were blazing. If Tiffany had been a Catholic, she'd have crossed herself and prayed for the soul of the scum who had made the terrible mistake of stealing Dee's car.

'No one,' Dee waved her finger, 'no one does this to me. That tea leaf is going to regret the day he ever stole one of my dreams.'

As soon as Dee heard her husband return she belted outside. Tiffany followed close behind.

'Have you found Marilyn?'

'No.' John was crouched, examining the drive where Dee's car had been parked.

'No? You've been gone two hours. What have you been playing at?' Then she noticed that his Range Rover was miss-ing. 'And where's your motor?'

John stood up and told her pointedly, 'It was hit by one of our neighbours. One of the neighbours *you* rang up and told to get on the road and look for your car. And the poor sod was too scared to say no.'

Dee pulled herself tall and got in his face. 'Where is it?'

John stared back. 'I don't know – he got away. But I do know this. The thief didn't break any windows to steal it, which means he's a pro and must have the contacts to sell it on. They're only half a dozen blokes in London with the front to nick that car and I know every one of them. I'll find it.' John's face hardened and he spoke with a chill in his voice that Tiffany had never heard him use before. 'Someone has had the brass balls to come into my house when my missus and boy are there? Everyone in the know knows you don't do that. I'm going to track him down.'

The sound of Dee's voice carried across the empty country-side. 'You better had, because if you don't, it won't just be my car you're looking for, it'll be a fucking good divorce lawyer.'

Forty-Seven

The next day Babs bashed her fist with such force on the front door of her new neighbours', she could have woken the dead at the local cemetery. 'Bloody open up or I'll bleeding kick the door in,' she shouted, even though she knew that would be pretty hard to do with the fluffy, rose slippers she wore, the ones she'd got from The Roman, from the bloke with a side-line in cannabis. The problem with The Devil now – like it needed any more problems – was that the council had decided to start housing what they called some of their more 'challenging' families on it. Challenging? More like head banging.

Babs' pounding had attracted the usual suspects – the nosey parkers on the landing and the twitchy curtain brigade, who liked to watch from within their four walls.

The door flew open and Babs was confronted by a woman who she knew as the mum of the house, except as far as she was concerned this idiot didn't know the first thing about parenting. Babs pointed her finger. 'Look, love, one of your boys was trying to break into my place when I got back from shopping. I saw the little bleeder from downstairs and he did a runner—'

'Shut the fuck up.' The woman's finger danced at Babs with every word she spoke.

'You what?' Babs reared her chest forward. Who the effing hell did this wannabe mummy bear think she was?

'You heard,' the other woman leaned right into Babs' space, practically foaming at the mouth. 'Piss off, off my doorstep. And don't you ever, EVER,' she yelled the last word, 'say shit about one of my boys again.'

Only when she got close to Babs did she realise that the mad moo's pupils were way bigger than God designed them to be. Her new neighbour was off her nut on drugs. Babs stumbled back. If there was one thing she'd learned in her years on The Devil, it was, stay well away from the druggies. They were so far gone they wouldn't even remember murdering you; they'd be sentenced by some judge who'd make sure they got rehab inside; and then, Bob's your uncle, they'd be back on the out in five, while you were still six feet under.

The crazy neighbour snarled, looked her up and down, gobbed a disgusting greenie at Babs' feet and then slammed the door.

'You wanna call the social on her,' someone yelled.

And then what? thought Babs instead of answering. The kids would end up in care and, as far as Babs heard it, there were rarely any happy-ever-afters for children in those care homes. Still, she couldn't be having no toddler toerags trying to rob her gaff. The next time it happened, she'd have to get some of the guys she knew to go around and have a quiet word or find out if the woman had any decent family to let them know what was going on.

'Mum, you alright?'

Babs' face lit up when she saw her two daughters coming along the landing.

'Yeah.' She kissed both her girls on the cheek. 'The new neighbour is off her head on God knows what. I saw one of her kids trying to abseil through my bathroom window like he's bleeding Spiderman.'

'You want me to have a word?' Tiffany asked already moving towards next door, but her mum caught her arm. 'Leave it alone. Those type of people always have trouble following them, so she and her witch brood will be on the move soon enough.'

After they got inside and Tiffany had dumped her gear in her room they all sat down for a brew in the sitting room. Babs had put a finger of gin in hers – alright a couple of fingers – not too much mind, just enough to keep her brain alert.

'I've got to get rid of Nuts,' Jen suddenly burst out. 'I can't do it anymore. The bastard has got to go.' Then the whole sorry mess poured out for Tiffany's benefit – the dinner money, the violence, the non-job. Babs' heart ached for her eldest. Who would've thought that nice Nuts would've turned into a geezer who used his fists as hammers once his front door was shut and stole his kids' dinner money.

Tiffany shoved herself to her feet. 'He's putting his hands on you?' She shook her head like she couldn't believe it. 'No fucking way. I'll teach him a lesson . . .'

Jen grabbed her arm and dragged her back. 'That isn't going to help. Sit down.'

As Tiffany retook her seat, she muttered, 'I tell you what, if a man laid a hand on me I'd fucking cut off his nuts and then come back later to do the same to his knob.'

'Come on, Tiff,' Babs said, 'you're meant to be making your sister feel better. It isn't Jen's fault her fella turned into Mike Tyson. Plus, let's get real, I doubt you've seen any man's family jewels with all that female company you keep touching up.'

Tiffany gave her mum a dirty grin with a teasing twinkle in her eyes. 'You want to come over to the dark side, Mum, you might enjoy it.'

Babs took a deep slug of her drink, like she had to wash her mouth out, just at the thought.

Jen let out a heavy sigh as she rubbed her palm against her forehead. 'Who would've thought it was going to be me who would make such a wreck of her life.' She caught her sister's eye. 'Ten years back, everyone said that I was going places and you were going to the dogs.'

Babs gripped one of her hands fiercely. She still couldn't believe that it was Jen who'd made a colossal cock-up of her life and not Tiffany. Tiff had been a train crash waiting to happen, but look at her now. Steady job, legit money in her pocket and a love life – although Babs would have wished it slightly different – that made her happy.

'That's the problem with life,' she told her daughter softly, 'you're on one path one day and the next you're on another, without understanding how you got there. The important thing is figuring out how to get back to where you want to be.'

'I just want him gone, Mum,' Jen said. 'All he ever brings to my door is a load of heartache. He slammed me into the wall the other day while the girls were in their bedroom and all I kept thinking was, what if they walk in? They'd be scared out of their bloody wits.' Jen shook her head, tears falling down her cheeks. 'I felt like total shit, total shit.'

'Fucker,' Tiffany let out between gritted teeth.

Babs grabbed Jen's other hand and squeezed. 'Maybe what we should do love is sit him down, explain the situation and maybe he'll get it and leave.' Even to Babs' ears, that sounded feeble. Men from Nuts' background didn't just up and leave after a bit of soul searching.

'Are you off your rocker, Mum?' Tiffany declared. 'The guy's strutting around The Devil like he's the dog's bollocks of Mile End, and you think he's just going to piss off, all peaceful like, thank you very much.'

'Well, come on then, Miss Clever Clogs,' Babs threw at her, 'what do you suggest Jen does?'

Tiffany made direct eye contact with her sister. 'I know it isn't the way we do things around here, but Jen could go to the authorities – tell them what he's doing. If you say he's hitting the girls, they have to do something. Child cruelty, ain't it?'

'No, no no.' Babs stood up. 'He'll find her and sort her out so that she won't ever do any talking ever again. I know women who've done it and, believe me, not many of them are around to tell the tale.' She moved over to the side-board and poured some more gin in her cup, a lot more this time. Once she was sat down again she continued, 'I know some people from the past. Faces. A couple owe me some favours . . .'

'You, Mum?' Jen sounded and looked scandalised. 'You know some dodgy people? Nah, never. You were always bleating on at us to walk across the street if we ever saw anyone like that coming our way.'

Babs flushed and there was something in her expression that neither of her daughters could place. She took a swig of her drink. 'I was a young girl too once. Made my share of mistakes long before your dad came along. Believe me, I made sure I made no more mistakes after Stanley did a bunk.'

Babs could see her girls looking at each other as if trying to square the image they had of their mum with the one she was giving them now. Bloody hell, if her Jen and Tiff ever found out about her past, she didn't know what she would do.

'The one mistake I never made,' Babs said, feeling choked up, 'was having you two. So I'll pull in some favours and get him bashed about a bit.'

'That won't work,' Tiffany shook her head. 'He'll just end up in the ozzie, get fixed up and, like some psycho homing pigeon, come back to Jen's. And if he gets a sniff that she was involved, who knows what the nutter will do.'

'It's just creeping me out,' said Jen. 'Every time I step foot in my place, knowing he'll either be there or about to come through the door.'

Tiffany's Nokia pinged with a text, so she checked it and then stood up. 'Look, I've got to go. I need to meet this kid I'm keeping an eye on for his parents. Get your brains into gear; we'll figure this out. There's more than one way to skin a cat.'

Forty-Eight

Nuts walked into his local boozer, The Old Swan (or The Knackered Swan as people on the estate called it, because it looked like it was standing on its last legs). He saw Kevin straight away at his usual spot, a small, round table in a corner, chatting on his mobile. His mate grinned as soon as he saw him and said into the phone, 'Catch you later, darling. Don't forget to warm my slippers by the fire.' With a chuckle he turned to Nuts. 'Where you been, my son, you've been a bit scarce.'

Nuts plonked himself down and smirked. 'Wouldn't you like to know?'

Kevin shuffled forward. 'You hiding something from your old mate?'

Nuts grinned back smugly. 'Let's just say I've got a little tickle – no, make that a big tickle – going. It's going to net me a pretty sum.'

Kevin didn't look pleased. 'You cutting me out? After everything I did for you while you were banged up in South London.'

''Course I ain't. Just something that came my way, lively like, and if there's one thing I am, it's a man of opportunity.'

Kevin still looked miffed, but Nuts wasn't about to blab about his potential good fortune. As far as he was concerned, he didn't owe his friend nish. Sure, Kev had made sure that Jen and the girls were taken care of while he was away and got him a few essentials through the back door of Brixton, but that didn't mean he had to tell him about every plump pie he had a finger in. Plus, if the truth be known, he was getting right fed up with his old friend. They had been knocking around together since he'd moved to The Devil and Kev was still talking about hitting the big time. You didn't talk it, you went out there and found it. That's what Nuts told himself he had done. This time he may have hit the jackpot.

'But what about that bizz I was telling you about, the one I said can open the doors for you?'

Here we go, Nuts thought, Kevvie boy singing the same tired tune about doors that swung open when he declared, 'Open sesame'. The problem was, Kev's doors turned into walls that got so high to climb they were dangerous.

'That's going to have to . . .' Nuts didn't finish as he eyeballed a group of women chatting away as they came through the door. They were young, fresh and with enough flesh on display to make Nuts forget he had a lady and kids waiting indoors. One in particular caught his eye. Now that's what you call a finger lickin' piece of meat. Colonel Sanders eat your heart out!

'I fancy my chances there.' And with that he swaggered over to the bar where the women gathered, not hearing Kevin whisper, 'You wish.'

'You alright, girls,' he presented himself. He kept his eye on the one he was interested in and dismissed what he considered to be the two trolls beside her. She couldn't be more than twenty, with buffed-out platinum-silver hair and legs that made him almost come just gazing at them.

'Nuts is the name ladies – not because I am nuts but because I've got lots of them.' He raised his eyebrows and winked. 'You know what I mean?' His signature chat-up line never failed to please. 'So, can I buy you a bevvy, love?' He flashed his teeth at Miss Long Legs.

She stared at him for a few seconds. 'I know you, don't I?'

Nuts puffed his chest out and then leaned cockily on the bar. 'I'm a name around here, you get me, a bit of a legend. People want anything done, especially with motors, I'm your man.' He leaned in. 'In fact, I've got a beauty of a ride that's got the right shade to go with your hair.'

'No, that isn't it,' she said. 'You've got two girls in Marshall Lane Primary School.'

Nuts straightened up. 'Nah, you must be getting me mixed up with some other fella.' He got cheeky again. 'Although I'll be your daddy anytime you say darlin'.'

She twisted her lips. 'You're Sasha's dad, or Little Bea as the other kids call her. Know how I know? Because I'm the teaching assistant in her class, Mr Taylor. Mr Lesley Taylor, that's who you are.'

Bollocks. Nuts made a swift exit towards Kevin, but that didn't stop him hearing what she said loudly to her friends: 'Word is, he was nicking Little Bea's dinner money.'

He almost did an about turn as his blood started to boil. He wanted to rip the tell-tale tongue out of her fucking head. Who did that blonde woof-woof think she was, coming into his boozer and batting her eyelids and dishing the dirt to any and everyone? He should grab her hair and drag her out the back and fuck the shit out of her until she moaned her arse off about him being boss. But he kept his thoughts and hands to himself; bashing up some woman in public was not a good look.

Kevin was creasing up with laughter when he got back to the table. 'Lesley? I thought you said your name was Leonard?'

Nuts wasn't about to explain how that name had haunted him through his early life, with the other kids taunting him with the nickname Lez.

'The dumb bimbo's got it wrong.'

He ordered a pint and thought of the day he'd be splashing cash all over the place when his deal came through. He wanted to see bitch teaching assistant's face then.

Tiffany ended her phone call with Jen and placed her mobile in her pocket as she approached the Blacks' house. She could hear Dee loud and clear before she reached the door. But couldn't hear John so it was like listening to one end of a phone conversation.

'My motor's been gone twenty-four hours already and you ain't got it yet? And the little bastard who stole it is still at large with both ears, both arms and both legs still attached? Call yourself a man? You useless twat. Some fucking gangland face you are – more like a garden gnome . . .'

Tiffany rang the bell. When Dee answered it, her contorted face managed a smile. 'Oh, hello, babes. You'll have to excuse me, I'm just having a domestic here with the old man.' She raised her voice and yelled over her shoulder. 'Of course I shouldn't need to raise my voice but when you've got a useless prick for a husband, you don't have much choice.'

She turned the volume down, to say to her part-time nanny, 'He's fucking useless. Don't you find men are a bit like dogs, babes? They need a kick now and again if you want them to go for a walk.'

John was sitting in an armchair with a mobile in one hand and a pencil in the other. He was scribbling in a notebook. Tiffany could see he had a list of names in it, some with ticks, some with crosses and some with question marks. He seemed to be about halfway down his list.

'You're sure about that are you?' he said into the mobile. 'He ain't been released early or anything? Alright, mate, thanks for your help.' John ended the call and turned to Dee. 'Do you think you could turn the abuse down when I'm on the phone to people? It's bad for business. I've got a reputation, remember?'

Dee was stalking the room, a drink in one hand, a ciggie in the other. She turned to Tiffany and scoffed, 'Hear that, babes? He's got a rep? Fuck me . . .' She looked back in anger at John. 'And did Ronnie Lemons steal my car?'

Her husband sighed wearily before he corrected her. 'His name is Lemmy Lemons.'

'I don't care if his name is Petticoat Lane Fruit and Veg Lemons, did he steal my effing car?'

'No, he didn't. That was his brother on the phone. Lemons is doing a stretch for possession with intent, so it can't have been him . . . Don't know how he got into that, high end car blags was always his thing.'

Dee wasn't interested in the suspect's career change. 'And how do you know Ronnie Lemons is in HMP? Have you checked? His brother could be stringing you along.'

'What would you like me to do? Pop up there on visitor's day? Would you like me to check his cell while I'm at it and see if he's dug a tunnel?'

Dee was seething. 'Don't get sarky with me cowboy or you'll feel the back of my hand.' She suddenly remembered Tiffany standing there. 'Oh, you wanna see Nicky, don't you, babes?' She went to the bottom of the stairs and screamed, 'Nicky – get your aris down here.'

John threw his phone, pencil and notebook down on the wooden floor and shouted at her. 'He hasn't come in from school yet.'

'Well, where is he then?'

John closed his eyes, held his fingers to his temples and pretended to communicate over the ether. 'Nicky, mate, come in, where are you?'

Dee picked up a crystal figurine from a table, raised her arm and aimed it at her husband. But when she caught Tiffany's eye she changed her mind and threw it at a wall where it crashed, shattering into glass shards, which showered the room. 'Find my Marilyn, you idiot!'

Somewhere in the house, a phone began ringing and John climbed out of his chair and went to answer it. Tiffany decided that, with no Nicky to look after, she might as well nanny his mum instead. She walked over, put her arm around the massively distressed Dee, and led her to the leopard print sofa where she refilled her glass and lit another fag for her. Tiffany made positive noises while Dee wailed that her marriage had been a terrible mistake and that John wasn't the man she thought he was. There were dark hints that John was going to have to go, and Nicky and she would now be reduced to poverty, but that she was strong and she would get through this. Looking around, Tiffany couldn't help thinking that, even without the figurine, poverty was going to be the least of Dee's problems.

When John returned to the room, he picked up his notebook, pencil and mobile. He was clearly waiting for Dee to ask him who'd been on the phone. When she didn't, he told her anyway. 'I've got a lead on the car. The person on the blower has put a name in the frame. And would you believe it? He's on my list of possible suspects, I just hadn't got to it yet. Even better, I know the bastard. He used to work for me. He's a definite probability for a job like this.'

Dee quickly forgot about divorce and poverty. 'Well, what are you waiting for? Go round and knock him about until he tells you where Marilyn is.'

John very deliberately drew a large circle around a name in his notebook. 'How little you understand of the ways of London's seedy underbelly, my dear. First, I have to make some enquiries and find his haunts and where he hangs out these days. He probably knows I'm after him already. Softly, softly, catchee monkey.'

To Tiffany, it looked as if John thought he'd done the work tracking his man down, so out of curiosity she went over to have a look at the highlighted name on the list. She stood frozen for a few seconds when she saw who it was, but said nothing as she stepped back.

'Now if you'll excuse me,' John continued, 'I have to pursue my enquiries as our friends down the station would say.' As he turned the handle on the room's door, Dee called after him. 'Who was this phone call from?'

John wrinkled his nose. 'I dunno, she didn't give a name. Some posh bird. But it'll be his best friend or his wife. They're the people who usually sell you out.'

Forty-Nine

Nuts splashed money around like a drunken sailor at Tommie's Snooker Hall off Chrisp Street Market in Poplar. He was a regular at the place where he liked to masquerade as a Cool Hand Luke figure with his mates. It was dark, quiet and had the advantage that few people knew he was a regular there. Plus it was a fanny free zone – no women allowed.

As Nuts lined up his shot, one of his mates slugged the double short that he'd been bought and wondered aloud, 'You had a win on the horses then, mate?'

Nuts held his finger to his lips and explained, 'Can't talk about it, except to say your man Nuts is back on the sunny side of the street.' Then he lined up his shot again, sending the cue ball down the table where it completely missed the green he'd aimed at. His mates were too happy drinking his booze to cry, 'Foul – and a miss.' But they couldn't stop themselves smirking. Nuts examined his cue but knew he couldn't blame that as it was a new one that he'd showed off to his friends earlier. Instead he turned to the manager and shouted, ''Ere Neville, I think this table's screwed. You need it rebalancing.'

Neville, who was told dozens of times a day that his tables needed fixing when a customer missed a shot, promised to look into it. Upset, Nuts propped his cue against a chair and told a fellow player, 'Take my turn for me, I need a leak.'

When he emerged from the gents, Nuts realised that Neville was a few paces away, having a quiet conference with two heavies that he'd never seen before.

He heard the manger tell one of them, 'Nuts ... ? I know the name but I can't put a face to it.' Neville threw the briefest of secret glances at him but that was enough to serve as a warning. Instead of returning to the table, he sauntered as casually as he could over to the bar where he took a swig from a drink that someone had left behind. Then, without looking round, he went down the stairs to the exit, hoping against hope that one of his mates didn't shout 'Oi, Nuts! Where are you going?'

He weaved through the market and then took a seat in the window of a café opposite the snooker hall, where he could keep watch on the door. Five minutes later, the two heavies who'd been looking for him emerged. They stood on the pavement whispering to each other for a while, looking at the tinted windows above. One of them made a call on his mobile and then they walked to a black Merc parked further down the road. For fifteen minutes they waited, keeping an eye on the entrance, before finally driving away.

Nuts carefully studied the street in both directions, then headed back across the road and up the stairs. As soon as Neville saw him, he hurried over, took Nuts by the arm and led him to his office.

'You're in big trouble, mate.'

Nuts tried but failed to play it cool. 'Why? Who were they?'

'They mentioned John Black's name and said they wanted a *word* with you.'

'Me? What the fuck does he want a word about? I ain't done nothing.'

Neville seemed nearly as worried as Nuts. 'They weren't saying – but I don't think the word they want to have with you is *peace*, if you know what I mean.'

'How did they know I was here? The reason I come to this joint is because no one knows I come here.'

Neville suddenly seemed in a hurry to have Nuts off his premises. 'I dunno. But you know how guys like John operate. If they want to find something out, they spread some money around and find it out. Seriously, mate, you'd better go; if I were you, I'd get in touch with John and get it sorted.'

Nuts threw his chest out. 'That's alright, I know John, I used to work for him. I'll give him a bell and find out what's what. Probably have a laugh with him about it.'

His bluster didn't convince Neville or himself. Nuts headed back to the tables, grabbed his jacket from a chair and headed towards the fire exit without saying anything to his friends. One of them called after him, 'Where you been, mate? Come on, bruv – don't sulk – we've all missed an easy green.'

But their bruv wasn't listening. He pushed the handle on the emergency exit door and fled down the fire escape outside. As he hurried away, to where he didn't know, he kept muttering, 'John Black? What the fuck? What the fucking fuck?'

Jen was woken up from a dream in which she was walking down the aisle with that dishy doctor from *Casualty*: the one with the sexy-hot hazel eyes who was a heart surgeon. Oh, how she needed a heart specialist in her life. She was woozy and squinted, groaning, as the intrusion of the bedroom light pierced her eyes. She shuffled up to find Nuts moving frantically around the room.

'What's the time?' Her voice was groggy. She checked the clock near the bed. 'It's bloody after two in the morning. What you doing?'

But he didn't answer her, just tore the suitcase down from the top of the wardrobe. He looked like shit. His face was stone white, his T-shirt stuck to his chest with sweat like he'd been running and his hair was sticking up in tufts at the front. He opened the case and flung open the doors of the wardrobe and started grabbing his clothes with such speed some of the wire hangers crashed to the floor.

'Nuts, what the effing hell's going on?' Jen flung her feet over the side of the bed and pushed down her imitation Jasper Conran, turquoise satin night-shirt. A dog was furiously barking outside and there was the faint sound of music coming from one of the other blocks. Typical Devil's Estate, it never sleeps.

As he dashed over to the chest of drawers, Nuts said, 'Has anyone been asking for me?'

Jen frowned as she stood up. 'Why would they?'

He sent her a quelling look. 'Just answer the question. Has anyone been looking for me?'

Jen's mouth settled into a grim line. 'You need to tell me what's going on?'

She got a grunt in reply, which royally ticked her off. He left the room and she followed him to the bathroom. He shoved his shaving gear into the suitcase.

'Where are you going?'

He finally answered her. 'I'm just going away for a few days. You know, I've got a bit of work on for that new job I told you about.'

Jen had to hold herself back from saying the job was as make believe as her winning the lottery. She folded her arms. 'What have you done now?'

'Leave off, Jen.' He brushed roughly by her and headed into the sitting room.

She marched after him. 'I told you that if you dragged trouble to my door again you're out. So you better start talking.' Close up she could smell a perfume she didn't like on him. 'You been with some scrubber?'

Jen was distracted by a whimper coming from the girls' room. Quickly she entered their room to find Courtney with her arms wrapped around Little Bea who looked like she was trying really hard not to cry. God, she hated this life. It brought too many memories of what life had been like with her dad, when she was little.

'Mum, what's happening?' Courtney asked, staring at her mother with her dad's eyes.

'Nothing.' She rustled up a smile for them. 'Just get back into bed and shut your eyes, yeah.'

She closed the door and nearly slammed into Nuts. 'I want the truth and I want it now.'

'All you say to anyone who's asking is that we've split up and you don't know where I've gone.' Then he headed for the door.

'And why would I say that?'

He threw the door open and looked back at her. 'I don't need a mouthful, alright. Just remember to say what I told you.'

A car screeched somewhere outside, another dog joined the early morning barking chorus; Nuts slammed the door, leaving Jen standing alone in her night-shirt.

'Mum, you alright?'

Jen turned to find Courtney standing in the doorway of her bedroom. The poor love was trembling. Jen went over to her, got on her knees and hugged her. 'Nothing to worry about, my little angel.'

'Is Dad going away again? Will he be gone for six months again, like before?'

Jen pulled back so that she could see her daughter's beautiful, small face. 'Your dad's got some special work on, which means he's going to be gone awhile. But I bet you, when he comes back he'll have a prezzie with him for you.'

That brightened up Courtney's face. There was a loud knock at the door.

'Bedtime, my girl.' Jen gave her daughter a quick peck on the cheek and closed the door behind her.

'Probably forgotten his friggin' keys,' Jen muttered to herself as she approached the door.

'Nuts . . .' she said as she flung the door wide, but the words dried in her mouth when she saw two big bruisers and a smaller man with a bald head standing between them.

The smaller man smiled. 'Is your husband in?'

Something about him just made Jen feel funny inside. Her hand held tight to the doorframe. She shook her head.

'My name's John Black and I want a word with him. Urgently.'

Fifty

The car was covered in so much straw, Tiffany had to use the wipers to clear the stalks off the windscreen. When she'd done so, she gently manoeuvred the vehicle down a dirt track and out onto a country lane. Ten years earlier, this job she was doing would have been all in a day's work for a teenage joy rider who got her kicks from taking extreme risks. Ten years on though, she was a very worried young woman. There were so many things that could go wrong with the act she was about to commit. She drove quickly, out onto the lane at the bottom of the road, and moved off before she had the time to throw the car into reverse and give up on the whole idea.

She looked at her watch. Almost three in the morning. The roads would be deserted which was good, but for any traffic that was around, she'd stand out like a sore thumb, which was bad. If that traffic included a solitary police car with nothing to do but pull cars over, she was sunk. On the passenger seat was an A–Z of Essex on which she'd traced a route with a marker pen. On top of the book was a torch. The path she'd chosen included just about every quiet side road in the county and doubled the length of her journey. But she was sure it was worth it.

About ten minutes after she'd set off, she had a bad omen. As she glided down the road at a steady twenty, she saw a fox crossing in her headlights. The animal stopped halfway and stared at her. She drew to a halt and it craned its neck examining her car. A few moments later, wagging its head, as if in disbelief and amazement at her nerve, it disappeared into a hedgerow. It seemed, even the local wildlife knew what Tiffany was up to and they didn't approve.

At every junction in these Essex Badlands, she slowed the car, examined her map and kept her fingers crossed she was going the right way. At every signpost, she stopped for reassurance that she was moving in the right direction. But slowly and surely she became confident that she would reach her destination.

Tiffany picked up speed and began to enjoy her ride. The car was sumptuous, with a seat that seemed to shape itself around her and caress her body. The pedals and steering responded to every light touch and seemed to know what she wanted to do before they were told. But as she lay back and whispered, 'Ah, this is the way to travel,' she felt her guts tighten as a warm red glow appeared on her dashboard. In disbelief, she picked up her torch, hoping against forlorn hope that it was telling her the temperature in Monaco or somewhere a car like this would be driven. But there was no doubt. On a deserted country road in the middle of nowhere, she was running out of petrol.

'Oh fuck ...'

She brought the car to a halt in front of the gate to a farm and checked her map. She had no idea how much further she could get without filling up and no idea where she could get petrol. She picked up her A–Z. The A13 was about ten miles further to the south. That was a main road and there was bound to be a twenty-four hour station there. But on a main road, there would be other cars and possibly the Bill. Worst of all, the car might grind to a halt, leaving her isolated and exposed in the last place she would want to be stranded.

'Oh hell.'

Tiffany put the car back into gear, drove off and began to look for the next side road heading south. As she went, she tried to keep her foot as light as possible on the accelerator and from time to time the red glow would dim and vanish before reappearing. The glow became steady and then deepened. The roads became wider and two-laned; houses appeared and street lamps began to shine. She found a slip road down to the A13 and she joined it, anxiously scanning her rear-view mirror for any sign that she was being followed.

At first the car seemed more relaxed now that it was going at a decent speed but Tiffany's eye-line kept drifting from the road ahead to the red glow on the dashboard. It looked to her as if it was turning the colour of blood.

'Come on, baby, come on . . .' and then, 'Don't they have petrol stations on this soddin' road . . . ?' The car seemed to be caught by surprise when the first signs that the abrupt end of its journey was about to happen. It coughed and spluttered before resuming its steady pace. The engine juddered slightly. Tiffany was running on fumes. A sign went by. '24 Hour . . . Ahead . . . One Mile . . .'

She began to plead with the car. 'Please, baby, give me another mile, I'll love you forever . . .'

The car responded and did its best, like an exhausted long distance runner trying to crawl over the line. Tiffany begged the car, 'Please, please . . .' The lights of the petrol station appeared and she turned onto the slip road. But the engine was spent; it cut out and went with the pumps in view, gliding to a halt. Tiffany paused slightly because while she wasn't turning the ignition there was still hope. She turned the ignition and was met with silence. 'Please, please . . .' The car was a

luxury one and soft-hearted. With one final effort, it spluttered back into life and gave Tiffany the final fifty yards she
needed before dying for good as she pulled up by a pump.

The station was deserted, apart from a solitary man in the
kiosk and two police officers resting on the bonnet of a patrol
car in a parking bay, drinking coffee and eating sandwiches. It
seemed to Tiffany that the vehicle she was driving was now
very large, very obvious and very, very suspicious. The two
boys would have been advised to keep an eye open for it and
the car was the type that was likely to stick in their memory.
She pulled fifty quid out of her purse and went to fill up.

As the petrol gushed into the thirsty tank, Tiffany could
hear the voices of the two cops chatting.

'That's right – John Black of all people . . . His missus'
motor . . . Don't know what make it is . . .'

'Black? Fuck me, if I'd done that, I'd be on a plane to South
America by now.'

Tiffany shook the last drops from the pump and went to
pay. As the guy on the kiosk took her money, he admired her
car. 'Nice motor.'

She said nothing, just took her receipt with the key gripped
so tightly in her hand it was digging into her fingers. She carefully avoided looking at the police as she headed to the car,
but she noticed that they'd stopped chatting. When she got
back into the driver's seat, she stole a glance. One of the cops
was standing with his arms folded, staring at her with a beady
eye. She started the engine but it wouldn't fire. She knew it
would take some time for the fuel to feed through. She gave a
brief look at the police. Now the other cop was standing next
to his colleague, sipping coffee and staring in the same direction. She turned the ignition. It failed. She looked again. One
of the cops was speaking into his radio. These were turning
into long moments. She didn't need to turn a third time; she

could see the police were approaching her out of the corner of her eye.

'Come on, treacle, you've been so good . . .'

The engine started. Wheels spinning, Tiffany sped out of the station onto the road. In the rear-view mirror, she could see the cops running back to their car. Out on the main road, any speed she asked of the engine, it supplied without any apparent effort. She went up to a hundred, a hundred and ten and then a hundred and twenty, flying down the empty road. For a brief time she could see the revolving blue lights in her mirror but then they vanished, never to reappear. Speed cameras merrily flashed to record her progress but she figured by the time any tickets were delivered, her problem would be resolved, one way or another.

It took her only fifteen minutes before she was in a scruffy suburb of Southend. She found her way to a small garage that was owned by someone she knew as absolutely discreet. She opened the gates and drove into a lockup at the rear of the premises. Before she turned the key on the door and headed down to the station to catch the first train back to London, she ran her hand over the bodywork which was as smooth as velvet. Daylight was starting to appear in the sky.

She smiled broadly.

She totally understood why Dee loved this car.

Fifty-One

John used his large hand to push Jen's door back. 'You don't mind if I come in, love, do you? The boys will wait outside. They're good like that. I'm sure there's going to be no unpleasantness anyway.'

Jen stumbled back. There was no violence in what he did but his every action was soaked in menace.

'He's not here,' Jen called out lamely as he pushed past her into the sitting room. She hurried after him.

It was an age before John spoke. 'No, I guessed not . . . But you know where he is, don't you?'

Jen didn't reply, her fingers madly fluttering at her side. He was inspecting the ceiling. He breezed around her sitting room as if taking a relaxed walk along the beach, picking up ornaments then carefully placing them back down. He peered behind the sofa, as if that might supply a clue as to where Nuts was.

Terrified, Jen took a deep breath and finally replied. 'No, I don't. We split up ages ago. He moved out. He's living with some tart up north.'

John put a vase down – the one her mum had given her as a house warming present – and turned to her. 'Dearie me, I hope you're not teaching your children to lie when they're in a tight spot, especially when a little honesty would pay everyone dividends.' He moved over to the window and opened it, looking down onto one of the long dark courtyards of The Devil's Estate. The wind rustled the ragged net curtains and, in the distance, music pumped from one of the blocks on the other side of the estate. From below, the sound of a youth being taunted by other boys could be heard and in the middle distance, from another open window, a woman was screaming. 'Don't hit me, you cunt, don't you fucking hit me . . .'

As if the sounds from the estate had served his purpose, John pulled the window shut. He turned back to Jen. 'How did a nice-looking girl like you end up with a prick like Nuts on a place like this? I don't get it.'

Jen said nothing, not least because it was a question she'd often asked herself. Slowly, John moved from the living room into the kitchen where he opened and closed a few drawers before he went into her and Nuts' bedroom. Jen followed, breathing deeply as she went. Her visitor had opened the wardrobe and was examining the men's shirts that were hanging there. There was a gap between them where Nuts had grabbed some when he'd fled.

'Nice shirts. Mind you, your Nuts always had an eye for a style. I remember that from when he worked for me. I called him Knobby for knob head back then.' Jen's eyes widened; finding out her fella had once worked for this criminal was news to her.

His voice veered over into sarcasm and he showed a shirt sleeve to her. 'I'm assuming he left these here when he ran off with the skirt from up north? Is that right? Or have you moved in another geezer with a taste for Hugo Boss shirts in the meantime?'

Jen was too scared to open her mouth. Then she caught two pairs of eyes staring at them through a crack in the door. Oh hell, the girls. She hurried over and found her daughters white faced, with Courtney holding her sister tight to her side. Jen faked a smile and said as gently as she could, 'Come on, girls, you're supposed to be in bed.'

They ignored her, their gaze fixed on the stranger. Jen's heart jumped when she felt John beside her.

He gave them a friendly wave and a grin. 'Sorry to disturb you, little ladies. I'm a very good friend of your dad's so I've popped round to see how he's doing but he seems to be out. Sorry, I know I'm a bit late . . .'

Horror ran through Jen. She didn't want him anywhere near her kids. She wanted to yell and scream at him to get away from them, but she didn't. That would only make the situation worse; much worse. So she thrust an arm around each of her children and lifted them up just like she had when they were younger.

'Mum . . . ?' Courtney started, looking over her shoulder at the strange man in her home as her mother motored towards their room.

'Be quiet,' Jen said severely. She hated the tone she was using, but she couldn't allow – wouldn't allow – her girls to be anywhere near that man.

As soon as they were in the bedroom she got them into their bed and pulled the duvet up around their necks and kissed them both on the forehead. 'Now go back to sleep.'

Courtney's voice was harsh. 'Where's my dad? Has that man really come to help look for him?'

Jen grasped at the straw she'd been thrown by her daughter. 'That's right, he's come to help find your dad – now go to sleep.' Her tone softened. 'Please, baby, just do it. Please.'

Closing the door firmly behind her, Jen found John sitting in Nuts' armchair. Her fear had gone, now she was angry. She hissed, 'You're a big man, aren't you? Scaring little girls in the middle of the night.'

John looked hurt, but she knew different. 'That's a nice thing to say, ain't it? I'm not here to scare anyone: not you, not even Nuts and certainly not your kids. Look love, I don't know what cock 'n' bull story your husband told you before he skipped town, but let me put you in the picture. Nuts has stolen something from me and I want it back. I don't know if he knew it belonged to me or not, and it doesn't really matter. So, the next time he gives you a little tinkle on the blower, tell him I popped round and if I get my property back in one piece, we can call it a day and have a good laugh about it.'

His voice and face turned hard. 'Tell him if he doesn't, then obviously I'll be left with no option but to tear London apart looking for him and, if that doesn't work, then I might have to consider scaring a few people. You know what I mean? But it shouldn't have to come to that, should it? I mean seriously – should it?'

Jen's anger had drained away and she now realised the full enormity of what had happened. 'Look, I don't know where he is; I don't know anything about any property and, if I had my way, I'd never see Nuts again. Now, please, leave me and my children alone. I thought you people had rules about that?'

John nodded and grimaced. 'Well, we do of course. But I'm afraid this situation is rather unusual . . .' He stood up. 'If he calls, tell him he's not in trouble, I just want the car back. If I don't get it back, then he'll be in trouble . . . as will other people.' He looked in the direction of the girls' bedroom. Jen tensed again.

He picked up a takeaway flyer lying carelessly chucked on the low-level glass coffee table. He took out a pen and wrote on the back of it, then put it back down. 'Nuts comes back, you call me, love. Because believe me, you wouldn't want me to come around again and ask your daughters this time.'

A stunned Jen walked a few paces behind him as he headed for the front door. He opened it as one of his boys yelled over the landing at a group of youths loitering near John's car. Once they heard the words 'John Black' they scattered.

John looked on, depressed, and turned back to Jen. 'Honestly, what a dump. If I was you, Jennifer, I'd consider moving. But obviously, don't do it before this sorry affair is settled. You keep in touch – OK?'

As soon as he'd gone, the girls opened their bedroom door and flew into Jen's wide-open arms. She hugged and kissed them tightly, still hearing the click of the door. That's what terrified her the most, that John Black hadn't slammed it, just closed it with a quiet but determined purpose. This was a man who wasn't giving up.

'It's going to be alright, everything is going to be alright,' she repeated over and over.

'Wait for me in the car, lads,' John ordered his crew as soon as they got downstairs.

He wasn't finished with The Devil's Estate yet. The whole place made him feel dirty. It stank to high heaven of desperation, of people trying to claw their way up from a cesspit they were never going to get out of. Worst of all, it brought back all those memories of him growing up in an overcrowded two-bed in Bethnal Green. And now he was on his way to visit someone who would make the stench of that past even stronger.

Five minutes later he was banging at the door in another block on the estate.

'Sod off,' came an irate female voice. 'If you're the Bill, he ain't here. He ain't lived here for years, so whoever's grassing him up is well out of date.'

'If I was the coppers I wouldn't be knocking, you stupid bint. I'd have the door on its hinges by now.'

'Charlie?' Her voice was excited now and she soon had the door wide open.

Of course she would use his real name, being one of the few people who knew it. John waltzed in past Melanie Ingram and wished he hadn't. The place smelt of stale fags, days-old rubbish and a disgusting odour that could've been the stain of beer or puke.

'Fuck, Mel,' he said with disgust as he placed a hand over his nose, 'you reek like a wino.'

No one would guess in a million years that he and Mel had grown up together and once stepped out together. She'd been real easy on the eyes back in those days, all feather soft, black hair, smooth skin and a body a man would cut out his heart for. All the local lads had fought tooth and nail to be the one to be seen on her arm. She'd been a right goer in the sack too, with legs that could twist around him like string and boobs that could crush him to blissful death. Now look at her: worn out, fat and, as he saw it, a downright disgrace to the memory of the girl she'd once been.

'Yeah well,' she hit back at him, 'my shit don't smell like Chanel anymore since my Mickey got banged up in your car ringing screw-up.'

'That was years back. Mickey got done because he's a one hundred per cent dickhead. Anyway, he's been out for donkey's. It isn't my fault he didn't come back to you and found a new bird to live it up with, in Portugal.'

'I'll make us a cuppa,' she said, showing her tobacco-stained teeth.

He shook his head. 'I'm not stopping.'

She looked at him and fluttered her eyelashes. 'That isn't what you used to say, when you couldn't wait to get me to drop my knickers.'

John suspected if she did, he'd be gagging from the smell. He put his hand in his pocket and pulled out a brown envelope and passed it to her. 'There's a couple of grand there. I want you to spread it around the estate. I want you to keep an eye on the comings and goings of Nuts Taylor's missus. Anyone hear anything or clap eyes on that ponce Nuts, they're to pass the info up to you and you let me know.'

No one had to tell John the type of place The Devil was – filled with toerags ready to sell their kids for the right money. Chuck some cash around and it wouldn't be long before he had Nuts good and tight by the balls.

'The fucking Millers,' she swore. She puckered her dry lips as if she was going to spit. 'If my Stacey had never got mixed up with their girl, she'd never have gone on the needle.' Her voice broke. 'She's letting any Tom, Dick or Harry stick it up her to get her next fix.'

What a total fuck up she's made of her life, John thought, looking around. How could that beautiful girl have come to this? He was sorry about what had happened to her girl, but if he'd been living in this hellhole he'd probably be banged out of his head on H as well.

'What's Nuts done?'

'That's my business. Just get the dosh flying and the tongues wagging.'

As he reached for the latch on the door he heard her say, 'It's going to cost you.'

John slowly turned back to her and stared into her greedy little eyes, seeing only the funny, laughing girl he remembered. 'Take what you need, Mel.' He almost told her to use it to get this fleapit cleaned up, but it wasn't his business. His business was finding that scum who'd taken his wife's car.

'You'll come back, won't you, John?' said his one-time girl-friend. 'We'll have a proper cuppa then. Talk about old—'

But John had opened the door and closed it firmly behind him.

Fifty-Two

On Saturday morning John found Nicky and Dee in the gym at the back of their house. Dee was furiously pumping a cycle machine with earphones on while Nicky was sitting on a bench, resting between sets, although his workout seemed to consist mainly of all rests and no sets. It appeared to John that he was even more sullen than the day before. Banshee sat admiring her mistress's workout as she sat curled near the treadmill.

Pausing only to take off her earphones, and without breaking stride or looking at him, Dee demanded, 'Where have you been? You didn't come home last night.' Her pedalling speeded up with fury. 'You better not have been shafting some slag.'

As if. Her demands in the bedroom department didn't leave him anything in the tank to spread around. 'Don't talk crap, Dee, you know what I've been doing.'

'Have you found it?'

John flinched slightly before saying, 'No.'

'Have you found him?'

'No.'

Dee's exercise became even more furious. 'I don't suppose you managed to find your way to their rat hole of a flat? Or did you lose your way?'

John felt he had something positive to report, by way of consolation for not finding the car. 'Yeah, I found my way. I saw the wife.'

Dee slowed her pace and mopped her brow with her sweat-band. 'And? Bloody well spit it out.'

John folded his arms. 'Do you do anything, except workout, primp and preen yourself and sit around eating chocolates all day? I mean, how about I give you the money and you open a little antique shop in the village – get yourself out of the house now and again?'

The wheels on Dee's bike slowed and stopped. 'Yeah – or, you could carry on just giving me the money and we'll skip the antique shop part. How about that?' She climbed off her bike. 'Does the wife know where he is?'

'She says not.'

Dee jumped out of her pram again. 'She's lying.'

John shook his head. 'I don't think so. The boy's not going to tell her that anyway, is he? He's not that stupid.'

Dee suggested, 'He was dumb enough to steal my ride. And he'll be in touch with her to find out what's going on. Why don't you tap her phone?' Then she shrank slightly and John got the distinct impression that she wished she hadn't said that.

'He won't say anything on the blower; he's not that stupid either. Nah, I reckon the best bet for now is to keep an eye on the family. She'll pass on the message that I want a word, and if he don't cough up, we'll have to think about putting on the pressure another way. He's got a couple of little girls. No father's gonna be able to withstand that kind of pressure, even a no-mark like him.'

Dee was shocked. 'He's got two girls? You never told me that.' Then she was angry. 'And you went around there in the middle of the night, frightening the bejabbers out of them?

What's the matter with you, you stupid animal? Right, you'll have to think of something else. I'm not having kids being scared out of their little jim-jams.'

John waved his hands in the air. 'I give up, I really do.'

He sometimes wondered if the answer to his domestic problems was to turn himself into a cat or a kid. It seemed to him that all her hatred and anger against the adult world was a mirror image of her sugary softness for children and pets. And not just pets either. After the appearance of a mouse in the kitchen, he'd bought a battery of traps from a local DIY store. Dee had thrown them all in the bin, reminding him that mice were innocent creatures that did no one any harm. When John agreed but suggested that didn't mean he wanted them eating his dinner either, he was called a murderer for his trouble.

'I'm not going to harm his kids, am I? I won't need to anyway. I'll find him, I know all about this guy. I told you, he used to work for me. Went by the name of Knobby in those days . . .' John was suddenly alarmed by the look on his wife's face. 'Are you alright, bird? You look like you've had a bit of a turn.'

Dee wiped her sweatband along her cheeks, looking down. 'Of course I'm alright, I just want my Marilyn back.'

John gestured at Nicky and whispered, 'What's the matter with him? He's in a right strop.'

Dee whispered back, 'I think he's got the hump because Tiffany said she was coming around this morning and hasn't put in an appearance. I don't know where she's got to; I'll have to remind her who's paying her wages. Poor boy's probably got a crush on her or something – not that it will go anywhere. She likes her bedmates with a bit on top and a bush downstairs, you get me? He'll get over it.'

John had been saving his most interesting revelation for last. 'Which reminds me, there's another bit of news I've got about the guy who pinched your car that you might be interested in.'

In the morning light, as Jen marched across the estate to the Old Swan, she bumped into Bex. Her best mate looked very pleased with herself, her flesh squeezed tight into a black number that looked like a thick elastic band and her face made up from chin to hairline. Shame about that awful perfume she still wore.

'Where you off to?' Jen asked. 'Your new fella taking you for a spin?'

Bex gave her head a breezy, little twirl like she was a teen going on her first date. 'Nowhere special, just enjoying life.'

Lucky bitch. Wish I had a fella who treated me like Madonna and Whitney all rolled into one.

'So when are we going to meet Prince Charming?'

Bex lifted her shoulders. 'He's a bit shy. He's still getting used to being around these parts—'

'Well, that will be some getting used to. I'm looking for Nuts—'

The smile fell from the other woman's face. 'What's up? He hasn't walloped you again?'

Jen didn't have the time for talking, so she started motoring away and, over her shoulder, threw out, 'We'll chat when I've got time.'

It was a real shame she didn't have the time to talk because she could do with chatting her problems through with her bestie. Other people might've come and gone from her life, but not Bex. Bex had been a real rock to her through some of the rough patches, especially during those periods when Nuts got banged up. And her flat had always been a safe haven for her and girls to flee to if Nuts' fist were getting a bit too leery.

As soon as Jen reached the Old Swan she banged hard on the closed door. 'Open up.'

No answer. She wasn't budging until someone opened the flippin' door. Eventually Jacko, the landlord, opened up.

'He ain't here,' was what he told her.

'And if he was, would you tell me?' She barged past him.

She wasn't surprised to see a small group of people inside. The Old Swan was one of those boozers that had a lock but never really closed its doors. In fact, much of its money was made after hours. The topless ladies wrapped around men's necks told her all she needed to know about how it had been raking in extra cash after the last orders bell had rung. Jen didn't see Nuts but she did see his friend Kevin. One of the women was sat on his lap, his fingers treating her nipples like he'd just discovered sweeties for the first time. As she moved closer she realised that the woman was Stacey Ingram. Jen could've wept at the state of her: eyes glazed over, ribs on display and track marks trying to hide under the layers of powder she'd coated on her arms.

'You want to be ashamed of yourself, you do,' Jen savagely chucked at him. 'How can you even think about having it off with her when she's in such a state?'

Kevin squeezed his hands deeper into Stacey's breast. 'It's supply and demand, Jen girl. I'm supplying it, she's demanding it.' He laughed like the situation was the best joke in town.

'Oh yeah? Your Sharon know where your wick's dipping when you ain't indoors?'

That got the smile wiped off his face. By this stage, everyone else was looking at them.

'Hop it.' Kevin patted Stacey's arse and she staggered towards the bar, obviously totally out of it. 'If you're looking for Nuts, I don't have a clue where he is.'

Jen looked him up and down. 'Don't believe you. You two are like Siamese twins. I need to see him now.'

Kevin suddenly noticed all the eyes on them and puffed out his chest like he was the man of the house. 'Who the soddin' hell do you think you are, coming in here and mouthing off at me?' He stood up so suddenly his chair fell backwards and whacked onto the floor. 'I wouldn't blame Nuts if he did do a runner. All you do is give him grief morning, noon and effing night. A man should be able to get peace in his own home.'

Jen's face went hot. 'That low-life was the worst thing that ever happened to me. You come and talk to my girls about the type of peace they've had since their dad got home–'

'That's on you, Jen,' he cut in. 'He said you wouldn't even bring them to visit him this time around.' He stepped menacingly towards her. 'No wonder he has to slap you around–'

'Don't you fucking touch her,' a voice yelled. Jen and everyone else looked around to see a furious and shaking Stacey at the bar. 'You lay one hand on her and I'll . . .' She picked up a bottle and threw it at Kevin's head. He ducked just in time and the bottle crashed against the wall behind him. Stacey went mad, totally out of control, picking up glasses and ashtrays and pelting them as she screamed blue murder at Kevin. Jacko finally reached her and wrapped his arms tight around her as he lifted her off the floor.

'Get your hands off me, you dirty bastard, you filthy . . .' Her curses flew as she kicked her legs in the air, only stopping when Jacko shook her so hard her head snapped one way and then the other. And then, as if she were in a dream, she flopped silent in his arms.

Jen was shaken and as stunned as the silence all around her. That poor girl needed help. Tiffany would be heartbroken if she ever heard about this.

'Piss off, Jen,' Kevin snarled at her.

But Jen didn't even hear him; she just kept looking at her sister's one-time best friend and felt an incredible sadness that such a girl's life could have ended up like this. Jacko let her go and Stacey stood there like a block of ice.

'Stacey,' Jen said, with her mum voice on, 'I'm taking you to your mum's.'

Stacey's lip curled as she shook her head. Jen walked over to her and knowing that Stacey wasn't going to leave with her, she did the one, decent thing she could do – she placed her jacket over the younger woman to cover her chest.

Then she turned to Kevin and pointed her finger at him. 'You tell Nuts that I want him home.'

As she turned to leave, out of the corner of her eye, she saw Kevin walk over to Stacey, cruelly grab one of her breasts and use his hold on her to drag her out towards one of the back rooms. By the time she got outside Jen thought her head was going to burst. Sometimes living around here just did her head in. If one of her girls ended up like Stacey, she'd die. There was nothing she could do for the junkie she'd left inside. She couldn't open her trap to the authorities to try and get her some help; you didn't do that type of stuff on The Devil, you took care of your own. Sadly, Stacey wasn't one of her own.

Jen's mobile started ringing dragging her away from Stacey Ingram.

'Yes?'

'It's Nuts.'

The Old Swan's landlord, Jacko, went around the back after signalling for the tarts he'd hired to get back on with their work – doing what they needed to do to get the blokes to buy the overpriced drinks. He pulled out his mobile and contacted Mel and, only after she'd guaranteed him two hundred, told her what went down in his pub.

* * *

'Where the bloody hell are you?' Jen blasted Nuts as she took their conversation to a spot behind one of the concrete walkways so that no one could hear them.

'Calm down, Jen—'

'Don't you flippin' well tell me to calm down. Do you know what happened last night when you left?' She didn't let him answer. 'Some man called John Black and his two not-so-nice friends came around and frightened the stuffing out of your kids.'

'What? Bloody hell.'

'You better tell me what's going on?'

She heard him take a deep breath. 'I didn't do it, Jen—'

'Do what?'

'I swear on my daughters' lives that I never nicked his wife's motor.'

Jen switched the phone to her other ear in her agitation. 'You leave my girls out of this. I told you what would happen if you started tea leafing again—'

'But I didn't do it.'

'How many times, how many ...' She drew in a harsh breath realising she was shouting. In a quiet, but still furious tone, she continued, 'You're a complete ponce, that's what you are. Always lying, never keeping your hands to yourself. Courtney and Little Bea were terrified out of their minds. I can't be dealing with this anymore.'

'Listen, Jen, I'm telling you straight up that John's got it all wrong—'

'John? What, don't tell me you know this geezer.' She played it like John Black had never told her about his previous association with her fella. She wanted Nuts to sweat.

'It was years back. I did a bit of work for him. He owned that posh club I took you to the first night we met. Remember, that black bird who spilled a drink on me? Well she's his missus now and a bit of a livewire.'

'Oh, so not only do I have to look over my shoulder for some major league Face but also his crazy old girl. You've really put us in the shit now, you top wanker. Where are you?'

'Scotland.'

'Scotland? What the hell are you doing up there?'

'Jen I needed to put as much distance as possible between me and John and Dee.' He paused. 'Maybe I should come back—?'

'No, you can't do that. I might think that you're a complete and utter wally, but they're going to do you if you set foot anyway near The Devil. That John Black really means business.' She shuddered. 'He said if he sees you you're a dead man.'

After Kevin had roughed her up and done things to her body she tried hard not to remember, a tear-stained Stacey contacted her mum about Jen's appearance in the Old Swan. Her mum reassured her that she'd done good and the fifty was on its way for her next fix.

Fifty-Three

Dee spotted her mum at their usual table inside the small café tucked away behind Bank Station. They met there because it was out of the way and no one they knew was likely to notice them. Christina Aguilera's 'Beautiful' played softly in the background.

'You look awful, love,' her mum said as soon as she sat down and pulled off her shades.

Dee still wasn't sure sometimes how she felt about this woman opposite her. Most of the time she was happy to see her, but there was still that piece of her, leftover from childhood, that couldn't understand how a woman could give her infant away. You're carrying a defenceless baby for nine months and then, just like that, you turn your back and go on your merry way. How could someone do that? That would be like Dee not giving an eff about what happened to Nicky when his dad disappeared. It just wasn't natural – not natural at all. But this woman held some kind of control over her because, whatever she might think, it was Dee who just couldn't turn her back and walk away.

'Things are a bit bonkers at the mo,' Dee answered.

Her mum's hand covered hers. 'Tell me all about it; I'm a good listener.'

So Dee told her about what had happened to Marilyn, but didn't mention any names. 'Mum I just want to go out there and find the fucker and choke him until he stops breathing.'

Dee only knew that her voice had got louder when she caught the disapproving look of a woman – one of the two, smartly dressed city workers, seated at a table nearby.

'What?' she challenged the women. 'What you looking at? You never seen a black woman before? And yeah, the woman sitting with me at my table is my mum and she's white. You got something to say about it?'

'Dee,' her mum warned, trying to restrain her.

But her daughter shook her head. 'No, Mum,' Dee waved her finger in the air once. 'I'm fed up with this. I've worked my arse off to be able to come to a place like this and just have a cup of tea without two twats who look like Princess Margaret with a broom shoved up her rear end thinking they've got the right to cut their eyes at me.' Dee leaned towards them: 'Boo!'

Both women rushed to their feet, left money on the table and were gone. Dee wasn't surprised when the owner came over, a middle-aged man with a moustache like a matinee idol.

'Ladies, I will have to—'

Dee slapped a ton on the table, which had the man smiling and shuffling off.

'You know what you need?' her mum said softly. 'You need a bit of prepping up. Something to make you feel better.'

'The only way I'm feeling top of the morning again is when my Marilyn is back home.'

Her mum smiled nervously. 'Why don't I come over tomorrow for lunch? We can have a girls' afternoon in.'

They were both silent because they knew that another line in their relationship would be potentially crossed. Dee had never been to her mum's and her mum had never been to hers. John knew all about her and had no problem with meeting her mother; it was Dee who had the problem. Letting someone into your home was really personal. She didn't know if she was ready to let her mum come through that door yet.

'I've never met your fella or your boy, it would be good to finally see them.'

There was such a yearning in her mum's voice that Dee knew she wasn't going to be able to say no.

'Nicky's my grandson, I'd be tickled to give him a hug.' Dee had told her mother all about how Nicky had come into her life and that it didn't matter that she hadn't given birth to him; he was her son.

'Alright,' Dee finally decided slowly. 'I'll get a lovely, slap-up lunch sorted. But don't think this means you can waltz into my house anytime you like.'

Her mum covered her hand again. 'I love you, Dee.'

Dee looked at her sadly. 'I just wish you'd been there to say that when I was a little girl.'

The dirty pictures on the wall of the locker room in the garage didn't even make Tiffany blink. Having porn pushed up in her face every day had narked her when she first came to work here as a teenager, but she'd long ago got used to working in an all-male workplace. They might as well have been snaps of Snow White for the effect they now had on her. She quickly put on her overalls, having just returned from a spot of lunch. For once she wasn't pissed that she was working on a Saturday because her mind was consumed with thoughts of Dee Black's motor. What she had allowed herself to get into still made her shudder. If John and Dee ever found out . . . No, they weren't going to find out. They couldn't find out. If they did, she was a goner for sure.

As soon as she entered the work room, Big Ron – Richie's eldest son or, in Tiffany's books Tweedle Dumb Arse – crooked his finger her way, signalling for her to come over. Big Ron was in fact a small man with a bald head and a very big mouth, which he exercised way too frequently for Tiffany's liking.

'You heard about what went on with John Black's missus' ride?'

Tiffany played it all innocent, shaking her head. She hadn't let on to him or his brother that she was working for the Blacks. 'Who's John Black? Never heard of the geezer.'

He gazed at her as if she were from a planet that hadn't yet been discovered. 'That's Mister Black to you, girlie. Let's just say he's a bit of legend in these parts. Anyway, the story goes that some idiot nabbed his wife's motor right from under his nose. Whoever the fool is, John's gunning for them.'

Tiffany couldn't help but swallow. 'What's that got to do with me?'

'If anyone tries to ship a classic Pirano FS in here during out of hours, you let me know.'

Tiffany stuck her hands in her overall pockets. 'Out of hours? Didn't think you and Little Sam did any of that crap in here. That's the first thing Richie told me when I came here: he says, I only do wheels that are above board.'

She took some delight in seeing Big Ron's face going beet-root red. He must think he was dealing with a wanker if he thought she didn't know about the secret, tax-free and highly illegal business he and his brother were also running.

''Course I didn't mean us,' he threw in quickly. 'But this guy has got to be desperate because that motor is as hot as . . . as . . .' Too dumb to even know how to finish his lame joke, Tiffany thought.

She wanted to say, 'As hot as your brain thinking, mate,' but instead said, 'As hot as Jennifer Lopez's bum.'

'Yeah,' he agreed, 'yeah. Anyway, if you hear anything, Mum's the word.' He tapped a finger to the side of his nose, 'And you come and tell Uncle Ron.'

As she watched him walk away, Tiffany knew that she was going to be triple careful now that word was circulating on the street about Dee's precious car.

A shiny, black Merc with tinted windows pulled into the garage. Sensing a ready stream of good money, Big Ron rushed over to it as it came to a stop. One of the back doors opened and a huge beast of a man, wearing shades and a dark suit, got out.

Big Ron flashed his teeth as Tiffany and the other mechanics watched. 'How can I help—?'

But the man interrupted in a deep voice. He pointed a large finger at Big Ron. 'You, piss off.' Tiffany's boss stumbled back. The goon swivelled his finger until it fell on Tiffany. 'You, in the car.'

Tiffany lost all the colour in her face as she felt like that finger was a knife stabbing her through the heart. 'You what?' Her voice shook.

His answer was to move his finger until it pointed at the opened door at the back of the car. Tiffany quickly looked around the room for help from her workmates, but it soon became clear from their downcast eyes – including Big Ron's – that she was on her own. There was no point running; the beast and whoever else was in the Mercedes would be on her in a second. No one had to tell her she was wasting her breath asking any more questions.

Gulping, she made her way to the car and with each step the man waiting beside it seemed to grow bigger and bigger. It wasn't until she dipped to get inside that she realised another hulk was already seated in the back. Startled, Tiffany started to retreat, but it was too late, the beast used his body to propel her forward. And then the car sped off, with a shaking Tiffany sandwiched between two thugs in the back.

Fifty-Four

They took Tiffany to a place she hadn't been to in ten years – the Pied Piper pub. Now it was a swanky wine bar with an Italian name that Tiffany couldn't pronounce. They took her up the back stairs to the top of the building, shoved her inside a room and shut the door behind her. Her heart nearly stopped when she saw who waited inside – John and Dee. Both of them stood, John with his arms folded, Dee with a fag in her hand, either side of an open window.

'Has something happened to Nicky?' Tiffany asked.

'It's got quite a view from up here,' John said instead of answering her question. But he didn't look out of the window to admire it. When someone talked about the view from a top-floor window, Tiffany knew to be scared.

'Mister Black, Mizz Dee, is there a problem?' Other than I've got your motor, her mind screamed. Oh my God, I knew I shouldn't have got involved in this. Shouldn't have listened . . .

Dee drew hard on her ciggie, and with smoke drifting out of her mouth and clouding her face, she said, 'I was saying to John here that it would be a real shame if someone had a nasty accident, falling head first out of this window. But these things happen, don't they?'

Tiffany knew that the other woman was reminding her, loud and clear, about the time she'd told Dee about that geezer, years back, dangling her out of this same window. She suspected that Dee hadn't told her husband about their past association because then she'd have to admit her part in the screw-up of John's car ring. Tiffany knew she could blab to John, but no way was she doing that; she might be a lot of things but she weren't no grass. Plus, she was up to her neck as much as Dee in putting the kybosh on John's chop shop scam.

The married couple didn't move from the window but Dee got straight down to business. 'What we're trying to figure out is why you didn't tell us that the dead man – and he will be annihilated when I get my hands on him – who pinched my Marilyn is your sister's other half?'

'You saw the name we fingered on that list when you came over and had a look,' John swiftly joined in, 'and yet you remained schtum. Didn't say a dickie bird to either of us. Now, we're thinking, why would someone who we let look after our boy, who we embraced into our family, treat us like a pair of two-bit mugs?'

'And you must've known that your very-soon-to-be dead brother-in-law worked for my John back in the day.' That shook Tiffany up and Dee could plainly see that. 'He was a runner for John.'

And was probably up to his lying neck in John Black's car ring when I worked for mad Mickey Ingram, Tiffany quickly worked out. That's probably why Nuts had been banged up when Jen was preggers with her eldest. Jen was too ashamed to tell Tiffany and her mum what he went down for and in respect to her feelings they never asked. Now she wished she had.

She shook her head. 'I never knew about any of that. Come on, leave it out. I would never–'

'Shut the fuck up,' Dee shouted, lunging towards Tiffany; her husband grabbed her arm and she bounced back like an elastic band. Dee was steaming. 'If you don't answer the question in three seconds flat, I'm coming over there to rip your tits off.'

Rip my tits off? I'd like to see you bloody well try. The old Tiffany came in the room. She'd been trapped in enough corners in her youth to remember how to get out of them by swinging her fists. She popped her hands brazenly on her hips, letting Dee know straight off that she was no pushover. ''Course I knew it was him.'

The other two looked stunned; they hadn't been expecting her to admit that. 'So why did I keep my mouth zipped? I'll tell you why. Because I hate that scumbag's guts and didn't want to have anything to do with any shit he might be up to his neck in.'

'But you could've told us where to find him,' Dee said. 'You're meant to be loyal to us. What you've done is rank, out-and-out betrayal.'

'What? And bring you straight to my sister's door?' She stopped because she saw the truth on their faces. A chill instantly started cooling her blood. 'Tell me you haven't been to Jen's?' Their silence gave her the answer she didn't want to hear. 'My sister's a good person; it isn't her fault that the fella she hooked up with turned out to be the ponce from hell. All she wants is a quiet and decent life for her kids. What mother wouldn't want that?' She looked straight into Dee's eyes. 'That's why you got me in to work with Nicky – because you want him to have a decent life too.'

'But if you'd spoken up we could've maybe sorted this out a different way,' Dee said, some of her anger disappearing.

'I ain't buying a word of it,' John jumped in. 'You know what I think? I think you're involved in this, right up to your lying gob. There was no glass in the driveway, which means that someone left the keys in Dee's motor. That someone was you Tiffany.'

Tiffany mentally belted herself up for the hard ride she knew was coming. 'And when would I have done that? As soon as I came back with Nicky, both of us came into the family room together and I didn't leave. I was there with you when the car was taken. So you tell me, when was I supposed to nick Dee's car key and leave it in the car?'

Dee looked indignant. 'You saying I left the keys behind?'

Tiffany quickly shook her head again. 'No. What I'm saying is that Nuts could've hotwired it—'

'No way,' Dee said. 'As soon as I bought my Marilyn I got someone to sort her out so no one could tamper with her.'

'Come on, Dee, Nuts is more nifty with his fingers than friggin' Houdini. He might be a total moron but if there's one thing he does know, it's cars.' She saw the doubt creep into Dee's face and so pressed on. 'You've got to believe me, I wouldn't in a million years help that scrote. As far as I'm concerned if you want to burn him at the stake I'll bloody well light the fire for you. All I ask is that you leave my sister well out of this.'

'We can do that, but all you've got to do is tell us where he is,' Dee said.

'Don't you think if I knew where he was, I'd be telling you? I know that Jen hasn't seen him because she would've let me know. No one has clapped eyes on him. He's probably done a runner and scarpered out of London.'

'Well, that's a real shame that is,' John said moving towards her.

'What do you mean?' Tiffany could feel something bad coming.

'By coming to my home where my son is and taking my wife's motor, your whack job of a brother-in-law has involved *my* family.'

'No,' Tiffany let out desperately.

John got right into her face. 'If that car isn't back in my driveway without a scratch on it by tomorrow evening you better tell Nuts that I'll be coming after his family.'

John's heavies dumped Tiffany outside the first tube station they came to, but she was in such a state she didn't even check which underground station it was. Once the car was out of sight, she desperately dragged out her Nokia.

'We're in deep shit . . . Just effing listen . . . You need to meet me now . . .'

Fifty-Five

Babs was buying some chocolate chip Cornettos for her grand-kids in the twenty-four hour mini supermarket when she heard that slapper Mel Ingram's voice carry over to her. She didn't want a run in with the old trout so she remained hidden in the frozen food section until her number one enemy was gone. She recognised the voice of the person Mel was speaking to: Ryan Mallory, The Devil's resident booze artist. Ryan would sell his own daughter (if she wasn't tucked up in the care system, away from him) if it meant money for another bottle of the hard stuff.

Mel didn't sound happy at all. 'I've already given you a score and I'm not giving you a penny more unless you've got something new to tell me, you piss head.'

'Don't be like that, Mel . . .' Babs heard hard footsteps walking away. 'Alright, Mel, I'll tell you what I heard the neighbours say.'

Footsteps coming closer again. Mel was back. 'Spit it out, I haven't got all day.'

'Give me the dosh first–'

'If you're pulling a fast one–'

'Swear on my life, Mel, I'm not.' There was the sound of rustling which Babs took to be the exchange of hard cash. 'The neighbours heard slamming doors and stuff. Then the fella scarpers and a little while later some posh motor turns up with some guy – not a hair on his head – in it. He pays her a visit and while he's doing whatever he's doing . . .' He winked at Mel . . . 'he leaves two of his gorillas on the landing.' He looked around, as if checking no one else was listening and then stepped closer to her. 'One of the neighbours hears the two goons chatting about a car their boss is asking after. After he leaves the two little girls start bawling their eyes out.'

The two little girls. A shiver went down Babs' spine.

'What car?'

'Dunno. But, I did hear something else.'

'Well, what you waiting for? Midnight mass? Spit it out.'

He smacked his lips and whined, 'I'm a bit dry at the moment. My mouth could do with wetting. So why don't you jack me up with another tenner . . .'

Babs heard a bit of a scuffle and then Ryan let out a long ouch. 'Mel, let go of my balls.'

'You keep pissing me about and I'll tear them off and leave them in the freezer section.'

'Alright, alright. They were looking for that geezer of hers, the one that did a bunk out of the flat. Sounds like he had something to do with the car disappearing in a puff of smoke.'

Geezer of hers. If this was about her Jen, Babs knew the geezer was that no-mark Nuts. The judge should've instructed the prison authorities to sling the key away once they slammed the cell door on him in Brixton.

'You sure about that?' Mel went on.

'I'm only telling you what I was told . . .' Footsteps clacking away. 'Hold up, where's my tenner?' The shop door tinkled as it was opened and then shut. Ryan waited a few seconds then let out in a menacing tone, 'Bitch. She doesn't know who she's dealing with. I used to be king of the ring. The undisputed champ at Jo-Jo's club . . .'

Babs came out of her hiding place and approached him as he still ranted. He looked like a proper dosser – dirty clothes and he stank of urine; he must've wet himself sometime during the day. 'How are tricks, Ryan?'

He stopped mouthing off and his bloodshot eyes widened. He tried to hurry away from her, which confirmed to Babs that he'd been gossiping about her Jen. She grabbed his arm and decided to treat him differently from Mel and give him the ole softly-softly routine. 'That Mel's a right old cow. I mean, she should have respect for someone like you.'

He shuffled his feet like he was back in the ring and nearly toppled over with the liquor inside him. Once he righted himself, he agreed, 'You got that right.'

As they talked, Babs steered him towards the counter where the spirits were kept safely away from anyone trying their hand at the five-finger discount.

'I was going to have a nice evening in with a little something to hold in my hand.' She looked up at the bottles of drink. 'I just don't know which one to choose. Brandy, whiskey, no, maybe some gin; I just don't know which one to choose.' She looked at him and wasn't surprised to see his inflamed, purple tongue licking his cracked lips as his mouth watered.

'You know what, Ryan son, I think I'll come back when I've made my mind up.' She half-turned away, but his hand on her arm stopped her.

He leaned in close to her and Babs had to hold her breath when the stench of his unwashed mouth hit her. 'Tell you what, Babsie babe, I'll give you a little tickle about something if you get me a bottle of Johnnie Walker.' His eyes went all innocent. 'Not that I need you to buy me a bottle because I would've come to see you to tell you anyway.'

The lying scrote. ''Course you would've.'

Half a minute later, Ryan was guzzling away at the bottle like he was at his mother's breast.

'So what's that you've got to tell me?'

He wiped his mouth with the back of his dirty hand. 'Heard there was a bit of bother at your Jen's last night. Some geezer and his associates give her a hard time looking for her fella.'

Babs already suspected what had gone on but hearing it still rocked her foundations. 'What did they want?'

He swayed and would've fallen if it weren't for the counter. 'Something about a car . . . Dunno . . .' He pulled the bottle back to his lips and Babs knew that she'd lost him to the booze.

She left him behind as he started singing some dirty ditty and the shop owner tried to hustle him out of the shop. Babs popped two steady pills and, heart racing, moved as quickly as her feet would take her to her daughter's.

'Don't want to go, Mum,' Courtney said stubbornly as Jen hurriedly put on Little Bea's coat.

'Cut it out, Court,' Jen snapped. 'Just do as you're told.'

Jen could've slapped herself when she saw the look of hurt sweep across her eldest daughter's face. If there were two people who had never done anything bad to her, it was her girls. She softened her voice. 'But I thought you liked going to spend time with your nan.'

Courtney wrinkled her nose. 'I do, but do we have to stay on Sunday as well? I might not be able to play on the landing with my mates.'

Jen crouched down and straightened the collar of Little Bea's coat. 'I'm sure she'll let you if you ask nicely. Mind you, I don't want you playing with that Dexter Miller.'

Courtney got all sulky again. 'Why not? Dexter's nice. I like him.'

'I know you do,' Jen muttered, so her daughter wouldn't hear. 'Let's just get you over to your Nanny Babs and then we'll decide what you can do this weekend.'

'Jeeeeen!' Oh hell. Jen heard her mother calling her from the landing like a foghorn on speed. Babs sounded agitated about something and Jen prayed that she hadn't heard about her visitors last night. But one look at her mum's face when she opened the door told her she had.

Jen played it all bright and breezy. 'I was hoping you could look after the girls for me this weekend, so I was just bringing them over.'

Babs didn't answer; instead, she turned to the girls and handed Courtney a tub of ice cream. 'Put that in the freezer for me, love.' Once the girls were out of the way Babs turned to her with her fists planted on her hips. 'What's going on, Jen? And don't give me no flim-flam nonsense.'

'Nothing.'

'Some little birdie told me that some Face and his thugs came around to yours last night looking for that toerag who's my grandkids' dad. And I heard that bitch Mel Ingram sticking her beak in and asking questions about it. I want to know chapter and verse about what's gone on.'

Jen knew there was no way out of telling the truth. 'Some top geezer came knocking for Nuts and when I told him I didn't know where he was, he made a little bit of noise. Scared the girls a touch, but he didn't lay a finger on me.'

Babs was alarmed. 'Oh my God, are you alright?'

Jen nodded. 'I don't think he'll be back, but just in case, I thought it best for the girls to be somewhere safe for the next couple of days.'

'And what about you, love? Who's going to keep you safe if he comes banging on your door again? Why don't you come and stay with me and Tiff as well?' Babs pursed her lips.

'I blame myself. Why did I keep pushing you towards Nuts all those years ago?'

Jen touched her mum's hand lightly. 'I was a big girl and made my own choices. And do you know what? I'd do it all over again because I wouldn't have my beautiful, pretty angels if I'd never met Nuts.'

'So what's that berk done now?'

Jen waved her hands hopelessly in the air. 'I don't even really get it, but this geezer was all hot and bothered because he said that Nuts pinched his motor. The car must be twenty-four carat gold the way he was shouting the odds about it. Anyway, I wouldn't like to be in Nuts' shoes when he catches up with him.'

'If he's keeping his head down he needs to stay off the estate because I saw him earlier.'

Jen looked surprised. 'Nuts?' She shook her head. 'You can't have, Mum; he's laying low up in Scotland.'

Jen looked puzzled. 'I swear it was him . . .' She frowned, then relaxed the skin on her forehead as she shrugged. 'Must be my mistake.'

'So will you take the girls?'

Babs squeezed her shoulder. 'You don't even have to ask.'

'Courtney's bellyaching about wanting to play out.' Jen grabbed one of her mum's hands tight. 'If you let her, Mum, I'm begging you, don't let her out of your sight.'

'It's alright, love,' Babs said softly feeling the tension vibrate in her hands, 'like I would on a place like The Devil. Plus, I don't want her mixing with that new lot next door to me. Their kids should be in cages in London Zoo. When I told the mum that one of her eldest animals had tried to break into my place she just gobbed at my feet and slammed the door.' Babs shook her head like she couldn't believe what the world was coming to. 'What are you planning to do while I've got Court and Little Bea?'

'Probably stop indoors. Maybe ask Bex to come over to do my nails.'

Babs pulled Jen to fully face her. 'If he comes calling again, don't let him in. The first thing you do my girl is lock yourself in the bedroom, get on that fancy mobile of yours and let me know.'

Fifty-Six

Sneaking out of the house wasn't the problem for Nicky. It was making sure no one noticed that he was gone. He considered claiming that he was doing homework but he knew not even his mum was going to buy that. And it was Dee who was the problem. Nicky knew he could be gone for a month before John would ask, 'Where's the kid?' But Dee had a nasty habit of poking her nose in when he was after a little privacy, and on that evening he was looking for maximum privacy. Nicky sat on his bed thinking long and hard before he realised the answer was staring him in the face. He got dressed to go out and then went downstairs.

Dee was lying on the sky blue chaise longue with two slices of cucumber on her eyes. Nicky got that. She'd shed a lot of tears since the car had been stolen and her eyes needed a rest. John was enjoying the break that his wife's rest cure was providing. He had one of his favourite books to hand – a true-crime book about East End gangsters. He enjoyed bringing his expert knowledge to the genre and correcting the author under his breath. 'That's rubbish, I know who did that blag and it wasn't him . . . Only hurt bad guys my arse – he was a proper fucking psycho that bloke . . . The guilty man might be a mystery to the author but I know who it was – it was me.' And so on.

Neither of the two adults acknowledged his presence, which was just how he wanted it. Nicky walked to the middle of the room, lit the blue touch paper and prepared to retire. "Ere Mum, has Dad found your car yet?'

The fireworks went off immediately. Dee pounced on his words. She tore off the cucumber, sat up and turned on her husband. 'No, he fucking hasn't. He's too busy reading a fucking book by the look of it.'

John looked at Nicky with something approaching shock mixed with displeasure, before pleading with his wife, 'I've got half of London looking for that car. What do you want me to do? Go out myself with an A–Z and a torch . . . ?'

With the job done, his parents arguing away like cats and dogs, Nicky went in to the hall and let himself out of the house without even bothering to keep his departure too quiet. He knew mum. The row he'd started would last until she collapsed, exhausted. Dad would grin and bear it. Even in the unlikely event that John asked, 'Where's Nicky?' the response would be, 'Never mind about Nicky, where's my car?'

He walked down the drive with a smile on his face, kicking gravel as he went. There were times when having a bat-shit crazy mother was an advantage in life. And this was one of them.

Tiffany had chosen a twenty-four hour burger bar out in the suburbs where London begins to merge into Essex – one of those flat places that don't even have a proper name of their own – as she assumed that would mean she wouldn't be recognised. But sitting at the window, watching the continuous stream of customers come out, she began to worry. She worried that someone might recognise her, or worse, identify who she'd come to meet. There was a car park outside and, in the distance, a sign for a tube station. She was desperate to get this meeting done and dusted before fate played a hand and someone shouted, 'Hi, Tiff! What are you doing here?' Looking at her watch became a nervous twitch. Looking at the clock on the wall became another as she hoped one or the other would speed up so this could be over.

A Ford Escort circled the car park before pulling up about as far away from the burger bar as it was possible to be, in a place where there were no lamps and light. A shadowy figure climbed out of the car, cap pulled low and then a hood over it. The figure walked slowly, head nodding, weaving and ducking as if an unseen attacker was lying in wait between the car and the swing doors into the outlet. After peering through the window a couple of times and giving the car park a lingering look, the person came in and drifted around like a ghost before finally settling nervously opposite Tiffany at her table.

Tiffany smiled and whispered, 'You can take your cap and hood off now. If anyone knows we're here, they'll know we're here – if you know what I mean, Jen.'

Jen prayed hard that no one knew she was here. Flippin' hell, thinking about what she'd done still made her heart race way too fast. She did what her sister told her to, and catching the expression on Tiffany's face told her what she looked like with her face exposed – tired, pinched, skin as white as snow.

'Is he here yet?' she asked quietly.

'No.'

'Are you sure he's coming?'

Tiffany faked a grin. 'Sure.' Then she stared into her milk-shake and admitted, 'He promised – but then he's about as reliable as a reformed junkie in a chemist.'

The two sisters stared out into the car park. Tiffany caught sight of another figure in black trackie bottoms, pumps and a black jacket. This figure too had a cap on, pulled so low it

covered the top half of his face. He too was weaving between
the cars, occasionally looking up from under his cap. But to
Tiffany, it seemed that, unlike Jen, he was enjoying this cloak
and dagger moment. When the figure reached the doors, he
flung them both open and entered like a cowboy gunning for
trouble in a Western. Looking out from under his cap, he spotted Tiffany and sauntered over to their table where he sat
down. She reached over and pulled his cap off as if she were
his mum. 'Jen – this is Nicky. Dee and John's son. He's also the
young man who stole his mum's car.'

Fifty-Seven

'Howay man, Bernie Gallows is the name.' The young man in overalls, who had just walked into the garage, announced his arrival to one of the workers, before adding, 'Can I speak to the owner?'

The mechanic noticed his Geordie accent straight away. The owner, Felix, was not going to be best pleased at having to speak to someone so late in the day; the boss was hoping to get off for parents' evening at his daughter's school. His daughter was a bit of a handful so Felix was always touchy when he had to go to speak to her teachers.

'I'll get him for you.'

The first thing an irritated Felix noticed about the fella was his hair. It resembled a badly fitted, curly wig that looked like it wanted to be anywhere other than on someone's head. Plus, the geezer wore a pair of glasses that would look better on a woman.

'You want to speak to me?'

'The name's Bernie Gallows.' Umm, Felix thought, that's a very strange Geordie accent – his bitch of an ex-missus had come from that part of the country; he'd drawn the short straw in the divorce settlement and ended up with the wild kid. But Felix let the customer talk; he'd had all sorts come in here.

'I run my own car maintenance business out of Grays and I'm looking for an engine for a 1987 Ford Escort and can't find one anywhere. One of my customers drove his car around with no oil in it and it's a bust. I don't suppose you have one you could sell me, do you?' His accent seemed to fade and he sounded more like a young chancer from *Coronation Street* as he went on. 'I'll pay good money for it like.'

'Well Bernie, as you can see, I run a little garage not a breakers yard, so I can't help I'm afraid.'

But Bernie Gallows seemed to have lost interest in the engine and seemed to be carefully scanning the yard and lock-ups outside. Then his attention seemed to wander to the gates. Even when Felix said, 'You're a long way from home, Bernie, aren't you?' he didn't notice for a few seconds before he turned his attention back to the question.

'Howay, came south for the work like and met a girl – you know?'

'I meant Grays – you're a long way from there too.'

Bernie obviously wasn't keen on being questioned and was now checking the walls of the office. 'Grays? Howay, I move around a lot, you have to in this business.'

Felix got impatient. He was not looking forward to this parents' evening lark. 'Well I'm sorry, I can't help you and I'm afraid we're closing now.' Bernie took no notice so the owner repeated his goodbye more firmly.

His visitor finally got the message and slowly and gradually began to make his way out. 'Thanks anyway.'

'You're welcome.'

Felix walked back to the office and said to Gladys, his secretary 'Google Bernie Gallows.'

A minute later she reported, 'Can't find nothing about him or a car business in Grays with his name.'

Felix walked back into the workroom and stared hard at the closed door. He turned back to his secretary. 'Make sure everything is shut away and locked up and I'll take care of the burglar alarm. I've got a feeling we haven't seen the last of Mr Bernie Gallows.'

Although Tiffany kept interrupting and insisting they were here to discuss the matter at hand, Nicky couldn't help trying to impress Jen with what a lad he was. At the same time he was half apologising for stealing the car in the first place while clearing himself of blame.

'Thing is, Jen, I totally sorted myself out, right?' Nicky leaned across the table and told her. 'I mean, if I had a kid and he had issues and he overcame those issues – did I tell you I suffered from low self-esteem? – I'd mark the occasion with a little something, like a motorbike for my kid. But what did I get? Nothing. Fu–'

'Oi,' Tiffany pointed at him, 'watch the tongue.'

Nicky carried on as if she hadn't spoken. 'They gave me nothing for turning myself around, not even a pat on the head. So I took the spare car key from the office and drove off in my mum's car to wind the bitch up. I mean, I was going to bring it back a couple of hours later but then the old man chased me and crashed his Range Rover and I thought, uh-oh, I'm in trouble now. Not that I was scared of course, coz I'm well hard, me.'

Tiffany interrupted again. 'Nicky mate, my sister doesn't care why you took the car. Anyway she knows already because I told her that when I sussed that it was you. You've already given me chapter and verse on why you did it.'

But Nicky wasn't listening. 'So I thought, fuck – what now? So my mate I'm at school with, his parents live in this massive farm about five miles from us and I took it up there and I says to the geezer, can I hide this motor somewhere? Because it's like a bit hot. So he says to me, yeah mate, no problem. So we hid it in a barn on their estate and covered it in hay bales. Sweet eh?'

If Jen thought it was sweet, she wasn't saying. In fact, she said nothing at all. Nicky took this as an accusation. 'I mean, you can bloody talk.' He ignored Tiffany's look of displeasure at the cursing. 'You and your sister, taking advantage of my mistake and blaming her husband for the blag so my dad would run him out of town. That's bang out of order that is and no mistake. Now my old man is running round talking about shooting people. I'm well in the crap now.'

Jen cringed, hearing Nicky put into words what she'd been party to. Why, oh why did I get involved in this? You know why girl: because you wanted Nuts to sling his hook for good.

Tiffany put her nanny face on. 'Nicky, do me a favour, shut the hell up, mate.'

The car thief wilted and muttered. 'Well I am, ain't I?'

'We're all in the crap,' she reminded him. 'That's why we're here, so we can take some action together before anyone gets hurt. As long as we're smart, none of us need to get into any trouble.' She stared at her big sister. 'Did you know that Nuts worked for John Black years back? Must've been the same time he was going out with you.'

Jen rubbed her forehead like she couldn't believe she was in some burger bar talking about her involvement in a stolen car instead of at home with her beautiful girls. 'I didn't know until John Black told me, after he invited himself into my home. I suspect it had something to do with Nuts getting nicked that time I was pregnant with Courtney.' She gave her sister a strange look. 'Hang on a minute, you were nicked because of your involvement in some car ring and so was Nuts. Did you—?'

'I swear, Jen,' Tiffany patted her palm over her heart while her other hand in her lap crossed two fingers, 'it wasn't the same thing. And if it was I never knew Nuts was a player.' Her fingers uncrossed; at least the last was true.

Jen leaned across the table looking murderous. 'I swear, Tiff, if you've been lying I will swing for you.'

'I am still here you know,' Nicky butted in.

Both women swiftly turned to him and collectively ordered, 'Shut up.'

Tiffany carried on talking. 'Forget the past. It's the here and now that matters. We have to be smart.' She looked at Nicky 'What's happening up at the house?'

Nicky shrugged and gave her an outline of what he'd heard, assuring Jen that her kids were in no danger because he knew his mum and she wouldn't have it; his mum loved kids.

Tiffany exploded. 'Yeah – and I know what your dad's like. He'd blow up a children's home if he thought it would get Dee off his back. Alright – you go home and only get in touch if you've got something important to report. And don't forget, your dad may be tapping phones, so make sure you use a call box somewhere.'

Jen watched her sister's face and knew that she was holding back on something. What wasn't Tiff telling her?

Nicky was disgusted. 'Is that it? I've taken two buses to get here. You could have asked me what was going on by phone. I thought we'd be doing something a bit naughty to straighten things out.' He turned to Jen and wrinkled his eyebrows. 'I'm well naughty, me.'

Tiffany took his cap, put it on the youngster's head and pulled it down so his ears stuck out. 'I just wanted to know what's happening at home.' But that wasn't quite the truth. She wanted to make sure that he wasn't weakening or going to 'fess up to his parents and wreck any chance she had of devising an escape route. But the kid was cocky, stupid and seemed to be enjoying the drama. There was no danger from him. 'So, get two buses home. Or, there's a car park outside, go and steal a car and go home that way.' She added with affection, 'Look after yourself.'

With Nicky gone, the two women sat alone. Jen's voice was nearly breaking. 'I can't believe that kid's old enough to drive a car.'

'He's not; he's fifteen, the little bastard. Some of the kids I used to hang around with were joyriders and could handle a motor like they'd come out of the womb with a steering wheel in their hand. And you better believe me that Nicky's just like them.'

Jen sat motionless for a few seconds, the remaining colour drained out of her face and tears began to run down her parched cheeks. Tiffany reached out with both hands and took her sister's in her own. She held them tight but said nothing, knowing that words wouldn't help.

'This is all my fault, Tiff. I only blamed Nuts for nicking that car for my children's sake and now I've put them at risk, because I saw a chance and took it without thinking it through.' Tiffany knew her sister was too good-hearted to put this on anyone else and preferred to lumber herself with the blame. 'Now look what's happened. I don't care if that bastard shoots me, but what's going to happen to my children?' Her sister had that look on her face again as if she could barely look into Jen's eyes. 'Tiff, you're not telling me something . . .'

Tiffany took a deep breath. 'Jen, I don't want you to be worried, but John and Dee sent some hard nuts to pick me up . . .' Jen's hands formed into balls on the table. 'They know I'm related to Nuts through you. The long and short of it is, they say if that car doesn't make a miraculous reappearance tomorrow evening they're not only coming after Nuts,' her voice shook, 'they're coming after his family as well.'

Jen's hand flew to her throat as she found it hard to breathe. *Oh my God, I'm going to be sick, going to be sick.* She could see a concerned Tiffany moving her lips, but she couldn't hear a word. She brought her hands to her mouth and started crying. She didn't give a monkey's about herself, but those people were going to come after her kids. They were going to hurt her girls because of something she had started. Why oh why had she listened to Tiffany's plan when Tiff told her about the Black's boy taking their car? Tiffany had convinced her that it was the ideal situation to fit up Nuts. She'd played her part so well – making the anonymous call to John Black in a fake posh accent; playing the outraged wife and mother when he'd thrown his weight around her home; giving Kevin a right bollocking in public, so everyone assumed she had nothing to do with it; telling Nuts to stay in Scotland because it was too dangerous for him to come back. She hadn't even breathed a word to her best mate Bex, or her mum. And now it had all turned on her. All she'd wanted was to get Nuts out of their life for good – was that such a bad thing to want? *But you went about it the wrong way, girl.*

Jen didn't even remember Tiffany leading her outside until she felt the cold air against her skin.

'Jen, listen to me,' her sister said forcefully as she grabbed her arms. 'We're going to get this sorted. Don't worry about Courtney or Little Bea, no one's going to touch them.'

Jen swallowed and swiped a tear from her face. 'But how are we going to do that?'

'We'll draw the poison the only way we can. We're going to get that car back and we'll figure out how to deliver it back where it belongs. John and Dee will be happy and you and the girls will be safe. Which means you're going to have to drive me so we can pick it up.'

Once they got into Jen's Ford Escort, she asked, 'Where is the car?'

'I tucked it up nice and safe in a garage lock-up well away from East London. But we've got a problem.'

Jen let out a tight little groan as her head sank back into the headrest. Problems! Problems! That's all she'd got by trying to solve the one mega problem in her life – more flippin' problems. 'What now?' Her weariness coated each word.

'We can't get the car until tomorrow morning–'

Jen urgently lifted her head and turned to her sister, anxiety imprinted across her already stressed face. 'Why not?'

Tiffany didn't look at her sister. 'That doesn't matter. What does is if we collect it in the morning that will give us plenty of time to deliver it back to John and Dee.'

'But what if there's a problem–?'

'There won't be. Believe me.' Tiffany turned to look at Jen. 'Dee's car will be back with her by midday.'

Jen relaxed back into her seat. 'Well, at least I can go home and collect the girls.'

'Why bother doing that? We're only going to have to hit the road early come morning and you'll have to bring the girls back to mum.'

'What are you suggesting? That I go home and lay low?' Jen pushed her head to the side to look at her younger sister.

'No, I'm suggesting that we don't go home at all.'

Jen scoffed. 'What? Doss in this car for the night?'

Tiffany wrapped her hands so tight around the steering wheel, her knuckles turned a pale white. 'If I go home mum's only going to give me the third degree. There's a nice B 'n' B I know not far from where the car is. We put our heads down there for the night and Bob's Your Uncle – in the morning we get the car and motor off to the Blacks.'

Seeing the indecision on Jen's face Tiffany quickly added, 'Courtney and Little Bea are safe, so there's nothing to worry about. The only thing we need to keep our eye on is that bloody car. How are you going to feel if we go home now and some other shit crops up stopping us from getting it? You know The Devil, there's always some crap to hold people back.'

Jen pinched her teeth into her top lip. Finally she nodded. 'Alright. But there's one important thing you need to know.'

Tiffany looked confused. 'What?'

'I ain't putting up with your snoring, so get your own room.'

Fifty-Eight

Felix was right. He hadn't seen the last of Bernie Gallows, or at least his garage hadn't. Bernie walked down the street on which the garage stood and slowed as he reached the gates. Not only was it padlocked but an extra chain had been looped through to make it more secure. The chain was new and had clearly been added that evening. Bernie realised he'd overplayed his hand earlier and he mockingly spat 'Howay man' to himself as he carried on walking. A security camera was stationed on a corner of the garage's wall but he was confident it was a fake. It didn't move, had no lights on it and there was no sign in the office he'd visited earlier that there was any kind of feed to a screen.

The walls were tall and had serrated bricks on top but that was no problem to a man of Bernie's resources. There had been no sign of any dogs earlier, either. The place looked like what it was – a small garage in a town in the home counties that fixed cars. But it was a garage with a secret and Bernie knew what that secret was. He'd been tipped off by one of his extensive range of contacts, and he was confident that – new chain or no new chain – he could get to that secret.

The wall to the yard ran along a side street where the lights were dimmer and passers-by few. Bernie walked down it, waited for a woman and her yapping Alsatian to pass by, and then, when the coast was clear, he unwound a rope that looped like a cummerbund around his waist under his jacket. He attached a claw to it and threw it over the wall, clambered up and down the other side and then dropped into the yard below. He stood motionless for a minute, listening for any sign inside or outside that anyone had seen him: the running of feet or the sound of doors closing. There were none. At the back of the yard were five lock-ups. In one of them was the secret.

He found it soon enough. Four of the five lock-ups had grimy and greasy windows that you could use a torch to peer through. But the fifth had curtains loosely hung over the window. That was where the secret was kept. It was obvious. Around his neck was a holster in which was stored a king-sized set of bolt cutters, more than powerful enough to cut through the modest padlocks. One arm of the cutters doubled as a jemmy and Bernie used it to lever open the lock which buckled and gave with a couple of tugs. He stood and waited for a few moments to see if the noise had alerted anyone outside. But there was no response on the street or inside the garage. He was alone in the world.

He pulled open the double doors on the lock-up and his eyes feasted on the car inside. He was trying to keep the noise down but was unable to resist giving a low whistle and whispering, 'Fancy keeping a piece of machinery like that in a dump like this.'

He went inside and ran his hand along the bodywork, the way another man might caress a woman's lush body. And when he looked inside, he realised he had a lucky break. The garage had left the car doors unlocked. And even better, when he searched the glove compartment he discovered that the keys were in there. He turned the ignition and wasn't surprised to discover it started first time. Cars like that always did. They begged to be started and driven away at speed. He drove the car into the yard and lined it up with the gates to make his exit. All it required now was to go back over the wall and take the locks off the gate, and it was a nice simple job, quickly and easily done.

But he didn't need to open the gates. Bernie realised to his horror that they were being unchained and someone on the other side was coming in. He raced back to the car and waited. Through the open driver's window, it seemed that perhaps he'd been mistaken and a passer-by had rattled the chain as he went by. Then he heard voices on the other side and the double gates began to swing open. Three men were standing in front of him. Two of them were policemen holding torches. The third was the owner. The three men walked forward towards him at a slow pace.

One cop came round to the driver's side. 'It's traditional to wait until a place opens before collecting your vehicle, sir. Now would you mind turning off the engine and getting out so we can have a little chat?'

In front of the car, the garage owner, Felix, had a smug smile on his face.

Bernie didn't hesitate. He threw the headlights full on, so that the two men in front were blinded, and then pressed the accelerator down to the floor. The engine roared like a lion and he slipped into gear. The car lurched forwards. He saw one of the cops dive for cover while the owner howled in pain as he was clipped by the bumper as he tried to do the same. The car careered onto the street and, without looking where he was going, Bernie threaded the wheel through his hands as he manoeuvred it in a tight turn. As he went by the police car that had been parked up, he noticed another car had been parked, which had its door slightly ajar. He guessed that the owner had been holed up in it with a flask of tea, waiting for him to turn up. As he careered down the street, he whispered, 'You prat, it's not your car is it?'

The cops didn't follow, but he kept up the speed until he was a few miles away, then he stopped and checked the bumpers and bodywork to see if he'd hit anything during his escape. With no daylight, it was difficult to tell. But he was confident, even if there was any damage, a quick polish or a specialist hammer would soon take care of it. Anyway, he had to do a few other things to the car to get it ready. It was a job well done.

Bernie got back into his new car and shouted 'Howay man!' as he drove off into the night.

Fifty-Nine

I just need to hear my girls' voices. Jen desperately pulled out her mobile as she stood on the private balcony of the room of the bed 'n' breakfast. She could hear the noises that Tiffany made as she shuffled around inside. The place only had one unoccupied room left, so the sisters were having to share. But Jen didn't think about any of that as the chilly dark settled around her; all she wanted was to hear her kids' sweet voices. If anything happened to her girls because of something she had done she'd never, ever forgive herself.

'Mum,' she said desperately as soon as the line connected. 'Are the girls with you?'

'Of course they're with me,' Babs answered, outrage showing in her voice. 'What did you think, I dumped them in a basket on the steps of the Town Hall or something?'

Jen's head leaned slightly back. Just knowing that her daughters were safe made her feel so much easier. 'Can I talk to them?'

'A bit late for that, my girl, I've already put them to bed, which is where I was when the blower went.'

'Please, mum, I just need . . .' She was going to say that she needed to hear their beautiful voices, but she didn't. The last thing she needed was Babs realising that something was up. 'I just want to say goodnight to them.'

'What's going on, Jen? You don't sound like yourself.'

Jen pulled in a steady breath before she answered to make sure that her emotions were under control. 'Just want to say beddy-bye to them.'

Babs huffed. 'Now I'm going to have to get them up.'

'You wouldn't have to if you had a mobile phone.'

'Mobile phone . . .' Jen heard her grumble, and then the soft sound of her slippers on the floor as she moved away from the phone.

'Mum?' Jen smiled and closed her eyes, hearing Courtney's sleepy voice less than a minute later; it sounded like the most wonderful thing in the world.

'What you been up to with Nanny Babs?'

Courtney groaned. 'Mum, I'm tired. Can I tell you tomorrow when you come get us?'

'I know,' Jen whispered softly. She was tired too. Her eyes reopened. 'Put Little Bea on.'

'Nanny Babs and me tried to wake her but she wouldn't. Shall I try again?'

'No. Leave her to her beauty sleep.' Tears pricked Jen's eyes. 'Just wanted to say how much I love you, honey.'

'Love you too.' Courtney let out a noise that sounded like a big yawn. 'Can I go back to bed now?'

'You get yourself back under the duvet.'

'Shall I put Nanny Babs back on?'

'No.' The last thing she needed was Babs trying to dig more information out of her. 'Give her a soft kiss goodnight from me.'

As soon as Jen finished the call she held the phone against her heart. It never ceased to amaze her that the ugly, major league mess up that was her life could have produced two, pure, innocent human beings like Courtney and Little Bea. If she were a churchgoer she'd thank God every day for them.

*　*　*

'Do you remember what we used to do as kids?' Tiffany asked softly almost an hour later.

Both sisters were tucked up in the twin beds in the small, cosy room. Both lay on their backs, staring up at the white ceiling.

'You mean play "Knock Down Ginger" and run for our lives when someone opened their door?' Jen smiled, recalling how she'd loved that game. She, Tiff and some of the other estate kids would toss a penny to see who would get chosen to knock on someone's door and then do a runner before the victim opened their door to find no one there.

'No, Dumbo,' Tiffany answered. Her voice faltered slightly. 'I mean when I'd get upset and hide in my wardrobe and you'd come in and get me to think about being anywhere else other than The Devil.'

'Yeah.'

'If we didn't have to get that car tomorrow where would you like to be?'

There was silence as Jen's brain ticked over her sister's question. But Tiffany jumped in again, 'Come on, Jen, there's a big wide world out there. If you could shut your eyes, click your heels three times and open your eyes again, where would you wish to be?'

'A two up, two down.'

'You what?'

'Just an ordinary house. Nothing flash, something simple. A bedroom for me and one each for the girls. A garden – nothing big, you know – just a bit of green where they could play and run around in the fresh air. A dining room where we could sit down and have our meals together. I just want . . . want . . .'

Tiffany knew that her sister probably hadn't even realised that she'd started crying as soon as she talked about her dream home. Tiffany moved across until she held her sobbing sister in her arms. Funny how the roles had been reversed and it was her now who was giving comfort.

'I just want a safe place . . .' Jen drew in a harsh sob. 'You know, somewhere me and my girls can pop our heads down at night and not have to worry about waking up to a load of bellyache the next day.' Another sob. 'Is that too much to ask for? Too much to wish?'

Tiffany's only answer was to gently stroke her palm down the side of Jen's hair. She suspected that the gesture was much more soothing than any words she could have said. Tiffany didn't know how long she held her sister, but when she heard the soft snores coming from Jen she gently laid her back on the bed and pulled the blanket to her chin.

'It isn't me who's the snorer, sister dearest,' Tiffany muttered quietly with a small smile dancing on her lips.

The smile died as she thought about her own dreams; the things that she wanted in life. She inched back to her own bed, but didn't go to sleep.

Jen was alarmed to wake up on Sunday morning to find her sister nowhere to be seen.

'Tiff?' she called out, but there was no response, so she eased out of bed and walked into the tiny bathroom. She pushed the partially opened door back, but there was no sign of her sister. If bloody Tiffany had run out on her . . . Jen turned swiftly when she heard the room door open.

'Where have you been?' Jen asked as she looked her sister over. Tiffany was dressed, but looked tired.

Tiffany quietly closed the door. 'I went for a walk. I've been up most of the night; couldn't get to sleep.'

'Right,' Jen said slowly. 'Do you want to get an hour's worth of kip and I'll wake you up after?'

Tiffany shook her head. 'Nah. Let's get this over with. The sooner we see the back of John and Dee Black the sooner we can get on with our lives.'

Fifteen minutes later they were in Jen's car on their way to pick up Dee Black's motor.

The roads were clear and it took Tiffany and Jen less than twenty minutes to get to the garage in Southend. Tiffany left her sister in the car to retrieve the Pirano FS from the lock-up where it was parked. Jen sat and waited but became increasingly worried when her sister failed to reappear. When fifteen minutes had passed, she got out and followed the path Tiffany had taken. The door to the office was open and when she entered she found her sister standing by a desk with a phone in her hand. 'No, no, no. That's not possible . . .' When she realised that her sister was there, she slammed the phone down, folded her arms and looked very worried.

'What's happened?'

Tiffany was dismissive, but she wouldn't look her sister in the eye. 'Nothing's happened. It's just a mix up, that's all. I'm sorting it out now.'

Jen didn't like the look on her sister's face. It was a carbon copy of the one Tiffany would wear when she was lying to their mum about not going to the cemetery. 'What kind of mix up?'

'Nothing. Go and wait in the car, I won't be a minute.' Tiffany walked out of the office into the yard and began hunting around, as if Dee's car might be hidden behind tarpaulin or a barrel.

Jen followed her. 'What's happ—?' But the words froze in Jen's throat when she noticed a lock-up by a brick wall. The door was wide open and inside it was empty.

'It's gone,' Tiffany let out in disbelief.

'You can't mean the car?' A panicked Jen rushed over to her sister, who turned back into teenage Tiffany.

'What the fuck do you think I mean? Father Christmas's sleigh? I—'

Jen grabbed Tiffany, taking her by surprise, and shook her. 'You bloody well better not mean Dee Black's car. My kids' lives are on the line here.'

'And whose bloody fault is that?'

Jen reared into her face. 'But you told me this was the best way to get rid of Nuts.'

'Don't lay it all at my door, Jen. You didn't have to . . .'

They both stopped moving when Jen's phone went. Jen quickly released her sister, hunted in her bag for her blue Nokia and checked the screen. Her eyes flicked wildly to her sister's face. 'It's John Black. What am I going to do?'

Tiffany's eyes grew large and wild. 'Stall him. Don't tell him where we are or what we're doing, just stall him.' She rushed back into the building and picked the office phone up and dialled a number herself.

'Yes?' Jen answered, taking the call.

John was in a jovial mood. 'Hello, Jennifer. How's things?'

Keep your voice calm. 'Good.'

'I'm glad to hear it. Are your kids OK?'

Jen saw red, but pushed her teeming emotions back. 'Good, thank you.'

'I've been worried because you haven't called me like we agreed.'

'But you said only to that if I—'

'Have you got it?' He didn't sound jovial anymore.

'Got what?'

There was a long pause before John posed a question. 'Do you know what really upsets me, Jennifer? It's not people trying to pull a fast one on me. I don't mind that, it happens. It's when people take the piss and then try and pull a fast one on me. That really, really upsets me. You understand? Now I'll ask you again – it's not a very difficult question – have you got it? A straight yes or no will do.'

Standing alone in the yard, Jen was lost. 'Yes, I mean no, I mean sort of; we're getting it now.'

The silence that followed was more menacing than any threat. 'I see. Where are you, Jennifer? Is your sister there? Did she tell you about our little get together yesterday?' When he didn't get an answer, John went on, 'Listen, Jennifer, I've been very patient here but my patience is running out. You see a man in my position can't afford to be too patient or people think you've gone soft. I need that car back this evening and if I don't get it, I'll have to play hardball. Which I really don't want to do and which I shouldn't really have to do. That's not unreasonable, is it?'

Jen's body went electric with anger and she bared her teeth. 'Now you listen to me, mate, you touch my kids and you're bloody dead even if I have to do it with my bare hands.'

John laughed at her. 'You don't have to worry about killing anyone; you just get that car back later on. Tell your sister the same. Otherwise, you and your sister are knackered. And so will anyone else be if I have to knacker them.'

Even though John had rung off, Jen carried on swearing threats and curses down the dead line. She only stopped when Tiffany reappeared in the yard. Without saying a word, she indicated with her head that they were leaving. The two women walked in silence down the street and back to their car. They sat inside for five minutes before Tiffany asked, 'What did he say?'

'You know what he said.'

Tiffany nodded. 'Yeah. Well, we're really up the creek without a paddle now. And without a creek either.'

Sixty

The first thing Nicky heard as he came down the stairs was his mum hand-bagging his dad about her precious Marilyn. He'd nicked the car for a laugh and it had been funny, but that had stopped when he'd seen Tiffany's sister's face yesterday. He knew someone on the edge when he saw one and that was a bird on the edge, no doubt about it. Even if he'd been caught in the car when his dad was chasing him, he knew the worst he could expect was a bit of a hiding – and he didn't care about that. Mum would have done her nut but she'd soon have forgiven him and defended him against John. It was just a laugh. But now he'd met Jen, the laughter was over.

As soon as he got downstairs he went into the front room the same time his dad said to his mum, 'I've had it with those two. I'm going to sort them out, big time. Satisfied?'

'When it comes back I'll be satisfied, but not before,' his mum threw back.

His dad was pacing and his mum sat on the edge of the chaise longue, a drink in one hand and a smoke in the other. His dad stopped pacing as soon as he saw him.

'Why are you up so late?'

'It isn't late. Just gone—'

'While you're under this roof you will learn to get your arse out of bed at a reasonable time and stop behaving like some lazy, fuck-up artist.'

Nicky almost jumped at his father's tone; there was steel in John's voice that he wasn't used to hearing. And the fact that his mum kept schtum, not supporting his story, disturbed him even more. But he decided to spin his story out anyway. He thought it would be clever to ask after Tiffany. The way Nicky saw it, that would cover the fact that he'd seen her the evening before if anyone asked. So he wondered aloud, 'When's Tiff coming round again?'

The silence was stonier than Brighton beach before his mum answered him. 'She's not. I'm not having that little bitch in this house again.' Dee ground out her ciggie in the star-shaped ashtray. 'We'll find you someone else, someone a bit more upmarket and reliable – not a thieving slag from the East End.'

Nicky was stumped. His first thought was that he'd been followed to his meeting yesterday but he quickly realised that wasn't possible, otherwise he'd be tagged as a thieving slag from the East End as well. His voice went up slightly. 'She's not? What do you mean, she's not coming back?'

'It means she's not stepping foot into my home ever again. It's not a very complicated sentence so what's your problem?'

Nicky was horrified. Life without Tiffany? Sod that. 'You can't do that. It's not right. She ain't done nothing.' He only just managed to avoid adding 'It was me!' The panic began to rise. Not only had he landed Tiffany in the crapper but her sister too and there was also something else on his mind. He was starting to think Tiffany was the only proper friend he had. She clicked with him in a way no one else had, including not taking any bollocks from him. He was fucked if he was going to let her go.

'Whatever she's supposed to have done, she didn't do it; someone else must have done it.' When he noticed that he now had two suspicious sets of eyes fixed on him, he decided he might have gone too far and began to row back. 'And even if she did whatever it was, I couldn't give a toss. Get her back!'

His dad calmly folded his arms. 'Listen boy, why don't you go back upstairs and do that homework you're pretending that you do each day. And try and remember to speak to your mum and dad in a more civil tone in future, especially when they've got serious business to sort out. Don't forget, you're not too old to feel the back of my hand.'

Nicky nearly went. He knew he was losing it and didn't want to get Tiffany in any more trouble but he couldn't contain himself. 'Fuck off with your homework – you're not my real mum and dad, are you? They're both dead, so you can't tell me what to do.'

Nicky reeled backwards as Dee let out a distressed, wrenching noise like someone was trying to strangle her. 'Why you little–' John started saying with fury, but he never finished because his wife rose up like an avenging angel and stormed towards her only child. Nicky staggered backwards until his back hit the wall. Dee reached him and he cringed back because he'd never seen her face so twisted with rage and pain. She grabbed him by his T-shirt. 'How dare you, how dare you? We are your mum and dad and we've done everything for you, without a word of thanks, you ungrateful little runt. Now get out of my sight before I give you a kicking you'll never forget.'

Nicky was shocked when he pushed Dee backwards and even more shocked that he wasn't punched in the face for it. He clocked the mixture of hurt, disbelief and horror on her face at what he'd done. His dad cursed a blue moon as he started moving towards him; no way would John let it pass that his son had put a hand on his mother. But Dee held up her hand, halting her husband in his tracks as Nicky made his escape into the hallway. As he ran up the stairs, he shouted down with defiance, 'Get her back or I'm so fucking out of here. And I mean it, she ain't done nothing wrong.'

Dee sat with her head pillowed against John's shoulder, cuddled close to him in a way she hadn't done in years.

'We have been good parents, haven't we, John?' she asked quietly. She was still reeling from the words her son had chucked at her. Dee couldn't believe he'd said them. And he'd pushed her. He'd put his hands on her like she was a stranger: nothing to him. That made her want to weep and curl into a ball. She sometimes forgot that she hadn't actually given birth to Nicky, that two other people had been his mum and dad for the first five years of his life. Dee and John never talked about Nicky's real dad Chris. John would never allow it. The only time he did was when Nicky asked about him, which grew rarer as the boy got older. But that never stopped Dee from remembering the last words John had ever said to her about Chris: *'We won't be seeing Chris again – not tonight, not ever.'* It sent a shiver down her spine, just thinking about it now – thinking about what John had probably done; that she had been the one to release the bowling ball that knocked down all the skittles. She kept the guilt about Chris tucked away, but it was always there.

John's hand rubbed up and down her arm. 'Of course we have. He couldn't have wished for a better mum than you, love. If we hadn't taken him into our home, think where he'd be now – in one of them homes that don't give a shit about the kids they're meant to be looking out for.'

'I've given that boy everything he's ever asked for. If he wants a pair of trainers, I make sure he's wearing the latest fashion on his feet. If he wants tickets to see Arsenal, I get him a season ticket for the year. I'd kill for him.'

John didn't say it, but he thought that was often the problem. Dee gave Nicky everything he'd ever wanted. Their lad could've done with a dose of growing up the hard way, just like him and Dee, finding out first hand what it felt like to really have to graft for a crust. You thought if you gave your kids everything they'd turn out right, learn to respect life, but that wasn't how it turned out sometimes. He didn't have the heart to tell his wife that the way she'd been bringing up Nicky meant their son thought all he had to do to get something in life was to stick his hand out, no elbow grease necessary.

Dee sniffed, holding back the tears. The last time she'd really cried in her life was that time one of the kids at school had called her a chocolate drop. She'd screamed and railed at life many times since then, but she'd never allowed herself to shed a bloody tear; crying was for people who had too much time on their hands. But her darling boy had pushed her to a place where her heart felt like it was falling apart.

'You know what I love about you, Dee?' John said. 'Your strength. The way you stick two fingers to the world even when I can see that your heart is breaking. Nothing and no one is going to crush my Dee.'

She hitched her head away from his shoulder and looked up at him, really looked at him. Instead of seeing the wrinkles and creases that defined a man who was nineteen years older than her, a man who she'd set out to take full advantage of, she saw a man who had become her rock. Without John Black, where would she be right now? This man had given her every last thing that she'd ever dreamed of . . .

'I know what's going through your head, Dee,' John said, cutting over her thoughts. Dee gazed at him startled, but he carried on before she could say anything. 'That I'm some dirty old bloke who deserved to be picked clean by a young, tasty bird out on the make—'

'No, John—'

He shushed her by placing his finger gently on her lip. 'I came up the hard way, girl, just like you, which means I took advantage of a person or two in my time. That's just the way it is. You see an opportunity, you've got to go through the door. The only thing that matters is that I love you to bits and always will.'

That did bring tears to Dee's eyes. His finger left her mouth and wiped a tear running down her cheek. 'I know I give you a hard time, John, sometimes, but push me back in time and you'll always be the man I'd choose, hands down.' Her lips trembled. 'I couldn't bear it if Nicky hates me.'

'He don't hate you. He's just reeling from you finally putting your foot down and not getting his way. The next time you see him it will be all smiles again. Anyway, you need to get yourself sorted because your mum's coming soon.'

Blimey, how could she have forgotten Sunday lunch with her mum at the house? Dee jumped away from her husband. The caterers were going to be here soon and she didn't have any time to waste.

Sixty-One

'I'm leaving London.' Jen gave her sister a half smile as Tiffany drove the car back home at high speed. They both agreed that Jen was in no fit state to do it. 'Perhaps I'll go to Scotland like Nuts – winters or no winters.'

Tiffany was lost in thought as they ate up the miles, but finally she said, 'No one's going anywhere. We can sort this out. We just need to take some time out and think things through. Every problem has a solution; we just need to work out what it is, that's all.'

'We haven't got any time. You didn't hear John Black on the phone. He's serious. He's coming after us, which I don't mind and he's coming after my children, which I do. No, we have to get out of town, for good.' Jen seemed wistful for a few seconds before she added, 'Do you know what I was thinking?'

Tiffany's mind was on other things but she decided to humour her sister; she could see what a bad place Jen was in and she didn't blame her. 'What you thinking?'

'I was thinking if our dad was around maybe he could get this sorted out.'

The car swerved slightly, registering Tiffany's alarm. She hadn't realised things were quite this bad with her sister and she feared she was losing it. Not to mention that, given the banter and rumours she'd heard over the years, she was under the impression that Stanley Miller was about the last person who could help them. She looked in her rear-view mirror and pulled over into a lay-by where she switched the engine off. 'In the back, Jen, I want to talk to you.'

The two women sat in the back seat and Tiffany put her arm around her big sister. 'Listen, babe, I know you're scared and I'm bloody shitting a brick too, but you need to trust me, OK? I know this world. I used to work for Mickey Ingram and I know Dee Clark. I know how they think and how they behave – OK? Now, if you leave it to me, I'll sort this out.'

Her sister didn't move but she snarled, 'Sort this out? You were the one who got us into this eff of a mess in the first place. I don't know what I was thinking. Fancy ringing a character like John Black and telling him Nuts stole the car. I must have been off my flamin' rocker.'

Tiffany seized Jen by the arm. 'You've got a short memory. How long ago is it since Nuts nicked your kid's dinner money? Gave you some licks? Proved beyond any doubt that he's a useless, sponging waster? You're worrying about what John Black might do? What about the things Nuts has already done and will carry on doing if you give him the chance? Sometimes you only get one chance to change your life, sis, and you have to take it and then accept the consequences. Yeah, we've got some problems now but if we play our cards right, we can come through. And despite what you may think we've still got some cards to play with – so toughen up and help me out. And the best way you can help me out is by cutting out feeling sorry for yourself and putting the shoulder to the wheel.'

Jen was unimpressed. 'It's alright for you, you've got no children. I have.' Tiffany tried to keep the hurt off her face but she knew she'd failed when her sister hugged and kissed her. 'Sorry, I didn't mean that to sound the way it did. I know you're doing your best for me and I know we had to get rid of Nuts somehow; I just wish we hadn't done it like this.'

They hit the road again. Tiffany's hurt went way beyond the jibe about her not having children. When it came to playing cards, she knew she was playing two games at once and some of the cards she was turning were marked. When she saw her sister's distress, Tiffany wasn't happy about what she was doing. There were high stakes on the table and Tiffany still wasn't sure who was going to win them.

Tiffany saw that her silence was upsetting Jen even more, and insisted, 'I know you're doing your best.' But could she say the same about herself, she wondered? She couldn't do this. She had to say something. 'Jen look, I need . . .'

Her words dribbled away when they drove onto The Devil and saw a cop car outside of their mum's block and a crowd of people looking up towards Babs' flat.

Sixty-Two

Dee stared at the decorated dining-room table ready for lunch and went ballistic: 'What the fuck is that?' she screamed at the two catering staff who had laid the table, her hand pointing at a huge floral arrangement in the centre. 'This ain't bloody Kew Gardens. I don't want my mum to think she's nattering the afternoon away to a flippin' giant daffodil!'

Dee felt as nervous as hell about her mum coming around, and it was showing. For many years, she had been preparing to welcome her mother to her home, but the nature of their relationship was such that this had never happened. There was always a reason. Dee was too busy or her mum was too busy. Something happened to one or the other at the last moment that meant the date they'd set wouldn't work. Dee had arranged for her mum to visit sometime 'next week' or 'next month' and then, when that week or month came around, neither of them had made the phone call. The two women had never been able to turn their mother/daughter relationship into a reality. They both knew and understood why. And it was the real reason why Dee was so soppy over children: because she remembered how it had been when she was one.

The situation baffled John. 'Get your mum over and then you won't have to do it again. How long's this been going on for?' Then he would add in an undertone, 'She's not a nutter is she? I don't want a nutter over here.'

Her Mum wasn't a nutter, but that was no comfort to Dee. When she finally made a firm date with her mum, she became panic stricken and spent the hours before frantically trying to prevent herself from calling back and saying the visit was off, because something had cropped up. Then she began to hope something would crop up so she could call the visit off for real. Nicky still wasn't talking to her and John, but she could hardly use that as an excuse, because it might make her look like a bad parent. Then there was the car, of course, but she couldn't use that as an excuse for obvious reasons. Dee had to face the awful truth – her mum was really coming for Sunday lunch and there was nothing she could do about it.

'Get that off the table,' Dee demanded. 'In fact, you can all leave now that the nosh is all sorted.'

After she paid the catering company an outrageous fee, Dee got the Dyson out and started madly hoovering the family room for a third time, like she was under strict orders from Kim and Aggie from *How Clean Is Your House?*

'How many more times are you planning to run that vacuum cleaner around?' John asked, looking at her out of the corner of his eye.

'I don't want my mum thinking I'm a slut.' She watched carefully to see if her husband whispered anything under his breath. When he didn't, she picked up an ornament and began frantically rubbing it as if hoping a genie might appear. Without looking up she asked, 'Where's Nicky?'

'I don't know. He's not talking to us, is he? In his room probably, planning to murder us in our beds so he can bring Tiffany back.'

'Bitch.'

'Well, quite.'

'The thing is I need him talking and on his best behaviour when my mum comes round.'

John pulled a face. 'You'd better go and find Tiffany then.'

Dee put the ornament down, abandoned the Dyson and pelted upstairs to Nicky's room where she tapped respectfully on the door. 'Nicky darling . . .' There was no reply so she tried again with gentle knocking and her best voice. This seemed to work as she got a reply.

'Knob off.'

Dee swallowed her bile and had another go. 'Babes, you haven't forgotten your new grannie's coming round? Best bib and tucker required.'

No answer. Dee decided to cut to the chase and drop the mummy act. 'Alright, what do you want? Help me out here.' When she got no response and saw that her son was beyond even bribing she realised how bad things were. She tried for a last time with an effort to make it sound as if the family dispute was all a bit of a joke. 'I know you won't let me down, babes. I'm your mum after all. We'll go out tomorrow and have a laugh about it. Could you wear your school uniform? I want Mum to see what a clever little soldier you are.'

This was too much for Nicky who shouted, 'Really, fuck off.'

As she ran back downstairs, she cursed the boy out. 'If that little bastard shows me up, I'll get Tiffany back and ban *him* from the house.' She went back to the front room and put the hoover back on before switching it off and shouting at John, 'When are you getting changed then?'

John was nonplussed. 'Changed?'

'You're not wearing that, are you? Slacks and a football shirt? Go and put on one of your five grand suits, a shirt and a tie. I'm not having my mum seeing you dressed like that or she'll think I'm married to a right Harris.'

John put his book down with a smile and went upstairs to change without saying a word. But Dee knew what he was thinking – at least her mum's arrival has taken her mind off the car.

And he was right. Dee flew up to her bedroom and entered the massive, connected dressing room, stuffed with clothes and shoes that Harrods would be proud to stock. She bit the inside of her cheek trying to make up her mind what to wear. She didn't want to come across as slaggy or overdone, like a turkey for Christmas dinner, but she did want to make a good impression: one that showed off her style and good taste. She turned her attention to her clothes. Florescent pink, electric blue, eye-grabbing gold with sequins – none of her stuff was the type of gear a daughter should put on to welcome her mum into her home for the first time. Bollocks, what was she going to wear? Her mind in a proper whirl, Dee decided to leave the bedroom and give the house a nervous once-over again. That's when she caught her gobby son trying to sneak out of the conservatory.

As he opened the double doors to leave, Nicky turned and saw her run in. Defeated he closed them again and began to head back to his bedroom. As he went by, Dee grabbed him gently by the collar and led him over to a chintz sofa by a picture window that looked out over the countryside. She sat him down and took his hand, which he reluctantly let her do. 'Listen, Nicky love, I know how you feel about Tiffany. I really do, because I feel the same way. Me and her go back a long way and we've done each other a few favours along the way too. And I don't blame you for getting the hump because we've had to ban her from the house, because I wouldn't like it if someone did that to me either. So get the nark if you want to. But the thing is, I've got my mum coming over and I want to put on a bit of a show. She's an old dear and seeing her grandson looking proud will cheer her up. Now please, help me out.'

Dee could see from the sneering look on his face that Nicky was about to say, 'But I'm not her grandson,' so she dug him gently in the ribs with her elbow and begged again, 'Please, help me out.'

Nicky looked down at the floor and then it seemed he'd had an idea. 'OK, if you let Tiffany come back, I'll be a good grandson.'

Now he was taking the piss. Struggling to control her temper, Dee told him, 'We've been through that; she can't come back. It's nothing personal, but believe me, she can't come back.'

Nicky fixed her eyes. 'Then it's nothing personal but I can't help.'

The boy might not have been her blood son but he shared her determination and single mindedness. 'It's your dad who's got the problem with Tiffany. If you behave while your nan's here, I'll have a word with him.' Dee wasn't sure if she was lying or not, but she was so desperate, it hardly mattered. 'I'm not promising mind.'

Nicky nodded. 'Fair enough.'

Dee held her arms out and they gave each other a hug, like a couple of mafia bosses who'd just agreed a deal but were already trying to think of ways to double cross each other. As they embraced, the front doorbell rang. Alarmed, Dee looked at her watch but saw that it was far too early for her mum to put in an appearance. She left Nicky and walked out to the hall where she met John who was coming from the family room. The two walked up to the heavy, oak-panelled front door. John peered through the peephole and then drew his head back in surprise. He looked again before whispering, 'I don't fucking believe this.'

He undid the lock and threw the door open. Dee followed John out and looked at the scene in shock. Her car, valeted like a jewel, was sitting outside and a man was standing beside it, like a salesman. Holding the keys up to be inspected, he said proudly, 'Hello, John. Remember me? I'm Nuts. I've brought your car back.'

Sixty-Three

'It's probably nothing,' Tiffany said, her voice shaking as she tried to reassure her frantic sister.

But Jen wasn't listening as she hustled through the crowd downstairs, everyone whispering to each other as they looked up at her mum's flat. She moved urgently towards the single cop near the car. 'What's happened?'

'Break-in, by the look of it. Probably the local scrotes trying to raise money for drugs. Nothing serious.'

One of the onlookers tutted and said, 'It's getting terrible round here. They should bring back hanging, if you ask me.'

'A break-in?' Jen heard her sister say, from behind her. 'What number?'

Jen bombed up the stairs when she heard the number for her mum's place. *My girls. My girls. My girls.* Her heart raced like crazy as she took the steps, two at a time. If anything had happened to her girls, she would never forgive herself. *This is all your fault. All your fault.*

Jen sucked in a shocked breath as she came face to face with what had happened to her mum's flat door. It had been nearly knocked off its hinges in a frenzied attack. She dashed inside the flat, her hand flying to her mouth. It looked like a pub after a bar room brawl. Courtney's and Little Bea's toys were scattered everywhere.

'Is this your home, madam?' a policeman in the sitting room asked her.

But Jen ignored him as she flew to the bedrooms, screaming her daughter's names. Both rooms were turned upside down, with no sign of her children.

'Jen,' she heard Tiffany shout, but she ignored her too and ran into the kitchen. No children. No Babs. Her face started to crumble as she headed back to the main room, legs like lead.

'Jen?' She heard Tiffany say again, but it felt like her sister's voice was coming from some far-off place, as if Jen were in her own little world – a place where her daughters should be but weren't. She could see the policeman's mouth moving, but couldn't figure out what he was saying. *Please God, not my girls. They haven't hurt anybody. What am I going to do? What am I going to do? What am . . . ?* That's when she noticed an old toolbox her mum had told her belonged to her Dad. Her face hardened as she got down on her knees, wrenched open the rusty top and emptied it onto the carpet, making the cop jump back.

She took no notice as the cop behind her started speaking: 'I understand a burglary's very upsetting madam but it would help if you could answer a few questions. Have you seen any suspicious-looking characters hanging around your flat lately?'

Jen ignored him and picked up a claw hammer and a screw-driver from the various tools that were lying in front of her. She put them in her handbag. She also noticed another object, wrapped in oilskin, which was tied up with ancient elastic bands. She felt it and dropped that in her handbag along with the other tools. Then she got up and pushed her sister out of the way as she headed for the kitchen.

* * *

Tiffany turned to the officer. 'This is our mum's place but my sister's very upset. Give her five minutes.'

The cop was frank. 'Well, there's not much we can do anyway, to be honest. But we'll file a report. You'll need to get the front door seen to. You can ring the council for that.'

Tiffany nearly groaned. 'Yeah, thanks for the tip, mate. Very helpful.'

She went to the kitchen and closed the door behind her. Jen was ferreting around in the cutlery draw.

'Sis, what are you doing?'

Jen picked up a fearsome-looking bread knife and turned to face her sister, who stood behind her. She shook with fury. 'This is your fault,' she spat. 'It's all your fault. It was your bloody idea in the first place and now . . . now . . .' Her voice broke with emotion. 'And now they've taken my kids. You're a bum and a crim, Tiffany; you always have been and I must've been off my nut to think of listening to you. Now get out of my fucking way.'

She slipped the bread knife into her belt and put a smaller one in her handbag.

Tiffany moved closer to her. 'No one's been taken. It's a–'

Jen pulled the knife back out of her belt so quickly her younger sister didn't see it until it was waving like a sword in her face. 'So where are they? Where are my girls? Answer me that.'

'Let's give Mum a ring.'

'On what? Two tin cans with a bit of string?' It was true, their mum didn't own a mobile. In fact their mum thought a landline was a bit racy.

Tiffany was terrified. She'd never seen Jen like this before. 'She's probably taken them up Vicky Park or something, or down The Roman, you know. Please, Jen, put that knife–'

Slap. Tiffany reeled from the impact of her sister's open palm against her cheek. Pain and shock stung her face.

'Victoria Park or Roman Road Market with all that's going on? You stupid, silly bitch.'

A raging Jen left the kitchen and headed to the toilet. Moments later, Tiffany heard the chain being pulled and Jen emerged with a glint in her eye, heading for the front door.

'Oi, where are you going?' Tiffany followed her sister, her palm rubbing her reddening cheek.

'To get my children. I know where they are.'

Tiffany's stomach churned as she realised what Jen was planning on doing. 'You can't go up there if that's what you're thinking. Those people are killers; you'll come out in a box. The girls aren't gone. Look, if you're worried, talk to the cops.'

'Talk to the Bill?' Her sister didn't stop her manic pace as she headed downstairs. 'Why? What are they going to do? Those people you've just called killers have probably got the police on their payroll.'

The two women emerged from the damp, dark, piss-stained stairwell into the cool daylight. Jen pulled her car keys from her bag and got into her motor with grim determination. Unable to think of what else to do, Tiffany quickly slipped into the front seat beside her. 'Please, think about what you're doing.'

'Get out.'

'No chance.'

'Please yourself.'

Jen turned on the ignition and the car lurched backwards before shunting forwards again, heading off towards the Mile End Road. When they reached the junction, she didn't hesitate but put her hand on the horn and pulled out in front of the oncoming traffic. Cars braked and swerved to avoid her before sounding their own horns in response to her honking. Jen ignored them, attempting to nose in front of any vehicle in her way, flashing her lights and shouting abuse as required.

Tiffany realised that her sister meant it. She laid her head against the rest. She had an hour, maybe more, maybe less, to come up with a plan. Otherwise . . . She looked at her sister's grim face and the tight icy grip she had on the wheel.

There was no doubt about it. Someone was going to get killed.

Sixty-Four

'Well, aren't you going to say something then? I mean, I ain't expecting a reward or nothing but a thank you very much would go down a treat.' Nuts let out a nervous laugh.

John looked at him in total disbelief. The fuckwit seemed to have no idea of the danger he was in. Dee barrelled past her husband, snatched the keys from Nuts' hands without looking at him and walked over to her car. John had one eye on her as she inspected the bodywork and peered inside and the other on Nuts. He put his arm around the young man's shoulder and led him some distance away to talk to him.

'What the fuck are you playing at? Eh? Seriously?'

Nuts widened his eyes as if he were hurt. 'Well, I heard your missus' car was nicked and there was a lot of slanderous verbal going round that I might have had something to do with it. And, err, you must have heard those cock 'n' bull stories too. Obviously it was nothing to do with me – I mean, as if. Anyway, although I've been out of the car business for a while now, I thought I'd show willing and track it down for you. I kept me ear to the ground, spoke to some of my contacts and traced it; caught the bloke who thieved it and gave him a kicking; and now here I am with the motor. Cushty eh?'

John looked over at Dee who was subjecting her recovered vehicle to a forensic examination. He also noticed Nicky at an upstairs window staring down at the scene. He turned back to Nuts. 'So who was this bloke?'

'What bloke?'

This bloke really is a knob head. 'The tea leaf who stole the wife's motor.'

John could hear Nuts' voice had become slightly hesitant and the younger man's shoulder was stiffening under his grip. 'Just a bloke, you know. From South London, I believe.'

John pursed his lips. He looked over his shoulder at Dee and then up at Nicky. He looked at the gravel under his feet, sighed deliberately and whispered, 'So what's this fella's name then?'

'Does it matter? I mean, Dee's got her car back, which is the important thing.'

'Dee?' John said harshly. 'You don't have the right to let my wife's name touch your lips.'

Nuts frantically nodded. ''Course, Mister Black. No disrespect intended.'

John clasped his one-time employee even closer. 'I need that name.' At the same time, John noticed his wife disappear inside the house, but he was drawn back to the dipstick when he started answering him.

'Well, I mean, I don't know his real name. He uses the handle "the cat" though. Out of Croydon I think . . . or maybe Tooting, I'm not sure.'

John Black was a proper criminal. He only believed in using violence for business reasons rather than personal ones. He believed feuds, vendettas and revenge belonged in the playground, not in the world of professional guys like him. It was true that he'd promised Dee that he would sort out the tosser who'd helped himself to her prized possession. But now that she had it back and he could look forward to a quiet life again, or at least as quiet a life as it was possible to get with a woman like his wife, he could see no reason for any further unpleasantness. And he couldn't possibly regard a small timer like Nuts as worthy of the effort anyway.

It was time to wrap this up, all nice and neat like. 'Listen, my old friend, I'm going to do you a massive favour. By now I should be breaking every bone in your body before handing your remains over to a reliable associate, to dispose of them in a responsible way. But I'm in a good mood.'

John saw his wife reappear, clutching something in her hand, and resume her examination of her car. 'You see that gate in the fence over there?' he asked Nuts quietly. 'I want you to run very fast to it, climb over and then follow the foot-path a couple of miles until you reach a small village where's there's a bus stop. Get a bus back to London, collect your gear and then piss off somewhere far away. For good. Because if I ever see you anywhere, or if I hear you're still in town, my mood will turn very dark indeed—'

'John!!! Come here right now.'

John turned to see Dee standing by her car and realised she was holding a torch in one hand. She wore that hard look on her face that told him loud and clear she was bursting to do significant damage to somebody. He guided a shaking Nuts back to where she'd opened the car doors for him, so that he could look inside.

Dee leaned in and pulled up the armrest to display the slim compartment inside. 'I had Marilyn customised so that she would fit my sunglasses.'

John felt Nuts try to tag away from him, but he held him tight. Dee slammed the door and shone the torch along its distinctive painted white trim. 'You notice anything, Nuts?' she challenged the now terrified man. He shook his head. 'What most people don't know is that, me being a right flash cow, I had tiny diamantes encrusted into the trim. Now it should glitter with this light.'

There was no glitter. Dee pulled a nail file from her pocket and scraped at the classic black paintwork. She shone the torch again. Under the scraped paint was a navy blue. 'It's a re-spray.' She looked up at Nuts. 'This ain't my car.'

Sixty-Five

'Stick a duster in his gob. I don't want him weeping and wailing while my mum and me are having a chat on the chaise longue upstairs. That'll put us right off our coffee and cake.'

The basement of John and Dee's house had been turned into a safe room in case any of their enemies decided to stage a house invasion, or the cops did a raid. It was empty, apart from CCTV screens, phones and some weapons for self-defence. The only furniture was a couple of chairs, and on one of these Nuts had been bound with a length of rope and a pair of Dee's stockings. Dee was torn between fixing her face for her mother's visit or venting her fury on the car thief. The fury was winning.

'The fucking front of it. He nicks my Marilyn and then brings a fake around by way of apology and imagines I'll fall for it. Then I suppose we were all going to have a good laugh and go for a drive. What a fucking tosser.' She let fly at her victim with a kick to his leg. Nuts groaned behind the gag. Dee screamed, 'You wanker. You're dead, you're . . .' She could think of no words that would do justice to her anger so she gave him another kick to make her point.

John straightened the suit and tie he was wearing for the visit of Dee's mother and took her by the arm to lead her away.

'Alright, calm down. We'll sort him out later. Your mum will be here anytime now. Go and play happy families with her. Only remember, when you give her the grand tour, don't bring her down here.'

Dee pulled her shoulders back. 'You're right. Plus, I'm better than this. I'm not a violent person.' But she gave Nuts an additional kick anyway.

John took her to the steps that led back up to the house. He looked back at Nuts and tried not to show any sympathy but he felt some anyway. The small timer's wrists and face were already going red and he was desperately professing his innocence, although with his mouth stuffed, it came out as the sound of someone slowly being suffocated. Too bad for him he wasn't an animal or a child – in that case, Dee would be getting him a bun or a saucer of milk, whatever it was he'd done. John was confident that Nuts would tell them where the stolen car had gone, now he was under lock and key. He had no choice. Whether that meant they'd be able to get the car back or not, and what was to happen to Nuts afterwards, were other matters. But John knew he had a little time now to make up his mind.

When they reached the top of the steps, they were startled to find their son waiting there. Nicky seemed agitated. 'Who's that bloke?'

John looked at Dee and then back at his boy. 'What bloke? There's no bloke.'

'The geezer who brought mum's car back. The one you roughed up on the drive. The one you've just dragged down to the safe room.'

John put his arm on Dee's shoulder. 'I'll tell you what, my dear, why don't you go and powder your nose and plump the cushions for your mum's arrival while I deal with this.'

John took Nicky into the dining room and closed the door. 'There is no bloke, OK? You haven't seen any geezer round here because he doesn't exist. This house isn't public school and we don't play cricket in this place. Instead, think of your home as a miniature East End. And in the East End, you don't see things that you don't need to see or hear things that you don't need to hear. And above all, you certainly don't say things you don't need to say. So, as far as you're concerned, there is no bloke. Are you getting me here, son?'

John could see the boy got him but it didn't seem to be helping. Instead, Nicky looked really spooked, which he didn't understand. 'You think he nicked Mum's car, don't you?'

'Perhaps I would if he existed but he doesn't exist, so it's not an issue.'

'He didn't nick it; you're so wrong.'

John's patience ran out. 'If you've got a problem with your hearing perhaps a cuff on the ears might help clear the tubes?'

Nicky said no more. He left the room with his head down. John was disappointed but he'd always suspected that if they sent the kid to public school, he might turn out straight. Nicky should know better than to flap his gums when his mum and dad were taking care of business.

Dee was madly rushing around the house. She'd changed into a hot pink number with so much bling attached it would have made 50 Cent looked underdressed. She seemed to have forgotten the man who didn't exist. 'Nicky! Get in the front room. Why aren't you in your school uniform? And have you got the prizes and certificates you've won out, to show my mum?'

'I ain't won no prizes or certificates,' he answered back in a sulky voice.

Dee's head was spinning, nerves eating her up. The bloody doorbell was going to go any minute. 'Right waste of money your education's been; you're a right show up. Never mind, tell her about your prizes and certificates anyway, she won't know the difference. Oh, and talk fucking posh.'

A car pulled up outside the house. Dee hurried to the window crying, 'She's here, she's here.'

She disappeared into the hall and touched up her Halle Berry cut in the mirror before heading to the door.

John walked into the family room and, after clocking a deeply depressed-looking Nicky on the sofa, he went to the window himself. Outside, a woman, who he suspected wasn't much older than himself, was paying a cabbie. John studied the scene with a weary look, as he could see this was going to be a long evening with Dee on tenterhooks, taking care of her mum while he came up with a plan to deal with the scumbag they had trussed up like a chicken downstairs. Then he noticed something outside. He pulled back the curtain and had a closer look before whispering, 'Who the hell are they then?'

The cab carrying Dee's mum had passed Jen and Tiffany who were parked in a lay-by on the way to Dee's house. Not that either of them had noticed. Jen's gaze was fixed on the chimneys to the property, where she was convinced her children were held captive. It seemed to Tiffany that her sister had finally calmed down and was ready to listen to reason.

'Let's go home and call the Plod, eh?' she said, keeping her voice very calm. 'Even if Dee's got the kids, they won't be in the house. But she hasn't got the kids, I promise you. It's not her style, I know her. Kidnapping adults? Yes, I get that. But kids? No chance ... Mum's probably home by now and wondering where we are.' She squeezed her sister's arm. 'Come on eh? Let's go home.'

Jen didn't look at her sister but just carried on staring.

Tiffany had spent the entire journey trying to come up with a plan but the only thing she could think of was to wait for Jen to cool it and then use common sense on her. It wasn't working.

Jen drew a deep breath and began rummaging around in her handbag. 'Right, I'm going in. Are you coming? If not, you can wait here and pick us up after the job.'

Tiffany drew a deep breath in turn, before saying. 'They're not in there, Jen. Even if they have taken the kids, they won't be there. Those two aren't stupid. They're proper criminals; they'd be keeping them miles away. Please listen to me. I know how upset you are but what you're doing is fucking bonkers, babe.'

Jen didn't even look at her; that's how far she was lost in her own world of revenge. 'So you're not coming then. Suit yourself. It's probably better you're not involved anyway.'

Tiffany madly shook her head. 'You'll go to prison! What use are you going to be to the kids if you're banged up? Have a think about that.' Jen opened the car door to get out but Tiffany grabbed her arm and dragged her back. Her voice turned rough and angry. 'What do you think is waiting in there for you? Some soppy old goat from a sweet shop? This is John Black we're talking about. He's armed and dangerous. He's killed people. And you think you're going in there with a busted hammer and a bread knife to take him on? Have you gone nuts?'

The two women began to struggle. There were scuffs, bumps and thumps in the confined space and it seemed that Jen was trying to whack her sister with her handbag. Tiffany clenched her fists, determined to knock Jen out as a last resort and drive her home unconscious. But she unclenched her fist and gasped with horror when she saw that she was staring down the barrel of a battered and stained Browning pistol, which was being held against her face.

Sixty-Six

Tiffany reared back in stunned horror. 'Oh my God, Jen, where the fuck did you get that from?' This wasn't the soft-hearted sister she knew. Jen appeared cold, determined – a woman who'd suddenly realised that you had to harden your heart sometimes to deal with the world.

Jen clasped both hands around the butt of the gun. 'It was in our old man's toolbox, wrapped in oil skin.'

Tiffany shook her head in utter disbelief. 'You picked that shooter up in front of that cop? Now I know you've lost it . . .'

'I didn't know it was a gun until I went into mum's toilet and had a look. Anyway, what do they care?'

'I think the courts do. Five years, isn't it? And I think you get more if you actually kill people with them.'

Jen pushed the driver's door open with her foot and began to back out of the car while keeping the pistol trained on her sister. To Tiffany, she appeared both unnaturally calm and wild at the same time, with the deadly weapon in her hand and her hair hanging over her face. Tiffany didn't know much about firearms but the gun looked so knackered she wasn't sure it would shoot anyway. And that was supposing Jen knew how to fire it, which Tiffany very much doubted. She watched her sister slink away. A few yards down the road, her sister stopped and began to inspect and fiddle with the gun, holding it up to get a better view of it.

Tiffany put her head in her hands, rubbed her face with them and reached for the car door. Her sister had been right, back at their mum's flat. This was all her fault. Framing Nuts for the car theft had been mega stupid. But barging into John and Dee's place with a shooter was about the craziest idea anyone could think of, and the last thing she'd intended. Then again, this was all her fault and she had to go with her. She couldn't let her sister go in there alone; Jen was too good a person and too good a mother. Plus, the guilt was starting to eat away at Tiffany. She should confess to Jen – tell her the full story of what was going on. If anything happened to the girls because of her . . .

Resolved to tell Jen the truth, Tiffany opened the door, but before she could say anything there was flash of yellow and orange, a rumble of thunder and the windscreen crashed backwards into thousands of pieces, showering her with shards of glass. For a few seconds, she sat rigid as an ironing board while her head tried to understand what had happened. It was only when Jen came rushing up to her, showing her the gun and crying, 'I'm sorry, I'm sorry. It went off. Are you alright?' that she understood that her sister had accidentally fired it.

Tiffany climbed out of the car and snatched the pistol from her hand. 'I'll look after that. Some fearsome gunslinger you are.' She checked the gun and tried to find the safety catch. 'Mind you, the old man is partly to blame; fancy keeping a shooter in a toolbox with the catch off. What a prat Stanley Miller was.'

She could see her sister was desperately trying to fight the tears – tears of utter madness and rage. She put her arm around Jen and gave her a hug. 'Alright, come on, we'll go up there together and see if we can find out what's going on. But the shooter's for self-defence, OK? And chuck those knives and the hammer away. We won't be needing them.'

There were clanks as Jen did as she was told and threw her various weapons into a ditch. Through muffled sobs she asked her sister, 'How are we going to get in there?'

Tiffany laughed. 'Hadn't really thought this through, had you, sis? Don't worry; I know how to find my way in. They're too arrogant to make the place really secure; they think no one would dare try and break into their home. Although having seen Dee in full sail, I'm not all that surprised.'

They reached the perimeter wall of the house. 'But I'm afraid we might have lost the element of surprise. Your gun shot will probably have alerted everyone for miles.'

In the walls was a wooden gate that led through to the back garden. Tiffany turned the latch and led her sister through. They walked past the flowerbeds, avoiding the lawn where they might be seen and over to the conservatory. Inside the house there was no sign of life.

'Hide by the shed while I check the front.'

Tiffany made her way down the decking that joined the back garden to the front, that Dee had named 'Lovers' Lane'. She ducked low as she passed the kitchen window, then very carefully peered inside. A miffed-looking John was struggling with the popcorn maker. He seemed unhappy but not like a man who'd just organised the kidnap of two children. Tiffany was more convinced than ever that she was about to break into a gangster's house on a wild goose chase with a crazy sister and a gun. She carried on down Lovers' Lane until she reached a wooden partition with a gate in it that led out to the front gardens and the drive where various vehicles were parked, including John's Range Rover, which looked in a sorry state after the crash. Over by the gate was another car, covered with a tarpaulin.

There was no sign of visitors and no sign that John had stationed anyone out front to keep an eagle eye open for unwanted ones. When Tiffany got back to Jen, she shook her head. 'Let's go. The kids aren't here. John's in the kitchen making popcorn for Christ's sake. Kidnappers don't make popcorn.'

Jen's expression grew stubborn. 'They're in there. I know they are. Mother's intuition.'

Tiffany gritted her teeth, felt the gun in her pocket and gestured with her head for her sister to follow. 'Alright then, mad bird. Let's go.'

Nuts had twisted and turned to avoid the reach of John and Dee, for a crime he hadn't committed. But that was then. Now it was just a case of staying alive. Christ he'd only tried to make the situation right by nicking another Pirano FS that he heard was being kept safe in a garage in Broxbourne. The only problem he had foreseen was that it was bloody blue and that had been easily sorted (or so he thought) by a re-spray. But he'd got that totally wrong, not realising that mad woman Dee also had her car customised.

He sat in darkness, bound hand and foot with a duster taped to his mouth, the only light coming from a couple of CCTV screens showing footage from the garden and the drive. He knew he wasn't the sharpest tool in the box but he also knew how to keep his nerve and he had some time. Dee had visitors. He was safe until they went and the deadly couple upstairs came down to lay into him again. Using his tongue as a make-shift fork he began chewing the duster into pieces, slowly but surely, and then storing the shreds in his cheeks like a hamster. When there was enough space in his mouth he began levering the tape that closed his lips, using his tongue again. Filling his lungs with air, he blew through the small spaces on the sticky surface of the tape covering his mouth while grinding his jaws to loosen it. Finally, he moved himself and the chair he was tied to across the floor and over to a bench, by bumping it from side to side. He pressed the dislodged tape against the wood with his head and rocked it backwards and forwards. The tape finally came free. He spat the chewed duster on the floor.

He looked upwards. Dee and John had visitors. But who? If it was a team of police officers, they might come down if they heard cries of help. If it was friends of John's, they would still be coming down but not to help out. He shuffled his chair along the floor to inspect the weapons John had stockpiled in the makeshift safe room. They included knifes, an axe and a ceremonial sword. They were all temptingly sharp but he had no spare limbs to use them with. He knew he only needed one. He moved himself over to get some more light from the CCTV screen to examine the bindings on his arms and legs. His hands were tied with rope. It would take some cutting. Nor could he wriggle free from the knots. He knew the more he struggled, the more his wrists would swell and the more firmly he would be trapped. But the bonds around his feet were stockings and Nuts could see they had ladders in them. They might give, under enough pressure.

He shuffled back to the weapons and managed to pull a knife off the wall between his teeth, then went back to the door where he dropped it, before tipping the chair and his body along with it onto its side. Working himself and the chair along the floor like a snail with cramp, he drew up against the blade and used his teeth to wedge it into a gap in the doorframe so the fearsome-looking edge was pointing outwards. Finally, he worked himself back so that John's mad bitch wife's stockings were resting against the blade. He rocked the chair and himself against it, bending and stretching his body in agony as he tried to cut through his restraints. Within seconds he managed to take down the first stocking without injury. He bit his lip in pain rather than cry out and alert his captors as

he turned the chair over with his now free leg and tried the
same trick on the other side. That worked too, but at the cost
of a gash through his trousers and sock and into his ankle,
which dripped blood onto the floor.

With his legs free, he struggled to his feet, his wrists still
tied to the chair. He soon realised that the drops of blood were
turning into a trickle. He knew that time was short. If his foot
seized up, it was over. If he'd cut an artery, he might be over.
He had more freedom of movement now his legs were free but
he knew that running the ropes on his wrists against the knife
risked slashing them. And even if he was unbound, he still had
to get the fuck out of this room. He willed the bleeding to stop
but as his haunted eyes flashed around the room, his attention
was caught by a CCTV screen where two figures were moving
along a garden wall, taking care not to be seen. Transfixed, he
could see they were both women and that they were both of a
certain size and build. They disappeared from one screen and
then reappeared on another. Finally, a lone woman appeared
on a third screen, her face fully on display. No doubt about it
this time. It was Tiffany. He knew without having to see her
who the other bird was.

For a few moments, Nuts forgot the rope and his wound and
wondered aloud, 'What the fuck are they doing here?'

By the conservatory door was a water butt, which collected
rain from the gutter above. Tiffany pushed it back and took a
key from underneath, which she used to turn the lock. She
went inside followed by Jen. Tiffany could tell that her sister
was struck by a bad case of nerves when she giggled, 'I should
be locked up in St Clements . . .'

'You're not wrong there,' Tiffany whispered, agreeing.
thinking they both deserved to be sectioned in the local psychi-
atric hospital, a couple of minutes' walk from The Devil. 'Now

shut up. And remember, we're here to see if they have the girls, that's all. Dad's shooter is just insurance.'

Tiffany was beyond anxious herself. As she held her ear to the door to see if anyone was on the other side, she understood the full enormity of what they were doing when she heard John's heavy and unmistakable footsteps on the other side. She listened as they faded and headed to the back of the house – the snooker room probably, or Dee's 'Hollywood' room, where guests could watch films on a big screen, sitting in plush seats. That was more likely. John had been making popcorn in the kitchen so perhaps they were watching a film together; in which case, there would be time to go around the house undisturbed.

She pulled the door open, went into the hall and listened. She could hear no noise and she was confident her ex-employers were at the pictures. Tiffany gestured to her sister to follow. The two women came to a halt at the top flight of steps that led down to darkness. Tiffany listened intently to the house but could hear nothing. 'Wait here. Down there is their safe room. If the kids are anywhere, they'll be in there.'

'I'm coming too.'

'No, we can't get in. It's got a keypad. Don't worry, I'll knock. If there's anyone in there, I'll hear.'

Tiffany crept down the steps into the gloom where the forbidding door was flush against the wall. She tapped on it gently and pressed her ear up for any sound on the other side. There was none. She tapped more loudly the next time and listened even more intently but there was still no noise. At the top of the steps she shook her head. 'No, listen, if they were going to be anywhere, it would be there. Let's quit while we're still ahead.'

Jen grew pissed again. 'Give me the gun and I'll bloody do it myself. I'm not leaving here until we've checked everywhere.'

For crying out loud . . . But without another word, Tiffany took her quietly and quickly upstairs and, very gingerly, they looked into all the rooms. Only Nicky's door was closed and had a light inside.

Jen was curious. 'Whose room is this? Could they be in there?'

'It's the kid's. You met him in that burger bar . . .' She didn't add, 'and he's the author of all our misfortunes,' but she didn't need to. Tiffany opened the door and went in. She knew, without the tell-tale sound of computer games being played, Nicky wouldn't be there. Those beeps and bumps were his signature tune, his fingerprints. Jen followed. 'Where is he?'

'I don't know. He's probably out joy riding.'

As they made their way back down the stairs, Tiffany heard a door swing open below and John's footsteps. She turned in panic and hustled her sister back to the landing. Leaning over the bannister, she saw John pass and heard him muttering, 'What am I, a fucking usherette-come-waiter now?'

Frozen to the spot, the two women waited until John returned the way he'd come, holding a bowl full of popcorn under one arm and a pot of tea in the other. His footsteps faded and a door swung shut. Baffled, Tiffany sat her sister down at the top of the stairs. 'Something's not right here. They don't have tea; they're coffee drinkers. And what's with all the popcorn? Dee watches her figure and John can't eat that much, he'd be sick. They've got no visitors or there'd be cars outside. I don't get it.'

Jen drew a deep breath. 'I do.' She rose to her full height and scampered down the stairs as if she were in her own home, turned and headed towards the back of the house. Panic stricken, Tiffany chased after her. 'Sis, please, they'll hear you; the whole fucking house will hear you.'

'Let them hear me. Now get the shooter out, we're here on business.'

She pushed through a connecting door and, as Tiffany followed, she could hear the voices of John and Dee on one side in the snooker room and the sound of cartoon music coming from 'Hollywood' on the other. Jen turned to her sister in triumph. She pointed at the music. 'That's where my kids are.'

Jen kicked open the double doors to 'Hollywood', reaching for the light switch on the wall. She threw it and everything in the darkened room became clear. In the middle of the front row of plush crimson seats was Nicky with a bowl of popcorn on his lap. Jen's two daughters sat either side of him with their hands in the bowl. Nicky picked up the remote and hit the pause on the film, *Finding Nemo*.

For a few brief moments, everyone in the room froze, too shocked to speak. Even Nemo looked stunned on the screen. Nicky rose to his feet, tipping the bowl and scattering popcorn on the floor. Horrified, he hissed, 'Tiff, Jen, what the fuck?' He then turned to the little girls and said, 'Pardon my language, ladies . . .' and then, back to the two women, 'What are you doing here? Get out, flippin' hells bells, before Mum and Dad see you.'

Tiffany ran to pick up the girls so they could make their escape but Jen was too quick for her. She got there first and Tiffany could almost feel the delayed hours of anger welling up inside her sister as she flew at Nicky screaming, 'What are you doing with my kids, you fucking, kiddie napping little bastard?'

Nicky looked at the door in fear and whispered loudly as he could, 'Your kids?' His eyes nearly jumped out of his head.

Jen ignored him as she hugged and smiled at her children. 'Are you alright, my little angels? Nothing bad has happened has it?' She turned to Tiffany. 'Come on, let's leg it.' She turned her attention and anger on to Nicky. 'As for you – if you've hurt my kids, I'll make you suffer until you wish you'd never been born.'

But Nicky wasn't listening; his eyes were firmly fixed on the door, dreading what was going to happen next. As if on cue, the doors flung open and Dee waltzed in like a cowboy in a saloon. 'What's the racket? We're trying to have a quiet chat in there.' It was Tiffany that her eyes alighted on first and she didn't seem in the least surprised to see her. 'Oh, it's you, is it? I had a feeling you might turn up again, sooner or later. Still, it's no great shakes; you can join the party.' Then she clocked Jen. 'And who are you?'

Jen put her children down, jerked her hand into her sister's pocket and grabbed the pistol. She levelled it at Dee.

Sixty-Seven

'Get out of the way.' Jen's voice wobbled as she held the gun tight, keeping it trained on Dee. No one moved. 'Let us go and there won't be any drama. Otherwise, I'll fucking splatter you all over Essex.'

The two small girls seemed unsure if this was all a game or not but they held on tight to their mother's legs. But they released their grip slightly when they saw Dee walking across 'Hollywood' until the pistol was only a few inches from her chest. 'Put the piece away babes. You're upsetting the children.'

'Get out of the way.'

But Dee stood her ground. 'I don't know who you bloody well are or what the effing hell you think you're doing in my house, but you touch a hair on these kids' heads and you're finished.'

Jen twisted her mouth with rage as she pushed the pistol into Dee's chest. Then she screamed, 'You stay away from my bloody children.'

Dee reared back, her face smothered in shock. 'Your kids? What the hell is going on here?'

Before Jen could respond Courtney tugged her mum's leg. 'Mum, why are you being nasty to Auntie Dee?'

Jen used her spare hand to pull her daughter close and

snarled, 'Don't ever call this evil woman "Auntie" darling. She's not and never will be your Auntie.'

Another voice intruded as the door swung open again. 'How are my girls getting on? I . . .' Dee's mother's voice froze in her throat as she took in the scene before her.

'Mum, stay back,' Dee shouted.

'Mum?' both Jen and Tiffany said, stunned.

Babs Miller's heart sank as she stared at all three of her daughters.

'Mum, wh . . . what's going on?' Tiffany asked, her head still spinning. 'Dee says she's your daughter. Is that right?'

They were all in the snooker room, John and Nicky teaching Courtney and Little Bea how to play while Babs and her daughters sat in a corner across the room. The atmosphere was tense, all of them on edge, and Babs knew that she was the only one who could get this sorted. But first, she wanted some answers of her own.

'Jen, what the hell are you doing here, waving that shooter around? I nearly had a heart attack in the flippin' doorway.'

'And you will have heart failure if you don't tell me and Tiff what's going on,' Jen stormed back.

Jen's girls giggled as John praised Courtney for popping a blue.

Babs badly needed a glass of Blue Ruin to steady her nerves. No, make that a whole flamin' bottle. 'It was before I met your Dad. Let's just say that I was a girl who liked life – you know, parties, meeting fellas.' Seeing the astonished look on Jen and Tiffany's faces, she added, 'I was a young girl once, just like you two. I wanted a bit of razzamatazz in my life. What girl wouldn't?'

'But why didn't you ever tell us that you had another girl? That we had another blood sister?' Tiffany asked. Her eyes turned to Dee. 'And of all people, Dee fucking Black.'

'Bloody hell . . .' Jen muttered under her breath.

Dee finally spoke. 'That's right, dear sisters, Babs here fobbed me off on a foster parent while you two were getting the full-on mum treatment. I ain't saying it was because my dad was black or nothing but you've got to ask a few questions there, haven't you? Still, we've kissed and made up now – ain't we, Mummy? On the other hand, at least I missed out on having Stanley Miller as a stepdad. He sounds like a right chancer. Mind you, at least you know who your old man is.'

Babs could hear the pain in her eldest daughter's voice, under all her bluster. 'You were never a mistake, love; I just couldn't keep you. It was different back then; people weren't so forgiving of a young girl straying from the straight and narrow.'

'But I don't get it, Mum?' Jen burst in. 'What are you doing here with the girls? Your place has been turned over–'

Babs swore. 'That will be the little bleeders who've moved in next door. I've tried to get their mum to do something about it but she's high as a balloon in the sky.' She took a breath. 'This was the first time Dee was having me over to her home and, as I had the girls, I thought it would be a nice little treat for them if they came along too. But what are the two of you doing here. That's what I don't get.'

Jen and Tiffany shared a look. Then Tiffany explained. 'Remember some Face came looking for Nuts at Jen's? Well it was John here, on behalf of Dee looking for her car because the word was Nuts nicked her motor.'

Babs gasped as she fixed her gaze onto her eldest girl. 'You can't go around threatening your sisters . . .'

'I didn't bloody well know they were my flesh and blood then, did I. I would've come straight to you, Mum, if I'd known, to get it sorted. But then, Mummy dearest, you've been keeping us all in the dark.'

Courtney laughed out loud as Nicky patted her on the head, which Dee saw. She turned to Jen with a slight smile. 'And what a pair of princesses they are, if I might say so, sis.' She called across the room, 'Aren't you girls?'

Both children nodded happily at their newly found Auntie Dee. Tiffany noticed that Dee's smile was blazing like the sun but that it suddenly faded. She looked across the room to see Nicky frantically pointing downwards with his finger at her. Dee looked over at John. 'Oi, we've forgotten about the B-I-L.'

John put his cue down. 'The B-I-L? Oh yeah – that B-I-L.'

'B-I-L?' Jen asked.

'Yes, sis.' Dee was clearly enjoying calling Tiffany and Jen 'sis'. 'You see, you're not the only one of my relatives who's turned up here today. My brother-in-law–'

Jen shot to her feet. 'Nuts?'

'The one and only,' Dee confirmed. 'Although we had another name for him, back in the day, but I wouldn't use it in front of children. As you know, the fool stole my motor and instead of giving it back and taking his punishment, can you believe the dickhead brought a fake round and tried to pass it off as the real thing.' Dee suddenly realised what the implications of Nuts being Jen's husband were. She dropped the piss taking and muttered at Jen, 'So is Nuts, like, the father . . . of your little princesses there?'

Jen slumped against the wall of the snooker room as she caught Tiffany's eye. Now Nuts was here, was the whole sorry story of how they'd fitted him up going to come out?

Dee coughed. 'Well, Nuts is waiting downstairs in another room having, shall we say, a smoke and a drink. We were going to have a word with him later, after Mum had gone. He only had to tell us where my car was and help get it back, that's all. We weren't going to do anything to him. We're not animals, are we, John?'

John gave her a sarcastic grin and confirmed, 'No, we're not animals.'

Dee was doing a reverse ferret faster than a ferret could manage. She looked at Courtney and Little Bea, who were mucking around with the balls on the snooker table. 'I mean, now we know that Nuts is family, I'm sure we can come to some arrangement. Can't we, John?'

John picked up his cue and started hitting balls again to the delight of the girls. His sarcasm was leaden. 'I dunno, dear, it's your ride after all.'

Dee pleaded with the rest of her family. 'I mean, he only has to give the car back, that's all. We don't care if he's sold it on. He can keep the money, we'll retrieve the car from whatever toerag bought it . . . I mean, I'm not being unreasonable here, am I?'

Tiffany stole the briefest of glances at Nicky whose expression begged her not to drop him in it. Tiffany tilted her head back, her brain thinking like crazy. She wanted to claim that she'd stolen the car but she knew that wouldn't work. She decided to tell as much of the truth as she could get away with, to get Nuts off the hook and keep Nicky out of trouble.

'Nuts didn't steal the car. I don't know who did but it wasn't Nuts. I got a mate of mine to make the anonymous phone call blaming him.' That got Dee ominously to her feet. 'Hear me out. I knew he'd be on John's list of possible culprits and I was hoping John would exile him out of London and he wouldn't be able to come back. Jen needs Nuts out of her life. He's the husband from hell.'

John looked at her as if she'd grown three heads. 'Exile the bastard? He stole my wife's car. What did you think I was going to do? Of course I was going to track the Herbert down and give him a hiding. Never mind exile, I've got my reputation to think about. Ask any judge, you can't let people get away with things like that or they start to take liberties.'

'Well, he didn't steal the car.'

Dee looked over at Jen. 'Bad hubbie is he, sis? Rough you up and that?'

Jen's head was sunk low, so Tiffany explained. 'He's worse than pond scum. He belts her one, anytime he feels like it. He nicks the kids' dinner money.'

Dee clenched her hands as she vibrated with anger. But she kept her silence.

'Look, Tiff, it's very nice of you to try and get Nuts out of trouble,' John said, 'but I'm afraid it's his thieving prints all over Dee's motor. We want it back and then we'll think about what happens next afterwards . . .'

Nicky cut him off as he called out, 'He didn't steal Mum's car. I did.'

Dee and John looked at their son like they were seeing him for the first time. Dee's brown skin had turned a sickly grey. She shook her head and blinked rapidly. 'Don't be silly, Nicky. This is not the time to wind me up. You're not even old enough to drive.'

'I stole it,' he continued in a high tone. Dee's face fell, hearing the truth in his voice. 'I was upset because you and Dad didn't give me something special for getting back into school, so I took your car to get my own back. I was going to bring it back but then everything got out of hand . . .'

'You little . . .' his father started saying, then he briskly walked towards him and grabbed him by the collar. As he was dragged bodily out of the room, Nicky started sniffling. John growled, 'I should've taken my belt to you years ago. You're spoilt rotten, that's what you are.'

'Leave him, John,' Dee demanded.

John couldn't believe his wife. 'Are you for real? He's taken us both for mugs and caused enough problems to create World War Three and you want me to leave the little shit alone?'

'John!' Knowing he wasn't going to get his own way, John reluctantly let Nicky go. 'We'll deal with him later.' Dee added, 'We don't want our guests – our family – to think that we're running one of those catholic homes for boys.' Her gaze snapped onto Tiffany. 'So, if my boy took my car and you all cooked up a story together to kipper Nuts, where is my Marilyn?'

Jen lifted her head and answered: 'When Nicky told Tiffany about the farm where he'd hidden the car, she went down there and drove it to a safe garage she knew in Southend.' She touched her heart. 'On my life, when me and Tiff went to get the car, it was gone. We looked up and down for it—'

'I swear, Mum,' Nicky pleaded. 'I never took it. I didn't even know anything about this garage in Southend.'

Dee sighed. 'Well, that's Nuts defo off the hook, because he says he found the car in a garage in Broxbourne. Silly sod, didn't think I would realise it was a fake.'

Tiffany quickly held up her hands. 'Like Jen said, when we went to get it from the garage in Southend, it was gone. Someone must've seen me put it there and, when I was gone, they saw their chance and took it.'

There was total silence until Little Bea's soft voice piped up, 'Nicky said we could do "The Birdie Song". I like "The Birdie Song". I'm really good at it. Watch.' Then she proceeded to hum the tune as she moved her hands, arms and hips around like a chicken. 'Come on, Auntie Dee,' she said as she stretched her hands out. 'Come and do it with me and Courtney.'

Dee at first looked as if someone was pointing a double-barrelled shotgun at her. Then she smiled and moved to her

newly discovered nieces and started humming along and joining in the actions. 'Come on, you lot,' she called out. 'Join in.
We might have our troubles but we're family. A new family.'

Babs was the first to join the party, then Tiffany and soon
everyone was prancing around doing 'The Birdie Song'. No
one kidded themselves that there weren't one or two problems
that still needed ironing out, but for now they were going to
celebrate the Millers and Blacks being one big happy family.
Soon the food and drink was flowing as Nicky hitched up his
stereo system and put on some music – although 'none of that
bitch and ho rap stuff' his father warned him, quietly in front
of the girls.

Dee moved over to John and whispered, 'Well, I suppose I'd
better go and get him – my brother-in-law, the innocent man.'

She did one final Birdie Song turn with Little Bea before she
left the party behind and was soon walking down the steps to
the safe room. When she reached the bottom, she typed the
code for the door, stepped inside and switched on the light,
and was greeted with a scene of carnage. Blood was splattered
on the floor and the walls. The stockings and rope that had
been used to secure Nuts were stained with red and scattered
around. The chair he'd been bound to was broken into several
pieces on the ground. The ceremonial sword and a knife lay on
the ground, flecked with scarlet.

But there seemed to be no Nuts.

Until a wild-eyed figure wielding an axe lunged at her from
behind a box case.

Sixty-Eight

In the moments before Nuts swung at Dee with the backside of the axe, she hardly recognised him. His light coloured shirt had both sleeves missing. One was clinging around his ankle, damp with blood. The other was wrapped around his wrist. His face was white and had a straggly fringe of hair falling over it. His one bare wrist was swollen and red. His lunge gave the impression of a toy whose batteries were about to run out.

Dee avoided the blow by smartly stepping to one side, while the momentum carried Nuts face down onto the floor, howling in pain. She made no attempt to stop him as he struggled to his feet, turned the axe blade out and tried for a second time to hit her. She held her hands out, grabbed the stock as it came towards her and wrenched it out of his feeble hands. She pulled up a chair and pushed him into it. He lolled like a puppet with cut strings. She was behind him now, axe in hand.

'You little prick.' She ran a finger along the blade. Even with only a little pressure, it was sharp enough to cut her skin. 'Do you know something? I'm going to regret what I have to do now – really, really regret it – which is why I'm going to do it quickly, before I have the chance to change my mind'.

She rested the sharp blade on his scalp like a chef about to chop a melon in two halves. Upstairs, the music was playing and the sound of the girls' running feet could be heard. She paused for a moment.

'But circumstances mean I've got no choice.' She examined the blade of the axe. 'We need to talk.'

Shrunken and looking as if he were about to pass out at any minute, Nuts said, 'Look, I've told you, I didn't steal . . .'

But she cut him short. 'Not about the car. I'm done worrying about the car. No, I'm talking about your marriage and your role as a father.'

Nuts blinked in disbelief and seemed to recover his composure slightly. 'My marriage? Look Dee, if I was you, I'd leave the off-the-wall interrogation techniques to the cops. Stay focused, eh? I've told you, I didn't take the car; I only nicked one for you to get you off my back. That's it, OK? Even if I had taken it, as soon as I found out it was yours, I'd have brought it right back pronto, straight up. I don't even know where you got the idea it was me who pinched it. Come on, Dee, you know me from the old days.'

'You're not listening, are you?' She ran her finger along the blade. It was sharp enough to cut silk. 'I know you didn't steal the car. But you did steal your kids' dinner money, didn't you? And in my book, that's far worse than stealing my ride.' She stared at him over the top of the axe head. 'But you know what makes it even worse? You stole dinner money from my nieces. That really deserves having your head split in two.' She got up from her chair, swinging the weapon by her side.

'My kids? Your nieces?' Nuts stared at her as if *she* should have the moniker Nuts. 'Are you popping pills or something? We'd have to be in an episode of *The Black and White Minstrel Show* for that to happen. Seriously, pack it in. Gimme a beating if you want to, but stop fucking about. I didn't even know you had any nieces. How would I?'

Dee walked around to the back of her man's chair and gently laid the axe on his scalp. 'Of course, it doesn't help that you've been mistreating my sister. Did you know Jen and me are half-sisters?' The stiffening of his shoulders gave her the answer she was expecting. 'That really pisses me off too. And she must be really distressed to give John an anonymous tip that you nicked my car so that he would force you to leave London.'

'She did what?' Nuts would have exploded out of the chair if Dee wasn't standing behind him still making up her mind whether to split him in two.

Dee ignored him. 'Like battering women do you? You're a big hard boy, aren't you. Why don't you slap me around then?' She leaned over and offered him her cheek. When he didn't move she pulled back. 'Bashing women around? You piece of stinking shit. You know what else really does my head in? What really gets on my tits is you pinching money from defenceless little kids.' She turned the axe and rested the blade on his head again. 'I know I'm going to regret this. It's not really my style but I've got to do it.'

'I'll change. I'll be better.' He sounded like the pathetic man that he was.

'It's too late for that, Nuts.'

For several seconds they were frozen in time while Dee gently jabbed Nuts' hairline with the axe. Then she pulled it back and slipped it into her belt. 'I'm really going to regret doing this.'

She put her hand under his arm and pulled him to his feet. She dragged him to the door of the safe room and then forced him up the stairs to the hallway, warning him to stay quiet. Grabbing him by the collar, like a little boy, she shoved him through the front door and onto the drive, taking care to close it quietly behind her. The avenger and her victim walked together through a high wind to where John had left the car that Nuts had stolen. The key was still in the ignition and Dee ordered him into the driver's seat to start the engine.

Nuts was now beyond scared and too frightened to argue anymore. 'Where are we going?'

'I'm not going anywhere. I've got visitors to look after. It's you who's going somewhere.' She laughed when she saw Nuts anxiously looking at the wheel and pedals and wondering if he had an opportunity to escape.

Dee leaned into the car and whispered, 'I'm going to regret this, probably every day of my life, but I think I have to do it. Here's how it's going to be. You can fuck off to A&E and get your wounds seen to. Then you'll go to whatever rat hole you scuttle about in. First thing in the morning, you're going to call a solicitor and tell him you want a divorce.' She pulled a roll of banknotes out of her Ultimo cleavage-enhancing bra, where she always kept an emergency stash. She threw it on the dashboard. 'You pay for it with that. You can cite unreasonable behaviour in the petition, if you want, I think your wife marrying you in the first place was pretty unreasonable actually. Of course I should split your head open with this but I wouldn't want that for my niece's dad, even a crap father like you. So, you can go where you like and do what you like but if I ever, *ever* find out that you've laid a finger on my sister or mistreated my nieces, I will hunt you down, Rambo style, chop your fingers off and stick them up your scrawny arse. Do I make myself clear?'

It was obvious that Nuts suddenly saw a chink of light in the dark hole he'd got himself into. 'Sure, we're about done anyway, me and Jen. What about this car?'

'What about it? I don't want it. You stole it; you do what you like with it.'

Nuts nodded and pulled the door to, exhaling breath like a deflating tyre as he did so. Dee heard him squeal with pain as he tried to put his foot on the accelerator and then the car shunted unsteadily backwards. Dee turned to go into the house but thought better of it. As he left, she turned back and threw the axe with as much force as she could muster so that it crashed through the rear windscreen.

'You fucking bastard.'

Back in the snooker room, the atmosphere had lightened. Jen had managed to convince the children that their day out in Essex was all a bit of playacting. Babs was telling no one in particular that forgetting to mention that Dee was her other child was the sort of thing any mother was inclined to do. John had told Nicky that he was lucky there were little kids around or he would have a snooker cue stuck up one end and poking out the other. Tiffany in turn had taken Nicky to one side and thanked him for 'fessing up – it was all her fault in the first place, she added. He'd given her a grim smile and told her, 'That's alright. I'll go and get a fluffy kitten from the pet shop and wear it round my neck. Mum wouldn't dare touch me then.'

John quietly took the Browning, disabled it and put it in a drawer, for disposal later.

But Tiffany, like everyone else, was anxiously awaiting the return of Dee and Nuts. When the door to the snooker room opened, all eyes turned on her and necks craned to look for her rogue brother-in-law. She closed the door behind her and made a beeline for her nieces who she took from Jen and held in each arm. 'Love 'em!'

John asked the question on everyone's lips. 'Where is he?'

'I've done a terrible thing which I'm already regretting.'

'Oh great, I've got to play gravedigger again have I?'

'Let's just say I had a little word with him. The scumbag has gone home.' Seeing Jen's face fall in despair, Dee added, 'I wouldn't worry about him showing his face for a while. He's probably gone to lick his wounds somewhere.'

Dee then paraded herself in the middle of the room with the children. 'Right, who's up for a nice cup of Rosie Lee?'

Darkness was settling in when Tiffany walked down the lane to fetch her car and brought it back to pick up the rest of the family. John fitted plastic sheeting over the shattered windscreen that Jen had shot out by accident. There was an awkward silence on the doorstep as the two sisters and their half-sister stood without quite knowing what to say. Eventually they agreed to meet the following lunchtime at Dee's to 'have a little talk'. But there was laughter too, when Jen asked, 'Can I have my children back now, Dee?' The two girls were as snug as two bugs, fast asleep, Courtney curled up by Dee's side and Little Bea in her lap.

'They're great kids,' Dee replied, sounding almost shy as she gave the girls gently back to their mum so she could settle them into the car.

Jen pushed her hair back as she looked at her new sister. 'They like you. Don't be a stranger. Anytime you want to see them, pop over.' She leaned in close and whispered, 'I can tell the girls like their new auntie.'

Dee wiped a single tear from her cheek. 'It feels good to have a family. Not that I didn't have one – my Auntie Cleo brought me up. Not that she's my real aunt or anything . . .'

'You don't need to explain to me. Where we come from our real family are the good people around us, whether they're blood or not.'

'But we are blood,' Tiffany joined in. 'Blood sisters. We've had our ups and downs, but now we're on the straight and narrow together.'

Tiffany held her hand out to Dee, who took it. Dee held her hand out to Jen. Finally, Jen and Tiffany held hands completing their new blood circle.

Inside the car, Babs smiled. Life was far from perfect but it made her heart swell as she watched her daughters hold hands.

Sixty-Nine

The following morning, Jen stood on the outdoor landing watching the comings and goings on The Devil Estate. Except, there weren't many comings or goings. The place was unnaturally quiet. No kids roaming after doing a bunk from school; no music blaring from the flats; no public bust-ups between men and women no one could believe were husband and wife. Jen smiled as she remembered how, back in the old days, Babs and her mates would sit out in chairs on the balcony, taking in the sun and gossiping about life. Back then, people would leave their doors open, most feeling safe in their community. The peace she felt reminded her that this had once been a good place to raise a family.

With a sigh she went back inside to get ready to pay Dee a visit, with Tiffany. She hadn't taken two steps into the passage when she heard an envelope come through the door. She picked it up to discover that it was hand delivered; it looked like it had already been unsealed and then clumsily stuck down again. When she opened it, she discovered a letter from a local solicitor announcing that it was her husband's intention to initiate divorce proceedings and that all communications should come via the solicitor. But at the bottom was a handwritten postscript from Nuts. He apologised for not contacting her in person. He felt, in light of the fact that she'd put his life in danger, by falsely grassing him up to John and Dee, that there was no future in the marriage and that he wanted a divorce. He expressed hope that at some future time she might have the decency to take responsibility for what she had done and apologise to him.

Jen's response was to mumble. 'If you fuck off out of life, mate, I'll take responsibility for the Great Train Robbery.'

When Tiffany came round and read the letter she burst out laughing. 'Be honest, he's got some front, hasn't he?'

'Yeah, the one thing we've never been short of in this home is front.'

Jen folded the letter, put it in her bag and the two sisters set off to do lunch with their half-sister in Essex.

Things got off to a bad start when Dee realised Jen's two little angels hadn't made the journey. When Jen explained that they had to go to school that day, Dee's response was, 'Yeah . . . OK . . . I suppose.'

When Dee asked in a lighter manner if Nuts had come home in the night, Jen was surprised. 'No, actually a funny thing happened this morning. Either he or his solicitor came round and popped a letter through the door saying he wants a divorce. So it would seem that Tiffany's little scam might have worked after all.'

Dee gave a half smile and said no more.

The three women swapped gossip about their lives. It was clear to Tiffany and Jen that there was a lot of anger from Dee towards their mum.

Jen gave Tiffany a look out of the corner of her eye and asked, 'Do you ever see your dad, Dee?'

Their eldest sister was grim. 'Mum won't tell me nothing about him. But one day, one day soon, I'm going to find out who he was.'

*   *   *

While they were having lunch on the lawn, John returned and gestured to Dee to join him for a private word. In the conservatory he shared the results of his morning's investigation.

'Right, I've asked around and there's no sign of your car anywhere. My guess is, whoever nicked it, knew who to sell it onto and it's probably been broken into bits and sold abroad. So that's the end of that. Although I've got to say, given the fact that that little fucker of a son of ours—'

Dee snapped back, 'Don't talk like that about my lad. He was upset and he was going to bring the car back later. You leave the boy alone. He's sensitive, that's all. And you can forget about Nuts as well. As long as he leaves my nieces and sis alone, we'll leave him be.'

'It's going to be hard to find that make of car again.'

'Don't trouble yourself. I was getting bored with it anyway. I was thinking I need a new one, something more up-to-date with all mod cons.'

John looked balefully into her eyes. 'Do you know something? I think I'm going to turn myself in. A bunk in HMP has got to be better than this.'

Dee, Jen and Tiffany finished their lunch and then Dee escorted them back to their car. They'd swapped stories about their lives in the East End, and the people they had in common, which turned out to be a surprisingly large number. Jen began to notice that, as long as they stayed off the subject of their family, there was no cause for friction. Stanley Miller and Dee's father turned out to be two men who were strictly off limits. They exchanged kisses and Dee was already pressing Jen for a date when the girls would be paying a visit.

'It's Courtney's tenth birthday soon, so obviously we're hoping you can come. Give the girls a chance to show off their Auntie Dee.'

Dee became wistful. 'I'll be there. I always wanted a little girl babes – give her all the things I never had. But it wasn't to be.'

After they'd left, Dee went to her bedroom and locked the door. She didn't want John or Nicky barrelling in unexpectedly. She walked into the dressing room and rummaged in the back of the dress closet until she found a cardboard box. She pulled it out and placed it on the bed, then sat down and opened it. Inside were all her old *Vogue* and *Country Life* magazines and the torn photos from mags she had once upon a time stuck on the wall. She still got a thrill looking at them.

This had been her way – admittedly by hook or crook – of getting what she thought she deserved in life. The Dee Clarks of this world didn't get handouts – they had to find a way of taking it. But that was no good if you didn't have a clue what *it* was. She grabbed the photo of the classic Italian sports car she'd once stuck on the wall and smiled as she stared at it. Then she crushed it in her hand. She put the box back, minus the car, and went online to search for a new motor.

Seventy

A week later a blonde woman in DKNY Jackie O shades drove to a service station on the M25 and parked her car in a darkened and shaded corner where it wouldn't be noticed. She went into the twenty-four hour café and waited until a confused looking middle-aged man appeared at the entrance. She knew him but he didn't know her. His name was Andy K. He was a business associate of John Black's but a rather unusual one. As a rule, John refused to have anyone from the 'business' in his house but Andy K he let in the front door. She had made some discreet enquiries about him and the word was he was a top guy who owned a dealership in an expensive area of West London selling classic cars to foreign residents. She'd given him a bell, told him she had a property she wanted to sell and given him the make. Andy agreed to meet her without breaking a stride. He was obviously used to doing business in motorway cafés and when she said, 'I'll know you when I see you,' he knew she wasn't a time waster. Even if she was, the property was worth the risk.

She discreetly waved a newspaper at him and he came over. He looked the type, with a baggy, but expensive suit, open-necked shirt, gelled hair and an array of expensive rings on his fingers.

'Nancy?'

'That's right.'

'I'm Andy.'

She kept it deadpan. 'I know who you are; I made the arrangements.'

'Of course, alright. What have you got for me?'

The blonde woman reached into her handbag and pulled out a brown envelope. Inside was a photo, which she handed over. He studied it for a while before putting it down on the table. Then he picked it up again and looked at it before pulling a face and saying, 'The thing is Nancy, there's not much demand for a car like this these days; the market's topped out I'm afraid, so I probably won't be able to help . . .'

She fixed him with a hard stare. 'Come off it. Those cars are like gold dust and you know it. The Arabs would sell all their wells for one and the Russians would give you all their fur coats. Don't fuck about, mate, I don't like fuck abouters.'

Andy sighed and picked up the photo again. 'OK, maybe . . . I could probably sell it for you. Is it yours?'

'No.'

Andy pursed his lips. 'Ah, now that might be a problem if the paperwork isn't in order. It might be stolen you see.' He looked hard at the photo. 'Funnily enough, a friend of mine had a motor like this stolen recently.'

She didn't blink. 'I know, that's it.'

Andy nearly jumped two feet in the air and dropped the photo on the floor as if it was coated in acid. He looked around like a hunted animal and whispered, 'Are you out of your soddin' mind? I can't buy that; if John found out I'd be under a motorway not driving on one, and so would you.'

She gave him a half smile. 'He's not looking for it anymore so you don't have to worry.'

'Since when?'

'Since last week . . . Don't look at me like that. If you don't believe me, give John Black a little tinkle; you've got his mobile number.' She paused for effect before adding, 'You can have it for fifty grand.' She paused again before saying, 'Yes, I thought that price tag would tickle your fancy. It's worth two or three times that. All you need to do is get a couple of engineers over from the Gulf, break it into bits, ship it out there as machine parts and Mister Black won't be any the wiser anyway. Go on, ring him up, see if I'm right.'

Andy picked up the photo and sat looking at it for a long time. Slowly he reached into his pocket, pulled out his mobile and made a call. 'Hello, John, it's Andy. Listen, are you still trying to trace the wife's car? Only I had a guy in earlier with a similar model – not the same obviously – but I wanted to check . . . Oh really? OK, well, it's probably long gone anyway . . . Bastards . . . Yeah.'

When the call was over, Andy carried on looking at the photo. He looked like an internet porn addict – guilty and excited at the same time.

The woman went in for the kill. 'I'll want cash.'

'Oh piss off, no one carries that kind of cash, this ain't the movies.' When he got no answer, he admitted, 'Probably better if there's no trail anyway.' He paused before saying. 'OK cash.'

The blonde woman drove for a good twenty minutes before she slid her rental car into a lay-by. Then she pulled off the blonde wig and sunglasses and dumped them on the passenger seat.

Tiffany Miller grinned as she looked at herself in the rear-view mirror. She'd played a cunning and clever game, shifting everyone around like chess pieces. She hadn't started out with any thought of taking the car, but that had all changed when she'd passed the estate agent's window on Mile End Road. For there she had fallen head first for a one-bed flat for sale. This money would give her the deposit she needed. To be given the chance to move out of her mum's and have her own place was simply a dream come true. And hanging on to Dee's car was going to give her the readies she needed.

It had been easy to move the car from the garage in Southend. After she had held a sobbing Jen in her arms while they were in the B 'n' B, once her sister was asleep she'd stayed awake for a while and then slipped out of the room. She'd gone to the garage, removed Dee's car and hidden it elsewhere. By rights, with all this shit going on she should have driven it straight around to Dee's and just 'fessed up. Taken Jen and the girls out of harm's way. But when she saw Dee's plush motor again – God forgive her – she couldn't take it back; just couldn't do it. Watch all her dreams drive off into the distance? That was too much to ask a girl from The Devil. So she'd decided to leave everything in motion and see where things ended up. Mind you, she had almost spilled the beans to Jen when they drove back to The Devil, but when they were distracted by the cops outside their mum's, the moment had passed. She'd then decided to confess all to Jen if the girls weren't at Dee and John's. But they had been, so Tiffany had kept her mouth shut. Dee had written off her beloved car and moved on. So had Tiffany – to a mega payout that was going to set her up for life.

'*Sometimes you only get one chance to change your life, sis.*' That's what she'd told Jen while they were in the B 'n' B. And, as far as Tiffany was concerned, this was her chance and she'd taken it.

Tiffany popped the radio on and grinned hearing her favourite track of the year blaring out. Swaying, she started singing at full blast to OutKast's 'Hey Ya!'

Seventy-One

'Happy birthday to you.
Squashed tomatoes and stew.
I saw a fat monkey,
And I thought it was YOU!'

The gathered crowd roared the last word and then raised the roof with thunderous applause. Babs beamed as she watched her granddaughter Courtney chuckling away, starry-eyed at the surprise birthday verse. The house was packed with children, streamers, balloons and party food. Babs was as pleased as punch to see her Dee's Nicky at the stereo system, ready to take control of the music. At a nod from Babs he hit the music and the kids started running around, some dancing while others played a rowdy game of catch. Babs was so pleased to see Courtney get over her earlier sulk. She'd been gutted when she found out Dexter Ingram wasn't invited to the party, and just didn't get it when her mum muttered about him having 'bad blood'. The poor girl couldn't understand why the boy she was sweet on wasn't allowed anywhere near her. It did seem unfair. But then, that was life; you couldn't have everything you desired and the sooner Courtney learned that, the better her life would be.

Babs walked over with pride to where her three daughters stood chatting with each other. Things had gone a lot more smoothly than she'd anticipated. Sure, she still had to take the heat sometimes from Dee wanting to know about her father, but getting to know Jen and Tiffany had mellowed her eldest out some. Babs was keeping her fingers crossed that it stayed that way.

'Shall I get the cake?' Babs whispered to Jen. They'd got a gorgeous pink-and-white cake with Courtney's name written across it in gold and silver glitter, especially made by Percy Ingles. Oh, little Courtney's face was going to light up when she saw it.

Instead of answering, Jen gazed around the beautiful front room where the party was being held. 'I still can't believe that Mrs Jackson let you use her wonderful house. This place is just cor blimey gorgeous.'

Babs had spoken to Mrs Jackson, one of the clients she cleaned for, who lived in one of the huge houses in the Georgian Square, across the road from The Devil's Estate. Well, that's the story Babs had told her daughter.

'I'd better go and get that cake then. Get Nicky to turn the music off in thirty seconds flat.' And with that she hurried into the kitchen at the back. She placed ten candles on the cake and, when she got the signal (the music stopping), she headed, with a big grin, towards the main room. She thought it was a bit strange that she couldn't hear any noise. She hoped her daughters hadn't told everyone to shush-it because then Courtney would know her cake was coming and Babs so wanted it to be a surprise. Never mind.

But when Babs got inside and saw the man standing near Courtney and Jen, she realised why it was so quiet. The cake slipped from her hand with shock and crashed to the floor.

'Babs, I can't believe you never sent me an invite to my own granddaughter's birthday,' announced Stanley Miller.

acknowledgements

Blood Sister would never have been written without the spot on expertise and encouragement of my super editor Ruth Tross and the amazing editing machine Zelda. Thanks also to Becca and Lucy for all the PR and marketing. Total kudos and thanks, as always, to my incredible agent Amanda Preston.

A special thanks to all you wonderful readers for all your loyal support and for spreading the word.

Thank You!

Thank you for reading *Blood Sister*. I'm keeping my fingers crossed that you enjoyed it. If you did I'd love to hear about it – you can get in touch with me by:

Email: dredamitchell@yahoo.co.uk
Twitter: @DredaMitchell
Facebook:/dredasaymitchell

I always love to be linked to reviews and ratings on your blogs or online!

If you enjoyed BLOOD SISTER, look out for the gripping
new novel in the FLESH AND BLOOD trilogy

BLOOD MOTHER

1972
Babs is a girl in trouble. But when she falls for charmer
Stanley Miller the trouble gets worse. Much worse.

Coming February 2017

Read on for an exclusive sneak peek.

Blood Mother: Sneak Peek

1972

'You're a whore! And a murderer!'

As if the spitting rage coming from the normally quiet and gentle Doctor McDaid was not enough, there was worse to come. Babs Wilson had, unfortunately, left the door to his surgery open as she fled out of it back into his waiting room so that several rows of patients could all hear him tearing a strip off her.

A few minutes earlier she had been sitting among them, waiting her turn, fists clenched white, hoping against hope that there was some mistake in the test results she'd got yesterday. In his surgery McDaid had soon killed that off; fear and last-minute hope turned to horror and a thin film of sweat appeared on her face. Then, when he turned on her in fury, she'd gone into shock. Now she stood in front of the other patients like an actor who'd forgotten her lines.

Some of her audience looked away in embarrassment, while others watched her with curiosity. Among them were several proper gossips who were already eagerly trying to work out what was going on so they could spread the word. She could imagine what their malicious patter would sound like once it started doing the rounds: '*Did you hear about the Wilson girl? I was down the quack's when Doctor McDaid called her a whore and a murderer. Old Jim McDaid was in a right two and eight, I can tell you. I wonder what that was about. As if we didn't know . . .*' Babs caught the eye of the Jackson woman, aka Dirty Laundry Jackson, who lived on her street. She'd be straight to work on the gossip mill, no doubt adding her own poisonous flavour and flesh to the story. The old bitch.

Babs was eighteen, a proud girl from a proud family. Her father had always told her to keep her head up and walk tall, no matter what. So she raised her head, stared down the gawpers and tried to walk tall. But when everyone heard the doctor call out again, to no one in particular, 'Whore! Murderer! The shame of her honest family!' she caved. Her shoulders sagged and tear-drops stung her cheeks.

The receptionist called out, 'Mrs Donovan? Doctor McDaid will see you now. Could you remember to close the surgery door on your way in?' Then she gestured at Babs to tell her to sling her hook. Babs moved with gathering speed.

Out on New Road in Whitechapel, she pulled in gasps of air. Without realising it, she found herself wandering into the traffic. A car slammed on its brakes and squealed to a halt a few inches short of her. The driver shook his head and pointed at his eyes before shaking his head again and driving round her. For a brief moment, Babs wished the motor had hit her at speed and dragged her down the road into oblivion, because she was a young woman in Big Trouble. In fact she was in Big Trouble twice over.

She might have been able to cope with one or the other but not both. She couldn't go home to her parents' house and she couldn't go and see her friends. But as she tramped the streets of the East End, she realised she didn't have to. She would just go and see Nev straightaway. He would sort her out. It was almost his catchphrase. 'There's nothing I can't sort out, baby. Nothing – you only have to ask and I make it happen.'

She hadn't seen Nev for a week or more. He was busy at the moment and couldn't fit her in. But she was proud of how busy he was. He wasn't a lazy bloke like some of the lads she'd grown up with. No, her Nev had prospects. Ambition. Perking up without realising it, she began the trek, crossing over Commercial Road, towards the Bad Moon boozer in Shadwell where Nev held court most lunch times, although he'd never taken her there himself. He would sort things out. Then she whispered out loud to no one, 'He'll have to, won't he?'

Nev was Babs' fiancé. Of course it wasn't official like; Nev didn't do 'official'. He didn't buy engagement rings or hold cele-bration parties; that wasn't his style. He was his own man who went his way and lived by nobody's rules but his own. That was one of the things she loved about him. But it was 'understood' that they were engaged. When she stopped outside jewellers and gave lingering glances at the array of silver and gold rings, Nev would squeeze her arm and say, 'No need to rush things, baby. We're happy as we are. All in good time. Everything comes to him who stands and waits.'

So she'd waited. And waited. And waited.

When Rosie Wilson clocked old Ma Jackson coming down her street, wearing her trademark black hairnet, she picked up speed so she could get into her house before the evil old crone collared her and wasted her time spreading the malicious natter that she specialised in. The big slob of a woman was legendary for sticking her snout – misshapen and red from years of stout and gin – into any and everything that wasn't her business.

Rosie always wore her headscarf when she went out because it was proper for a woman of her age, just like her George wore his tie without fail. The Wilsons were a respectable family, unlike many of those who lived in the streets behind the London Hospital in Whitechapel. That's why she didn't care for back-fence talk. Besides, most of Dirty Laundry Jackson's was made up anyway. But the old dear was too quick for her. As Rosie got her key out, Jackson caught her on the doorstep.

'Hello, Rosie love. Long time no speak. How's the family? Everything alright?' Then she added with a snide smirk, 'How's your girl Babs getting on? Everything OK?'

Rosie looked in the old woman's spiteful, watery eyes. Jackson had the manners of a door-to-door salesman. She was that annoying. Babs cut her short. 'Yeah, we're very well, thank you, and Babs is fine. Now if you'll excuse me . . .'

But Jackson wasn't fobbed off so easily. She was an expert at this game. 'Oh that's good, that's very good. So Babs is alright then, is she?'

Rosie pursed her lips, annoyed as hell that this woman wouldn't take her loathsome business elsewhere. 'Yes, Babs is fine. I just told you.' She turned the key in the lock.

Jackson moved in for the kill. 'Are you sure? You know me, dear, I don't like to spread gossip . . .'

Rosie interrupted with leaden sarcasm, 'No, I know you don't.'

'. . . But I was down Doctor McDaid's this morning and your

Babs was there having a right old barney with the Doc. He was
in a fair old state, thought he was going to burst a blood vessel
for sure. Effing and jeffing at her, he was, while your girl gave
it back to him like a proper fishwife. He was calling her all sorts
of vile names that I wouldn't like to repeat, dear – then Babs
marches out of the surgery giving him the old Harvey Smith.'
She rolled her eyes dramatically. Rosie couldn't imagine her
darling Babs sticking two fingers up at anyone, like that show
jumper Harvey Smith had done the year before.

But Ma Jackson cracked on. 'I've never seen the like in my
life. So I thought to myself, there's something not quite Kosher
here; I mean old man McDaid is always as quiet as a mouse and
your Babs is such a nice girl . . . usually.'

Rosie kept it zipped. The mud that this poisonous old trout
liked to sling around was always embroidered – though sometimes, just sometimes, there was a root of God's honest truth in
there somewhere. But Rosie found this particular bollocks story
impossible to believe on any level.

Fortunately, the two women were interrupted by the appearance of a striking girl dressed in flared slacks, a cheese cloth
blouse and platform heels.

'Hello Mrs Wilson, is Babs in?'

'Hello Denise – no, she's out I'm afraid.' Denise Brooks was
her Babs' best mate and Rosie liked her. She was a sweet girl,
unlike many of the young ones around here who were growing
into loud-mouthed replicas of their parents. The only problem
with Denise was her unfortunate 'lights on but no one at home'
expression.

Rosie could see that Ma Jackson was eagerly hoping that this
new arrival would shed some light on the incident at the doctor's
and was disappointed when Denise looked surprised and said,
'Oh? That's a shame; she said she'd be in. I thought we were
going to the pictures later to see the 'Steptoe and son' film. Can
you tell her I called?'

Rosie nodded and the girl turned and walked back in the
direction she'd come.

Ma Jackson put the needle back on her stuck record. 'So,
Babs alright then? You know me, if there's a problem and I can
help in any way . . .'

Rosie pushed the front door open. 'I think you must have got
the wrong end of the stick. I've got work to do.'

'Of course, dear.'

Rosie closed the front door behind her. Her husband did shift work and was dozing in his armchair in the sitting room. With a mixture of alarm and anger, she prodded him and asked, 'Have you seen Babs today? Did she say she was going down Doctor McDaid's?'

Her husband shrugged his shoulders. 'No, I haven't. What's she doing that for anyway? She's not ill, is she?'

'That's what I'd like to know.'

Her husband closed his eyes and turned his head away. Rosie walked around the house pretending to do a few things before marching back into the front room and shouting, 'Where the hell is Babs anyway?'

Even before she pushed open the door of the Bad Moon pub, gut instinct told Babs her fella wasn't there. There were only a few punters inside, a stocky barman and a busty, hard-faced landlady wiping down the surfaces. As soon as she reached the bar, the landlady stopped polishing and asked, 'What can I get you, love?' But she didn't seem very pleased with her new customer. The Bad Moon was a bloke's pub and Nev always took her somewhere else.

'Has Nev been in today?' Babs knew her voice sounded desperate, but she couldn't hold her emotions back.

'Nev? Don't know any Nevs.'

'Yeah, you know – Neville.'

'Oh, him.' The landlady looked at her with sympathy. Babs' stomach rolled. 'No, I haven't seen him around for a while.'

Babs' desperation grew as the other woman got back on with her cleaning. While there was some hope she'd kept things under control, but this was her first port of call and already hope was draining away.

'What do you mean you haven't seen him?'

The landlady looked back up, her eyes as tough as stone. 'What I say – I ain't seen him. It's not a very complicated sentence, is it?'

Babs clenched her fists. 'You're a liar. He's always in here. I know.'

The other woman put her dishcloth down and placed her palms on the bar. Her fingers twitched ever so slightly, showcasing knuckles that said she knew a thing or two about the hard knocks of life. 'Look, love, I'm not taking any lip from a slip of a girl like you. He's not here and we haven't seen him for a while. Now – do you want to order a drink or what? Otherwise I'll have to ask you to leave.'

Babs looked around at the patrons nervously. They were looking back at her in the same way as Doctor McDaid's patients earlier.

She left.

So she never saw the barman shift up to the landlady and ask, 'Who was that?'

'Some dopey bird looking for Neville,' she answered, pulling out a Virginia Slim and lighting up.

And Babs never saw the barman burst into laughter. 'Silly bitch. Her and half the other scrubbers in the East End.'

Once she hit Commercial Road again, Babs caught a bus to Limehouse. When she'd first met Nev, he'd had a pad there. In fact, it was there that they'd first had sex, later on the same night she'd met him. She'd gone up to the Reno nightclub in Stoke Newington with her friend Denise as they'd heard they had a classier clientele than the usual wide boys, spivs and pretend bank robbers they met on a night out in the East End. At first, it seemed what they'd heard wasn't true, but that was before she met Nev. He hadn't seemed that interested but when she turned him down for a dance, he suddenly became very interested indeed. Nev wasn't the kind of bloke who took refusals lightly. He spent the rest of the night pursuing her and chatting her up. Once he had his big strong arms wrapped around her for a slow dance in the small hours, she didn't remember making any more decisions. She followed him in a dreamlike state to a cab and then to his flat and then to his bedroom.

She'd had other guys, of course, but he was different. He was tall, he was strong and he was cool. He didn't show off or play act because he didn't need to. The hard boys in the Reno all got out of the way for him. The manager and the bouncers all knew him by name. So she knew no geezers were going to lean out of a car window and shout, 'Oi darlin, show us your tits!' while Nev was around. Not if they wanted to keep a matching pair of ears. He was polite, he was protective and he had good manners. And as guys like that were at a premium down her neck of the woods she wasn't going to let him go without a fight.

So the morning after the Reno, after she'd waited patiently for him to arrange to see her again, she got angry when she was finally forced to ask, 'Are we going out together then or what?' – and he didn't seem to understand the question. She got even angrier when he said nothing in reply. So she'd yelled, 'I'm not a fucking tart, Neville' so loudly that the neighbours must have heard.

He'd gifted her with his one hundred watt smile. 'Yeah – sure we're going out.'

Afterwards, she apologised to him for getting the nark. It was obvious to her later that he was just upset she'd even asked the question in the first place. And that was the first excuse she'd made for her new boyfriend.

As she looked out of the bus window at the estate in Limehouse, she realised in the pit of her guts that she'd been making excuses for him ever since.

She'd never seen the estate he lived on in daylight before. It was one of those old style thirties estates, on its last legs, looking dirty and dingy. She walked up to the fourth floor where the flat was. At first Nev had claimed it was his place but later he'd admitted that he was looking after it for a friend who was on remand for something that he totally and absolutely hadn't done. Of course, she believed him. She knew Nev wasn't at the flat anymore but kept her fingers crossed that he had left a forwarding address.

Whoever was occupying the flat now had a poster in the kitchen window that said, 'Demand the Impossible!' so she guessed they were squatters. The same poster had been in the window of a squat on the street where she lived with her mum and dad. That was before the Rozzers had come round and dragged the squatters out by their long, greasy hair, giving them a good kicking on the street before they'd been chucked in the back of a Black Maria.

The lock on the flat in front of her had been kicked off and replaced with cardboard. It was a squat alright.

Babs tapped on the door. It was opened slightly by a young man with long, straggly blonde hair nearly down past his nipples. He wore flared jeans and a Che Guevara T-shirt.

'What do you want?'

'I'm Neville's fiancé. He used to live here. Have you got a forwarding address?' Babs realised how stupid she sounded, standing at the door to this flat, on this estate, asking for a forwarding address for her 'fiancé'.

'Never heard of him . . .' The door slammed shut. But a few moments later it opened again, more widely this time. 'Neville, you say? Wait there a minute.' The freak disappeared before returning with a handful of mail. He passed it to Babs without a word and the door shut again.

As she slowly made her way downstairs like a mourner at a funeral, she quickly scanned the front of each envelope – all addressed to Neville but with various surnames. It was bad enough finding out her boyfriend maybe wasn't who he said he was, but she was in for another shocker when she tore open each letter and looked inside. They were final demands, summonses and threatening letters about unpaid loans and overdrafts. Nev had always told her he was 'in business'. That he had various 'irons in the fire'. That he was looking at 'investment options'. Now it was clear why he was so well dressed and could afford such expensive things. He wasn't actually paying for anything but living on the never-never.

Then there were the postcards. She'd cried no tears since her visit to Doctor McDaid hours earlier. Now they erupted again. But this time they were acid ones that stung her face.

'Hi Nev! Found a great spot for some nudey sunbathing! Can't wait to get back and show you my new all over tan. And I mean all over! Loads of love! Tania!!!'

Another one from Petra in West Berlin.

'Baby! Course finish next week. I'm in London from Monday. I call. Petra XXXXXXXXXXXXXXXXXXXXXXXXXXXXXXXXXXXXXX XXXXX ps but please don't call me Nazi anymore, yes?'

She checked the postmarks on the cards. They'd both been written after she'd met Nev at the Reno club.

All those nights the little bastard was 'busy' or doing 'business'. Or 'seeing his family'. Of course he never asked her to meet his family. It seemed that Nev had taken the same view as Doctor McDaid all along – she was a whore. What a proper fucking moron she'd been. And worse, what a fucking moron he must have thought she was.

When she got down to the courtyard below, she scattered the envelopes and letters in the gutter. She took the postcards, tore them into tiny pieces, spat on them and threw them on the ground before grinding them with her heel in fury.

She was done weeping and wailing. Her back straightened and steel set in her spine. She raised her head, more determined to find Nev than ever. She was Barbara Wilson. And no one was going to make a divvy out of her.

As she walked on, she remembered something. One evening when she'd been in the flat upstairs, there was a knock at the door. After a brief chat on the doorstep, Nev had said he was popping out for ten minutes to discuss business with the caller. While he was out, the phone in the flat rang. She was absolutely forbidden to pick up Nev's phone and was sometimes ordered out of the room when he answered it. But as he wasn't there, she'd picked it up. The voice was smooth and Cockney. 'Alright, darlin? Can you pop Neville on the blower?'

'He's just stepped out.'

'No problem. Can you ask him to call the Go Go Girls Modelling Agency in Soho? We've got some work for him. He's got the number, sweetheart, but I'll give it to you anyway ...'

'OK. Can I tell him who called?'

The man seemed amused. 'Me? I'm the proprietor, love. My name's Stanley Miller.'

THRILLINGLY GOOD BOOKS FROM CRIMINALLY GOOD WRITERS

CRIME FILES BRINGS YOU THE LATEST RELEASES FROM TOP CRIME AND THRILLER AUTHORS.

SIGN UP ONLINE FOR OUR MONTHLY NEWSLETTER AND BE THE FIRST TO KNOW ABOUT OUR COMPETITIONS, NEW BOOKS AND MORE.